I0535005

THE LONG GAME

the *long* game

KATHY ALTMAN

AUTHOR'S NOTE

The Long Game is the re-release of a Harlequin SuperRomance, and was previously titled *A Family After All*.

THE LONG GAME

Copyright © 2023, 2015 Kathy Altman

Cover Design by: Sommer Stein, Perfect Pear Creative

Digital ISBN-13: 978-1-961992-01-6

Print ISBN-13: 978-1-961992-02-3

This book is a work of fiction. The characters, names, places, and events portrayed in this book are products of the writer's imagination and are not to be construed as real. Any similarity to real persons, living or dead, or actual events, locales, or organizations is entirely coincidental and not intended by the author.

All rights reserved.

No part of this publication may be reproduced, scanned, or distributed in any form or by any means, electronic or mechanical, including information storage and retrieval systems, without written permission from the author, except in the case of brief quotations embedded in critical articles and reviews. Please do not participate in encouraging piracy of copyrighted materials in violation of the author's rights. Purchase only authorized editions.

For more information on Kathy Altman and her books, visit her website: www.kathyaltman.com.

To my sister Mary.

I can thank you for making the long drive,

and for the snowy walks from the hotel to the hospital and back again,

and for the hot chocolates,

and the cheerfulness,

and the hugs and prayers,

but I can never thank you enough for simply knowing I'd need you.

You're all kinds of amazing.

SETH WALKER CURSED A streak bluer than the truck's oil-heavy exhaust as he slid out from under the chassis and blinked in the morning sun. Dammit. This was not going to be an easy repair.

He'd have to call the garage. Arrange a tow. And figure out how the hell he was going to manage to pay for either when his bank account balance hovered somewhere between pathetic and desperate.

He plucked his shades from his shirt pocket, jammed them back into place and reached for his phone. He'd find a way. If he didn't have a truck, he couldn't make his deliveries. And if he couldn't make his deliveries, he couldn't see Ivy.

The clutch in his chest had him shaking his head. Maybe that would be a good thing, considering what he planned to tell her.

Then again, maybe she wouldn't care.

After dialing the garage, he lifted the phone to his ear and turned away from the road. Traffic was sparse, but the occasional passing car still made it difficult to hear. He wandered to the edge of a vineyard that stretched all the way to Lake Erie, a hazy strip of blue in the distance bordered by the lighter blue of the sky and the vibrant green of the grapevines. Off to the left, a yellow monster of a harvester straddled a row of vines. As it lumbered through the crop, it shook the purple grapes onto a conveyer belt that led to a massive storage bin in the back. Seth had been up close and personal with a harvester more than once while making his deliveries, and he didn't know how the drivers did it. They had to climb a ladder just to get to the cab. He liked his steering wheels closer to the ground.

He made arrangements for a tow while breathing in the sweet scent of Concord juice, pressed End and dialed again. One call down, two to go.

His thumb hovered over the Send button. He exhaled. Screw pride. All he had to do to save himself the cost of a rental was call in a favor. And suck up the ribbing next time he got together with the guys.

Joe Gallahan answered the phone, saying, "Your ass better not be backing out of poker night, 'cause I'm feeling lucky."

"You're feeling lucky 'cause you're getting lucky."

"Hey, that's my girl you're talking about."

"Yeah, well, she's lucky, too."

Joe snorted. "I can feel myself being hit up for a favor."

"You always were a sensitive kind of guy."

"Kiss my ass. Now, what do you need?"

Less than a minute later, Joe had agreed to lend out his truck for the two to three days it would take the mechanic to fix Seth's ride.

"Hang tight," Joe said. "I'm on my way."

Two down, one to go.

Bradley answered on the first ring. "'Sup."

"Try again," Seth growled.

A protracted sigh, then, "Tweedy's Feed and Seed, how may I help you?"

"Better."

"Dude. Why do I have to answer your calls like that? You're the owner. You should know the name of your own business by now."

"Cute." Seth turned back to his truck. If only he could afford to abandon the damned thing. "I'm stuck at the side of Route 5, waiting for a tow. The brake line's leaking. Joe's going to lend us his pickup so we can handle deliveries until Pete can breathe life back into Bertha here."

"That sucks. About Bertha, I mean, not about Joe."

"Point is, I'll be late getting back to the store. You okay watching the kids till I get there?"

"Not a prob. Or you could let me make the deliveries."

"I got it."

"You sure? Because I don't mind. Anyway, isn't it my turn to deliver to the dairy farm?"

In your dreams, kid. "You don't get a turn at the dairy farm."

2

"I used to. And, dude, I know Ivy misses me. Just the other day, she told me how much she misses me. I saw her at the post office and she came up to me and said, 'Oh, Bradley —'" the kid started talking in a high-pitched voice, though God only knew why he added the Southern accent "'—I've missed you so much, Bradley, you big, strong, handsome hunk of man, you —'" Abruptly, Bradley switched back to his normal voice. "Sorry, Mrs. MacFarland, I didn't see you standing there. Weed killer? Try aisle three." He got back on the phone. "Awk-ward."

Seth didn't know whether to laugh or groan, so he did both. "Stop tormenting my customers. And don't forget to dust."

"Give my love to Ivy," Bradley said, and disconnected.

Not long after, Joe pulled up. Seth climbed into the passenger seat and stuck out his hand. "I appreciate this."

"No sweat. I can always use Al's car if I need to run errands."

"How's Allison doing?"

As he pulled back out onto the highway, Joe gave his head a shake that failed to dislodge his goofy grin. "She's great," he said. "Just great."

"Glad to hear it. I know the motel's doing well. Whenever I drive by, the parking lot's full."

"That website she put together is really bringing in the business."

"The renovations must have helped, too. I still hear horror stories about the turquoise ceilings."

"Bet you hear more about the python behind the wall."

Seth didn't have to fake his shudder. "I'd rather talk about the ceilings."

"I know what you'd rather talk about. Or should I say *who*. Ivy still thinking about opening a riding school?"

Seth frowned. "Where'd you hear that?"

"From Al. Ivy asked her advice on creating an 'online presence.'" Joe glanced over at Seth and winced. "Damn, man, I'm sorry. I figured you knew. You're at the farm all the time."

"I'm at the farm when I have a delivery to make."

"That's all there is to it?"

"She's determined to keep things casual." Which was a never-

3

ending source of frustration for him. They'd met a year ago, when he and his kids had moved to town and he'd taken over the feed store. The tall blonde fascinated him. She was industrious, smart, sexy and playful—a constant tease to the deliberate side of his personality. Unfortunately, she was also determined to keep their relationship shallow. He'd been just as determined to coax her toward the deep end.

But some things weren't meant to be. Like his marriage, which had ended two years earlier. Maybe it was just as well Ivy wasn't into forever, because his kids were still struggling to deal.

Joe's next words reinforced that notion. "Between your kids, your store and that cranky-ass truck of yours, it sounds like you have your hands full anyway."

Seth grunted. "So does she." *A riding school.* When would she find time to run a school? The woman worked too damned hard as it was.

What really bothered him was that she hadn't mentioned it. Yeah, they kept it laid-back, but over the past several months they'd talked about everything from the nutritional value of the cottonseed in her cows' feed to the healing properties of oral sex. His groin perked up at the phrase. *Down, boy.*

They never talked much about his kids, though. And that was the thing.

His kids came first.

Joe turned into the crumbling asphalt lot of his motel, Sleep at Joe's. Seth smirked, even as wistfulness whispered through him. Joe and Allison had gotten back together in the spring after a year apart. He doubted there was a lot of sleeping going on.

He met up with Joe on the sidewalk in front of the truck and offered his hand again. "Thanks. I'll take good care of her."

"You're welcome. And yeah, you will."

"Anything I can do in return, you let me know." Seth waved at Allison, a curvy blonde who was working at the other end of the motel, spreading mulch around the base of a young tree. She returned his wave and blew Joe a kiss before turning back to her yard work.

Seth gave his head a mournful shake. "I get a kiss and you get a wave? What'd you do, leave the toilet seat up again?"

"Smart-ass. The kiss was for me." Joe pushed him off the sidewalk and trailed him to the driver's side. "You heading out to Ivy's now?"

Seth gestured toward the empty truck bed and opened his door. "I need to get back to the store and load up first."

Joe slammed the door shut after Seth had buckled himself in. "Hey, I thought of something you can do for me," he said through the open window.

"Name it."

"Spring for some decent beer for poker night."

Seth raised an eyebrow. "What do you care?"

"That cheap-ass crap you buy gives everyone else gas. I may have quit drinking, but I still have to breathe."

*   *   *

IVY MILLBROOK SHOULD HAVE been working. Instead she was staring at the backside of the man she'd lusted after since the day he'd moved to Thistle Hill.

A year was a long time to go hungry, but Seth was tougher than a cheap cut of meat. Since her livestock needed feed and Seth was the only game in town, Ivy had no choice but to respect his preference to sit tight as friends.

Plus, he was a genuinely nice guy. Damn him.

When he turned and caught her staring, the flare of heat in his brown eyes stirred up a jittery warmth in her belly. But then he looked away, and a squeeze of panic put a hitch in her breathing. He had something on his mind. Something she probably wouldn't want to hear. She squinted up at him as he shifted on the truck bed, surrounded by flecks of dust floating in the afternoon sun, straw rustling beneath his boots. What the heck had happened to the laid-back, naughty camaraderie they usually shared?

He lifted his ball cap away from his hair and swiped an arm across his forehead, resettled his hat and finally returned her stare, his own gaze reflecting half amusement, half frustration and half speculation.

She frowned. Wait. That was too many halves. But with all those gorgeous man muscles mere inches from her nose, no one could blame her for not being able to do the math.

"Ivy," he said.

"Seth," she drawled, proud of the lack of urgency in her tone.

He propped a boot on the nearest hay bale. Despite the green-apple crispness of the October day, he was sweating. And no wonder, considering he'd already unloaded most of her order — and hers was not the first delivery of the day. His long-sleeved cotton shirt clung to impressive pecs, and the deepened rhythm of his breathing had her wishing that she, and not hard labor, had made him pant.

An explicit mental image of just how she might achieve that shoved her own lung action toward the red zone. A swell of lust left her fidgeting. She shifted her thighs against the ache and Seth made a growling sound of impatience.

"Are you going to just stand there eyeing my ass, or are you going to help?"

The warning behind his words kept her from pointing out that he'd turned around. It was no longer his ass claiming her attention.

"Help," she said.

Not realizing she was answering his question, he crouched on the truck bed and held out a gloved hand, jaw firm, eyes distant. Seemed Seth Walker was in no mood to play today.

"You can push the rest of these bales onto the tailgate while I finish unloading."

Ivy sighed. "Fine." She stepped onto the bumper and let him haul her up beside him. She pressed her palm against his chest to steady herself and had only an instant to appreciate his solid, sweaty warmth before he jumped to the ground. He hefted a bale as if it weighed no more than his battered ball cap and swung toward the barn.

"Where is Wade, anyway?"

"Home with his wife," she called after him, her gaze lingering on a very fine rear view. She exhaled, pictured his handsome face and sucked in her bottom lip. What had put that furrow between his brows?

No matter what was troubling him, she'd only make it worse by letting him do all the work. She pulled her gloves from the back pocket of her jeans. As she stuffed her hands into the scarred leather, a gust of autumn air skated past the pickup, carrying the comforting scents of meadow grass and manure, lifting her bangs off her forehead. Pride surged. She scanned the fields of her Pennsylvania farm, waves of vibrant green lolling under a thin, hazy streak of Lake Erie blue.

Seth emerged from the barn, one eyebrow lifted. With a squeak Ivy lunged forward and started shoving.

He leaned an arm on the nearest bale and she noticed his faded navy Henley was ripped at the elbow. "Becky still recovering from her accident?"

She stopped pushing, flipped her braid back over her shoulder and nodded. "He's working fewer hours until he's confident he can leave her on her own." It was proving to be rough handling Wade's chores on top of hers, but at this particular moment she was grateful for her farm manager's absence. It was nice having Seth all to herself.

Even if they had strayed from their routine. Usually they took their time, engaging in nonstop innuendos and dirty jokes. It was why he always saved her stop for last. They'd end the visit with his asking her out and her asking him to bed. Both knew nothing would come of it. Seth didn't do casual, so Ivy didn't do Seth. Because she was all about casual.

But as much as their sexual standoff frustrated her — and drove her to ride her own fingers almost every night — she looked forward to their time together. He respected her. Challenged her. Cheered her.

At least he had until today. He was probably just tired. The man worked harder than she did. *And* he was a single father of two.

"I'm sorry she's not doing well." Seth gripped the twine binding the nearest bale and tugged it toward him. "I'd heard the accident wasn't serious. Just the one car involved, right?"

"She broke her collarbone."

Ivy must not have managed to keep the cynicism out of her voice, because Seth cocked his head. "And?"

"And...it's a collarbone. Collarbones heal." She wondered at the relief that skated across Seth's face. Sweet of him to worry about a woman he didn't even know. "But I think Becky's gotten used to having Wade around the house. And I think he likes feeling needed."

"So a husband misses his wife. What's wrong with that?"

"I need him, too," she said, and cringed at the petulance in her tone.

Seth dipped his head and looked up through his lashes. Good God, the man had gorgeous eyes. "You're not thinking about breaking your own collarbone, are you?"

She rolled her eyes, watched as he hoisted the bale and blurted, "Do you?"

"Do I what?"

"Miss your wife?"

He stopped, adjusted his grip and headed for the barn. "Ex-wife," she heard him mutter.

Guess that meant she wouldn't get an answer. She was still trying to decide whether to press the issue when Seth reappeared. Quickly, she leaned over again and braced her hands on another bale, feeling like a football player performing preseason drills. She slid the bundle over to Seth but didn't straighten, liking that his face, with its stubbled jaw and concerned expression, was so close to her own.

"Hey, what's with the sign?" he asked.

She knew what he meant. The big fancy Millbrook Dairy Farm sign at the end of the driveway had become the pet project of some smart-ass with artistic skills. He — or she — liked to monkey with the middle word. Currently the sign read Millbrook Funny Farm. The moniker probably had Ivy's father rolling over in his grave, but it was fairly accurate.

"I've decided to stop wasting energy trying to fix it," she said. "At least it's always G-rated. Though I have to admit, I didn't much like the Fat Farm edition."

Seth grunted, took off one glove and freed a hunk of hay. "You got someone seeing to Wade's work while he's gone?"

In her dreams. "Yes."

His gaze narrowed. "So you don't need help picking up the slack?"

"You offering to stop by more often? Give me a hand when I need it? Or —" she propped her chin in her palm, arched her back and gently swayed her hips, enjoying the stretch of the muscles at the backs of her thighs " — maybe there's another body part you'd be

8

willing to contribute to the cause."

Seth slapped a palm down on the hay bale. "Need to get this inside," he said.

His voice carried an edge. She peered at him, watched his gaze flick from her face to the front of the truck, saw the color streak his cheekbones and glanced behind her. Oh. *Oh*. It wasn't the front of the truck that had snagged his attention but her reflection in the sliding window. With her chest nearly touching the hay bale and her ass in the air, her position seemed somewhat...suggestive.

It was affecting him.

And now it was affecting her.

She straightened slowly and treated herself to an unhurried inspection of some serious muscles. "You're looking flushed," she managed. "Too much sun, I expect. How about a beer?"

"Love one." He swallowed and with a tilt of his chin indicated his pickup. "But this thing won't drive itself."

"So stay."

"You know that's not going to happen."

Yeah. She did. She shrugged. "Why're you driving Joe's truck?"

"My brakes are shot."

"On your pickup?" A curt nod. "You couldn't use your box truck?"

"Didn't have that many deliveries to make. Anyway, the box truck uses too much gas for everyday use."

She frowned. "Business okay?"

"No."

Her stomach dropped, but his next words made it clear his "No" had nothing to do with her question.

He removed his ball cap again. The brown hair plastered to his skull looked black. "We're not going to just step over this and keep on walking. Not again. We've been circling each other for a year. But we both know it's not going to happen. We want different things. And neither one of us will get it unless we back away from each other."

"How do you know I'm not getting it?" she asked archly.

Her face heated under his steady gaze. "Point is," he continued, "while we're doing whatever this is we're doing, I haven't felt free to see anyone else."

"But you want to."

He moved to the side and held out a gloved hand, offering to help her jump down. When her boots hit the ground, she almost dropped to her knees, which were suddenly and inconveniently loose. He stared down at her.

"I'm looking at the woman I want to date. You've made it clear that won't happen."

"You want more than I can give."

"How about what *I* can give? You don't think you deserve love, but you do."

Oh, God.

When she didn't—couldn't—respond, he tapped a knuckle under her chin. "This thing about not wanting kids...it doesn't make sense. They arrive by the bus full and you enjoy the tours as much as they do. If you'd just give it a chance—"

She jerked away from him, the warmth sparked by his "you deserve love" comment vanishing faster than an apple under her stallion's nose. "You don't know that." Her hang-up when it came to kids might not be rational, but she had her reasons—reasons she didn't plan on sharing with anyone, let alone Seth.

"You don't know *me*," she continued.

"You won't let me."

"But there are so many incredible things I *will* let you do."

He blew out an exasperated breath. "Come on. This is about more than sex. You like me. You look forward to my visits. We have fun together. My kids don't bite." He flashed a grin that threatened her knees all over again. Damn that dimple. "All right, they do, but not often, and never when there's a chance they'll talk someone into playing Uno. Look, you have a lot in common. All three of you love horses, hate Brussels sprouts and live to cause me grief. Why not give this a shot?"

"Because I'm looking for sex, not a happy-ever-after."

"Got it." He put his hat back on and reached again for the hay bale, his motions smooth but his stubble-roughened jaw as hard as the steel toes of his work boots. "Olivia over at the DMV has been asking me out for a while now. Guess I'll take her up on it. Maybe it would be better for both of us if I split your deliveries with Bradley."

"Did you warn him about me? Tell him not to turn his back on the cougar at the dairy farm?" She was being unfair. She wasn't winning any points, either—there was no mistaking the disgust in Seth's expression.

Time to pretend the past fifteen seconds of conversation had never taken place, because otherwise she'd dissolve into tears right in front of him. Besides, she knew how busy the feed store kept Seth and his part-timer... Chances were their delivery schedule would stay the same.

She also did her best to ignore the sudden scorch of indignation she had no right to feel. Olivia Duncan was a petite, bubbly brunette with big breasts and a notorious affection for children, if not for their teeth. She kept a bottomless bowl of candy at her window for the kids whose parents had dragged them along on their errands. No way could Ivy compete with that, even if she wanted to.

"Wise choice," she finally managed.

"Bradley? Or Olivia?"

"Olivia. I didn't think Bradley was your type."

Seth gave her a look she couldn't interpret. "You know her?"

"Not personally. But I'm sure, after you wine and dine her once or twice, the next time you go in to renew your license she'll wave you right up to the front of the line."

He never cracked a smile. "It'll be nice to have a woman put me first for a change."

* * *

THE MOMENT HE PLACED his left boot on the long-faded pavement, Seth heard the arguing. Two all-too-familiar voices, raised in earsplitting fury. He shook his head and shoved the pickup door shut, heading toward the noise. If he was honest, playing referee was exactly the distraction he needed.

Damn Ivy Millbrook and her lovely blond hide.

A shriek echoed inside the building. He winced at the faded brick structure he'd owned just over a year, an investment that made him alternately proud and scared shitless. Tweedy's Feed and Seed. The worn wooden sign was placed strategically over the strip of etched cement that read Thistle Hill Fire Company No. 6.

He'd fallen hard for this two-story slice of history, with its boxy shape, bell tower and masonry arches that curved like eyebrows over tall white-framed windows. The pair of fire engine–sized bays behind white mullioned doors provided more than enough space for loading and unloading supplies. The oversize front door, capped by a battered aluminum awning striped with white and green, added a welcoming retro touch.

The rat-infested interior, Seth hadn't been so impressed with. The old guy who'd turned the firehouse into a feed store had run it for decades before eventually getting too sick to manage it. His daughter had kept it going for a while, but she wasn't all that young, either, and by the time Seth had come along, the place had contained more dust and droppings than merchandise.

But after everything that had happened the past few years, he'd been desperate for a distraction. The opportunity to own his own business in a country community by the lake? Too good to pass up. The weeks he'd spent hauling and scrubbing and hammering and painting—and sweating bullets at the bank—had been worth it.

Now he just had to convince his kids he'd made the right decision.

"Da-ad!" Nine-year-old Grace emerged from the nearest bay, hands steepled against her forehead to protect her eyes from the afternoon sun. She was all legs and nut-colored hair, just like her mother. He grinned through the usual hot prod of regret and pulled her into a hug. Her little body remained stiff—she wasn't liking him much these days.

She wriggled free, her eyes on Joe's pickup. "The truck broke down again?"

He didn't know whether to be amused or bothered by her world-weary tone. "The brakes need work. Joe's letting us use his until Bertha's out of the shop."

Her on-the-warpath gaze returned to his face. "Travis took my marker. My favorite marker. The purple one. How am I supposed to finish my project? I have to turn in a weather report and I'm drawing a rainbow and without purple it'll look stupid and I'll fail." Her voice ended on a squeak shrill enough to shatter glass.

"I hear you, G, I hear you. Take it down a notch, all right? Let's go inside and talk to your brother."

She flounced back into the store, her bright turquoise tennis shoes smacking the concrete. Seth followed more leisurely, blinking in the dim interior. He nodded at Bradley, the lean, shaggy-haired, just-turned-twenty part-timer who'd opted out of community college in favor of another year of playing video games on his mother's couch. He was slouched behind the counter, a bottle of glass cleaner in one hand and a smartphone in the other. Didn't take a genius to figure out which he'd been using.

The kid might be lazy, but he had good business sense and Seth liked him. More important, Grace and Travis loved him.

"Everything good?" Seth asked. Another argument erupted from the office in the back and he grunted. "Besides the noise level, I mean?"

"Old Mr. Katz called. He's on his last bucket of feed. Wants to know if we can make a special delivery."

"Got time to swing by on your way home?"

"I guess." He frowned. "You ever going to make him pay his bill?"

"That horse of his is all he has left of his farm. The odd bag of feed won't kill me."

"You, no. Your business, yeah. I lose this job and I won't be able to pay my phone bill."

"Your concern is touching," Seth said wryly. "But I'm not going anywhere. You won't, either—" he lifted an eyebrow at the glass cleaner in Bradley's hand " —as long as you *do* your job."

Bradley grinned, snatched up a rag and flicked at the countertop while humming in a falsetto tone.

"Smart-ass," Seth muttered, and continued on to the office, a half-wood, half-glass corner structure left from the building's firehouse days. A battered metal desk took up one half of the room, and waist-high shelving lined the other. In the center stood a rickety round table Seth had set up as a homework station for the kids. The school bus dropped them off about half past three and they were stuck at the store until six, when Seth closed for the day. They hadn't been thrilled with the arrangement at first, but they'd settled into a routine — snack and playtime until four thirty, homework till closing. Most days they finished their assignments before piling into Seth's truck for the short trek home, which meant that once dinner and cleanup were behind them, they could veg in front of the TV until tuck-in time. Traditionally, tuck-in time included hearing a chapter from whatever book they'd voted Seth should read them. Every now and then they veered off course and had a sing-along. Grace insisted she needed the practice for sixth-grade chorus tryouts.

Never mind she was still in fourth.

"Where *is* it?" Grace's voice was thick with tears. "Tell me!"

Seth stalked into the office wearing his best "heads are about to roll" expression. "All right, what's the problem here?"

"I told you," Grace cried. She had both palms on the table and was leaning toward her brother, who sat steadily coloring, a fistful of crayons in one hand and half a chocolate bar in the other.

Dammit, Bradley. No wonder they loved his part-timer.

Grace opened her mouth again and Seth held up a finger. "I'd like to hear it from Travis."

With a beleaguered exhale, his daughter pushed upright and crossed her arms over her chest. Seth waited. Grace fumed. Travis poked the green crayon back into his fist and plucked out a yellow.

"Travis," Seth prodded.

His seven-year-old looked up from what appeared to be a drawing of a food fight. Chocolate ringed his mouth and it was all Seth could do not to grin. That would be fatal, though. Grace was already convinced Seth loved her brother more.

"Hey, Dad," Travis said brightly, as if he hadn't just been trading insults with his sister.

"Hey," Seth drawled. "We're looking for a purple magic marker. Have you seen it?"

Travis blinked but remained mute, his normal MO whenever talking would mean telling a lie. Seth gritted his teeth around a sigh. Either Travis had the marker, or he knew Grace had it and didn't want to tattle. Lately G had taken to "losing" things in a bid for attention. Or maybe she just wanted to drive her dad crazy.

She was doing a good job of it.

Thing was, he could never tell when the tears and the drama were real. G's pediatrician back in State College, along with Seth's mother and his good friend Parker, who operated a nearby greenhouse and had her own challenges with a daughter who'd just turned ten, had advised him not to sweat it, assuring him it was just a phase. Decent advice, except that a week ago he'd spotted his checkbook in the recycling bin. Hard not to sweat that.

He'd reasoned, scolded, pleaded and suspended all kinds of privileges. He understood his daughter's frustration. Still, there had to be a better way for her to express it.

Back to the matter at hand. His son had resumed his coloring, the tilt of his white-blond head casual, his grip on the crayon anything but. "Travis isn't talking, G. How about we all look for it together?"

"I don't have time," she whined. "I need it now."

"Can you use a different color?"

She dropped her arms and snatched up her drawing, a tidy rendition of a rainbow arching behind a soggy pair of trees and a horse. She stabbed a finger at the innermost arch of the rainbow, currently colorless, and shot him a look that screamed, *Duh!*

He surveyed the markers scattered across the table. "If you mix red and blue, you get purple. Maybe use red, then color over it with blue?"

"Good idea," Bradley said behind him. G's shoulders lost some of their height, though she shot a dirty look at her brother.

"Whatever," she muttered. She grabbed the red marker and dropped into her chair.

Seth turned away and bumped knuckles with Bradley. "Remind me to give you a raise."

"You can't afford it." He shoved a message pad at Seth. As per usual, there were more doodles than writing on the paper. "Pete Lowry called again. He needs another payment for the work he did on the truck."

This was the work he'd done the *last* time Bertha was in the shop.

15

"I'll take care of it." Somehow. Seth noticed Bradley fighting a grin. "Something else on your mind?"

"Olivia Duncan's on the phone again. Want me to take a message?"

Seth pictured the curvy brunette with the open smile and kind eyes. Last time they'd talked, she'd offered to arrange a picnic lunch for Seth and the kids. Sandwiches and Frisbee by the lake.

"You three should enjoy the beach more often," she'd said. *Like a normal family*, she'd meant.

He glanced over his shoulder at his kids, one secretive, the other sullen. Thought of the hell they'd been through the past few years.

They could use some normal.

His brain flashed from Olivia to Ivy, whose elegance, beauty, stubbornness and lusty sense of humor were far from ordinary. Ivy. Who'd made it clear she'd put up with children only if they arrived on a school bus and left the same way, in ninety minutes or less.

He didn't want to date anyone else. Hadn't wanted to date at all after his divorce, until he met her. But he had to make it clear — to himself and to her — that what little they had wasn't working anymore.

"No." Seth took off his cap and tossed it at his desk, rolled his shoulders and headed for the door. "I got this."

*   *   *

IVY SWEPT THE RUBBER currycomb over the stallion's gleaming coat, over and over, each circular stroke carrying her closer to calm. She still had a long way to go, though, because she hadn't quite managed to convince herself that Seth Walker didn't deserve a good, swift kick in his stupendous ass.

She knew he hadn't been playing hard to get. But it ticked her off that he'd simply up and walked out on the game. The jerk.

What ticked her off even more? The burning sensation behind her eyes. She blinked, cleared her throat and focused on the one male in her life she knew would never let her down.

"He doesn't know what he's missing, does he, Cabana Boy?"

16

The dark bay's coat rippled and he scolded her with a snort. She was brushing too hard. Ivy lifted the comb away.

"Sorry about that." She moved to the corner where she'd stashed the plastic grooming tote and exchanged the currycomb for a soft-bristled body brush. She hesitated and stared down at the fresh straw covering the floor. Her shoulders ached from mucking out stalls—she'd gotten a little too carried away with the pitchfork. And she still had to close up the milking shed, pay bills and record the production numbers before she could call it a day. A tuna sandwich would have to do for dinner. She didn't have the energy to manage anything more exciting.

Crap, did she even *have* mayonnaise?

She leaned forward until her forehead rested against the iron grill forming the upper half of the stall. The slim bars provided better lighting and ventilation than a solid floor-to-ceiling wall and saved Ivy—and her horses—from claustrophobia. She closed her eyes and breathed in the rich, sunshiny scent of dried straw and the mint toothpaste she used every time she washed her hands to get rid of the smell of manure.

She pictured Seth with Olivia, and regret knotted her stomach. Maybe he'd understand if she explained why she couldn't have children in her life. And maybe he'd hate her forever.

It wasn't worth the risk. Seth was right. He and his kids deserved a woman who'd put them first.

Would he really stop playing deliveryman, though?

She opened her eyes, pushed away from the wall and turned back to Cabana Boy and his soothing beauty. He was brown, and his points—mane, tail and lower legs—were black, but Ivy's favorite feature was the bright white star on his forehead, a star that looked more like a backward comma. Her parents had brought the stallion home as a sort of consolation prize for leaving Ivy behind while they cruised the Mediterranean. One month later, they were both dead.

That had been eight years ago.

Cabana Boy nudged her shoulder. "I should have brought an apple," she murmured. Her stomach grumbled, and she huffed a laugh. "For each of us."

A scuffing sound behind her had her swinging around while her heart bounced against her breastbone. Wade leaned over the stall door, and Ivy struggled to keep the disappointment out of her face. How pathetic, that she'd think for even a second that Seth might have changed his mind.

"Hey there," she said. "Heading out?" It was late, but he'd made it into work only a couple of hours ago.

He nodded, gaze locked on the stallion. "I fixed that one pulsator. Just needed to adjust the pressure. We're back to ten milkers again."

"Bless you," she said, and got the first inkling of trouble when his lips thinned under his gray-flecked mustache. She patted Cabana Boy's flank and turned toward her farm manager. "Everything okay with Becky?"

He shrugged, still not looking at Ivy. "Her brush with death has got her to thinking. What she wants to do with her life and such."

"Brush with death?" Ivy gaped. "Wade, she backed into a Dumpster at the dollar store. Broke her collarbone after slipping on a half-eaten egg-salad sandwich when she got out to check the damage."

"There are people who can take something like that in stride. Others feel the need for the kind of understanding only a family can provide."

He stuck out his lower lip, signaling his disappointment in her reaction. Ivy sighed. Such a fine damned line between being judgmental and showing righteous scorn. Apparently she'd crossed the line. Again.

Then Wade's words registered. *Oh, God.* "You're moving back to Montana?"

"Soon as we can get packed."

An icy dread coated Ivy's stomach. "Does that mean you're not giving any notice?"

"Like I said, she needs her family." He sucked his lower lip back in and raised conflicted eyes. "I'm sorry, Ivy. I really am."

Shock held her immobile, and her heart felt heavy in her chest. Becky had obviously put her foot down, and Wade had never been able to tell his young bride no. Somehow, she willed a smile to her lips. "I'll miss you," she said thickly. "You've been a top-notch manager and a good friend."

How the hell am I going to replace you?

He shuffled inside the stall and held out a thick, scarred hand, but Ivy ignored it and drew him into a hug. He stiffened, then squeezed her hard, and squeezed even tighter when she made to step back. Once he finally released her, he was blinking rapidly. He turned his head and took his time plucking a piece of hay free of his shoulder.

Ivy concentrated on giving Cabana Boy's head a good solid scrub. "Do you need a reference? I'd be happy to write one up and email it to you."

Wade moved to the other side of the stallion and started stroking the bay's ears. "I appreciate the offer, but I won't need it. We'll be helping out at her folks' ranch."

"Cattle?"

"Dude."

She almost laughed aloud at the disgust in his expression.

He met her gaze, his pale blue eyes brimming with doubt. "Sure wish I didn't have to leave you in the lurch like this."

Me, too. "Don't give it another thought. Everything will work out. It always does. Of course Becky should come first. Give her my best, okay? Anyway, lately you've been mooning over Montana like I've been mooning over that robotic milker that feeds the cows and mucks out the barn at the same time."

Wade's mustache stretched as he grinned. "I am looking forward to getting back out on the prairie. And you can't beat the fly-fishing."

"There you go. Now come on into the house. You can make sure I'm caught up on everything, and I'll print out your check."

An hour later, after sending Wade off with another heartfelt hug and a severance check too small for her liking but too big to be prudent, she left the house in search of her two farmhands, who were no doubt fretting about the extra work they'd have to take on now that Wade was leaving. Normally, they'd have left hours ago, but Wade had asked them to stick around until he'd talked with Ivy. She bet they'd loved that—*not*—but there was always plenty to keep them busy, and she'd put a little extra something in their paychecks to help make up for it. She'd just have to squeeze a little extra milk out of the girls this month.

Padding paychecks might even win her some points when it came time to ask the guys if they'd be willing to take on Wade's duties until she could hire a new manager. She didn't even want to think about how long that could take. She glanced at the clock and closed the lid on her laptop. If Gary and Dell hadn't left yet, she might as well get this conversation over with. Though it promised to be more of a beg-fest than a dialogue.

She grabbed a sweatshirt, stepped out onto the porch and stood for a moment, getting her bearings. Shadows crowded the outbuildings and rolled across the yard. In the distance, the band of navy that was the lake swallowed the remainder of the sun. Only the faintest curve of glimmering orange lit the sky. A barn owl bid daylight a high-pitched, rasping goodbye.

Okay, then. No wonder she was hungry.

Ivy glanced at the gravel lot beside the dairy barn. Two pickup trucks. Gary and Dell were still here. She jogged down the steps and was heading for the barn when a figure ambled out of the milking shed. Gary. If his thin, six-foot frame hadn't given him away, the pale yellow sheen of the outdoor lights reflecting off his hairless head would have.

When he spotted her, he changed course. She met him halfway across the yard, her boots squelching over grass already slick with dew.

"Gary. I was just about to come and check in with you and Dell. Can you give me two minutes before you leave? Is Dell closing up?" If Dell secured the barns, that was one less thing she'd have to worry about before grabbing that tuna sandwich. Yay. She took a step toward the milking shed.

Gary moved in front of her. "You going to promote one of us to manager?"

Oh. Ouch. She hid a wince. "Why don't we find Dell so we can all talk about this together?"

"That means no." His jaw was tight, his eyes narrowed. He spread his legs and planted his hands on his hips, making it clear he wasn't going to move until he had his answer.

Fine. She'd do this twice. "That means no," she agreed. "You and Dell are each a valuable part of the farm, but neither of you has the business experience I need in a manager."

"You'll have a hard time finding a replacement for Wade."

"Yes, I will."

"Dell and I have worked here a long time. We deserve a shot at that job."

"I couldn't run the farm without you or Dell. And I appreciate your loyalty, Gary. But I don't have time to provide on-the-job training. I need someone who already knows how to manage a dairy farm."

He dropped his arms and took a step backward. "And in the meantime, Dell and me'll have to pick up the slack. Screw that."

Ivy held out a hand. "Wait. What does that mean?"

"Means I'm outta here."

This couldn't be happening. "You're quitting?"

"Goddamn right."

"Gary." The knot of frustration in her chest tightened, gathering into a dense, aching mass of dismay. "Please stay. We'll all have to pitch in more, but it'll be temporary. I promise I'll make it worth your while."

"Yeah?" Like a cardboard villain in a cheesy Western, he paraded his gaze up and down her body while tracing a slow hand over his chin. "What did you have in mind?"

NOTHING CLOSE TO WHAT you have in mind," Ivy responded drily. Revulsion warred with disappointment. Why had it taken her so long to recognize that Gary was a sexist asshole?

"Forget I said anything. You can pick up your last check tomorrow."

Wade, she realized. He'd been her buffer, and she'd taken him for granted.

Why were epiphanies always so costly?

She watched Gary stalk toward his truck. It was too dark to make out his expression as he looked back over his shoulder, but she could guess it carried an ugly promise of payback. Just what she needed. Would he try to talk Dell into leaving, too? God. Two men out of her life in a matter of minutes. Three if you counted Seth, who would no doubt cut her off completely any day now. She was on a roll.

Her stomach gurgled again. *Roll* reminded her of cinnamon. And the steaming pile of cow crap that was her day explained why *cinnamon* reminded her of the unopened bottle of schnapps she'd stashed in the cabinet over the kitchen sink.

She wheeled around and marched up the porch steps, chin held so high she tripped on the last one. She stumbled forward and fell into the screen door, one arm outstretched in a vain attempt to catch herself. The mesh fabric parted from the aluminum frame with a growling *zzzzzzzip.*

Oh, for Pete's sake. She pushed herself upright and scowled down at the ruined door. This wasn't something she could fix herself. And now Wade wasn't around to take care of it. She'd have to call someone.

Or maybe she'd just quit screen doors, cold turkey.

Of course, *cold turkey* made her think of Wild Turkey, and the thought of bourbon reminded her she had a date with a bottle of schnapps.

Thankfully, she could open it all by herself.

Ten minutes later, Ivy decided that drinking alone, especially from a bottle covered in five Christmases' worth of dust, was as pathetic as it was dissatisfying.

She needed something else to distract her. A reflexive glance at the calendar yielded the perfect solution. How could she have forgotten her monthly investment club meeting? Her fellow members of Dollars and Divas would provide the perfect diversion.

And chances were good the booze would be dust-free.

*   *   *

HALF AN HOUR LATER, after a hasty tuna sandwich and a conversation with Dell that saved her a return trip to the liquor cabinet, Ivy parked in the gravel lot belonging to Thistle Hill Growers, a local greenhouse run by her friend Parker and Parker's husband of less than six months, Reid MacFarland. At least, Reid *would have* been helping to run it if he weren't serving his final tour of duty in Iraq. Ivy couldn't imagine how difficult the separation must be, not only for the couple but for Parker's daughter, Nat, who adored Reid. It hadn't always been that way, for Nat *or* her mother. Reid had sought Parker out to apologize for his role in the friendly fire that had taken her husband's life. Parker and Reid had ended up falling in love, and now Parker couldn't wait to have her new husband home for good. She'd moved to Thistle Hill a year and a half ago, and it had taken her a while to warm up to Ivy — to anyone, really — but Ivy had finally talked her into joining the local investment club, and Parker was now one of Ivy's closest friends.

Ivy hopped out of her truck and breathed in the heady scent of damp mulch and those ruffly red blooms Parker had once told her were camellias. The early-evening gloom was thickening, and an autumn chill edged the air. Ivy made her way along the concrete path that crossed the yard, connecting the empty gravel lot to a driveway crowded with cars. Seemed she was the last to arrive.

Not that she should have been there at all. What she should have been doing was writing up a help-wanted ad, making phone calls and working up some kind of a schedule from hell for her and Dell. She'd simply have to squeeze that in sometime in the morning, between chores.

Hesitating in the warm yellow glow of the porch light, she let the muted laughter and chatter and the pumpkin-pie smell of Parker's signature muffins soothe her.

Oh, yeah. She needed this.

She was reaching for the door when it swung open. Parker had exchanged her usual denim overalls for black pants and a sapphire-blue cowl-neck sweater. She smiled and pushed at the screen door.

"About time you got here, Farmer Jane," the redhead teased, waving Ivy into the comforting chaos of a Dollars and Divas meeting. Ten women of varying ages and backgrounds formed the group, but they all had one crucial thing in common — they liked each other. A lot. They also liked wine, desserts, romance novels and laughing.

And talking about men.

Ivy felt better already.

Inevitably, the conversation turned to sex, which did *not* make her feel better, because it had been so long since she'd had any. But hoo, boy, had she learned a lot over the years.

Especially from the Catlett sisters.

When Ivy stepped into the cottage-style living room and began her hellos, it was the seventy-something Catletts she spoke with first. Hazel and June liked their makeup bright, their gossip salacious and their man candy shirtless. Hazel's white hair was pixie short, and tonight's shade of lipstick looked like a blueberry had got it on with a box of Christmas tinsel. June wore her silver hair in a similar style and tonight rocked a yellow sweater dress Ivy couldn't have carried off half as well. Ditto on the turquoise eye shadow.

"Audrey has a boyfriend," June said in a singsong voice as she guided Ivy over to the dining room table, where Parker had set out a selection of wine and soft drinks. June was referring to Audrey

Tweedy, the Catletts' close friend and coconspirator. Audrey was a woman who believed staunchly in the power of protein. Her father had opened the feed store Seth now owned, and Seth had won himself instant popularity with most of Thistle Hill's old-timers — especially Audrey — by keeping the name Tweedy's Feed and Seed.

Ivy helped herself to a glass of wine and took a hefty sip. She'd promised herself, no thoughts of Seth Walker tonight.

Yeah. As if she'd really manage *that*.

"Hazel's furious. She thinks it's her own main squeeze, Pete Lowry," June said in Ivy's ear. Her "whisper" bounced off every flat surface in the room and quieted all other conversation.

"The guy who owns the garage?" Allison Kincaid moved closer and clinked her glass against Ivy's in greeting. Despite having been in Thistle Hill the shortest of any of the women present, the petite blonde was Ivy's closest friend. She was also co-owner of the town's only motel, Sleep at Joe's. Allison gazed down at Hazel, who was tucked into the corner of Parker's pale-blue-and-cream-striped couch. "You and Pete have a thing?"

Hazel offered up a wink that failed miserably at being playful. "He really knows how to twist my gas cap, if you know what I mean."

Allison wagged her head. "No, I don't, and I'd consider it a personal favor if you didn't tell me."

Ivy joined Allison in frowning down at Hazel. "You don't really think Audrey's messing around with Pete, do you?"

"She's had that Lincoln of hers in his shop five times in the past month. *Five times.*"

From the connected dining room came a snort. Parker looked up from the tray of hors d'oeuvres she was arranging in the center of the large oval table.

"Hazel Catlett. You do realize that car of hers is older than I am? Things are bound to give out."

Hazel rolled her eyes as she emptied the wine bottle into her glass. "Parker MacFarland, you're twenty years younger than me. You can't even begin to know what you're talking about."

"*Twenty* years younger?" June scoffed. "More like forty. Better ease up on the wine, sis."

A door banged open and shut out in the hall and twenty-four-year-old Liz Early appeared in the archway in black jeans, boots and a purple turtleneck, her curly ebony hair gathered up in a thick ponytail that reached halfway down her back.

"What are we talking about?" she asked brightly.

"Getting old," Hazel said.

"Oh." Liz dropped into the chair opposite the couch, crossed her legs and pulled out her phone. "Should we call someone who actually knows what that's like?"

Everyone laughed, and Ivy stretched forward from her position by the couch to offer Liz a knuckle bump.

Parker pushed a hand into the air, as if she were summoning a waiter, then pointed at Liz. "Someone give this girl a drink."

While June and Allison converged on Liz's chair, June with an empty glass and Allison with a wine bottle, Ivy sank down onto the couch beside Hazel.

"Have you asked Audrey if she's seeing Pete? I think you should, Hazel. You two have been friends since...well, since forever. She wouldn't do something like that to you."

"And how do you know that?"

"You wouldn't do it to her, would you?"

"I wouldn't do it *again*."

Ivy stared. Hazel shrugged. "It was a long time ago."

June pivoted to face them and flapped a hand. "Don't listen to her. She doesn't really believe that, about Audrey and Pete. Besides, we all know Audrey has the hots for Snoozy."

"We do?" Allison whipped around so fast she almost fell sideways. That was what she got for wearing those ridiculous designer heels. Which Ivy totally coveted and would have said so if she weren't preoccupied trying to imagine the skinny, mournful-looking owner of Snoozy's Bar paired up with the brawny Audrey Tweedy.

Allison gaped at Hazel. "Are you sure Audrey's crushing on Snoozy? I didn't think she was all that impressed with him *or* his snake."

Laughter erupted. Allison flushed when she realized what she'd said.

"It's true—Audrey's very impatient when it comes to Snoozy's snake." Liz leaned around Allison and looked earnestly at Ivy. "I was in the diner when she tried to convince him to let her eat it."

A moment's shocked silence, then the shrieking began. Ivy fell back onto the couch, hooting, and Hazel pounded the armrest and almost choked, she was laughing so hard. June dropped onto the arm of Liz's chair, giggling wildly and shaking her head, while Allison rocked back and forth and scrubbed at the tears dripping down her cheeks. Parker stood by the dining room table, both hands clapped to her mouth.

Liz's expression alternated between embarrassment and indignation. She started to say something a couple of times but no one could hear her over the laughter. Finally, Allison took pity on her and signaled for everyone to quiet down.

"Okay, okay, let's give Liz a break. We all know we're talking about Snoozy's python, which I had the misfortune of finding wedged behind the wall of my motel room." She shuddered. "I'm still hearing things behind the walls."

Ivy pushed off the couch and patted Allison's shoulder. "On the plus side, you reunited a long-lost pet with her grieving owner. And now you have Joe to handle your pest control for you."

"Yes," Allison murmured. "Now I have Joe." The way she said it and the sappy smile on her face made Ivy more envious than any pair of Jimmy Choo shoes could. But a happy-ever-after wasn't in Ivy's future, and she was fine with that. Though she wouldn't mind a happy-for-now with Seth. Especially if that happy could occur in bed, and even more especially if they could agree on terms. Like, say, for every one of his orgasms, she got two?

He was good for it. She just *knew* he was good for it, damn him.

"Okay, ladies." Parker pointed over her shoulder at the dining room table. "Refreshments are served. How about we help ourselves, then get down to business? I found a technology stock I want to tell you all about."

Liz started to snicker as Ivy poured a glass of iced tea. "Speaking of business, I saw someone's been at your sign again, Ivy."

She made a face. "I know, right? But they did a good job with it. These days, *funny farm* is an apt description."

"Oh, come on." Allison settled her glass next in line for tea. "You've got that place running like a well-oiled machine."

Liquid sloshed onto the lace tablecloth and Ivy hissed. She set the pitcher aside and snatched up a stack of napkins. "Dammit. Parker, I'm sorry—"

"Relax. Accidents happen. Be right back." Parker rushed off to the kitchen.

Allison came around the table to help mop up. "You're not yourself tonight. Want to tell me what's wrong?"

Ivy lifted her head. Everyone was listening, expressions full of shared concern.

She sighed. "My manager quit this afternoon. Less than an hour after that, one of my farmhands walked out when I told him he wasn't qualified to step into the position."

Her news was greeted with a chorus of sympathetic noises. Hazel leaned over and put a hand on her arm. "Sorry to hear that, hon."

Allison looked thoughtful as she dabbed at the tablecloth. "So you'll need someone to help out part-time while you're looking for replacements."

Ivy smirked at her designer-clad friend. "Why? You interested?"

"Dear God in heaven, no. Learning to milk a cow is *not* on my bucket list." Allison grinned. "See what I did there?" When no one else seemed impressed, she went back to dabbing. "How about Seth?"

Ivy set her glass down before it slipped through her fingers. "In the first place, he has two kids to look after and his own business to run. In the second..." She hesitated. Allison bumped her shoulder.

"C'mon, girl, spill it."

Parker chuckled as she came back into the room with a handful of dishrags. "She already did."

Liz tittered.

Ivy exhaled. "Seth and I... We're not on the best of terms."

June pursed her lips. "When are you going to stop rejecting that poor man?"

"As of today," Ivy muttered.

Allison clapped her hands. "You're finally going for it? For crying out loud, woman, what are you doing *here*?"

Ivy was shaking her head, her braid heavy between her shoulder blades. "I won't be rejecting him, because after today he won't be asking me out anymore."

"What did you *do*?" wailed Hazel.

Allison shrugged her slim shoulders. "All that means is you have to ask *him*."

"Ladies, I'm not interested in dating. Period."

"But this is Seth. What's the big deal about dating Seth?" Hazel fluffed her white hair. "Go on a few dates, do the nasty, decide if you're in it to win it."

It took a moment for Ivy to find her voice again. "The *big deal* is, he may very well realize that dating me is no deal at all. That I'm one big anticlimax, so to speak. What if he's so disappointed he decides he never wants to see me again?"

Parker turned and lobbed the dishrags at the nearest countertop, added a mini quiche to her plate and passed the platter. "Maybe I'm just being slow, but hasn't that already happened?"

"He didn't say he never wanted to see her again. He told her he was cutting back on seeing her." Liz paused, then made a face at Parker. "Dude. You're right." She turned a sympathetic smile on Ivy. "What are you going to do?"

"The only thing I can do." Ivy sank into the nearest chair and pushed at her plate. "Cut my losses and start saving for a wedding present for him and Ms. DMV."

Allison put a hand on her hip. "Is this about Evan?"

Liz frowned. "Who's Evan?"

"You remember." June nibbled at a cube of cheddar. "The guy Ivy was going to marry."

"That jerk." Liz finished off her plate with a ham biscuit and settled across from Ivy.

"Wait. I never knew you were engaged," Parker said.

Allison poured her own tea and pulled out the chair beside Ivy. "Two years ago, and she hasn't dated anyone since. And no—" she aimed a pointed glance at her neighbor " —casual sex isn't dating."

At the head of the table, Hazel grinned. "It's one hell of a runner-up, though."

"And of course this is about Evan." Allison flapped her napkin and dropped it into her lap. "A guy says he loves you and can't get a ring on your finger fast enough and all the while, he's scheming to sell your farm to a real estate developer? That's bound to leave a scar."

June sprang to her feet and brushed crumbs from her sweater dress. "How about we look at Seth as an investment? Run the numbers. Do a risk analysis. What do you think, dear heart?"

"I think we have better things to do." Ivy turned resolutely to Parker. "Tell us about that stock you mentioned."

Parker grinned. "I'd rather do a stock study on Seth."

"Thank you." June cast a stern expression on Ivy. "You going to make us take a vote?"

"Fine. Whatever." Ivy yanked her plate closer and wrenched a red grape free of its cluster. "But I'm telling you, this is a losing proposition."

"We won't know that until we've filled out the checklist." June bent down to the shoulder bag she'd stashed under the table and pulled out a clipboard. She put on her reading glasses, picked up a pen and got down to business. "Historical earnings?"

Ivy snorted. Allison flicked Ivy's biceps and June peered at her over the top of her glasses.

Ivy sighed. "He's only been running the feed store for a year."

"Insufficient data." June scribbled on the form.

Ivy shifted in her chair. "But he is the owner."

"Which means it'll be easy to find out what management's up to. Debt ratio?"

"Really? You think I know that?"

"What *I* want to know is—" Hazel looked up from polishing her bifocals " —what's his growth potential?"

Liz elbowed her in the ribs. "I'm betting eight inches."

Amid the whoops and high fives, Ivy dropped her head into her hands. *Please, God, just smite me now.*

"How about his current yield?" someone asked.

"Ivy's the one with the high yield." That was Allison. "If she had her way, she'd be yielding all over the place."

"That's enough." Ivy planted her palms on the table and pushed to her feet. "Thank you all for the advice. It may have been unsolicited, but it was definitely valueless. Now can we please start the meeting?"

June grinned. "I see what you did there."

"Ivy's right—it's time to get down to business." Parker opened her laptop. "Let's start with—"

"Wait, I have one, I have one." Liz was practically bouncing in her seat as she leaned toward Ivy. "Bite low and say hi."

Ivy couldn't help but laugh, Liz looked so delighted with herself.

"What does that even mean?" Hazel squinted across the table. "You want her to bite his crankshaft? I wouldn't think that would go over so well."

June was nodding sagely. "And do you really think that once she bites him, he'll stick around long enough for her to say hi?"

"Oh, please, give the girl a break. It was funny." Allison grinned. "Besides, every guy likes a little nibble now and then."

"Don't we all," sighed Hazel. Immediately, Allison and Parker took Hazel to task for finding fault with Liz's contribution in the first place. While they bickered, Ivy decided to ask Liz about her love life. It was way past time to put someone else on the spot.

She leaned across the table. "How's everything between you and Marcus?"

"Good. It's good." Liz hesitated, and her shoulders collapsed. "No, that's not true. We've been dating since April and I don't know him much better than I did when we met. I mean, I know he has...issues to work through, and he's told me some stuff, but we've—" her cheeks flushed and she lowered her voice "—we've hardly been physical at all, let alone had sex."

Ivy wondered how much Liz knew about Marcus's situation. Allison had come to Thistle Hill to shame her ex-boyfriend Joe Gallahan into helping her save her job at an advertising firm back in Washington, DC. Joe had agreed but only if she'd help with the motel's renovations. It hadn't taken long for them to fall in love all over again—despite serious challenges involving a python, an ex-con out for vengeance and a fire that almost destroyed the motel.

That ex-con had been Marcus Watts. Allison had stumbled upon him after he'd broken into her room at the motel. The twenty-year-old had been living in the woods, waiting for the opportunity to burn down Sleep at Joe's because of the horrific abuse he'd suffered while his stepfather owned the place.

Allison hadn't confided every detail, but Ivy knew enough to be both sickened and enraged on Marcus's behalf and to realize it could be a long time before he was ready for any kind of intimacy, emotional or physical.

She glanced around and saw that everyone else was still engaged in a good-natured argument. "Have you talked to him about it?"

Liz nodded miserably. "He gets so defensive. He's seeing a counselor, but I have a feeling a big part of the problem is that he doesn't think he's good enough for me."

"I'm sure you're doing your best to convince him otherwise."

"Yeah, but now I'm thinking I need to follow the same advice everyone is giving you. You know. Totally take the initiative." Her smile was both tentative and sly. "Is that what you're going to do?"

Ivy was saved from responding when Parker stood and tapped a knife against her wineglass. "Someone needs to call this meeting to order. Otherwise you'll all be spending the night and anyone still here in the morning will have to earn her breakfast by helping out in the greenhouses."

"Oh." June raised her hand. "Speaking of greenhouses, I noticed the floodlights on the hut closest to the parking lot aren't working."

"Those dumb things." Parker scowled. "There must be some kind of electrical problem, because Harris just changed those bulbs."

"I'll get Joe to take a look at them for you." Allison bit her lip. "And if there's anything else along those lines you'd like done, you might want to let him know now. He has another project coming up that's going to keep him extra busy."

"Hmph." Hazel pushed a strawberry between her blueberry lips and gazed at Allison, brown eyes twinkling. "And here he just put the finishing touches on that brand-new love nest above the motel office. What's next, a sauna? A swimming pool?"

"A baby." Allison aimed a sheepish glance at Ivy and pressed her palms to her stomach. "We're going to have a baby."

*   *   *

A SCALDING RUSH OF acid taunted the back of Marcus's throat as he gazed at the other employees gathered in the diner's kitchen. This was some bad shit going down, and everybody was looking at *him*.

One of the waitresses, Rachel, stood beside him, lower lip quivering, and he almost reached for her hand. She had that whole everything-has-to-be-a-drama teen thing going on, but in this case she wasn't exaggerating.

"It'll be okay," Marcus murmured, but how could he expect her to believe that when he didn't believe it himself?

Rachel ignored him, and continued to stare at the diner's owner. "You're saying one of us is a thief."

"I'm saying there's money missing." Cal ran a palm over his short, gray-black hair and Marcus shifted his weight. Poor Cal looked closer to tears than Rachel.

"If it were just one instance," Cal continued, "I'd chalk it up to a mistake. We all make 'em. But several times over the past month, the drawer's been short." His sober gaze traveled from face to face. No one spoke. Someone swallowed, loudly. It was Thursday night, and business was slow. As soon as their one customer had been served his maple-glazed salmon, Cal had gathered the entire evening shift in the kitchen.

Marcus, the cook. Rachel and Parvati, servers. And Noah, who manned the grill during the early shift but had dropped in to pick up his paycheck. All but Noah wore the diner's uniform of black polo shirts and khakis. They took turns staring at the reddish-brown tiled floor, the empty grill that still smelled of fish and fried onions, and the stainless steel shelves lined with neat rows of plates, glasses, napkins and condiment bottles with the labels turned out.

They looked everywhere but at Cal.

"We have to figure this out and put a stop to it," he said. "I'll have to sell a truckload of cinnamon rolls to make up for the revenue I've lost."

"I think just this past week I've eaten a truckload of cinnamon rolls." Parvati patted her ample stomach, trying to lighten the moment. But Cal wasn't smiling.

"Think about it, folks. Smaller profits mean smaller raises and fewer employee benefits."

"Are you having this same talk with everyone?" Marcus asked quietly. There were three more servers on the books, plus a busboy on weekends. "Or just us?"

Cal gave him a look Marcus couldn't interpret. "Everyone needs to hear this. The problem is happening at the cash register, but I won't tolerate theft of any kind. I don't care if it's a can of tomato sauce. You have a money problem, you come to me. We're family. We're supposed to be here for each other." He cleared his throat, but not before everyone heard the break in his voice. "I hate that we're even having this conversation."

Noah, a spongy-looking redhead with a sparse goatee, crossed his arms and squinted. "You said this started a month ago?" When Cal offered up a curt nod, Noah's gaze slid to Marcus. "Isn't that about the same time he started working the register?"

Marcus didn't flinch. He'd been waiting for this. He met Cal's gaze squarely, and after a moment his heart bobbed back up to the surface. How long would Cal be able to hang on to the respect Marcus was seeing in his eyes?

"Yes," Cal said simply. "But I trust Marcus as much as I trust each of you. Which is what makes this so hard." He went on to tell them he was available at any hour of the day, for anyone who wanted to talk. Then he went into his office and shut the door.

"Why don't you stay away from the register?" Eyeing Marcus, Noah folded the envelope containing his paycheck and slid it into his back pocket. "That way, if money goes missing again, we'll know you're not the thief."

"And if it doesn't go missing, everyone will think he is." Parvati raised her perfect eyebrows. "Nice try, Noah."

He let loose a smirk. "Maybe no one's stealing at all. Maybe someone's getting confused and making too much change. Maybe Cal shouldn't let anyone over fifty near the register."

Parvati's lined face went gray.

Rachel fisted her bony hands. "Shut up. Just shut up. How old do you think Cal is, you moron? Anyway, you're the one who can't inventory five boxes of steaks without using a calculator."

"All right, that's enough," Marcus growled. When everyone went quiet, he struggled to hide his surprise. He pushed away from the counter he'd been leaning against and angled his chin toward the office. "Cal's right. We're family. Instead of turning on each other, we should be helping each other out. I don't believe any of us is stealing, so let's work together and figure out what *is* going on."

"Who put you in charge?" Noah demanded. "You turn twenty-one and suddenly you think you're calling the shots?"

"Excuse me?" A hesitant voice reached them from the front of the diner. "Could I get a refill on my tea?"

"Be right there, baby doll," Parvati called. She scowled at Noah and bustled out of the kitchen.

Rachel's thin shoulders bounced. "So what if he's only twenty-one? You're only twenty-three."

"And you're, like, twelve, so get out of my face."

"There a problem here?" They all turned to see Cal standing in the doorway to his office. No one answered. With abrupt motions, Cal finished tying the strings of his black apron. "Marcus, don't you have somewhere to be?"

"Yes, sir." Marcus pulled his own apron over his head. He usually cooked in the evenings, but Cal had given him the rest of the night off. He'd worked a double over the weekend when Noah had called in sick, and Cal had insisted.

Which meant Cal would be cooking for what was left of the shift.

The diner's owner turned to his other cook. "You have your check. How about you let Rachel get back to work?"

With a nod, Noah scurried toward the back door. Rachel made a clumsy gesture toward the front, then spun and hurried to join Parvati.

Cal studied Marcus. "Usually when you have a date with Liz, you're out of here so fast all anyone can see is a blur. Everything okay?" When Marcus hesitated, Cal held up a hand. "Never mind. I

35

shouldn't have asked. But in case your lady needs softening up, I put aside a little something for you in the walk-in."

Marcus shook his boss's hand. "I appreciate that." Though a few cinnamon rolls wouldn't even start to make up for the hurt he was about to inflict.

* * *

TEN MINUTES LATER, MARCUS parked in front of Snoozy's Bar, where Liz waited tables. He eased the wheezing pickup in between two SUVs and let the engine idle. His palms were slick on the steering wheel, and his throat felt as though he'd spent an entire week breathing in flour.

She'd called him late last night. She'd said she needed to know more about him and asked that their date tonight include an exchange of secrets. He'd balked at first, but she'd been insistent.

Her voice had been soft, sleepy, coaxing. He'd pictured her curled up on her couch in flannel pajamas, sipping a cup of that chai tea she liked. How could he say no?

After their conversation, he'd barely slept. He'd struggled with what to say to her, with how much to reveal. By sunrise he'd known what he had to do. He'd keep his end of the bargain, and then he'd say goodbye.

The passenger door opened and he jumped.

Liz peered in, her face wary. "You look like you're about to make a quick getaway. Do you want me in or out?"

"In," he said, though that was the trouble. She'd already worked her way into his heart, and lately she'd been running a strong campaign to work her way into his bed. He could almost picture them building a life together.

Not going to happen, dude. She had no idea what she'd be getting into.

Sweat seemed to shoot out of his palms and he scrubbed his hands on his jeans. He glanced at Liz as she settled in her seat and did a double take as he noticed the heels on her sandals. They had to be as high as his hand was wide.

"You didn't tell me what to wear," she said, in half accusation, half challenge.

"Would it have mattered?"

She rounded on him and he tensed, but she didn't fire back. Instead she wore a delighted smile. "You *have* been paying attention." She made a satisfied sound, flopped back against the seat and started to hum as he backed out of the parking lot.

A funny, unfamiliar feeling settled between his ribs. She was right. He had been paying attention, since the day they'd met here at the bar after Joe Gallahan had cornered him in his motel. Marcus had been a homeless stalker with more attitude than sense, but Joe had ended up treating him to lunch. One look at the crinkly-haired server taking their order and Marcus had wanted to stay in Thistle Hill forever.

"How are things with Joe?" she asked, as if she'd read his mind.

"Better." Joe had lost it there for a while, letting guilt drive him to the whiskey bottle, but he'd managed to turn things around. It helped that he'd fixed things with Allison.

C'mon, Marcus. Don't go getting wistful.

"Have you talked to him lately?" Liz tried for an offhand tone and failed miserably.

Marcus shot her a look. "I take it Allison shared their news at your meeting last night?"

"Yes!" Liz bounced around in her seat, her grin wider than Lake Erie. "A baby! Isn't that exciting?"

He dragged in a breath. So that was what this was all about. Her friend was pregnant and now Liz was feeling domestic.

Shit.

"Well, I think it's exciting," she said. Her hand rested on his biceps, heating his skin through the sleeve of his shirt. "Where are we going?"

He blinked back a round of baby-ass tears and offered up a muttered "You'll see."

Twenty minutes later, he parked at an unused entrance to a golf course, divided from the lake by a strip of woods that, thanks to erosion, was a lot skinnier than Marcus remembered. Dusk was on its way. The autumn evening had taken on a grayish tinge, which meant the woods would be murky. He got out of the truck, grabbed a flashlight from behind the seat and tipped his head toward the lake. "Want to give it a go?"

"Is there a path?" She cast a doubtful glance at her heels. "Maybe I should take these off."

"There used to be a trail covered in pine needles. If it's overgrown, we'll turn back."

"Used to be? When was this?"

"When I was a boy." After she slipped out of her shoes, he hesitated and shook his head. "Wait. This is a bad idea. Your feet will get cold. How about we go grab a hamburger and I'll show you another time?"

"No way. We had a bargain. You'd show me yours and I'd show you mine." The naughty in her voice and the alluring curve of her lips thickened the breath in his lungs.

"I don't think our bargain included an X-rated show-and-tell," he said lightly.

Her smile sagged. She opened her door and hopped out. "When we're done here? You owe me that hamburger."

Wincing at the disenchantment in her tone, he joined her where she stood on the faded pavement in front of the truck. Her head was cocked. He heard it, too. The constant heavy rumble of a waterfall. His pulse kicked into an awkward sprint.

"Show me," she said.

He didn't have to use the flashlight. Not yet. He guided her along a path that led to the stream feeding the falls. The rich smell of damp earth rose up around them, and the rumbling grew into a thunderous rush as the woods opened up. He captured her hand, and together they stepped out onto a bluff that rose a good thirty feet above Lake Erie.

"I'd come to this spot whenever I could," he murmured. "The foaming fury of the waterfall next to the calmness of the lake — it fascinated me. Called to me, too." He looked over at her, admiring her pale features, flushed peach by the disappearing sun. "More than once I came close to jumping."

Briefly, violently, her whole body shook. She released his hand and swiped at the shocked tears that sprang into her eyes.

"All I wanted was to feel normal," he said, pushing the words over the hot swell of emotion in his throat. "You can't feel normal when everyone looks at you like you're a freak."

"You're not a freak. Your stepfather? The other men who molested you? They're the freaks." She swiped again at her cheeks, wiped her palms on her jeans and took a deep breath. "And anyway, if it's normal you want to feel, I can help with that."

A split second later she was on him, her hands sliding around to the back of his neck, her breasts getting cozy with his chest.

EVEN AS HIS BODY yelled, *Hell, yeah*, his brain shouted, *Bad fucking idea*. Marcus backed away but Liz followed. When a tree blocked his escape, she pushed even closer. He slid sideways, dropping the flashlight and grabbing on to her waist for balance. Her shirt had ridden up and the feel of her soft bare skin made him dizzy.

He froze. She froze. They stood chest to chest, zipper to zipper, and he could hardly hear the waterfall over the breaths ripping out of his throat.

She whispered his name and her mouth sought his. Before their lips could connect, he turned his head and reached for her hands. "I didn't bring you here for this."

"Maybe I came for this."

"You're sorry for me. I get it."

"I'm not sorry for you, Marcus. I hurt for you. I want to...to..."

"Ease my pain?"

"Show I care."

"This isn't happening."

"Tonight? Or ever?"

He nudged her away from him, intent on finding the flashlight so they could get out of there. He hadn't handled this well. He hadn't handled this well at all. She pressed close again and nuzzled his throat.

"Please, Marcus," she murmured. "I'll make it good for you."

His lungs seized. He shoved her away, harder this time, so hard she stumbled and fell. His hands—hell, his entire body—trembled. He collapsed back against the tree and struggled for air.

Don't fight it, Marcus. You know you want it, Marcus. Hold still and I'll make it good for you...

"What's wrong?" Liz was crying, gasping as she got to her feet. She peered through her hair at him, dark eyes wide as she swatted at the debris that clung to her jeans. "What did I do?"

"Those words. I don't want them in my head. Especially when I'm with you."

"I'm sorry, I... How could I know? I'm so sorry."

"Don't be," he gritted. "It's not your fault."

She wiped her face on her sleeve and crossed her arms. "It feels like it's my fault."

He found the flashlight and scooped it up. The dark was falling fast. He reached for her, thought better of it and faced her instead, hands awkward at his sides. "Liz, I'm not ready for this. I thought you understood."

"I wanted to show you how much I care. How much you mean to me."

"If you cared, you wouldn't try to manipulate me."

"Manipulate you?" She kicked at the freshly fallen gold-and-russet leaves. "I want to please you."

"Why? What do you want with me? I'm damaged goods. You have no idea how damaged. I have a minimum-wage job, I live on the second floor of an old lady's house and I drive a truck that's older than I am."

"I know all that. None of it changes how I feel about you. I *like* you, Marcus. A lot."

"Here's something you don't know. I'm an ex-con."

Her head came up at that. "You were in prison? What happened?" When he didn't answer, she frowned. "Am I supposed to guess?"

"Aren't you worried?"

"Tell me you're a serial killer and I'll worry. At the same time I'll wonder why you're already out of jail."

His turn to frown. "I didn't kill anyone. It was a fight. I started it. Pulled eighteen months for aggravated assault."

"Why did you start it?"

"I was angry."

"Because?"

"Point is, I'm an ex-con. You need to stay away from me."

She snorted, then laughed when she saw his outrage. "Don't be so dramatic. You're trying to scare me off because you're scared yourself." She moved closer and tugged at his shirtsleeve. "Tell me what started the fight."

He hesitated, then leaned against the tree again. She stayed where she was, and he breathed a little easier. "I worked in a kitchen. At a restaurant. The owner had a thing for one of the busboys."

"The owner was a man."

"Not a man. A monster. One day he cornered the kid in the storage room and tried to make him—" Marcus fisted and unfisted both hands. "So I beat the shit out of him."

"Was the kid okay?"

"Yeah. He was okay."

"Did the monster go to jail?"

Marcus grunted. "Got out before I did."

"When did you get out?"

"A few months before I came back to Thistle Hill."

"You came back to burn down the motel."

"And Cal recognized me. You know the rest."

"Do I?"

He didn't know what she meant.

Her spine sagged, as if he'd failed some kind of test. "How are things with Cal?"

Marcus shrugged. "He's still the same man who fed me whenever I ran away from the motel and ended up at the diner. He's the one who called the cops, the one responsible for getting my stepfather arrested." Too late to do much good, but at least the man had tried.

He stared through the gloom at the woman who was naive enough to think she could free him from his past. "Why are you still here?" he growled. "Why haven't you run screaming for the truck?"

"One, I'm not wearing shoes. Two, you have the flashlight."

He thrust the flashlight at her. She took it but didn't move. He paced away, paced back, picked up a stick and started breaking pieces off and tossing them to the ground. *Snap. Plop. Snap. Plop.* Still she

42

didn't speak.

"How can you want me?" he said finally, hating the need behind his words. "After what I've done?"

"It's true I don't know what you've been through," she said softly, her voice strangled. "I do know it was bad. I also know it's not so much what you've done but what's been done to you. You're a survivor. I respect that. I'm awed by that."

She clicked the flashlight on, then back off. "The first time I saw you," she whispered, "it was like I—I recognized you. Not your face but who you are. Inside." She turned the flashlight back on. The white-yellow glow illuminated her perfect features. "I can be patient, Marcus. I admit I'm feeling less than sexy, but I can wait. You're worth it. You're so worth it."

He had no idea what to say to that. To any of it. He couldn't have talked anyway, since it felt as if that same big-ass tree he'd leaned against was lodged in his throat. As if to demonstrate that she meant what she said, she remained silent, waiting, as he tried to speak.

"Liz," he said finally, his voice guttural. "You deserve better. I think it's time we both moved on."

He wasn't sure what he'd expected her response to be, but a dismissive sniff wasn't it.

"Why?" she demanded, one hand on her hip. "Because you've been in jail?"

He nodded, and she exhaled loudly.

"Whew," she said. "That's okay, then." Her grin outshone the flashlight's beam. "We're perfect for each other, because I've been in jail, too."

*   *   *

IVY'S EARBUDS SERENADED HER with the latest from Pink, which helped mask the mechanized roar of the Bobcat. Up and down the aisle between the bedding stalls she drove the loader, pushing manure, sand and wastewater toward the opening in the floor at the back of the barn. The opening led to a storage chamber underneath, where a horizontal auger pressed the manure into a pit. Thus Ivy had year-round access to her own fertilizer supply. She sold some of it, too — Parker used it for her greenhouses.

One more run down the center and she could start rinsing away the remaining manure with the pressure washer. Yeah, it was a dirty job. A twice-a-day one, too, because 110 Jerseys produced a lot of poo. Not as much as Holsteins, oddly enough, which was one reason Ivy was letting her Holstein population fade out. Sixty percent less poo to push.

Wade had teased that she enjoyed this part of the job way too much, but it made her feel good, spiffing up the place for the girls. She'd switched from organic bedding to sand for that reason — it was cleaner for the cows. Not that the barn stayed clean for long. Jersey girls knew how to party.

She steered the Bobcat out of the barn and into the sunlight, planning to park it near the milking shed, which was next up for a cleaning. She and Dell had already mixed the feed, fed and milked the cows and the calves, and washed the milkers after settling a cow into a separate pen when she'd come up lame. Ivy planned to check her out as soon as she finished with the Bobcat — hopefully, the poor animal had nothing more than a stone lodged in her hoof, which would easily be fixed with a hoof pick and a foot bath. But with Ivy's luck, the prognosis wouldn't be so straightforward. Already this morning she'd discovered she'd forgotten to order supplements and a truckload of sand. It had also slipped her mind that she'd agreed to board a friend's horse for two weeks, and she didn't have a stall prepared yet.

More mucking. Yay.

She caught movement out of the corner of her eye and turned to see Thistle Hill's librarian waving at her from the driveway. In fact, the big man was waving at her so hard he was creating a breeze. Ivy turned off the engine and jumped to the ground, glanced down at the sorry state of her boots and jeans, and shrugged.

No one should expect a dairy farmer to look fresh or smell sweet.

"Noble Johnson." When Ivy reached the paved drive, she peeled off her right glove and held out her hand. "What's my favorite python wrangler up to these days?"

Noble grinned, and despite the day she was having, Ivy found herself grinning back. With his massive frame and shoulder-length hair, the same white-blond as hers, he did not resemble the stereotypical librarian. Or book minder, as he liked to call himself.

The sound of an engine signaled someone else coming up the drive. Noble and Ivy both watched as Allison's gray Camry came into view. Allison parked beside Noble's pickup and Ivy bit her lip.

She had an apology to make.

"My snake-herding days seem to be behind me," Noble said, and turned back to Ivy. "Joe hasn't called to report any more exotic critters hiding out in his walls." Allison walked up and he flashed her a smile. "But I do hear your motel menagerie will soon be expanding by one." He pulled Allison close in a one-armed hug. "Congratulations."

"Thanks, Noble."

When Allison turned to Ivy, the latter spread her arms, revealing all her sweaty, dirt-streaked glory. "I'd hug you, but..."

Allison laughed and held up her hands. "Thanks. I'll pass."

"Decided on names yet?" Noble rubbed his chin. "I can give you a few suggestions."

"Let me guess." Allison winked at Ivy. "For a boy, Perry."

"That's right." Noble's face beamed with pleased surprise. "Can't do a boy a better honor than naming him after ol' Oliver Hazard."

"You told me all about the Battle of Lake Erie, remember?"

Noble nodded and narrowed his eyes. "Now, for a girl..." He tapped a finger against his chin and ignored the mock trepidation on Allison's face.

"How about naming her after Mary Boone?" he finally suggested. "She was born in Erie and was a huge influence in the New York art market in the '80s."

"Mary or Perry," Allison mused, and patted his brawny shoulder. "Not bad. Tasteful, even. I was expecting something along the lines of Cornelia or Epenetus."

"I have taste." Noble sniffed, running a palm down his lime-green velour tie.

Ivy eyed his pristine khakis and burgundy button-down shirt, which provided an interesting backdrop for his tie. "You are looking spiffy today."

"If you're impressed now, you should stop by the library tomorrow. Check me out in my suit and tie."

"What's tomorrow?" Ivy asked.

He frowned. "The new-member reception for my book club, remember? That's what the cheesecake is for."

Ivy clamped both hands on her head as a prickly heat surged up her throat and into her cheeks. "The cheesecake. Oh, Noble. I forgot all about it." His crestfallen expression made her feel worse.

"That's okay," he said slowly. "I'm sure I can pick something up from the diner. Unless..."

She ignored the panic roiling in her belly and concentrated instead on the fresh hope in his eyes. "Yes. Absolutely. I'll make it tonight and drop it off before the reception tomorrow."

By the time Noble finished pumping her hand in gratitude, her shoulder ached. After he left, she turned to Allison as she rubbed the sore spot.

"I owe you an apology. I should have called you yesterday to follow up after the meeting. I really am happy for you and Joe."

Allison reached out and squeezed her elbow. "I know you are. But I'm the one who should apologize. I should have told you first, in private. Instead the words were coming out of my mouth and I couldn't take them back and I knew I'd done a hateful thing. Please forgive me."

"You were excited. Of course you were excited — having a baby is a big deal. You were surrounded by your friends and you wanted to share your news. There's no need to apologize for that." When Allison quirked an eyebrow, Ivy let loose a sigh. "Okay, fine. Yes, I was hurt you hadn't told me first. Now that we've both said we're sorry, can we call it even?"

"Ivy. I was there. I saw your face. There's more to it, isn't there?"

Ivy's arms and legs felt suddenly heavy and she shivered.

Allison gave her arm a final squeeze and stepped back. "If you ever want to talk about it," she said softly, "I'm here."

"Thank you," Ivy muttered, and cringed when she barely recognized her own voice. She cleared her throat. "You do realize I'm going to throw you one hell of a shower?"

"I'm counting on it."

"I never did ask about Joe. How's he handling all this?"

Allison's smile was a beautiful thing to behold. "He can't wait. He's already changed his mind three times about the paint for the nursery. The good news is, he gets to do the painting." She poked Ivy in the shoulder. "Now. About those cheesecakes. Want help making them?"

"Them?"

"If I'm going to help, I should get something out of it, don't you think?"

A rush of gratitude warmed Ivy's chest. "That would be fabulous, thanks."

"Ivy." Allison winced. "I also wanted to apologize for bringing up Evan last night. I know he's a sore subject, and then we ended up having to explain to Parker who he was, and...well, I hope I didn't sound like I was trivializing what happened."

Ivy shook her head. "You were right. He's a big part of the reason I'll never be anything more than casual with a guy. It's not worth the heartache of finding out your boyfriend's a scheming asshat who only wants you because you can help boost his bottom line."

"You know most guys are not like that."

"No. I don't."

"Well." Allison shrugged, and her expression turned teasingly superior. "One day you will. So I'll see you around what? Seven?"

Ivy hoped like hell she'd have her chores done by then. "Tuna sandwiches okay?"

Allison considered. "Got pickles?"

"Bread and butter, baby."

"Then you're on."

Ivy watched Allison's car until it disappeared around a bend in the driveway. Once it did, she let her body sag and closed her eyes.

She'd have to do a better job hiding her feelings. It wasn't fair to Allison, Joe or anyone else. Ivy was the one with the problem. Her friends shouldn't have to walk on eggshells around her because of it.

The equipment shed on the other side of the free-stall barn

suddenly belched out a loud growling sound. Dell, checking out the tractor. Time to get back to work. Slowly, she turned back to the Bobcat and couldn't help wondering how she'd manage to get it all done. Once she finished pushing manure, she had to check on her injured cow, conduct an inventory, call in an order and make an appointment with the nutritionist, who regularly adjusted the mix she fed her stock. Then the feeding and milking would begin all over again. And somewhere in there, she had to find time to buy groceries.

As much as she loved the farm, she couldn't help wondering, every now and then, if she should have just sold it eight years earlier, after the cruise ship her parents were traveling on sank off the coast of Santorini. Seemed Ivy was still trying to prove she was capable of more than her mom and dad had ever given her credit for.

And still trying to make up for the mistakes she'd made.

She dragged in a breath and hesitated. More noisy rumbling, this time coming from behind her. Ivy turned and blinked. That was a school bus lumbering up the driveway.

Oh, God.

Apparently she had a tour today.

Her heart thudded dully, and it suddenly hurt to breathe. Two days without Wade and already she was falling apart. She'd thought she could manage. Why couldn't she manage?

She *had* to manage.

She rolled her shoulders up and back, shifted a grimace into a smile, and headed for the bus full of laughing, chattering children.

* * *

THE NEXT DAY, IVY hit her sleep-deprived stride. With a carefully crafted regimen of coffee, chocolate and the occasional ten-minute catnap, she figured she could handle being two men down, at least until she collected some serious prospects for Wade's job. So far her only applicant was the manager of a fast-food restaurant in Erie, who'd worn dress shoes and a silk tie to the interview. He'd had all kinds of nifty ideas for upgrading her recordkeeping, but the instant he set foot in the dairy barn, the dry heaves had started. He hadn't realized the position would be so hands-on, he'd explained.

"Feet-in," she figured he'd meant. But what did he expect from a building full of digesting Jerseys?

She was hunched over her laptop in her office, updating her animal healthcare records and trying not to visualize Seth with Olivia Duncan, when the doorbell rang. *Woot!* Dinner had arrived. No way could she face another tuna sandwich, no matter how much fun she and Allison had had the night before.

Ivy hurried to the door, her socks pulling her into a slide the last few feet. She tugged Liz Early inside and gave her a one-armed hug, careful not to bump the bag of goodies her friend carried.

"Oh, my God, that smells divine." She led Liz into the kitchen and patted the table. While Liz set the plastic bag down and struggled to untie the handles, Ivy produced a pair of scissors and snipped the knot right off. One by one she pulled out the warm containers, so excited by the freedom of not having to drag something together for dinner that she gave Liz another hug.

"You're a sweetie for delivering," she said. "Especially on a Saturday. I owe you one. Dell does, too. I made him two grilled cheese sandwiches for lunch today and I thought he was going to break into tears."

No response. Ivy looked up to find Liz staring, hand over her mouth.

"Jeez, Ivy," Liz breathed. "What happened to your eye?"

Ivy winced. "I've been avoiding the mirror. How's it look?"

"Painful. Did you put anything on it?"

"A bag of frozen Brussels sprouts."

Liz's expression graduated from dismayed to horrified. "Brussels sprouts? You don't actually eat those, do you?"

"A couple of years ago, when June Catlett was on her underappreciated-foods kick, I promised her I'd give them a try, but I've never been able to work up the courage."

"I remember that. She came into Snoozy's hoping we'd add cardoons to the menu."

"What the hell are cardoons?"

"They're like artichokes, only you eat the stalks. Snoozy never had any on hand, but there they were, on the menu. Luckily, no one ever ordered them." She leaned in for a closer look at Ivy's eye. "How'd you do it?"

"I tripped in the milking shed. Ended up with a face full of wall."

Liz hissed in a sympathetic breath. "You're lucky it wasn't worse."

"Oh, I have plans for this eye. If Dell calls in sick tomorrow because he can't face another grilled cheese, I'll moan and groan and lay it on thick. I'll describe in vivid detail the purples and greens. If that doesn't work, I'll tell him we're having Snoozy's chili for lunch. He'll be here before I hang up the phone. Thanks again for the special delivery."

Liz offered a smile that didn't carry her usual glow. Ivy wanted to kick herself. Even with one good eye, she should have noticed it sooner.

"Snoozy recruited someone to cover for me while I'm gone, so it's no problem," Liz said. "He was thrilled to get your order. He pretty much emptied the pot. I haven't seen him grin so big since Mitzi came home."

"Could that have anything to do with Audrey?"

Liz waved a dismissive hand. "Audrey made several visits to Snoozy's to apologize for the whole let's-barbecue-your-snake suggestion, but Snoozy kept avoiding her. He really was furious. Anyway, June teased her for a while about having a crush on the poor guy, but she was just trying to do the right thing."

Ivy winced at the word "crush." "How's that working out, by the way? Having her enclosure right there in the bar?" She fished her checkbook out of her purse.

"Freaked me out at first. But I'm used to it now. It's not like she moves around much, and as long as I don't have to watch her eat, I'm good. Besides, ever since Snoozy put that sign out front advertising his python petting zoo, business has definitely picked up. More customers means more tips, so I'm stoked."

Uh-huh. Ivy kept one eye on Liz as she ripped the check free. "You don't look stoked."

Liz accepted the check and flushed. "That's quite a tip."

"You did me quite a favor. Saved me a lot of time and heartache."

She tapped the nearest carton. "It's the heartburn that's really going to cost. But it'll be so worth it."

Liz tucked the check into her jacket pocket. "Do you have a few minutes? I was hoping we could talk. I know you're busy..."

"Never too busy for you." Ivy gave herself a mental pat on the back for sounding as if she meant it. She pushed the cartons aside, pulled out a chair for Liz and plopped down onto its twin. "Can I get you something to drink? Coffee? Wine?" Oh, damn. She didn't have any wine.

Liz shook her head and shrugged out of her jacket. Ivy shoved the cartons a little farther away. Did they have to smell so damned good? She glanced around the kitchen, desperate for a distraction from the spicy siren call of the chili. The forlorn look on Liz's face did the trick.

"What's going on?" Ivy asked gently.

"It didn't work."

"What didn't work?"

Liz bit her lip. "Marcus. Me. Sex."

Ivy grimaced. "I'm sorry to hear that."

Liz stumbled through a laugh. "No need to look so horrified. I didn't suddenly find out he's gay or into BDSM. He didn't fail to perform or anything. We never got that far. He blew up at me for pressuring him, then said he thought it was time for us both to move on."

"Oh, no. Oh, Liz." And oh, dear *Lord*, did that sound familiar. Ivy ignored the hollow feeling in her chest. *This isn't about you.* She cleared her throat. "Did Marcus give you any reason at all for the breakup? Besides feeling pressured, I mean?"

"He told me why, but it was totally not a valid reason, and I tried to argue, but..." Liz shrugged. "When he drove me home, he didn't say anything except to tell me to take care of myself." Her face collapsed, and she drew in a shuddering breath. "I screwed up. I wanted to show him how much I love him, and instead I ended up chasing him away. I couldn't even get him to kiss me."

Ivy leaned forward. "You can fix this. Just tell him you understand. Tell him if he needs more time, he can have it."

"I did say all that. He didn't go for it. Even if he had, how much more time do I give him? Months? Years? If I don't pressure him at all, then where's his motivation to sleep with me?"

Ivy didn't know how to answer that one. "I guess what you need to decide is how long you're willing to wait."

"I'm not sure that's even an option anymore." Liz hung her head, and her hair tumbled to cover her face. When she looked back up, her eyes had dulled. She rubbed a palm against her chest. "Ivy, he said goodbye like...like there wouldn't be another hello."

Ivy straightened, feeling as useless as a fork in a soup bowl. "I'm so sorry." She'd driven Seth away like Liz had driven Marcus away. What advice could she possibly give? "Have you considered talking to Allison? She knows Marcus better than any of us."

"I thought about it, but if he ever found out, he'd be humiliated. I couldn't do that to him." She tucked her hair behind her ear. Drew in a deep breath. "That's really something, isn't it? I mean that Allison's going to be a mom."

Ivy braced herself for the familiar little clutch of pain. Yep, there it was. *Hello, old friend.*

"I want that," Liz said softly. "I want with Marcus what Allison has with Joe."

An image of Seth taunted Ivy, and her ready words of encouragement faded. All she could manage was a nod.

Resignation chased the daydreams from Liz's face. "I need to get back to work. I'm sorry to bother you with all of this." She got to her feet and pushed the chair under the table. "Thank you again for the generous tip."

They hugged, Ivy's own desperation echoed in the rigor of Liz's fingers on her back. Minutes later, she waved from her porch as the little blue car disappeared down the driveway.

Some tip.

Sorry, I can't help you. Find someone else to talk to.

With a sigh, she shuffled back into the kitchen, grabbed two of the containers and turned to put them in the fridge.

So much for her appetite.

* * *

SETH SLAPPED HIS CARDS facedown on the table and sagged back against his chair. "Fold."

"Judas Priest, Walker." Joe shot him a disgusted look. "That's got to be the tenth time tonight. You don't get your act together, we're going to boot you out of the club."

"We can't boot him out." Noble brandished the remains of a sub thicker than his wrist. "He's the only one of us who knows how to make a decent sandwich."

Gil Cooper, owner of Cooper's Hardware and Seth's off-road-biking buddy, lifted his bottle of beer. "Plus he's just now learning that a good brew isn't supposed to look like lemonade and smell like three fat guys trapped in a two-man tent."

"And he has a daughter who bakes." Former marine Harris Briggs was a chewing-gum addict, an infamous grump and the part-time manager of Thistle Hill Growers. He waved a chocolate chip cookie in the air. "Forget quarters. We should be playing for these babies."

Joe snatched the cookie out of the air, took a bite and shook his head at Seth. "You know what your trouble is?"

"Yeah. I'm not getting enough sleep."

"Neither am I, but it's not because I'm too stubborn to take what's on offer." Joe dodged a balled-up napkin. "I'm just sayin'. She wants you, too."

"Who're we talking about?" Gil didn't realize his cards were angled for the whole table to see. There was a reason his stack of chips was shorter than everyone else's.

Seth hesitated, then muttered, "Ivy Millbrook."

"That's my kind of trouble," Gil said, and smirked when Seth glared.

"You're going to have trouble of your own if you don't keep your cotton-pickin' hands to yourself," Harris growled at Joe, who was hogging the plate of cookies.

"Now, boys, play nice." Gil stretched across the table, knocking over three towers of poker chips and an empty beer bottle in the process. The bottle clattered off the edge and hit the linoleum with a hollow clunk. Undeterred, Gil scooped a handful of cookies off the Hello Kitty platter. He tossed a couple at Noble and sat back down.

Everyone else exhaled and straightened up out of the human shields they'd formed around their own bottles and stacks.

"What about Olivia Duncan?" Noble asked through a mouthful of cookie. "She's cute. I saw you two in Mama Leoni's parking lot last night. How'd that work out?"

Seth scowled. "It didn't."

"Because it's not Olivia keeping Seth up at night." Joe tucked in his chin and peeked at his cards. "Now, are we going to finish this game or not?"

"He's got something good," Noble said, disgusted, and threw down his cards. Ignoring Joe's bark of protest, he squinted at Seth.

"What's up with you and Ivy? You two like each other, so why've you spent the past year ducking and weaving? Hit the canvas, already."

Seth squeezed the back of his neck. "That guy she was engaged to a few years back." He looked at Joe. "What was his name?"

"Evan."

"Evan. Right. Apparently the bastard did a number on her, because she's convinced commitment's a four-letter word."

"She's gun-shy." Noble nodded sagely. "I get that." When Joe snorted, Noble spread his hands. "What? Haven't you ever wondered why this prime piece of bachelor booty is still on the market?"

Joe checked out the big man's bright yellow *Read Books, Not T-shirts* tee, which he wore with a paint-stained pair of black leather motorcycle pants and emerald green high-tops. "No."

"I've been wonderin'," Harris spoke up. When everyone stared, he flushed. "On behalf of the ladies, that is."

"I'm no stranger to heartbreak." Noble patted his solar plexus. "It takes a brave human being to risk that kind of pain again."

Gil screwed up his eyes. "It takes a brave human being to risk looking directly into your outfit." He shook his head at Seth. "I don't get it. Sounds like Ivy wants no-strings sex. With you. What's the problem? I'd be all over that."

"Would you?" Seth asked softly.

Gil blanched. "The opportunity. I'd be all over the *opportunity*, not the lady in question." He grabbed his beer and cocked his head. "I take it back. I'd be thrilled to hit that and you should be, too."

Seth started around the table toward him and Gil popped to his feet. It took him two strides to get tangled up in a chair. He fell on his ass and Joe shook his head.

"You'd have to talk to her first," Joe said. "During and after wouldn't hurt, either. Sure you're up for that?"

Gil offered up a silly grin as Joe helped him to his feet. "I can talk to a girl. Just ask the one I'm dating."

"Virtual chicks don't count," Noble yelled.

"Neither do the ones who ask for money," Joe added.

"Screw all of you." Gil squinted at Seth. "You're seriously not putting out till there's a ring on your finger?"

"It's not about the ring, assholes." Seth dropped back into his chair. "It's about commitment. I don't want my kids to see a parade of women coming in and out of my house."

"So don't bring 'em home." Harris had given up on the cookies. He fished a pack of spearmint gum from the pocket of his plaid shirt. Cellophane crinkled. "That's what motels are for."

"Not my motel," Joe growled.

"Parade of women, huh?" Gil rolled his eyes. "Don't you need a permit for an ego that size?"

Seth ignored him. "Bottom line is, I have to set an example for my kids."

"Good for you, man." Joe nodded solemnly. "They'll erect a statue in your honor."

"A special-order one." Noble leaned forward. "With blue balls."

Seth gave him a dirty look while Joe hooted and Gil offered Noble a sloppy high five.

"Speaking of rings — " Joe leaned back in his chair " — I'm thinking about getting one."

Noble scratched his chin. "For your nose or your — " he raised his eyebrows at Joe's lap " — love muscle?"

Joe blinked. "Love muscle? Seriously?"

Gil's expression was dubious. "You going to pop the question?"

"Thinking about it," Joe said. "Though I don't know what I'll do if she turns me down."

An uneasy silence, broken by an occasional plastic *chink* as Gil busied himself restacking his chips. Abruptly, Joe straightened and turned to Harris.

"Harris, man, I'm sorry. I wasn't thinking."

The older man waved him off. "Don't go gettin' your dress over your head," he said gruffly. "Yeah, I turned Eugenia down, but I had good reason and she knows it. You get that ring. That young woman of yours won't say no."

Noble gave Joe an elbow to the ribs. "You planning on telling them what *is* going to happen, instead of getting us all worked up about what *might* happen?"

Seth stood and started gathering the empties. "I knew you were a little too happy about lending me your truck. What's up, Gallahan?"

Joe leaned back and linked his hands behind his head. "It's like this, guys." There was no mistaking the giddy in his gaze, and Seth figured it out the instant before Joe spilled. "Allison's pregnant."

Shouts and backslaps followed, quickly turning into whispers and knuckle bumps when Seth warned his guests that if they woke up his kids, he'd be serving tea and cucumber sandwiches the next time he hosted poker night. Ever the librarian, Noble asked, "When you say cucumber, you talking English or Armenian?"

Joe reached for the last cookie. "Any advice for a father-to-be?" He cut his eyes at Noble. "I'm talking to those of us who have a kid, not those of us who act like one."

Gil belched, long and loud. "That leaves us all out."

"Hold on." Noble folded his arms across his massive chest and watched Seth carefully set the empties in a recycling bin. "The kids are with your ex every other weekend, so why can't you do your parading around then?"

"Because that's not what I want," Seth growled. He offered up a half smile and a shrug. "That's not *all* I want. Besides, I won't have her thinking I'm ashamed of her."

With a snick, Gil popped the top of another brew. "But if s*he's* good with it—"

"I'm not. End of story. Now how about we turn the conversation back to our baby daddy here?"

A sob sliced through their banter. "Dad!"

For an instant, Seth went rigid.

"Daddy!"

He sprang to his feet and sprinted to his daughter's bedroom. His heart rammed his chest as his friends thundered after him. Grace's door was open, her room dark. Why was it dark? He slapped the light on and blinked in the sudden glare.

Grace had shoved herself back against the headboard. She sat with her knees to her chest, her small fists holding the edge of the blanket to her chin. "Someone turned out the light." Strands of brown hair clung to her damp cheeks, and mucus dripped from her nose.

Seth strode over and gathered her close. She sobbed and trembled against his chest as he rocked her.

"Bad dream?" Joe hovered inside the door while Noble and Gil peered over his shoulder.

Seth pointed to the outlet by the door. "Her ballerina night-light's missing." It had been there when he'd tucked her in. She'd never have let him leave the room otherwise.

Harris came in with a glass, water sloshing onto the carpet as he stepped around books and shoes and piles of clothing. Noble followed, head craning left and right as he searched the cluttered floor. "I don't see it. Could Travis have taken it?"

Seth was wondering the same thing.

Right on cue, his son staggered into the room, rubbing his eyes. "What's wrong?"

"Grace's night-light." Seth set the water aside and held out an arm. Travis shuffled over and Seth pulled him in close, loving the feel of his son's sleep-warmed body. "Have you seen it?"

Travis shrugged, and Seth swallowed a frustrated oath. Dammit, he was tired of things disappearing. Which one of his kids was playing games? Grace wasn't faking her fear. Had she removed the night-light, set it somewhere and then forgotten where she'd put it?

She'd stopped crying. Seth felt her jaw move against his heart as she yawned. "Hey." He eased her away and kissed her on the forehead. "How about we leave the hall light on for tonight and get you a replacement night-light tomorrow? Will that work?"

She nodded sleepily. Seth leaned over and kissed Travis, as well. "Okay, Tiger. Back to bed."

"I'll take him." Gil took Travis's hand and steered the little boy toward the door. "Maybe on the way you could tell me where I can find myself a pair of those killer jammies. Is that the Hulk?"

"It's Martian Manhunter," Travis said in a voice dripping with disgust.

While Noble picked up a doll from the floor and positioned her in a nearby chair, Joe stepped out of the room to turn on the hall light. Seth settled his daughter back under the sheets and smoothed her hair from her face.

"What if I have another bad dream?" she mumbled, eyes already closed.

"I'll come running."

"All of you?"

Seth grinned. "If you want."

"I want." She rolled over onto her side, rubbed her cheek against her pillow and fell asleep.

Two minutes later, the guys had resumed their seats around Seth's kitchen table. Silence reigned until Gil dropped his hands to the table and exhaled loudly. "Who the hell is Martian Manhunter, anyway?"

"Member of the Justice League. Pals with Superman?" When Gil still looked lost, Noble made a *tsk tsk* sound. "What'd you read when you were a kid, Cooper? Trixie Belden?"

Seth glanced around the table. Someone had to say it. "Who's Trixie Belden?"

Noble rolled his eyes. "Heathens."

Harris's cards lay abandoned beside him as he twisted his beer bottle in a halting circle. "Your daughter do that a lot?"

"Have bad dreams? Since the divorce, yeah. More often since these two geniuses—" Seth gestured with his beer at Joe and Noble "— found that damned python and couldn't stop bragging about it."

"Don't go blaming me," Noble protested. "Joe found her. All I did was help pull her out of the wall."

Gil exaggerated a shudder. "It's a wonder you two aren't having nightmares."

Joe waved a careless hand. "I haven't woken up screaming in weeks. Anyway, it was Allison who found her." He tapped a red chip against the table absently. "Parker said something once about Nat having nightmares. She said they read books together about kids conquering their fears and played flashlight tag so Nat wouldn't be so scared of the dark."

"Monster spray." Harris cleared his throat and lifted his beefy shoulders in a self-conscious shrug. "When my daughter was little, we put a bottle of monster spray by her bed. Worked like a charm."

"Judas Priest." Joe rubbed a hand over his mouth. "I'm not ready for this."

"You'll be fine." Seth lifted his beer. "To Joe. May he be a better father than he is a poker player."

"Like that'll be hard," muttered Noble, and considered the crumbs on his plate. "Know what goes great with pale ale? Cheesecake."

While Harris choked on his beer, Joe made a face. "Didn't you get your fill at the library last night?"

"I should have asked Ivy for two," Noble said. "Those book club members can eat."

Joe sobered. "You'll probably have to do without Ivy's cheesecake for a while. I doubt she'll be spending much time in her kitchen."

Seth frowned. "What do you mean by that?"

"Allison told me after she got back from her investment club meeting on Tuesday." Joe grimaced. "Two of her workers bailed. One of them was her farm manager."

Seth shoved to his feet, jarring the table and scattering chips in the process. Four days ago? He hadn't heard a thing. Wasn't a feed store supposed to be the male version of a beauty parlor?

He gripped the top rail of his chair so hard it creaked. "Stop staring, assholes, and tell me what happened."

"The manager and his wife are moving to Montana. I guess the other guy quit because he didn't want to get stuck with the extra work." Joe shrugged. "That's what Allie said."

"Who's filling in?"

"Nobody, far as I know." Joe spread his elbows on the table and leaned forward. "Don't do it, man."

Gil finished chugging a glass of water and swiped a hand across his mouth. "Don't do what?"

"Our buddy Seth here has some kind of hero complex. Seems he can't say no to a woman in need."

"Weren't we just talking about how he did say no?" Gil went back to the sink for a refill.

"That was sex," Joe said. "This is drama."

Harris snorted. "Whatever you do, stay away from the drama." He tossed his cards on the table. "Why do I get the feelin' we're through playin' poker tonight?" He pulled out another stick of gum.

Noble nodded and held out his hand when Harris offered him the pack. "What happened to your first piece?"

"Swallowed it when the kid screamed."

Joe shook his glass, rattling the remaining ice cubes. "This isn't your problem, Seth. If Ivy needs help, she'll ask for it."

"Not from me, she won't."

"She doesn't have to," Noble pointed out, around a wad of spearmint. "Joe's right. You can't help yourself. Remember that lady—what was her name—the one with all the goats?"

"Mad-as-a-Hatter Mattie." Harris sat back with his hands linked across his belly, as if settling in for a bedtime story.

"That's right. Old Mattie Fillmore. When it was time for her to move into assisted living, who's the one who handled it?"

"She bought hundreds of dollars' worth of feed from me in less than a year. I owed her."

"How about Parker?" As usual, Harris smiled when he mentioned his boss. "Wasn't long after she moved here that you were over at her place, helpin' me clear all that junk out of her greenhouses so she could open for business."

Seth rolled his eyes. "Her dog eats a lot. Guess where she buys the food."

Noble looked at Joe. "Mattie Fillmore, Parker, and God only knows how many other unfortunate souls our hero here has risked his life for." He ignored Seth's snarled oath and gave an incredulous shake of his head. "We're going to need a bigger statue."

Gil gave a solemn nod. "Which means we'll need a bigger park."

Harris popped his gum. "And more blue paint."

"Jesus," Seth muttered. "Give me a break."

He couldn't help Ivy if he wanted to. She needed a hand during the day, and it wasn't as if Bradley were up to—or would even be interested in—running the feed store. But damn, he hoped she found help soon, because she already worked way too hard.

"So what're you going to do?" Gil asked. He lunged over the table and started scooping up cards. Everyone else hastily lifted their drinks out of his way.

"What am I going to do?" Seth snatched the cards away from Gil. "I'm going to play another round of poker. Who's in?"

*   *   *

IVY HAD BEEN UP, dressed and drinking her first cup of coffee before four in the morning for years, but lately it was getting harder and harder to peel free of the sheets. Not just because she wasn't getting enough sleep. Or because wistful—okay, lustful—thoughts of Seth were keeping her awake. But more than that, starting each day meant accepting all over again that the farm was in trouble.

A lot of trouble.

And every day she operated with too few hands was another day she fell further behind.

She leaned into the sink, watching the fledgling sunrise as she sipped at her third—or was it fourth?—cup of coffee. The colors in the early-autumn sky made her think of her grandfather. "Condiment colors," he'd called them. Besides mustard yellow and ketchup red, she spied Thousand Island dressing orange, relish green and apple butter brown.

She grabbed a banana from the bowl on the counter and glanced once more out the window. She hadn't enjoyed a close relationship with her parents, especially after everything that had happened when she was eighteen. Her mother and father had never been the nurturing types, had always had more expectations than affection.

But because of them, she lived surrounded by beauty. Farm life wasn't easy, and at twenty-two, following their deaths, she'd resented the burden. As the years had passed, she'd managed to turn resentment into appreciation.

She scooped up her lavender cashmere scarf — a gift to herself for surviving her ex-fiancé — and let herself out of the house. Damn, it was cold. She zipped her jacket up over her scarf and trudged toward the barn, the motion sensor lights waking as she drew near, their ivory glow shining through the mist she created with every exhale. In moments they'd go off again, as the sunrise gathered strength.

Fifty feet from the barn she paused and squinted. Something didn't look right.

She sucked in air, dropped her banana and pushed into a run. The barn door was open. She swung inside, slapped at the wall and blinked like a madwoman when the light came on. She lunged toward the stalls.

Another door open.

Oh, God, no.

Cabana Boy was gone.

4

IVY WHISTLED. NO ANSWERING neigh. She spun in a frantic circle and whistled again. Listened as best she could with her heart whump-whump-whumping in her ears, but all she heard were the usual early-morning sounds — the chickens clucking sleepily in their coop, the snort and shuffle of the Jerseys as they lumbered into the milking shed, the hollow thud of hooves against wood as the remaining horses in the barn made it clear they were ready for breakfast.

They'd have to wait.

She whirled and ran back to the house.

*   *   *

AFTER MORE THAN AN hour of driving around, scouring roads and neighboring farms, Ivy received a call from the sheriff's department. Cabana Boy had made it to downtown Thistle Hill, where he'd had a run-in with a UPS truck.

"Oh, my God." Ivy steered her Volvo to the side of the road and pressed a shaking hand to her head. "Is he okay?" *Please tell me he's okay.*

"The vet's here now," the dispatcher said kindly. "He says your horse will be all right, but you're to come right away. Bring your trailer."

Dr. Wilmer Fish had served as Thistle Hill's veterinarian for almost thirty years. He was a short, stout man in his early sixties with a loud laugh and hair dyed so black it looked plastic. Wilmer complained every time she called him out to her farm, yet he always left looking forward to coming back. Because he never went home without a cheesecake tucked under his arm.

The dispatcher had told Ivy she could find the vet behind the courthouse. After doubling back to the farm for her truck and trailer, she drove slowly around the side of the building. Wilmer stood beside her trembling stallion. The vet was taping a bandage onto Cabana Boy's gaskin, the large muscle on the hind leg.

A hot surge of regret blocked Ivy's throat, and she coughed and sputtered it free. She had to brake and blink the liquid out of her eyes before she could park. Despite the urge to hurry, she forced herself to walk calmly across the lot. Cabana Boy nickered when he saw her, and it was all Ivy could do not to drop to the ground and sob in shame and relief.

She dropped a kiss onto his muzzle. "How is he?" She moved around to Cabana Boy's neck, closed her eyes and hugged tight, until he blew an impatient breath and twisted free.

"He'll be fine." Wilmer peeled away his latex gloves and swiped an arm across his forehead. "I cleaned the wound and stitched it up. The bandage should keep the site dry. He'll have a scar, but he's a lucky horse." He peered at her face. "What's with the eye?"

"Face-plant. I really should watch where I'm going." She grabbed both of his hands and squeezed. "Thank you, Wilmer." She turned back to her stallion and murmured to him as she ran her palms along his flank and all around the wound. He never flinched. "How's the UPS driver?"

"A little shaken. He had to finish his rounds. He left his number so you can call and talk insurance." He paused. "They'll want to know how the horse got out."

"The barn door. I don't remember leaving it open, but I must have." She leaned her forehead on the stallion's rib cage and breathed in the smell of sunshine and horsehide. "If anything had happened to him..."

"Check that door when you get home, and make sure the latch isn't broken. Let me help you get him loaded up. I'll come by for a follow-up tomorrow."

Ivy chuckled wearily against the stallion's hide. Guess she'd be making another trip to the grocery store, because Wilmer would be looking for his cheesecake. But she needed to stop by the feed store first.

Actually, she needed to make a call first, to her insurance company. That would be fun.

Not.

"Thank you again, Wilmer." She couldn't hide the catch in her voice.

"Accidents happen, Ivy."

Yes, they did. But lately she was experiencing more than her share. And she couldn't afford another one.

* * *

IF EVERYTHING HAD BEEN business as usual between her and Seth, Ivy would have sexed herself up for this next encounter. Unbound hair, black eyeliner, red lipstick and her plum-colored sweater dress, the one that covered everything yet didn't leave much to the imagination. She'd have cheerfully taken advantage of this new opportunity to show the man what he was missing, and he'd have cheerfully glowered and lectured while pretending not to check her out.

But business with Seth was not as usual, and Ivy couldn't afford to alienate him any further. So what did one wear to a business meeting that could very well involve good old-fashioned on-your-knees begging? Black seemed appropriate, but he'd only accuse her of being dramatic.

Ivy groaned and swung away from her closet. She did *not* have time for this. She yanked a dark green sweater out of her bureau, went back to her closet and grabbed a pair of hip-hugging jeans and brown ankle boots. Downstairs, she snatched up her bag from where she'd dropped it, just inside the front door.

The middle of the day was not the optimum time to leave the farm, but Dell had assured her he didn't mind. She hated to bother Seth at the store, but she hated the thought of bothering him at home even more.

Actually, she didn't want to bother him at all, but desperate times called for desperate measures.

She parked in front of Tweedy's, relieved to find only one other vehicle in the lot. A box truck was backed up to one of the bays, a heavy, rhythmic slap making the truck bed tremble. Someone was loading feed. She walked to the rear of the truck, her midsection turning to jelly.

But the figure that thundered down the ramp and scooped up another fifty-pound bag of horse feed belonged not to Seth but his young employee. He hefted the bag in his arms and turned, spotted Ivy and staggered back a step.

"Sorry, Bradley. Didn't mean to scare you."

"No sweat." He squinted. "What happened to your eye?" When she hesitated, he turned bright red, raised his left hand and flicked his hair behind his ear. "Never mind," he mumbled. "None of my business."

"It's fine," she said lightly. "I took a tumble in the barn. Hey, is Seth around?"

He shifted the bag onto his shoulder, crouched down and scooped up another. Ivy winced as he hefted it to his free shoulder and struggled to stand. Face beet red, muscles bulging, he gave her a wink — a wink that turned into a twitch as he fought to clear the sweat dripping into his eye. "I'll be done in a minute," he wheezed, "if you don't mind waiting."

"I don't, but I actually need to talk to Seth." She strode past him into the store, anxious to give him some privacy so he could dump the feed before he gave himself a hernia. She smiled when she heard a double thud echo inside the truck, followed by a low-pitched groan.

"He's in the storeroom," Bradley called out moments later. "Come back and see me if you can't find him. I'll be done by then. 'Cause I can load two bags at a time."

She waved an over-the-shoulder thank-you and kept moving.

The concrete floor, arched windows, high ceilings and heavy beams of the storeroom reminded her of the firehouse the building used to be. The stains on the floor and the cobwebs draped across the corners reminded her it hadn't served that purpose for a long time.

The room didn't smell musty, though. It smelled rich, like horse feed. And peanut butter.

She hovered in the doorway. Seth stood with his back to her, head bent over a clipboard. He didn't turn, so he must not have heard her boot heels click-clacking across the concrete toward him. Either that, or he was ignoring her.

Except Seth didn't play those kinds of games.

He wore a faded pair of jeans and a long-sleeved navy tee. He made a note on his clipboard, then reached down and grabbed a corner of the nearest bag. With a smooth flick of his muscled arm, the bag landed on a pallet a good ten feet away.

Hoo, boy.

Ivy ached with the urge to sidle up behind him and run her hands along the solid contours of his shoulders and back. His casual strength had always been a turn-on for her. Too bad he refused to let "casual" carry over into his relationships.

She was glad she hadn't said that aloud, because even in her head, it didn't sound as convincing as it once had.

Seth still hadn't realized she was there. She jiggled her hands, as if to shake off the need to touch him, and pulled in a breath. Peanut butter again.

"Let me guess," she said. "Grace made your sandwich today."

He turned slowly, a smile lifting one side of his mouth — until he got a load of her face. Then he hissed in a breath and tossed the clipboard aside without looking to see where it would land. The fury that flared in his deep brown eyes triggered an apprehensive tingling along her spine.

"Want to tell me how you got that?" He spoke in an ominous growl.

"I tripped. It's what happens when you're not watching where you're walking."

He scanned her face carefully, and after a while the menace in his own faded. "It's what happens when you're doing the work of three people and you're too stubborn to ask for help," he said.

Okay, then. "About that..."

His brows lowered. "Why didn't you tell me about losing Wade and another one of your guys?"

"It's my problem." She shrugged. "I wanted to fix it."

"Yeah?" He turned away again. Another bag sailed to the right and landed with a crunch. "How's that working for you?"

"Not so well."

He faced her again and this time stared at her hair. Instead of her usual braid, she'd gathered it up in a messy twist and clipped it to the back of her head. "You used to confide in me," he said gruffly. "We take sex off the table and suddenly all that's over?"

"I never took sex off the table. In fact, I'm all for sex on the table."

He made an impatient noise, but the flat line of his mouth gave him away. A dizzying swell of glee had Ivy leaning against the doorjamb.

"You're as frustrated as I am," she said lightly.

"No, Millbrook. I'm more frustrated than you are. A hell of a lot more." He stalked away along the row of pallets, spread his fingers and relaxed them, exhaled, and stalked back. "Are you really all right?"

When she nodded, the tension in his shoulders eased. "I heard about Cabana Boy, too," he said. "Will he be all right?"

"The vet says he will. Thanks for asking." She tipped her head. "Can we talk?"

He flashed a smile, though his dimple was nowhere to be seen. "Isn't that what we're doing?" He must have recognized the trepidation she was feeling, because he gestured at one of the hip-high stacks of feed. "Have a seat."

She crossed to the pallet, the sound of her footsteps echoing to the rafters. She dropped her purse and scooted up onto the nearest bag, her pulse stumbling into a pathetic flutter as she waited for him to slide up beside her.

Instead he propped a boot on the edge of the platform and leaned forward, crossing his forearms on his thigh. "What's up?"

"Remember what you said before, about me being too stubborn to ask for help?" She smoothed her palms up and down her thighs and smiled weakly. "This is me, asking."

He glanced down at her nervous hands. "What kind of help?"

"The early-morning-feeding-milking-mucking-then-do-it-again-in-the-afternoon kind."

He rubbed a hand over his mouth. The rasp of stubble against skin sounded loud in the storeroom.

Ivy threaded her fingers. "I know it's a lot to ask. I know it would mean taking you away from your kids and your store. But I promise it would be temporary."

"You're asking because I'm familiar with your farm."

It wasn't a question. Ivy half slid, half fell off the stack of feed bags trying to get to her feet. She ignored the hand Seth held out — ironic, much? — and smiled sheepishly. "And because I trust you."

Both eyebrows went up. "Bet that was tough to admit."

"You have no idea." She blew out a breath. "Did it work?"

He bent down and picked up his clipboard, slapping it against his thigh. "Want to know what chaps my ass?" he demanded. "You're here because of the horse."

She blinked. "That's right. I'm sleep deprived and stressed and I made a terrible mistake that could have cost me something very precious."

"Jesus, are you kidding me?"

"What?"

He tossed the clipboard again, gripped her upper arms and gave her a gentle shake. "You're worth more than a damned horse."

Warmth flooded her chest, and her throat went all prickly. *Really, Ivy?* How pathetic could she be, feeling all sappy because Seth valued her over her own stallion? "So you're not going to help because what happened with Cabana Boy is the reason I'm here?"

His gaze focused on her injured eye. He dropped her arms and stepped back. "I didn't say I wasn't going to help. I said it chaps my ass."

"I wish you'd stop talking about your — "

"Don't. If we're going to do this, we need to set boundaries and that's one of them."

Hope stirred. "Meaning?"

"It'll be business, all the way."

"Don't you think I want that, too?" *What a liar.* "I'm not a child,

Seth. I can keep my hands to myself." *There you go again.* "Anyway, I'm way behind. Neither of us will have time at the farm for anything but work. And like I said, this is temporary. Once I find someone to replace Wade, you and I will go back to being store owner and customer."

He didn't correct her, didn't say, *Friends, you mean.* Remorse pinched again, harder this time. She couldn't have made any more of a mess of this.

He skimmed a palm over the back of his neck and nodded once. "I'll adjust my hours so I can help you with chores in the morning. I'll handle the store and deliveries during core hours, then come back and help you milk again in the afternoon. If you don't hire a manager within a couple of weeks, you can put me on the payroll until you do. As a laborer, I mean. I don't know much about managing a farm, but I can help you with your recordkeeping."

"Thank you." She forced a swallow. "We need to talk wages."

"We need to talk logistics." Hands on hips, he angled his head toward the doorway that led back to the store. "Why don't you come into the office? I'll make coffee and we can hash the rest of this out."

"I don't have time," she said. "Just pick a morning and show up."

"When do you start your day?"

"Three."

"Bullshit."

She laughed and started walking backward toward the store. "Come when you can. We'll make it work." She paused in the doorway. "You'll miss your mornings. With your kids."

"I can live without soggy sandwiches in my lunchbox, as long as it's only for a month or so. And it was Travis, by the way, who made my sandwich this morning. I can always tell because he has a heavy hand with the jelly. Unless I slip up and buy strawberry, and then he eats the stuff before it can even make it to the bread."

"Will they be okay with this?"

He crouched, reached under the pallet she'd been sitting on and pulled out a small orange cylinder about the size of an index finger. A foam bullet, she realized, from a toy gun. Seth held it aloft. "I find these things in the weirdest places." He shook his head and stuck the piece of foam in his pocket. "Anyway, don't worry. We'll work it out."

She couldn't help herself. "What about Olivia? How do you think she'll feel when you're spending all of your spare time at the farm?"

"Not an issue. We had our first date the other night. There won't be a second."

"There won't?" Ivy cursed the gladness that tumbled through her veins.

"I kept comparing her to you, and not just in my head."

Ouch. Ivy swallowed, and it tasted like shame. That glee she was feeling? Not only mean but useless.

"Marcus broke up with Liz," she blurted.

"Uh...what?"

"She wanted to have sex with him and he told her she was rushing him and there was no sense being in a relationship when they wanted different things, so he called it quits."

"Damn." He scratched the back of his head. Then his gaze came up and locked on hers. "Damn," he said more softly.

"She's devastated. He doesn't even want to be friends."

"He'll come around. He cares too much about her to cut her completely out of his life."

"Saying hello in the checkout line at the grocery store doesn't count."

"Ivy—"

"Is this going to ruin the rest of what we have, whatever that is?" When her tone wavered, she crumpled a bit inside. "Am I making a mistake by taking advantage of your generosity?"

"You can't take advantage when I said yes. Anyway, what is this, your *Can we be friends?* speech?" he asked drily.

She ignored the edge in his voice and tugged at the waist of her sweater, trying as covertly as she could to give her armpits more air. "Oh, no," she said, giving her head a solemn shake. "We can't be friends. Not while I'm your boss. *After* I hire a full-time manager, *then* we can be friends."

His lips twitched. "I might be busy then."

"Ouch."

"Look. I want to be there for my kids, and I want to be there for you, too. So what do you say?" Seth offered his hand. "Partners?"

That last word put an instant halt to the warm and gooey going on behind her breastbone. Considering the last partnership she'd entered into had almost lost her the farm? Another one was *not* on her agenda.

She closed the distance between them and stared down at his hand, at the sun-browned skin and scarred fingers, the bruise discoloring the nail on his index finger. Finally, she reached out, watching as his grip smothered hers.

"I prefer the word *cohorts*," she said.

He gave her fingers a squeeze and let go. "You would."

"So I'll see you later?"

"You mean earlier." He glanced at a watch he wasn't wearing. "If I'm coming over in the morning, I have about an hour before I need to hit the hay."

Ivy laughed. "I see what you did there."

"Go away, Millbrook. I have work to do."

She was halfway to the cash register when she realized she'd forgotten her purse. She turned back. Seth stood in the entrance to the stockroom, her bag dangling from his outstretched arm. She accepted it silently.

"Ivy?"

"Hmm?"

"I get that you prefer to handle things on your own. I'm guessing you feel guilty about coming into the farm the way you did, and it's natural you'd want to protect it. I appreciate your trust."

Ivy faltered. No one knew her like Seth, damn him. She inhaled. "And I appreciate your..." She allowed her eyes to dip down and then up, admiring anew the crazy-defined muscles that crowded his jeans and cotton shirt. A tingling rush of desire sapped the moisture from her mouth — just the distraction she'd counted on.

"Your willingness to help," she finished lamely. When he lifted an eyebrow, she sighed. "This isn't going to be easy."

"Like you said. It's temporary."

The strain in his voice followed her all the way out to her car. Was he stressed because he couldn't imagine putting up with her sorry butt day after day, week after week? Or because he couldn't imagine working beside her while keeping his hands to himself?

She wouldn't blame him if it was the first, couldn't do anything about the second. It was bad enough being a shameless mass of want whenever she was around him. Adding *hypocrite* to the list meant permanently earning the label Lost Cause.

Maybe she could convince him to change the terms of their agreement. Since she couldn't imagine how she'd find the words to thank him for what he was about to do for her, maybe she could show him instead.

*   *   *

SETH DID NOT CONSIDER himself a morning person. He'd been faking it since he became the sole parent responsible for getting Grace and Travis up and fed and off to school every weekday. But it kind of sucked getting up at five thirty to make breakfast and lunches and fold the laundry he'd forgotten in the dryer the night before.

Not that he'd have traded being a dad for anything. Still, household chores had been easier when he'd shared them. Everything else he and Deb had tried to do together had been difficult as hell.

Guilt speared him. He should have tried harder, for the kids.

He parked his newly repaired truck next to the milking shed and switched off his headlights. The engine gave off a series of muted clicks as it settled back to sleep. Seth tried a yawn, but it fizzled out halfway through. He wasn't as tired as he should have been. The prospect of spending the day with Ivy had him revved up, even though he knew he'd be shoveling shit.

Still, he wished he'd taken time to make coffee. He pushed out of his truck. Five thirty was bad enough. But 3:00 a.m.? That wasn't morning. That was the middle of the frickin' night.

Thank God for Mrs. Yackley, their next-door neighbor. She was a generous woman and had twice handled getting the kids to school — once when Seth had had to leave for an early meeting with his ex-wife and her lawyer in State College, and another time when he'd contracted some sort of stomach bug and had been too sick to stand, let alone make lunches and meet the bus. Those occasions had meant crossing his yard at seven in the morning, though. Three might be pushing it. His neighbor had been game, but they'd settled on four.

And here he was at Ivy's, fifteen minutes after the hour. He shivered and congratulated himself for exchanging his usual ball cap for a knit hat, courtesy of Mrs. Yackley. The temperature gauge in his truck had read forty.

What was he doing, sacrificing what little time he had with his kids to play cowboy? Yeah, he liked to give his friends a hand when they needed it. But this was more than that. He'd been presented with a prime opportunity to show Ivy just how great a team they could make and he'd snatched it right up when he should have put more effort into thinking about how this would affect his family.

Then again, would it have mattered? All he could think about was saving Ivy from the breakdown she was headed for, helping her keep her farm running and getting her to trust him in the meantime. If she kept him around long enough, he might even be able to convince her to give him and his kids a go.

If Travis and Grace were lucky enough to end up with someone like Ivy in their lives, wouldn't that make this all worthwhile?

Hell, yeah.

So don't keep the lady waiting, Walker.

He glanced from the house to the barns. Lights blazed in all four buildings. *Eenie, meenie, miney, moe.*

He was halfway to the nearest barn when the thunk of the front door echoed across the driveway. He turned to see Ivy descending the steps, looking elegant as ever despite the god-awful hour and her standard farmer's outfit—knee-high rubber boots, faded jeans and a jacket that looked like a plaid shirt on steroids. Her pale hair was in its usual braid, her walk the sexy, determined glide he was used to seeing. What he wasn't used to seeing was the nervous edge to her smile.

"Good morning." She handed him a mug of steaming coffee. The smell of it was almost as delicious as the huskiness in her voice.

"Good morning," he said, and hefted the mug. "Bless you."

"It's the least I can do."

Seth took a sip and bent his knees at the rich snap of flavor that carried heat to his belly. Another sip, and he raised his eyebrow over the rim of his mug.

"Cinnamon schnapps," she said. "A little something to get you going."

He suppressed a snort. As if he needed booze for that when she was standing right in front of him.

She eyed his chest. "How much do you like that denim jacket?"

"A lot. But don't worry—I know how to use a washing machine."

"Do you also know how to use a needle and thread? Because trust me, it will get ripped."

"I'll find something else to wear tomorrow."

She wrapped her arms around her waist and bounced on her toes. "I can't tell you how much I appreciate this. It's bad enough to haul you out of bed this early, but when it's cold like this..." She shivered. "Just wait till it snows."

"Yeah, well, when that happens, you might just have to come drag me out from between my sheets."

She stopped bouncing.

Seth wrenched his mind away from the vivid image of tangling with Ivy in his sleep-warmed bed. Yeah, they'd agreed to keep this professional, but how was he supposed to make any progress with her if he couldn't tease her?

Be smart, Walker. The teasing thing worked both ways. Anyway, he had bigger things to worry about, like making sure his kids still recognized him at the end of this temporary gig.

He had a fine line to walk, but there was no way he could have said no to Ivy. Especially when she'd never asked him for help before.

He cleared his throat. "By the way, Bradley's got me covered all day. Talking me through everything is going to slow you down, and I didn't want to leave you with half the chores undone."

Ivy blew out a breath. "Thank you. I dreaded having to ask Dell to stay late again."

"He's not giving you a hard time, is he?"

"He's been great. I just don't want to push my luck, you know?" As though on cue, the sliding door to the milking shed rumbled open and Dell appeared, coffee cup in hand. He waved and jogged toward the house for a refill.

Ivy tipped her chin in the same direction. "More coffee before we get started?"

"No, thanks. I'm good." With his free hand, Seth pulled his gloves out of his back pocket. "Mind if I look in on Cabana Boy first?"

"Oh. Sure."

He followed her into the horse barn, a building that managed to feel cozy despite its size and the thick concrete floor. Maybe it was the warm glow of the pendant lamps, the dark weathered wood or the clean straw smell. Or the owner herself, who radiated a sensuality he found a captivating contrast to her ice-blonde beauty.

She waited for him at the third stall on the right. He'd expected to see Cabana Boy nosing for a treat, but the stallion remained in the far left corner, head bent, eyes closed.

"He's mad at me," Ivy said. Her voice was wry, but Seth didn't miss the disappointed angle of her mouth. "Either for shutting him up again or for letting Wilmer do that." She pointed at the bandage on his flank.

"He'll come around." Seth knew firsthand how tough it was to stay annoyed with Ivy Millbrook.

"Just the same, I'm glad Wilmer will be here later to check him out."

Seth eyed the latch on the stall door. "You sure you're the one who left this open?"

"Had to be me. Dell had already left for the day."

Since a row of bars lined the top half of the stall door, Seth couldn't accuse the horse of being too clever for his own good and letting himself out. He scratched his jaw and voiced the concern that had pestered him since he'd first heard of Cabana Boy's escape. "Could someone have done it deliberately?"

"You mean as some sort of prank?" Ivy frowned. "No. Who would do that?"

"What about your other farmhand? The one who walked out?"

"Gary? He was angry, yes, but not that angry. This was my fault. I'm sure of it. I haven't been getting enough sleep. I'm wearing the proof on my face." She gestured at the green and yellow smeared beneath her eye.

"You think you forgot to latch this door *and* forgot to close the barn door?"

She glanced at the main entrance and back at the stall. Apprehension seeped into her face.

Seth palmed her shoulder. "I'm not trying to scare you. Not trying to make excuses for you, either. I just want to make sure we know what we're dealing with."

"What *I'm* dealing with." She took a step back, and his hand slid free. "Remember earlier, when I said fixing you a cup of coffee was the least I could do? I also mean to respect your wishes and keep this arrangement business, all the way."

"I appreciate that." He managed to say it with a straight face.

"No problem."

He considered her a moment, enjoying the color staining her cheeks, then tipped his head back and checked out the rafters. "Ever consider getting security cameras? One at each end of the alley here would help you keep an eye on things, and if you post a warning, it might make a would-be intruder think twice." He gave her the side eye. "Might even discourage whoever's been getting creative with your sign."

"Not a bad idea. I'll think about it." She took his empty mug from him and set it on a nearby saddle stand. "Before we get started, there's something I want to say. I'm grateful you're here, and I don't want to take advantage. I want to put you on the payroll right away."

"We agreed I'd help out for a month first."

"We need to renegotiate. Unless you *want* the guilt to eat away at me, day after day, as you help save my farm for nothing in return but the occasional meal."

"Don't forget coffee. Which is exceptional, by the way."

"Thank you."

"You're welcome."

"Are we good?"

He sighed. "How occasional are the meals?"

"More occasional if you don't let me put you on the payroll."

"Then we're good."

*   *   *

TWO HOURS LATER, SETH had finally gotten the hang of the milking machine, but the backs of his legs were sore as hell from squatting. He'd better throw a few more burpees into his workout routine, assuming that from here on out he could find time to hit the weights. Then again, after hauling hay bales and buckets of feed twice a day on top of everything he did at Tweedy's, he might not need to.

The milking shed was smaller than the dairy barn, but it was set up in the same way, with open stalls lining either side, all facing a feeding trough that extended along each wall. A wide concrete walkway extended down the center of the barn, with manure gutters running parallel and backing up against the stalls. Steel railings separated the stalls and gave Seth something to hang on to when, after squatting four times for every cow he milked, he was starting to regret having to get to his feet.

Once he got into a rhythm, though, he found the work soothing. His only disappointment in learning how to work the apparatus was that Ivy had arranged for Dell to show him how to do it. How could he convince her they'd make a stellar team if she paired him up with someone else?

Only ten cows could be milked at a time. For 110 cows, that meant eleven shifts. Each shift went faster than Seth expected, taking maybe twenty minutes, tops. After the cows jostled into place for milking — the girls were actually eager to give up the goods, so eager that Ivy had to shut a gate outside the milking area to keep the other cows from crowding in — their teats were cleaned with warm water and dipped in an iodine solution to help prevent mastitis. Another swipe with a warm rag, and the Jersey was ready to be hooked up to the milking machine.

The machine had four elongated tubes called cups, one for each teat. An air tube provided vacuum pressure, and a second tube carried milk up to an overhead pipe that emptied into a receiving tank in a separate room. The apparatus made a *shook shook knock knock, shook shook knock knock* sound as it worked. If the cows had needed any calming, that probably would have done the trick. But Ivy's Jerseys were a laid-back bunch, probably because she treated them so well. Part of her milking routine was to groom the cows while they were being pumped, which explained why Seth's shoulders burned even more than his legs and he had cramps in both hands.

Wisely, he kept his aches and pains to himself.

By the time Ivy, Seth and Dell had finished feeding all the livestock and milking the cows, it was almost eight, and the apple Seth had eaten on his way to the farm that morning had long since lost the battle against hunger. He followed Ivy and Dell into the house, his stomach sitting up and paying rapt attention as he caught the scent of sausage.

Oh, yeah.

He'd just stepped into the kitchen, a sunny space with pale green walls, dark hardwood floors, and a multitude of red and yellow pots brimming with houseplants, when his cell rang. He recognized Bradley's reggae-like tune and excused himself. He wandered into the living room, toward the framed photos that lined the fireplace mantel. "What can I do for you, Bradley?"

"Do we offer free samples?"

"Do we what?"

Bradley slurped something through a straw. OJ, was Seth's guess — he'd probably stopped on his way to work for a breakfast biscuit. Seth's stomach applauded the concept.

"Mr. Katz is thinking about trying a different brand of dog food for Mona here," Bradley said. "He wants to know if she can try a sample first. He says she's a picky eater."

"He brought Mona into the store?"

"Yeah."

Dammit. The last time that dog had been left to wander, she'd crapped in every aisle. It had taken Seth a week to get rid of the smell. "Tell me she's on a leash."

"Even if she isn't?"

Seth ground his teeth. "No samples. That would mean opening a brand-new bag."

After a few seconds of off-line rumbling, Bradley came back with "Mr. Katz says he doesn't mind waiting."

Seth just bet he didn't. "It's not the time — it's the money. Once that bag is open, we'll have to sell it at a discount."

"He doesn't have the cash for his regular brand," Bradley whispered. "You're the one who keeps giving him stuff and now suddenly I get to be the bad guy?"

Shit. "Give him half off."

"I tried. He says he doesn't want our charity."

Seth laughed because otherwise he'd have drop-kicked his phone. He checked out a photograph of a pigtailed Ivy slumped in a high chair covered with chocolate frosting and his laughed turned genuine. "One sample. That's it."

"Hold on."

"Bradley?" The kid had set the phone down, probably on the counter. Seth could hear muffled voices, a *schwipp* as the bag was ripped open, a crunching sound and voices again. Bradley got back on the phone.

"Mona liked it."

"What a relief. Can I go eat my breakfast now?"

"Wait, how much do I charge him?"

"Charge him what's on the price tag."

"But...the bag's been opened."

Seth rolled his eyes and pushed away from the mantel. "Figure it out, Bradley. I have to go."

He returned to the kitchen but only Ivy was there, rummaging in the fridge. No Dell, no plates on the table, no sign of anything sausage scented.

"Everything okay?" Ivy peered at him over the top of the refrigerator door.

"Yeah." Seth moved to the sink. "If you need any dog food, today's the day to get it. Apparently we're having a sale." He spoke over the sound of running water. "Where's Dell?"

"He finished eating and went back out to the barn."

Seth glanced over his shoulder. "He finished? Already?"

"Mmm-hmm. Peach or strawberry?"

He hoped like hell she was wanting to know what kind of jam he liked on his big-ass biscuits. "Peach."

She stepped back and tossed him something. Water sprayed everywhere as he shot up a hand to catch it, and he knew what it was before he looked at it.

Yogurt.

Damn.

He dried his free hand on his shirt and scowled down at the label boasting fat-free contents. "Your own cows eat better than this."

A toilet flushed off to Seth's right as Ivy snickered. "Just kidding," she said, and patted the oven as Dell came out of the bathroom. "Breakfast casserole and biscuits are on the way." She turned and reached up into a cupboard.

"Cute." Seth put the yogurt back in the fridge and accepted the plates she handed him.

Dell met him at the table with the silverware. "Consider yourself hazed," he said in the wispy voice no one would ever expect to hear coming from a man built like a Brahman bull. Weathered features flushed from the heat of the kitchen, he nodded at the casserole Ivy pulled from the oven. "Lucky, too. My first day here, I got a jar of olives and a can of mandarin oranges for breakfast."

Ivy winced. "Going to the grocery store is not my favorite chore. And you're forgetting the toast I made to go with it." She set the casserole on a trivet Seth hastily provided and went back for the biscuits.

"So." Dell pursed his lips at Seth before dropping a fork and a knife beside each plate. "You have farm management experience."

Seth shook his head and grabbed a bunch of napkins from a bright red basket on the counter next to the microwave. "No experience. Just another set of hands to help out until Ivy finds a replacement for Wade."

Ivy shot Dell a frown as she transferred a dozen steaming golden biscuits from a cookie sheet to a cloth-lined basket. "He's here to take orders from you, not the other way around. I told you that before you left last night."

Dell's flush deepened, and he scratched at the black stubble on his chin. "Guess I misunderstood." He sat at the round table, his back to the window, and reached for a biscuit. "If he's taking orders from me, that makes me a manager, then, doesn't it?"

"Yes. But not the farm manager, Dell. Not unless you know how to manage breeding and calving schedules. You also need to feel comfortable projecting sales and expenses."

Dell grunted as Ivy handed Seth a jar. Seth looked at the label. Peach preserves.

"Thank you," he said, and continued to stand by the table.

Ivy flushed and dropped into the chair nearest the stove. As Seth took his own seat, Ivy handed the serving spoon over to Dell, who was halfway through his second biscuit. He flicked Seth a triumphant, less than friendly glance and cut into the casserole.

Seth set his jaw. Jesus, he hoped he wasn't going to have any trouble with Dell. The farmhand appeared to be in his late forties, but he also looked as if he could bench-press half a dozen of Ivy's cows. Seth was no slouch in the muscle department, but the last thing Ivy needed was the kind of trouble that could push her last hand into walking out on her.

* * *

AFTER BREAKFAST, SETH WAS looking forward to getting behind the wheel of the Bobcat, even if it did mean shoving shit around. Ivy, apparently, wanted him to get up close and personal with the poo, as she called it, because she traded the keys to the Bobcat for a pitchfork and pointed him to the horse barn.

"New guy has to pay his dues," she said, and tossed the keys to Dell, who walked away wearing a smirk that took up his entire face.

Seth stacked both palms on the pitchfork's handle and leaned in. "I'm only going along with this because of that breakfast you prepared." He rubbed his belly. "Thanks again."

Roses bloomed in her cheeks. "It's a pleasure cooking for someone with a healthy appetite. Anyway, you earned it."

"Now I feel guilty enough that I have to confess. I have an evil plan."

"To lure me into the loft and have your wicked way with me?" As soon as she said the words, her eyebrows gathered and her mouth dropped in penitence. "Sorry about that."

"Don't be. It'll take us some time to get used to keeping it clean."

Meanwhile, he had to angle himself away from her so she couldn't see that he'd given much more than a thumbs-up to her suggestion.

"What is your plan?" she asked.

"To show you how well we can work together." He handed her the pitchfork and grabbed another from a rack on the wall. "Which means we have to actually work together."

"Nice try." She handed the tool back. "I have spreadsheets to tend to."

"Convenient."

"I know, right?"

The sound of a car engine pulled Seth's gaze away from Ivy and toward her driveway. A silver hatchback parked beside his truck. *What the – ?*

He grunted. "This should be interesting."

"Who is it?"

Together he and Ivy watched Olivia Duncan emerge from her car and retie the belt on her light blue sweater jacket. Seth moved toward the door, and Ivy followed.

"I thought your date didn't go well." Ivy sounded peeved.

Seth fought a grin. "It didn't."

"Something went well enough to bring her chasing after you."

"How do you know she's here to see me?"

Ivy rolled her eyes and headed out into the crisp sunshine. "Olivia. How are you?"

The women chatted for a few minutes, Ivy tall and slim, Olivia shorter and curvier. A lot curvier. The woman was a knockout, but it was Ivy who drew Seth's gaze, again and again.

Finally, Ivy gestured toward the barn, then turned and headed for the house. Olivia waved at Seth and strolled over to meet him, a white waxed bag in her hand and a tentative smile on her face.

"Olivia." He leaned down and kissed her cheek. Somewhere in the distance, a door slammed.

She held up the bag and gave it a jiggle. "I brought you some of those chocolate-covered animal crackers you like so much, as a thank-you for dinner. When I stopped by the feed store, your boss told me you were here. I hope you don't mind."

"My boss, huh?" With a chuckle, Seth scrubbed a hand through his hair. One of these days, he was going to kick Bradley's ass.

"I got the impression he was exaggerating, but he was enjoying his moment and I didn't want to spoil it for him. Here." Olivia pushed the bag into Seth's hands.

"Thank you," he said, and knew it was inadequate.

She lifted a shoulder. "I know. I'm sweet. It's all the candy."

Seth grinned. "You do know how to rock a candy dish."

"I promise this is just a thank-you and not a ploy to get you to ask me out again. I like you. A lot. But I think we both figured out pretty quick you're not into me. Still, I had a really nice time, and I wanted to let you know." She wandered farther into the barn, the click of her high heels muffled by the bits of straw on the floor. "I wasn't going to come, but I thought maybe it would shake things up a bit." She tipped her head toward the house. "In a good way, I mean."

"About Mama Leoni's. I owe you an apology."

"Yes. You do. It was worth a try, though." She patted him on the arm and moved back toward the barn's entrance. "It's good of you to help Ivy out. Maybe she'll change her mind about dating you."

"I don't know anyone more stubborn, so I doubt it. But thanks. For the goodies, too."

"You're welcome. Save some for the kids." She offered up a shy smile and turned away. When she got to the doorway, she glanced back. "Oh, and I do, by the way."

"Do what?"

"Know someone more stubborn." She gave a little wave and click-clacked her way back to her car.

*   *   *

FOR THE NEXT HOUR, Ivy refused to get up from her chair, forcing herself to finish her recordkeeping without so much as one sip of coffee. She considered it punishment for that ridiculous display of jealousy. And what was with the flirting? She couldn't even last half a day without hitting on the poor man?

This was going to be tougher than she'd expected. But, oh, so very worth it. While Seth and Dell were busy with the chores, Ivy could get caught up on receivables and payables and on finalizing the latest contract with the dairy she sold her milk to. She might even have time to ride fence.

When she heard the distinct rumble of the vet's ancient Jeep, she finally pushed away from her computer. She grabbed her plaid jacket and hurried outside. Usually she'd release Cabana Boy into the pasture so he could enjoy some fresh air and exercise while the barn was being cleaned, but what if she couldn't get her hands on him again for Wilmer? The stallion was not happy with her. She could see him playing hard to get.

When she reached the barn, the vet was already inside Cabana Boy's stall. Seth stood nearby, his hair and long-sleeved tee soaked with sweat, his forearms reddened and scratched. He must have been tossing around hay bales again.

Seth quirked an eyebrow as he pulled off his gloves. "Mind if I listen in?"

She should say yes. She should remind him he had work to do. But it was her work, and she was quickly becoming addicted to having him around while she did her chores.

"No," she said. "I don't mind at all." She sidled into the stall and took hold of Cabana Boy's bridle. She scrubbed his forehead with her knuckles as Wilmer gently probed the stallion's wound. The horse closed his eyes and leaned into Ivy. Seemed all was forgiven.

"Looks good," the vet said. "I'll change the bandage and check again in a couple of days. No need for me to take the stitches out — they'll absorb into the skin. In the meantime, do what you can to keep this dry. If he can stand it, keep him here in the barn for another week." He removed his latex gloves.

"I'll do my best. Thank you, Wilmer. So much." She reached out.

He clasped her hand and gave it a fatherly squeeze. "Like I said, I'll be back. But I don't suppose you have a little something for me today?"

"You know I do. I'll run and get it while you pack up your stuff."

When she came back out of the house, Seth stood with Wilmer in front of the Jeep, one palm braced on the hood, the other low on his hip. Sunlight turned his brown hair amber and spilled over shoulders that looked impossibly broad in the faded jean jacket he'd shrugged back into.

If Ivy hadn't been so busy staring, she'd have rolled her eyes. How absurdly unfair, that a man could look that delicious without even trying.

"...check-engine light," Wilmer was saying.

"Chances are it's your catalytic converter. The ethanol in the gas ruins them. How's your mileage?" When the vet made a face, Seth nodded. "I hate to be the bearer of bad news, but you probably need to replace one of your converters. Take your Jeep in to Pete. Have him check your engine codes."

"Wait, *one* of my converters?"

Seth rapped twice on the hood. "This baby has two."

Wilmer sagged against his vehicle. When Ivy handed him the bottom-heavy plastic bag she carried, he shot upright again and his expression brightened. "Did you throw in a fork?"

She laughed. "It wouldn't do you any good. The cake is frozen solid."

"I'll turn on the heat in the Jeep."

Seconds later, he was behind the wheel and heading down the driveway, saddened that Ivy had recommended against thawing his cheesecake in the microwave. When Seth remained silent, staring after Wilmer, Ivy turned toward the barn for one last check on Cabana Boy before getting back to her computer.

Seth stopped her. "Did you stay up all night baking? Is that why you have shadows under your eyes?"

She bit down on a defensive rejoinder. "They're not shadows," she said, trying for a playful note. "They're bruises."

"The hell they are. Ivy, I'm here to make your life easier. I'm not here so you can add to your chores."

"You're not here to give me orders, either."

He let his hand fall away from her arm. "You work too hard."

"If I do, it's none of your business," she snapped. "You certainly can't begrudge that man his favorite dessert when you trip over your own tongue whenever you manage to talk me into baking a batch of ginger molasses cookies. And anyway, if I stayed up all night, it's because I was fixing that stupid breakfast casserole."

Seth's eyes flared, then narrowed. Regret tugged at the corners of his mouth and Ivy sighed. That stuff he'd spent the morning scraping off the dairy-barn floor? Exactly what she was feeling like.

In the paddock behind her, Priscilla Mae—Holstein, former Lilac Queen, adored by schoolchildren county-wide and the pride of Millbrook Dairy Farm—mooed a richly deserved scolding. Ivy scuffed the toe of her boot against the asphalt. "I'm sorry I said that. I got plenty of sleep last night. It's just that I'm not used to having someone worry about me." She peered up at him, squinting in the late-morning sun, and said it again. "I'm sorry."

"No." He stuffed his hands in his jacket pockets. "I crossed a line."

"It's a line we're playing tug of war with."

A moment's pause, then he swung toward the barn. "I need to finish mucking out the stalls."

She followed him inside, to the last stall on the right.

She stepped between him and the wheelbarrow he was headed for. "About that cheesecake for Wilmer. I'd forgotten I had an extra one in the freezer. This is what we do. I send him away with a treat, and he's happy to be there for me anywhere, anytime. Like when Cabana Boy needed him yesterday. He showed up, no questions asked."

"That's what he does," Seth said.

"Are you trying to say I'm letting him take advantage of me?"

"I'm trying to say you need to learn to say no."

"Well," she said huffily, "if that's the case, I couldn't have a better teacher than you."

He chuckled and started to step around her to get to the wheelbarrow, where he'd tossed his gloves.

Her hip brushed his as she shifted to block him. "And for your information, food has nothing to do with what keeps me up at night."

"I could say the same thing," he countered, almost idly. "And I'd mean the 'keeps me up' part literally."

5

IVY FELT SLUGGISH, HER blood warm and heavy in her veins. What she needed to do was get a grip, and not on Seth.

Oh, what the hell.

She moved in close and set her hands on his chest. The solid, sculpted chest she'd salivated over for an entire year. *Good God.* He went rigid beneath her touch, but he didn't speak, didn't protest. His heart thumped against her palms, and her pulse throbbed in greedy reply. She angled herself upward and hesitated, his mouth within licking distance. His breath warmed her lips. After a quick peek into eyes as conflicted as hers should be, she changed course and lifted her chin to the left. She scraped her teeth lightly along his earlobe.

His body jolted. She settled back onto her heels and did her best not to smirk.

"Ivy." His growl carried a warning. Still, he didn't step away. Was he as tired as she was of this game they'd been playing for what seemed like forever? After all this time, had curiosity about their kiss and what it would taste like won out?

She got her answer when his fingers curled around her upper arms. *Hel-lo.* He bent his head. She licked her lips. He paused, made a small satisfied sound, ignored her face and pressed his mouth to her neck instead. He dragged his teeth along her skin and she choked out a half laugh, half gasp.

She wanted to protest, but she was petrified that words would break the spell. Instead she speared her fingers into his sweat-dampened hair and urged his face closer.

When his mouth finally landed on hers she whimpered with pleasure. No gentle sliding of lips, no slow, unnecessary build — just a long-awaited fusion of hot want and slick desperation. The man had read her mind. She moaned her approval and wriggled closer. His arousal was evident, and the rigid pressure against her stomach kicked her yearning into overdrive.

The tingling press of her breasts against his unyielding pecs, the wet silk texture of his hair, the sweat and sunshine scent of an outdoors man all had her gleefully keeping pace as his mouth devoured hers. Never mind that it had been so long since she'd experienced any of those things. She'd never experienced them with *Seth*, and the fact that it was his tongue tangled around hers made her dizzy.

With a groan she could feel in her breasts, he changed the angle of the kiss. He squeezed her arms briefly and sent his left hand to her back, wrapping it in her braid. A gentle tug lifted her chin, freeing her mouth. She gulped in air, lungs shuddering as he scorched kisses along her jaw and down the side of her neck. His breathing rasped as loudly as hers. His right hand skated down her waist and around to her ass, caressing and at the same time pressing her even closer to his straining erection.

Need sparked and popped and shimmered. She flexed her fingers in his hair and quivered against his muscled heat as his barely there beard grazed her cheek.

"Damn, you taste good," he muttered.

She hummed her agreement, hoped he realized she meant *he* tasted good, too. She helped herself again to his earlobe.

He released her hair and ran his palms up and down her spine. "You're not saying much," he murmured. "I don't know whether to be nervous or smug."

"I'm afraid to say anything." She nipped at his corded neck, and it was his turn to quake. "I'm afraid this will stop."

He went still, and it did.

"Seth," she moaned, ashamed by her need but too turned on to back away.

He did it for her.

"Ivy." His hands slid back up to her shoulders and gently pushed. His face was flushed, his gaze troubled. "I meant to keep my hands to myself."

"Is it wrong to be thrilled you couldn't?"

"I was the jerk who set the conditions and I stomped them all to hell in what, four hours? Five?"

She watched helplessly as he swung away. Details of their surroundings filtered in, guilt chasing away the haze of desire she would really rather have lingered in forever. Behind her, Cabana Boy snuffled, and a low-pitched hum started as the barn's heat kicked on. Outside, the Jersey girls lowed as they plodded their way to the fields to graze. The steady drone of the Bobcat signaled that Dell was still on cleanup duty.

Dell. Her stomach clutched. What if he'd walked in on them? Anyone could have. Worse, what if one of the *Catlett* sisters had walked in on them? If Hazel or June had stopped by, all of Thistle Hill would have heard by lunchtime that Seth and Ivy had been about to get it on in the horse barn. How long would it have taken after that for Seth's kids to hear the rumor?

Ivy pressed an arm to her belly. He would have hated that.

"Stop beating yourself up," she told him. "It takes two, you know." When he turned back to her, looking disgusted, no doubt with both of them, she threw out her hands. "Fine. No platitudes. I've been trying to convince you for months that what I feel is okay, so I'm not going to dismiss what you're feeling. I enjoyed what we did just now. I'd enjoy doing it again. I know that's not going to happen, but I appreciate the break from reality. I also appreciate everything you're giving up to be here." She scooped his gloves out of the wheelbarrow and tossed them over. "Now get back to work."

Despite the gravity in his expression, one corner of his mouth twitched. "Once you get your farm back in order, we need to talk."

"What about?"

"What do you think?"

She wanted to tell him there was nothing to talk about, that nothing had changed. But with one heart-stopping kiss, they'd made everything twice as complicated.

She really needed to find that new manager. Tugging on his gloves, Seth headed once again for the wheelbarrow. He paused when he reached her side. "You're right. That can't happen again. It'll screw with this arrangement, and you need this to work." His eyes darkened. "That said, from here on out, every time you see me, know that I'll be thinking about that kiss. I'll be remembering that your skin smells like vanilla, your hair feels like silk and your mouth tastes like sunshine on a snowy day."

She blinked up at him. *Okay, then.* She swayed forward.

His hands came up to steady her, and his dimples flashed. "I'll give you a month's worth of free horse feed if you promise to never, ever tell anyone that words like that came out of my mouth." His face lost all trace of amusement. "Words I shouldn't have said. Look. I want to talk when all this is over, but let me tell you something that might help you understand where I'm coming from. Deb and I got married because I got her pregnant."

"Oh" was all Ivy could say. That explained a lot.

"You know how well that turned out." His phone rang. He peered at the screen and frowned. "I'm sorry, I have to take this. It's the store again."

Ivy waved her consent, grateful for the interruption. "I have to check on the calves anyway."

His low-pitched voice followed her out of the barn. She knew what that *I want to talk when all this is over* comment was about—Seth thought he might have a chance of changing her mind. After the way she'd behaved, who could blame him? Her body was still tingling from that spur-of-the-moment lip-lock.

But she remained determined to cling to her independence. Plus, there was the whole children issue. If they couldn't get this arrangement back on a professional footing, it was time to explain why kids could never be part of her future.

*   *   *

WHEN THE KNOCK CAME at the door, Marcus set his thriller aside and pushed off the bed. He'd heard the doorbell earlier. His landlady's lunch guests had started to arrive, which meant she'd hiked up the stairs hoping to talk him into potato-chip-covered chicken salad and canasta.

He trudged toward the door. He owed Audrey Tweedy. He owed her a lot. But he had some serious sulking to do. It had been a week since he'd broken up with Liz, and he didn't feel any of the self-righteousness he'd promised himself. Instead he felt like shit. The only time he'd felt worse was when his mother died.

Doing the right thing sucked ass.

With a roll of his shoulders, he reached for the knob. Since he was miserable anyway, he might as well keep pretending to be a hero and join the coffee klatch. When he opened his door, though, Audrey's plump face looked more apprehensive than inviting.

"Liz is downstairs asking for you," she said.

He hated himself for the excitement that bubbled over in his chest. Scrubbing a palm across the bristles of his short hair, he turned, scooped up his kicks and sat on the end of the bed to put them on. His fingers shook. If he'd had the early shift at the diner today, he wouldn't have been forced to deal with Liz now.

It was too soon. Her open smile, bright blue eyes and crinkly hair that smelled like honeysuckle... How was he supposed to keep his feelings, let alone his hands, to himself? Especially after that almost kiss? Remembering the press of her breasts against his chest took out his knees every time.

He clenched his jaw and toyed with the idea of asking Audrey to send Liz away.

"Don't be such a wuss," he muttered. He had to face her sooner or later.

"What was that, dear?" Audrey hovered in the doorway. "Is there something I can do?"

With a shake of his head, Marcus stood. Audrey adjusted the purple barrette that held her chin-length gray hair out of her eyes and crossed her meaty arms. He gave her an awkward pat on her shoulder and her eyes went wide.

And no wonder. He wasn't the touchy-feely type.

"No, thank you," he said. "I'll just — " He jabbed his thumb toward the stairs.

"Let me know if you need anything." Her Minnie Mouse voice

followed him as he made his way to the first floor. "I have meatballs in the slow cooker and ham-and-cheese rollups in the fridge. Eat some protein. You'll feel better."

Marcus rolled his eyes, but it was an affectionate eye roll. Audrey Tweedy firmly believed that regular doses of protein could solve the world's problems. She had to be the only Thistle Hill resident able to resist Cal's cinnamon rolls.

He turned right at the bottom of the steps and stopped dead. He'd been warned. He should have been ready. But the sight of Liz Early standing ten feet away punched the breath right out of his lungs.

Without another word, Audrey brushed past him on her way into the kitchen.

Liz attempted a smile, but her lips refused to cooperate. "I was hoping we could talk," she said huskily.

He couldn't stop staring. She didn't look any different, wasn't wearing anything other than the usual jeans and flowery top she waited tables in, but he couldn't take his eyes off her.

"Liz," he said. And that was it. That was all he had.

"I'm not here to try to change your mind. I just... I want to explain." She flushed and shifted her grip on the strap of the purse she wore over her shoulder. "Actually, that's a lie. I'm hoping my explanation will make everything blindingly clear and we'll suddenly be all right again, but I'm realistic enough to know that's not going to happen. So, will you let me explain?"

Hell, no, he wanted to say. The more he saw her, and the more they talked, the harder it would be to stay away. But if he couldn't even bring himself to listen to her side of things, even once, she'd figure that out and they'd be back where they started.

He nodded for her to precede him up the stairs. It took less than an instant to realize *that* was a bad fucking idea. He had to drop his head and stare at his shoes because the flare of her hips and her endless legs were turning him on.

He followed her into his bedroom, shut the door and leaned back against it. Having her here in his space was doing a number on his heart rate. Not that he would try anything, with a card party about to start downstairs. Still, he had to get her out of there.

Keep it together, dude.

She dropped her purse on his bed and wandered around the room, absently rubbing her hands up and down the sides of her jeans. Her high-heeled boots made shooshing noises against the carpet. She trailed her fingers along the surface of the massive oak desk Audrey had insisted he use, the rattan lid of his clothes hamper and the gray striped curtains he didn't have the heart to tell Audrey reminded him of the putty-colored prison walls he'd stared at for fourteen months.

Should have been eighteen, but keeping his head down and his mouth shut had earned him an early release.

Finally, Liz met him back at the door. "Do you realize that in the six months we were dating, I was only here once?"

He battled to keep his gaze on her face. "There was more privacy at your house. You don't have someone knocking on your door every twenty minutes offering protein shakes and hard-boiled eggs."

"Audrey means well."

"I know she does. But I don't think I've watched a movie all the way through since I moved in. Why are you here, Liz?"

"I told you. I want to explain why I acted the way I did."

He pushed away from the door and moved over to his desk, pulled out the straight-back chair and straddled it. He curled his fingers around the twin posts at the top. "You didn't do anything wrong. You have a right to expect sex with your boyfriend. I'm sorry I let you down."

"Marcus. I don't want your apology."

"I know what you want."

She shot him a reproachful glance and dropped down onto the foot of his bed. "Have you ever heard of the five love languages?"

He exhaled. "You mean like French or Italian?"

She fought a smile, and he fought the embarrassed urge to go lock himself in the bathroom.

"A love language is how you prefer to express your love," she said. "Like giving a compliment or spending time together or buying a gift. My love language is physical touch. That's a problem for us because you're not...expressive that way."

At one time he had been. He had vivid memories of being lifted up into a hug when he was maybe four or five, of good-night kisses, of being cuddled in his mother's sweet-smelling arms. But that was before she got married again. Before she died. Before his stepfather.

"I can't help it," he gritted.

"I know that. And it was wrong for me to try to force it. I'd just like you to understand why I tried. I wanted to show you —"

"Liz."

" —how much I love you."

Shit. He resisted the urge to rub at his chest. "This isn't a problem for us, because there *is* no us."

"What if I promise not to push?"

"That wouldn't be fair to you."

"No." She got to her feet. "You don't get to say that. If you wanted to be fair to me, you'd give us another chance. We're not ready to call it quits. We've been through too much together."

"Together? No." He got up from the chair. "I went through stuff, and you happened to be there."

He had to glance away from the devastation on her face.

"That was harsh." She pushed the words past whitened lips. "Why didn't you stop me? Why didn't you set me straight a long time ago?" Her voice had started to rise. "Is this about my age?"

"Your age?" He blinked. Had she lied? "You mean you're older than twenty-four?"

Outrage slashed color across her cheekbones.

"No," she snapped. "I'm not. But apparently three years is way too big of a gap." She grabbed her purse and yanked it onto her shoulder. "I made the mistake of thinking there was more to this than there really was. A heads-up would have been nice."

"Yeah, well, I didn't realize this was all about getting naked. I thought we were taking time to get to know each other."

"We are. Or we were. That night by the waterfall, we learned a lot about each other."

"Right." Marcus sneered. "Like how you think spending a night in jail for criminal trespass compares to a year and a half in prison for assault."

"Make fun of me if you want, but it still gives us something in common. Anyway, we've been dating six months. How much more do we need to know about each other?"

"Before hitting the sheets, you mean." Marcus inhaled. She'd left herself wide-open. If he took the shot, he wouldn't have to worry about her again. She'd forget about him and find someone who could give her everything she needed. Someone who didn't get suspicious looks or pitying smiles.

Someone who wasn't fucked up in the head.

"Look, if you're so horny, why don't you just find someone else to fuck? That way you don't have to miss out on another six months of sex."

Liz gasped. And stared at Marcus as if she'd never seen him before.

He couldn't stand it.

"Aw, hell," he choked. "Liz, I—"

Rap, rap, rap. "Everything okay in there?"

Their chests heaved as they faced each other. The twenty feet between them seemed like a thousand miles.

Rap, rap, rap. *"Marcus?"*

He swallowed and jerked his head toward the hallway. "This is why we never hung out here." He strode to the door and pulled it open.

Audrey squinted at him, then at Liz over his shoulder. Without looking away from Liz, she pushed a plate of bacon-wrapped shrimp into his stomach. "I thought you two might like a snack."

Marcus didn't take the plate. "This is nice of you, but we're not hungry."

"Don't blow smoke up my fanny. I know you think I'm an interfering biddy. This food isn't for your stomach—it's for your mouths. If you children can't talk, you can't argue."

"I'm sorry. We'll keep it down."

"I didn't come up here to ask you to keep it down—I came up to ask you to stop arguing." Audrey frowned down at the plate and repositioned one of the appetizers. "Also to leave the door open so we can hear what you're saying."

"There's nothing more to hear." A stone-faced Liz maneuvered around them. "Thanks for the snack, Audrey, but I was just leaving."

"Wait." Marcus reached for her and at the same time asked himself what the hell he was doing.

"I can't." Liz started down the stairs. "I have to get to work." She paused and looked over her shoulder. "Besides. I've already waited long enough."

*　　*　　*

SETH DID HIS BEST to hide his grimace as he dismounted, but the shit-eating grin on Dell's face told him he hadn't succeeded.

"Been a while, I take it." Dell jumped nimbly off his palomino and led the way to the barn.

Seth barely resisted the urge to flip the farmhand off. He lifted the reins over his own mount's head and followed Dell, stiffly, every step a burning ache.

"Try years," he grumbled.

Inside the barn, he adjusted his borrowed hat — he'd exchanged his knit cap for a tan Resistol to combat the sun — and guided the mare over to where Dell was already removing the palomino's saddle. Both horses had drunk deeply from the trough outside, and now the buckskin Seth had been riding — Poppy, according to the nameplate on her stall door — was nosing around for feed.

Seth fetched two apples from the bin in the tack room, tossed one to Dell and fed the other to Poppy.

Dell nodded his thanks but hadn't lost his grin as he hefted his saddle and walked past Seth on his way to the tack room. "You'll feel worse tomorrow."

"Bite me." Seth loosened the cinch that wrapped around Poppy's ribs and connected to each side of the saddle to keep it in place. He dragged the saddle free of the mare's back and trailed after Dell. "How much of the farm did we cover?" They'd ridden a solid two hours.

Dell turned from positioning his saddle on one of the dozen or so wooden racks that extended from the wall like mini ironing boards. He grabbed Seth's saddle and swung it up onto the next empty rack.

"Less than a quarter," Dell said.

Jesus. "It must take you days to do a complete circuit."

Dell shrugged, grabbed two currycombs, handed one to Seth and returned to the horses. They groomed in silence. Normally that would have suited Seth just fine. But the lack of conversation meant his thoughts were free to veer right back to Ivy and the smokin'-hot kiss they'd shared not twenty feet away from where Dell was standing.

From the moment he'd met the woman, he'd thought about kissing her. He'd thought about it a lot. Every red-blooded male with eyes in his head would think about kissing Ivy Millbrook. But the reality? A hell of a lot more satisfying than the fantasy. Satisfying and maddening, because it couldn't happen again.

His gut twisted, and he almost regretted the thick roast-beef-and-cheese sandwich he'd bolted down at lunchtime. If they didn't get this train back on the right track, he and Ivy would both end up doing something they'd regret. He yanked his mind away from that no-fly zone, moved around to Poppy's other side and went back to brushing. After a while, he squinted over the mare's back at Dell, who'd set aside his comb and was gathering up the palomino's reins.

"What's next on the agenda?" Seth asked him.

"Second milking, second feeding, second cleaning."

Seth grunted. "Second thoughts."

The farmhand didn't crack a smile. He led Silver Dollar back to his stall, secured the door and headed out of the barn. "Meet you in the milking shed," he called over his shoulder.

Seth propped his forearms on Poppy's back and watched him go. "Hell," he muttered, "even grouchy old Harris Briggs would have found that funny."

His phone rang. He winced, but Poppy never even flinched. She stood in what looked like the equine version of a slouch, head sagging, eyes closed. His brushing had put her to sleep.

He pulled his phone from his back pocket, pressed a button and lifted it to his ear. "Bradley, what part of 'You're in charge' do you not understand?"

"I can hear the smile in your voice. You must be with Ivy."

Seth gave the mare a pat and pushed upright. "No, though I am with a beautiful female." He collected the two combs and headed for the tack room. "Do you realize this is the fifth time you've called me today?"

"Dude. You need to relax."

"Stop calling and maybe I will."

"This'll just take a sec. Listen. We're closed on Sundays, right?"

"Right," Seth drawled, wondering where the kid was headed with this.

"What if I opened the store this Sunday? For, like, half a day?"

And now he knew. "Why would you do that?"

"So we can close early today." When Seth didn't say anything, Bradley rushed on. "Some of the guys are heading to Seven Springs and asked me to come along."

Seth tucked his phone between his shoulder and his ear and led Poppy over to her stall. The mare hadn't even opened her eyes. "You want to close the feed store so you can go skiing."

"Well, tubing, but yeah."

"We talked about this." Seth removed Poppy's bridle and shut the stall door. "You agreed to cover the store all day today."

"Yeah, but I didn't know about the tubing then."

Seth bowed his head and banged the end of the phone against his brow. "I hear you," he managed, "but I can't let you lock up early. I'll lose too much business. We'll get few if any customers on Sunday because no one will expect us to be open."

Bradley let loose a dramatic sigh. "I get it. A deal's a deal."

Better. Much better. "Thanks, man. I'll be there with the kids before closing." Seth ended the call, returned the bridle to the tack room and reached for his work gloves. Time to get his head in the dairy game. If he worked hard enough, maybe he wouldn't have the energy to want what he couldn't have. He slapped his gloves against his thigh and headed for the milking shed.

Half an hour later, Ivy came looking for him, and when he saw the panic in her expression, he knew exactly what she'd come to tell him.

"There's a school bus in the driveway," she said. "Why is there a school bus in the driveway?"

*   *   *

IVY DIDN'T APPRECIATE THE *What's the problem?* expression Seth was wearing. Despite that, she did her best to focus on his face rather than the way his crossed arms made his biceps bulge under his denim jacket, or the way the sun slanted in through the shed door behind her, gilding his rumpled brown hair.

The brakes on the big yellow thing coming up her driveway squealed.

School was over for the day. This was not about a tour.

She hitched a thumb over her shoulder and raised her voice so she could be heard over the milking machines. "What's going on, Seth?"

He shrugged. "What else am I going to do with the kids after school?"

"Oh, no. No way."

"I can't leave them at the store. That wouldn't be fair to them or to Bradley."

She threw out her arms. "The farm isn't childproof. There are a million things that could go wrong." Someone could take a tumble off a fence or get trampled by one of the Jerseys or fall into the manure pond.

Worry stabbed at her breastbone.

Seth turned and signaled to Dell, then stepped away from the gate that closed off the milking area. He picked up his hat. "Between the two of us, we'll make sure nothing does."

"That's not going to work," she said. "The whole point is to help me get my chores done. How will throwing two children into the mix do anything but slow us down?"

"We'll take turns keeping an eye on them. We'll make it work." He lowered his chin as he herded her back toward the door. "It's a package deal, Ivy. Take it or leave it."

"Why do you have to be so stubborn?"

"You talking to me or yourself?"

She growled, and he did a half-assed job of hiding a smile.

Ivy swallowed a sigh when she noted the speculation in Seth's eyes. She couldn't blame him for wondering why the prospect of hanging out with two elementary-age kids made her nervous. Heck, she entertained twenty or thirty of them at a time whenever she hosted a classroom tour, and never once had she broken a sweat.

But fewer kids meant more one-on-one time, and after showing these two around, she wouldn't be able to herd them back onto a bus. Plus, they were Seth's kids. Things were complicated enough between them, even more so now that they'd tasted each other. And whose fault was that?

Good going, Millbrook.

But oh, dear *God*, that man could kiss.

Desire pounded through her, slow and sweet. Deliberately, she turned her head away and latched her gaze onto Dell, who was shooing the latest group of ladies toward the milking area. They didn't need much encouragement, since they had food waiting for them in the bedding barn. Ivy shouted to Dell that she'd be back. He waved her off.

She swallowed the sour taste of guilt. Dell was looking forward to leaving the farm at a decent hour. As soon as the cows were milked, he planned to be gone, and rightly so. He hadn't left work before dark since the day she'd lost Gary and Wade.

Outside in the driveway, the bus rumbled to a stop. The door opened with a squeaking gush of compressed air. Travis appeared first, stepping sedately to the pavement like any self-respecting seven-year-old superhero in disguise. Ivy's heart warmed a little. Who could resist the big-eyed towhead with the brightly striped shirt and Captain America backpack?

Grace came off the bus even more slowly than her brother. She cast a suspicious glance around as the doors closed behind her and the bus pulled away. When she caught sight of Travis she sauntered toward the paddock fence to join him, her walk both graceful and full of disdain.

Did she take dance classes? Seth had never said. Ivy had never asked.

She took two steps forward and had to stop when her feet refused to keep up with her legs. Seth passed her from behind, touching her lightly on the arm as he walked by. A sign of support? Or a scolding?

She knew which she deserved. It was crazy pants how nervous these children made her.

After fumbling for her phone and sending a quick text, Ivy pushed herself forward. Seth leaned down and hugged his kids, and while he had his arms wrapped around them, Travis stole the Resistol Seth had borrowed from Dell. He put it on his own head and it promptly fell down around his ears and covered his eyes. Laughing, Seth took the hat back, then dropped into a crouch and listened intently as the children talked about their day at school. Travis's high-pitched chatter about the fish tank in his science class had Grace rolling her eyes, until Seth took her hand and jiggled it. She pouted but stopped making faces. When it was her turn and she talked about Egypt and the Nile and how she wanted to dress up as Cleopatra for Halloween, her expression grew animated and her pink mouth moved faster and faster. Ivy had never seen anything sweeter.

All the while, Grace kept a watchful eye on Ivy.

When the little girl paused to take a breath, Ivy strode the rest of the way up to the trio. Seth winced as he straightened, then gave her a wink.

"You remember Miss Ivy, don't you, kids?" Seth tugged lightly on Grace's hair, a curly shoulder-length mass a few shades lighter than his. "You met her at the spring festival."

"Welcome to Millbrook Dairy Farm. It's nice to see you two again." Not knowing what to do with her hands, Ivy jammed them into her pockets. "Sounds like you two had an exciting school day."

Lame, Millbrook. So lame even the kids ignored her comment.

Grace squinted up at her. "What happened to your eye?"

"I fell in the barn. I wasn't watching where I was going. Don't make the same mistake, okay?"

"I remember you from the festival. You rode that big brown horse that does tricks." Travis jerked his head left and then right. "Where is he? Can we ride him?"

"He doesn't do tricks, dummy — he dances."

"Hey." Seth shook his head at Grace. "No name-calling."

She turned away and crossed her arms, gazing across the paddock as if whatever was on the other side were the most interesting thing

102

in the world.

"You're right, Grace," Ivy said. "Dressage is often referred to as 'horse ballet.'"

Travis perked up. "What is that word you said?"

"Dressage." Ivy smiled. "It rhymes with *massage.* You know, like a back rub?"

Travis made a face. "Ballet is for girls."

"It isn't ballet, *exactly.* It's a stride that involves a lot of suspension. Think of a horse trotting underwater. It takes a great deal of strength and training. The horse you saw me ride at the festival is my Arabian stallion, Cabana Boy, and he's really good at dressage. I'm probably doing him a disservice by not letting someone show him, but I can't bring myself to let him go."

"You competed?" Seth lifted and resettled his hat, and the unconscious masculine gesture made her toes curl.

"When I was a teen," she managed. "But not with Cabana Boy. If I'd had him in the arena, I'd have won a lot more ribbons."

"Ever give lessons?" This in a small voice from Grace.

"Every once in a while. It's tough to find the time."

"You should make it happen more often." Seth cocked his head. "I wish you could see what you look like when you talk about riding. You're radiant."

Heat rolled into Ivy's cheeks and she seriously considered joining Grace at the fence. She doubted she'd be welcome, though—Grace's back had gone as stiff as a possum playing dead when Seth had made his comment.

"So can we ride your horse?" Travis brought them back on track.

"He's resting in his stall right now. I can take you to say hello, but I'm afraid it wouldn't be safe to let you ride him. He has a lot of energy, and when he gets excited, he doesn't listen very well."

"Daddy says that about us," Travis admitted.

"About me, too," Ivy said drily.

Seth coughed into his fist. "Hey, guys. How about we ask Miss Ivy to give us a tour?"

Grace turned her head, revealing a scowl. "You've been here all day and you still don't know your way around?"

Ivy snorted but resisted the urge to offer Seth's daughter a high five. Nothing could put a kid on the defensive faster than an adult who tried too hard.

"There's Priscilla Mae! She was at the festival, too." Travis threw himself at the fence and climbed up to the second slat before Ivy could bat an eye. "Can we ride her?"

Ivy walked over and leaned on the fence beside him. "I'm afraid she wouldn't like that. She's far too prissy." Of course the Holstein chose that moment to spread her back legs and relieve herself. This time it was Seth who snorted. Ivy glanced back at him, only to see that he was watching his daughter watch Ivy. Ivy turned toward Grace and did her best to look anything but condescending.

"But I'll tell you what we can do. Would you like to see the calves? Maybe help me feed them?"

Interest flickered in Grace's eyes. Her chin lifted in defiance of it. "Our mom lives in State College," she said. "She's real smart. She has a lot of degrees."

"That's great," Ivy said, trying to keep the *Where the hell did that come from?* out of her smile. "Do you like school as much as she does?"

"Did you?"

Ivy blinked. "Parts of it," she said. "Math, mostly."

Grace screwed up her face. "Math's no fun. I like English."

"I like science!" Travis launched himself away from the fence and began to hop up and down on one leg. "We made slime and we colored it green and Danny dropped it on the floor and there was a big green spot and we told Mrs. Oakley that Danny threw up and she sent him to the school nurse. Can we go see the calves now? I'm tired."

"Stop hopping," Seth suggested wryly.

Ivy and Seth led the kids to the nearside of the bedding barn, where a separate indoor/outdoor pen housed the calves. Making mooing noises, Travis ran up to the wire fence and peered in. Though Grace followed at a more leisurely pace, there was no mistaking the excitement on her face.

"There's, like, eight in there," Travis said. He'd started hopping again. "Are we going to feed them all?"

"That'd be a good idea, since I suspect they're all hungry." Seth rested his hands on his hips. "Once you're inside the pen, there'll be no going crazy. No running, yelling or quick movements, because we don't want you to get hurt, and we don't want the calves to get hurt. You're to do everything Miss Ivy tells you to do. All right?"

Both kids nodded, practically quivering with anticipation.

Ivy ran a practiced eye over the calves. They didn't seem the slightest bit perturbed by the kids' presence and in fact were already rushing the fence, eager to get fed. "All right, then. I'll be back with the bottles." Luckily, Dell had already prepared them for her. She returned to the pen towing a wagon loaded with eight bottles and couldn't help a sigh when she caught Seth's approving smile.

Despite everything, he still seemed to have hopes that his kids would charm her into wanting a family.

"How come they don't eat out of a bucket?" Travis wanted to know.

"They already have the instinct to take a nipple. You've seen how they latch on to the mama cow's udder?" When he nodded, Ivy shooed the calves away from the gate and opened it. "We'd have to train them to eat out of a bucket. Feeding them this way takes more time, but it's easier to make sure they all get their fair share."

Soon giggles and squeals replaced the sound of bawling calves as Travis and Grace — or G, as Seth called her — each fed four demanding babies. Seth helped Grace, while Ivy lent Travis a steady hand whenever a calf got pushy, which was pretty much all the time. When the bottles were empty, Seth had the kids carry them back out to the wagon. Ivy couldn't pull the wagon into the pen, because the wheels had little traction on the straw.

"How come they're separated from their mothers?" Grace stared at the calves, then turned and stared at the Jerseys grazing in the distance. Ivy shot a panicked look at Seth, but he was deep in conversation with Travis and hadn't heard the question.

Maybe the best way to deal with the subtext was to ignore it. Besides the fact that it was none of her business, Seth had never talked about his divorce.

"The calves are extremely vulnerable the first few months of their lives," Ivy explained. "That's why we put down straw and clean it several times a day. Manure has germs and we don't want the calves to get sick. And if they were in the free-stall barn with the heifers or the mature cows, they might not get enough to eat. We keep them in the pen for three months to make sure they get a strong, healthy start. Meanwhile, we slowly wean them off the milk and teach them how to graze and eat out of a bucket. As soon as they're ready, we let them join the herd."

She said it cheerfully, while bracing herself for sympathetic tears. She'd cried for the calves, too, when she was a girl. Instead of getting weepy, Grace regarded her with what looked a lot like disappointment, then swung away and marched over to her father and brother.

Ivy puffed air out of her cheeks. *What'd I do?*

She was locking up the gate and Travis was asking to see the horses next when a powder blue Buick crawled up the driveway. Hazel Catlett got out of the car, carrying a flowered tote under one arm and a salt-and-pepper schnauzer under the other. Travis gave an energized yelp and ran toward the dog. This time Grace wasn't far behind, until she suddenly seemed to remember adults were watching and slowed to a saunter.

Or was it just Ivy who was the problem?

"Is it me?" Ivy moved up beside Seth. "Or is she always like this?"

"Unimpressed, you mean?" He gave his head a shake. "You can't take it personally. G's just practicing."

"For what?"

"For being a teenager."

Hazel set Baby Blue on his feet, ordered him to sit and called the kids over. They dropped to their knees and introduced themselves while Hazel rummaged through her tote.

Ivy frowned. "I thought Grace was only nine."

"Haven't you heard? Nine's the new thirteen."

"You poor man."

He grunted. "I will be, once she starts caring about boys and makeup and designer labels."

Like two indulgent parents, they watched Travis and Grace fuss over Hazel's dog. Ivy caught her breath. *Whoa, Nelly*, she rebuked her

106

subconscious. Parents? *Ain't gonna happen.*

"You okay?" Seth murmured.

"Me? You're the one who's moving like you aged fifty years since breakfast."

An adorable flush seeped into his cheeks. "Been a long time since I got on a horse," he muttered.

She resisted the urge to tease him further. "I was wondering. You call Grace 'G.' Why don't you call Travis 'T'?"

Before he could answer, Hazel looked up and waved as though she were holding a winning lottery ticket in her fingers.

"I came as fast as I could, hon," she called. "Baby Blue couldn't find his squeezie."

Seth's eyes narrowed and he turned to Ivy. "What's this?"

"Reinforcements." She rolled her lips in, then tried to smile. "Hazel agreed to look after the children in the afternoons while we work. This will be safer."

"Safer." He raised an all-too-knowing eyebrow. "For who?"

With both hands she tugged at the hem of her jacket, her fingers curling into the scratchy wool. "Besides the fact that I promised Dell he could leave after the milking, having Hazel here will free us up to get the mucking and the health checks done. The faster we finish, the faster you can get your kids home."

He swore under his breath. "I suppose you know why I would have voted against this."

She forced herself to meet his gaze. "You want me to get to know them."

He showed off his dimples again, and she had an irresistible urge to kiss them. "Dumb idea, huh?"

"Sweet, actually."

"They're good kids."

"I'm sure they are."

He exhaled. "You're right. I've seen enough of the farm today to know this is better. But I want to split the cost."

"Done," she said.

Hazel let loose a triumphant cry. Ivy and Seth turned to see her brandishing a sandwich bag crammed with dog treats. She murmured something to the kids, and they obediently cupped their palms. When she peeled open the bag, Baby Blue was up on his hind legs, front paws digging furiously at Travis's jeans.

"You know better than that, Baby Blue." Hazel gave the dog a gentle swat and tipped the bag into first Grace's, then Travis's, hands. "Not too many," she said. "They give him gas like you wouldn't believe."

As the kids took turns feeding the dog his treats, Hazel pulled out her cell and snapped a few photos, then trotted over to join Ivy and Seth.

"Those young'uns of yours know how to play poker? Not the strip kind, of course." She squinted at Seth. "Unless you're available to play?"

Ivy fought a grin. A woman after her own heart.

"How about Gin Rummy?" Hazel rummaged in her tote and brandished a baggie full of quarters. "I'm hoping the kids are rubes so I can win enough to buy a tank of gas." She waved at the Buick behind her. "Feeding that baby ain't cheap."

After a glance at Seth's rock-hard jaw, Ivy covered the old woman's hand with hers and gently guided the quarters back to where they came from. "You're here to help them with their homework, Hazel, not fleece them."

"Got it." Hazel nodded and beamed up at Seth. "Don't worry, big boy — your kids are in good hands. Anything else I need to know?"

"Just that we'll be around." Ivy patted Seth's arm, which was rigid with tension. "Close by. Checking in with you. Often." Hazel continued to beam and Seth's arm relaxed a fraction. Shading her eyes, Ivy peered up at him. "If you want to help Dell finish up the milking, I'll get Hazel and the kids settled inside. After that, I'll be cleaning out the chicken coop." She tipped her head. "Or I can help Dell and you can — "

"I'll be in the shed," he said, and took off, heading back the way they'd come almost as fast as his son had headed for Baby Blue.

Okay, then.

"Just a minute, missy." Hazel stopped Ivy as she turned toward the house. She reached back into her tote, and something crackled as she pressed it into Ivy's hands. "Use them in good health."

Ivy looked down. Condoms. Tropical flavored. *Oh, dear God.*

Numbly, she murmured her thanks and stuffed the brightly colored roll in her pocket.

After ushering Hazel and the kids inside and showing them all of the important places — the bathroom, the fridge, the junk-food cupboard and the dining room table Travis and Grace weren't thrilled to discover would double as their homework station — Ivy grabbed her bucket of cleaning supplies off the back porch and headed for the coop.

She liked to change the bedding and scrub the coop once a month. If she could smell ammonia, the chickens could, too, and breathing that in wasn't healthy for any animal. After working her hands into her rubber gloves and herding the chickens out into the yard, she started sweeping.

Ivy carried armful after armful of soiled straw to the wheelbarrow. Then she dumped her supplies on the ground, filled the bucket with a mixture of bleach, dish detergent and water, grabbed the scrub brush, and went to town on the linoleum covering the floor of the coop. She also scrubbed the walls, the roosting bars and the nest boxes. As soon as she'd hosed the place down, she'd let it dry, toss in fresh bedding and cross one more chore off her list.

Hallelujah.

She backed out of the coop, turned and chest-bumped several feet of solid, stationary male. She staggered back two steps and clapped a gloved hand to her chest. "I didn't know you were there."

"Didn't mean to startle you," Gary said gruffly.

She started to ask, *What can I do for you?* then realized she didn't want to hear what was sure to be a disturbing answer. "I hope you're not here to tell me your check bounced," she said instead.

His jaw slid forward. "I'm here to get my job back."

Oh, hell no.

6

IVY SHOOK HER HEAD. "I'm sorry, Gary. I'm looking for a manager only."

"You mean that guy from the feed store? What's he know about running a dairy farm?"

"He's not running the farm. He's helping out Dell until I hire someone permanently."

"You have two openings." Gary held up two fingers, ironically making the peace sign while his face flushed red with anger. "Wade's and mine."

"I'm not hiring you back."

"Why the hell not?"

"You're not a good fit."

"You never had a complaint before."

"That's right. I didn't. Not until the day you made an inappropriate comment and walked off the job." She picked up the bucket and started tossing her supplies back inside, never turning her back on her former farmhand. Finally, she straightened, broom in hand. If he came after her, she'd jab him in the gut.

While screaming bloody murder.

"But Needle Dick over there." With a jerk of his head, Gary indicated the milking shed. "He fits?"

"I can't help you, Gary, so please go. I have things to do."

"I need the work."

She resisted sneaking a peek in the direction of the barn. "Let me remind you that you're the one who quit. I can't trust you not to do it again. Besides, I don't like the way you look at me."

"Maybe because you're wishing I'd do more than look."

Her stomach slid sideways, though he seemed more sullen than sinister. "I'm pretty sure that's not it."

He spit at the grass between his boots. "I wouldn't do a stuck-up bitch like you anyway."

Ivy frowned. "I'm not stuck-up." Was she?

"Prove it." He advanced on her, eyes narrowing when she held the broom out in front of her like a *bo* staff. "Give me another chance."

Over Gary's shoulder, she spotted Seth striding in their direction, and relief sapped the tension from her muscles. Her arms sagged, and the broom handle hit her legs, just above her knees.

"What the hell's going on here?" Seth, his face a mask of hostility, thrust himself between Ivy and Gary. "Are you *threatening* her?"

Gary ran a shaking palm over his bald head, and Ivy didn't blame him for being nervous. Seth stood with his hands fisted and his knees slightly bent, ready to launch himself forward. Ivy, meanwhile, wanted to roll her eyes and fan her face at the same time. As thankful as she was to have backup, and as thrilling as she found Seth's fierce defense of her, she would *not* be the helpless heroine tied to the railroad tracks.

She stepped out from behind Seth. "Everything's okay. Gary was just leaving."

Seth didn't take his eyes off the farmhand. "You all right, Ivy?"

"I'm fine. I was just explaining that I don't have any job openings." She swung the broom upright and planted it firmly beside her. "You don't need to check in again, Gary. I won't be changing my mind."

Gary hesitated, but when Seth took a step toward him, he turned and stomped away.

As soon as he disappeared around the corner of the house, Ivy exhaled. "You didn't need to come rushing over here. I could have handled it on my own."

"Yeah?" Seth faced her with narrowed eyes, jaw muscle jumping like mad. "Think he'd have left so readily if you'd been alone?"

"Yes. But you didn't give me a chance to prove it."

"And thank God for that. If you'd screamed, Dell and I wouldn't have been able to hear you. Not when we're in the barn running ten milkers and surrounded by a hundred cows. I only came out because

111

I needed to talk to you about a lesion we spotted on one of the Jerseys."

Ivy fought to suppress an unsettling mix of gratitude and resentment. "As soon as I hose down the coop, I'll come find you and you can show me which cow you're talking about."

"I have a better idea." Seth carved a hand through his hair, held it and let his arm drop. "Why don't you head into the house and call the sheriff? I'm going out front to make sure that asshole isn't hanging around."

"Why would I call the sheriff?"

"Are you serious right now?" Seth jabbed a finger toward the driveway. "He threatened you. Not only that, but I'm 99 percent certain he's the one who set your stallion loose."

"Gary has worked here over two years. I think I know him better than you do." Except she didn't, did she? His ugly innuendos the other day had caught her completely off guard. Still, this was her problem. "Anyway, there's no way I can prove he had anything to do with Cabana Boy getting out."

"So you're just going to sit back and wait for the next bad thing to happen? Like hell. If you don't call Sheriff Tate, I will."

"You're not in charge. Just because we shared a kiss doesn't mean you get to order me around."

"Order you—" He spun on his heel and paced away, startling a chicken that had wandered back to check out the status of her coop. The hen squawked a rebuke and scurried off. Seth paced back. "This isn't about anything but keeping you safe."

"It's my problem, Seth, not yours."

"Yeah?" With slow, deliberate motions, he picked up the broom and leaned it against the wire fence that surrounded the chicken compound. "Neither Dell nor I would've heard you scream, but I bet Hazel could have. Or one of the kids. Gary was pissed off before. A few minutes ago, you humiliated him, so now he's furious. What if Hazel or Travis or Grace had come running? What if something had happened to one of them?"

Ivy sucked in a breath. He was right. Oh, God, he was right.

Seth's fingers dug into his hips. He kept his distance. "You value

112

your independence. So much so you're willing to pay a hell of a price for it. That's your decision. I don't get it, but I respect your right to make it. What I can't respect is you assuming everyone else will chip in, no questions asked. That's not admirable, Ivy. That's selfish."

She flinched, and willed the depth of her hurt to stay hidden. He was disappointed enough. She didn't want him to think she was making a play for sympathy. He didn't understand, though, how thoroughly she'd failed her parents, and how much she had to prove.

Not that it mattered when her debt endangered others.

"You're right," she said softly, through the shame that thickened her throat. "I'll go see the sheriff tomorrow. If I call this in now, they'll send out a deputy and the kids will want to know why."

"Good." Seth backed away, and she sensed it was more than a physical retreat. "I'll check out front, finish up with Dell then wait for you in the barn."

She watched him go, accepting that things between them wouldn't be the same. Which was okay, right? It was what they both needed to happen.

Still, it stung like nobody's business.

*   *   *

LATE THE FOLLOWING MORNING, Ivy exchanged her rubber boots for a pair of the low-heeled leather kind and drove downtown to the courthouse. The overcast sky and wet chill in the air were a perfect reflection of the melancholy she'd been trying to shake off since Seth had arrived with his own coffee at four thirty. They'd worked well together, but they'd worked mostly in silence, with Dell tossing them the occasional bewildered glance. She'd never been so grateful for Dell as she had been at breakfast that morning. He'd carried the conversation single-handedly, alternating between asking Seth questions about fly-fishing and describing his former life on a Texas cattle ranch. Ivy didn't get the chance to apologize to Seth, because she hadn't wanted to do it in front of Dell.

The sheriff's department shared with county officials a faded single-story brick building that had been around since the '60s. The oak trees dotting the property were as big around as an upended bale of hay, and the camellia trees at each corner, lush with layered pink blossoms against glossy green leaves, had to be fifteen feet tall. As Ivy walked the path to the courthouse entrance, red-, brown-and gold-toned leaves rattled and crunched beneath her feet. The earthy scent sparked a yearning for ginger snaps and apple cider.

Ivy tried not to dwell on the number of chores waiting for her back at the farm as she pushed through the glass doors separating the sheriff's office from the rest of the building. Clarissa Dodd, the redheaded dispatcher who also served as receptionist, looked up from her computer, her black-rimmed cat-eye glasses, pale face and scarlet lipstick putting Ivy in the mood for a Doris Day movie.

Clarissa wore a cordless headset. She angled the microphone away from her mouth. "May I help you?" she asked.

"I'd like to see Sheriff Tate," Ivy said. "Would you please tell her Ivy Millbrook is here?"

"Ivy." The dispatcher stood, revealing a pencil-skirt-and-cardigan combination as delightfully retro as the rest of her. "We talked on the phone the other day. How's your horse?"

Ivy smiled. "He had to have some stitches, but the vet says he'll be fine. Thank you for asking."

Clarissa nodded. When she walked away, Ivy's smile widened. Instead of the pumps that would complete the look, the dispatcher wore lime-green tennis shoes, the exact shade of the necktie Noble had been sporting the other day.

When Clarissa beckoned Ivy into the sheriff's office, Lily Tate had her head bent over her desk, making notes on a steno pad with her left hand while taking a bite out of a hard-boiled egg in her right. She held up one finger of the egg hand, wrote a few more words and tossed the pen onto her desk. Relaxing against the back of her chair, she regarded Ivy.

Ivy regarded her back as Clarissa slipped out. Sheriff Lily Tate was a slim brunette with a pretty face beneath a pixie cut much perkier than her personality. Without waiting for an invitation, Ivy sat. She had a feeling that otherwise she'd be waiting a long time. "How are you, Lily?"

"As busy as you, I'm sure." Lily leaned forward again, set aside the egg and wiped her fingers on a napkin.

Okay, then. Ivy squared her shoulders. "Yesterday I had a run-in with a former employee. Seth Walker suggested I bring it to your attention."

"He do that to you? Your former employee?" Lily nodded at Ivy's black eye.

"No. I did that all by myself."

Lily studied her a moment. "You're here talking to me instead of one of my deputies because, what?" Her voice was as crisp as her tan uniform shirt and mud-colored tie. "It's a sensitive matter?"

Ivy leaned sideways, reaching for the purse she'd dropped by her chair. "You're right. I admit I came straight to you because you're a friend." Lily was also a member of Dollars and Divas, though she wasn't often available to attend meetings. She took her position as sheriff seriously. Too seriously, some said, but wasn't that better than the alternative?

Ivy stood. "I should talk to someone else about this."

Lily held up a hand. "No. You're fine. This is fine. I'm sorry. I had a late night and I still haven't shaken it off. Please. Sit back down." Her gaze shifted to a black frame on her desk. Ivy couldn't see the photo, but she could see the edges of the frame. Since they were stamped with pumpkins and ghosts, it was probably safe to say the frame held a photo of Lily's daughter.

Halloween had been little Elodie Tate's favorite holiday. Lily's husband and daughter had been on their way to shop for Elodie's trick-or-treating costume when a driver too drunk to notice a stop sign had killed them both. October 31 was right around the corner. No wonder Lily was having trouble sleeping.

The sheriff shoved at the items on her desk and placed her palms flat on the newly cleared surface. She offered Ivy a brittle nod. "Tell me what brought you in."

Ivy caught her up, and when she described Gary's attempt to intimidate her, Lily frowned. She angled her body toward her computer and started typing. "You said Seth Walker interrupted the encounter. Did he overhear any threats?"

"It wasn't so much what Gary said — it was the way he said it."

Lily continued to tap at her keyboard. "So the answer is no." *Tap, tap, tap.* "Hazel Catlett and Seth's two children were in the house at the time?"

"Yes."

"They didn't witness your encounter?"

Ivy shook her head. "I don't think they even knew he was there."

Lily swiveled back to face Ivy, her expression grimmer than usual. "Seth Walker was right. You should have reported this immediately. His kids will be spending a lot of time at the farm. Their well-being should be your priority." Abruptly, she stood. "Children are precious. You should do everything in your power to keep them safe." She leaned forward and slammed her palms on her desk. Ivy jumped.

"Everything." Lily coughed to cover a sob. Slowly, she sat back down, her spine even straighter than her necktie. Her eyes went wide and she began to blink, frantically scanning her desk. Ivy plucked a packet of tissues from her purse and held it out.

"What can I do?" Ivy murmured. "Tell me what I can do for you."

Lily dabbed at her eyes, cleared her throat and lifted her chin. The aloof law enforcement officer was back. "You can keep me posted. I'll have a talk with this Gary. Make sure he understands we'll be watching the farm. We'll run his name through the system, see if he has any priors. This kind of thing usually ends at the point you've reached now. Times are tough, and losing a job can make anyone go a little crazy, but not usually violent crazy."

"Thank you. I appreciate your time." Ivy got back to her feet and hesitated. "We missed you at last week's meeting. Will you make the next one?"

"I'll try." Lily had turned her attention back to her computer. "But you know how it is. A sheriff's work is never done."

"I don't know...exactly how it is. That doesn't mean I don't hurt for you."

Lily's fingers hovered over her keyboard. "I don't need your sympathy. I need your common sense. Keep an eye on those kids."

Outside the courthouse, Ivy walked slowly along the sidewalk toward her car. Too bad she'd given her tissues away, because her own eyes were leaking.

A jangling sound made her look up in time to step out of the way of a heavyset man half walking, half jogging with his dog, a black Lab who trotted serenely beside her red-faced owner. Ivy watched them as they moved away, the dog's tail in a perpetual wag.

She rolled her shoulders up and back. What real reason did she have to feel sorry for herself? So her friendship with Seth was on the rocks. So things between them would change forever once he found himself a wife. So what? People suffered heartbreak every minute of every day.

At least she hadn't lost her husband and only child in one senseless, brutal, irrevocable moment.

* * *

SETH SMELLED HER BEFORE he saw her. Vanilla and mint. A heady combination that made him think of sugar cookies and ice cream. And Ivy.

He wiped horse spit on his jeans, marveling at how quickly the stallion could make an apple disappear. He turned away from the stall to find Ivy watching, an expression he couldn't quite decipher in her hazel eyes.

"You'll spoil him," she said softly.

"He's been through a lot. The occasional treat won't hurt him." Seth managed a grin. It killed him, the remoteness between them. He'd known working with her would be a challenge, but she'd needed his help.

Then there was his plan to convince her to lift her dating embargo. That wasn't going to change, especially now that he'd tasted her. It would have to wait, though.

"Don't tell the boss," he said. "She's a mite touchy when it comes to her horse."

"She's a mite touchy when it comes to just about anything these days." She smiled when he didn't refute it. Her lips didn't stay curved for long, though. "I spoke to Lily." He must have looked confused, because she added, "Lily Tate."

Seth sent an eyebrow skyward. "You call Sheriff Tate 'Lily'?"

"I think she's more upset with me than you are. She said that you were right, that I should have called the sheriff's department immediately. She also said she'd talk to Gary and have the cruisers on duty do a drive-by whenever they could."

"Sounds good."

Ivy reached through the bars on the stall door and stroked Cabana Boy's muzzle. "I think we need to renegotiate our agreement," she said quietly.

"By 'renegotiate,' I take it you mean 'cancel'?" Panic wriggled its way into his chest and he shook his head. "No. We're not rehashing this."

"Even after I made a poor choice yesterday? One that endangered your children?" He started to speak and she shoved a hand between them. "That was a rhetorical question. I see the way you are with them. How much you value your time together. I can't continue to take that away from you."

"You're not taking it away. I'm giving it to you. Temporarily. By the way, you're pissing me off."

She snorted. "I'm getting good at that."

"Yeah, you are. Look, somebody offers you a gift, you accept it. Gracefully."

"A gift? Your ass is costing me."

"I knew the real Ivy was in there somewhere." He pushed away from the stall, hoping he could find the words to make her understand. "Yes, my knee-jerk reaction is to help out if I can. But a decision like this, with a direct impact on my kids, I don't make lightly. This is a learning opportunity. My kids see me help out a friend in need, they learn a little self-sufficiency, and it starts to sink in that they shouldn't take things for granted. Besides. I gave you my word."

"You're right. Graceful I'm not. I don't like having to ask for help. That doesn't excuse my lack of good manners, though. I apologize." She paused. "I seem to be getting good at that, too."

"Apology accepted."

"Friends?"

Remorse rolled through him at the hesitation in her eyes. "Depends." He rubbed a hand over his belly. "You plan on feeding me lunch anytime soon?"

"I'll get right on that."

"Hey." He held her in place with a hand on her arm. "I was wondering. You ever consider getting a dog? For protection and maybe even help rounding up the ladies?"

"I wasn't allowed to have a dog when I was a kid. Now I wouldn't know what to do with one."

The mix of wonder and regret in her tone had Seth cringing. Why wouldn't her parents have let her have a dog? Hell, she didn't even have any cats — a frickin' miracle, considering she ran a dairy farm.

Though it was a good thing when it came to having Grace around, since she was allergic. His daughter still hadn't gotten over having to give that kitten away.

"Maybe that's something we can work on together," he said gruffly, giving Ivy's arm a squeeze. "There are plenty of dogs out there that need adopting."

Her expression faltered. With a nod and a mumbled comment about lunch, she tugged free of his grip and practically ran out of the barn.

Cabana Boy gave a snort that bordered on smug.

Seth sighed. "No shit, she likes you better." He turned his head and eyed the stallion. "Tell me your secret and tomorrow I'll bring you two apples."

This time when the horse snorted, Seth ended up with snot all over his shirt.

*   *   *

SETH AND DELL WERE just loading their lunch bowls into the dishwasher after making short work of Ivy's hamburger soup when the doorbell rang.

Ivy swore under her breath. "It's the roofer, here to give me an estimate on the north end of the milking shed. He's early." She frowned at the bread and butter still out on the table, along with the remnants of the soup. "I don't suppose..."

"See you out in the barn," Dell said, and scooted out the back door.

Seth shared a head shake with Ivy and shooed her out of the kitchen. The least he could do was clear the table.

The phone rang as he was stacking containers of soup in the fridge. After Ivy's voice invited the caller to leave a message, Seth heard the words that struck fear in the hearts of parents everywhere. "This is Mrs. Quesenberry, calling from the elementary school. I was trying to reach—"

Seth slammed the refrigerator door and grabbed the phone. "Hello?"

The woman stuttered for a moment. "O-oh, hello. Is Ivy Millbrook there?"

His shoulders sagged. Of course the call was for Ivy. If something had happened to one of his kids, the school would have called his cell.

"I'm sorry," he said. "She's busy at the moment. Can I take a message?"

"I'd appreciate that." The woman's voice warmed. "Could you let her know I was hoping to bring my kindergarten class by the farm for a tour this Tuesday?"

Seth bit back a sigh. As if Ivy didn't already have enough on her plate. "I'll tell her you called," he said.

"I know she sells her milk to a dairy that makes cheese," the woman continued enthusiastically. "I'd love it if she could arrange to have some samples on hand. And she'll have time to let the children ride, won't she? Just around the paddock?"

Plastic squeaked in protest as Seth's fingers tightened around the phone. He pictured Ivy, purple shadows of fatigue competing with the green and yellow bruises under her eye, running the farm and offering tours and stressing about Cabana Boy and dealing with Gary and cooking and baking and keeping the books—Jesus, she never caught a break. He looked at the stock pot she'd prepared the soup in and tugged at the collar of his T-shirt. "Hello? Are you there?" The teacher's voice jerked him out of the argument he was having with himself.

Ivy would be pissed with a capital *P*, but enough was enough.

"Ivy isn't giving tours right now," he said. "Why don't you try back after Halloween?"

* * *

A WEEK AFTER CAL had first gathered his evening staff to talk about money missing from the register, he held a reunion. Noah, Rachel, Parvati and Marcus waited in the kitchen while Cal finished up a call in his office. Once upon a time, the cheeseburgers sizzling on the grill would have smelled like nirvana to Marcus, especially since he'd skipped lunch. But he didn't have much of an appetite these days.

Noah scowled at the clock above the stove and folded his arms across his chest. "Man. I should be out of here by now."

Parvati settled her bulk in the chair someone had wedged between the bathroom and the sink. "Hold your horses. It won't kill you to stay over a few minutes."

"Says the woman who doesn't have a date," Noah said sourly.

"But I do have a date. With a romance novel, a shot of Amarula and a tortoiseshell cat who's good at pretending she doesn't like me."

Noah exhaled hard through his nose, pulled a handful of change out of his pocket and started counting. Since he didn't seem interested in plating the burgers he'd cooked, Marcus donned an apron and did it for him. When he'd added fries, coleslaw and a dill pickle spear to the plate, he handed it to Rachel.

"Thank you, Marcus," she said pointedly.

Noah ignored her. He ignored them all.

Rachel shrugged and headed for the dining area. She turned briefly in the doorway. "Maybe Cal figured out who's been stealing."

Parvati's eyes went wide and she tangled her fingers in her lap.

"Nah." Noah shoved his hands in his pockets and slumped against the stainless steel sink. "If he'd figured it out, the cops would be here."

The office door opened and Cal stepped out. Marcus winced and set aside the spatula he'd been using to scrape the grill. The diner owner looked exhausted, which meant he didn't have good news.

Rachel rushed back into the kitchen, fumbled a smile and scurried over to stand beside Parvati. Noah stood straight.

Cal rubbed his hands together, as if he were washing them. "I promised you an update. Fact is, we're still coming up short at the end of the day."

A chorus of groans.

"I'm going to start switching out the drawer every two hours, see if we can establish a pattern. Some of you have made suggestions on how to combat this, and I appreciate your input, but at this point I have no intention of installing surveillance cameras or gluing tracking devices to every twenty-dollar bill."

Rachel backhanded Noah's biceps. "And just who did you think would pay for all those little locator chips?"

"Ow," he said, and rubbed his arm. "How'd you know that was my idea?"

Marcus cleared his throat. "Maybe now would be a good time to limit register access."

"Great," Rachel said. "How'm I supposed to take a break if I'm the only one on shift who can ring up tickets?"

"We'll work something out." Cal nodded at Parvati and Noah. "Thank you both for staying late. I'll email everyone the new procedures." He disappeared back into his office and shut the door gently.

The others stared at each other, the only sound the distant rattle of ice in a plastic tumbler as whoever had ordered that hamburger drank the last of a soda. With a sniffle, Rachel left the kitchen to offer her customer a refill.

Noah shook his head at Marcus. "You better hope the register comes up short at least one more time, or they'll be here to drag your ass to jail."

Someone knocked on the back door.

"Told you, numbnuts." Noah jabbed a finger at the door. "Hope you stole enough to cover bail."

"Pound sand," Marcus muttered. The distress on Parvati's face was harder to take than Noah's taunts. He gave her a wink as he crossed to the back door, some small, ridiculous part of him hoping Liz stood on the other side. Not that he would have a goddamned clue what to say to her if she was.

He pulled the door open and went rigid.

Silence dropped over the kitchen like a pan lid over a grease fire. Marcus stepped back, and Sheriff Tate stepped in.

She nodded a terse greeting. "Cal here?"

There wasn't enough spit in Marcus's mouth to swallow the dread coating his throat. Having a uniformed official around generally spelled bad fucking news.

He gestured toward the office. The sheriff knocked twice on the door, then let herself in. During the two seconds it took the door to close behind her, Marcus locked eyes with Cal, who was pushing up out of his chair.

Cal looked apprehensive, sure. But mostly, he looked old.

Marcus didn't realize he'd dropped his hand towel until he tripped over it on his way back to the stove. He snatched it up and tossed it into the dirty-laundry bin under the sink, then gripped the rounded stainless steel edge and stared down at the lukewarm water and the grayish suds floating on the surface. He reached in and pulled the plug.

"Holy shit," Noah whispered. He glanced around and caught Rachel's gaze as she came into the kitchen toting a plastic tub filled with dirty dishes. "This shit just got serious."

"Would you please stop saying that word?" Parvati shifted in her chair and plucked at her tight mahogany curls. "You sound like a gangster."

Noah waved the older woman off. "Seems they did figure out which one of us has sticky fingers. Or they're close, anyway."

"Or maybe they're just trying to scare us into confessing." With a clattering thump, Rachel set the tub down beside the sink. She turned to find everyone staring and frowned. "What? Doesn't anyone else around here watch cop shows?"

The office door opened and Cal stuck his head out. "Marcus. Could you come in here, please?" Cal's solemn gaze traveled to Noah. "Keep an eye on the grill." The door closed again.

The redheaded cook whistled, staring at Marcus as he pushed away from the sink. "It really was you."

"Be quiet, Noah." Grunting, Parvati got to her feet. "You don't know what you're talking about. We're probably all about to be questioned." She patted Marcus on his shoulder as he walked by. "We're rooting for you, baby doll."

Nausea writhed in Marcus's stomach as he stepped into Cal's space. The cloying scent of the microwave popcorn Cal had fixed earlier didn't help any. Marcus prayed he wouldn't hurl.

Cal and the sheriff stood on either side of the desk, the sheriff passing Cal's phone back to him as Marcus walked in. Dread turned to confusion when he saw that both Cal and the sheriff were smiling. Confusion turned to certainty that he'd somehow hurtled into an alternate reality when Sheriff Tate turned her smile his way.

"Dogs," she said.

"Excuse me?"

"Your boss was just showing me pictures of his Rhodesian Ridgeback. I'd consider getting one myself if I thought I could afford to feed it." In a flash, her expression morphed from friendly to detached. She pulled out a notebook and opened it. Took out a pair of reading glasses next and slid them onto her nose. "I'd tell you to sit, but this won't take long."

Marcus didn't know whether to be relieved or scared shitless.

Inwardly, he winced. Maybe he did need to watch his language, even inside his head.

"Someone reported a man and a woman trespassing on the golf course off Lake Cliff Drive. They provided a license plate, which matches the plate on your pickup. Were you parked at the southeast entrance of the Birchside golf course last Wednesday evening?"

"Yes, ma'am." His chest ached as he remembered the giddy, healing warmth of Liz's body pressed against his.

"Even if access to the course was public, it wouldn't be lawful after sunset." She peered at him over the top of her half-moon glasses. "Were you aware you were trespassing?"

"Yes, ma'am."

"Want to tell me what you were doing there?"

Funny how cops phrased things. With defensiveness and hostility, assuming a witness had something to hide and at the same time inviting a confidence, one potential friend to another. Couldn't they just ask outright, instead of making it seem as if confessing were the bad guy's idea?

Marcus looked up to find the sheriff watching him closely. Wariness had seeped into Cal's quiet regard. Marcus sighed.

"I lived in Thistle Hill when I was a kid. I spent a lot of time in the woods, walking around and stuff. One day I discovered that spot above the waterfall. I used to go there a lot, to think, and I wanted to show it to my girlfriend." The girlfriend he no longer had.

The sheriff shot him a wry glance. "I remember you used to live here, Mr. Watts. I doubt you've forgotten that four months ago, I arrested you for arson."

He wanted to say something smart-ass like *We all make mistakes*, but the misery behind her eyes stopped him. He recognized that kind of bone-deep, humbling, relentless pain. He respected it. He lived it.

She nodded once, as if they'd come to an understanding, then tucked her glasses and notepad away.

"You want to visit that spot again, Mr. Watts, you'll have to secure special permission from the golf course. If they do grant you a permit, you'll need to keep it on you at all times." She offered her hand. "I appreciate your time."

Marcus shook her hand, impressed by the solidness of her grip. "You're not going to write me a ticket or anything?"

"I'm satisfied that you didn't visit that spot with the intent to perform mischief, Mr. Watts. However, I will write you a ticket if you trespass again."

The hot, tight knot in his belly loosened. "Yes, ma'am."

As soon as she left, Cal came around his desk and perched on the edge, arms folded across his chest. "How do you want me to handle this?"

"What do you mean?"

Cal tipped his head toward the kitchen. "Everyone out there will assume I called in Sheriff Tate to handle our missing money issue. The fact that she didn't want to talk to anyone but you will convince them you're the culprit. You want me to make sure everyone knows that's not true?"

"The people who matter already know," Marcus said slowly.

"And if everyone thinks you suspect me, maybe the real thief will relax enough to make a mistake."

"That's a possibility. More likely they'll stop stealing, since the blame has conveniently fallen on someone else. Either way, it'll put a stop to the thieving. But I don't want you to feel manipulated, son."

Marcus shook his head. "If there's anything I can do to help, I want to do it. You don't deserve this."

Cal put a hand on his shoulder. When Marcus barely flinched, his boss gave him a slight smile. "Not many of us deserve what we get in this life. No one knows that better than you."

*   *   *

"COME IN," IVY CALLED out as a knock sounded on her office door. She braced herself, wondering if it was Seth on the other side. But when the door opened, it was Grace who stood there, just beyond the threshold. Instinctively, Ivy minimized the spreadsheet she'd been working on, though even if Grace could see the monitor from where she was standing, she probably wouldn't know what artificial insemination was, let alone care about the rising cost.

Ivy jumped to her feet, yanking on the hem of her sweatshirt as she rounded her desk. "Grace." She glanced over the girl's shoulder. Did Hazel realize Grace was wandering the house? "Is there something you need? Are you hungry?"

Grace shook her head, but Ivy was already on her way to the kitchen. "Did you give Hazel the slip?" she joked. She glanced back as she opened the fridge, and the guilt on Grace's face made it clear that was exactly what had happened.

"We were visiting the calves when I told her I had to go to the bathroom. And I did," she added quickly.

"That's fine. But we might as well get you a snack while you're in here." Ivy scanned the shelves for something kid friendly. "How about some yogurt? Or an apple?"

"No, thank you."

Damn, Seth's kids were polite. Ivy shut the refrigerator and turned. Grace was shifting from foot to foot, not looking at all as though she'd already gone to the bathroom. Then Ivy noticed she was sneaking peeks at the front door. She was waiting for Hazel to catch up to her, Ivy realized.

"Was there anything else you needed?"

Grace tugged at the seams of her jeans. "I wanted to ask you something."

Oh, God. "Ask away."

Grace dropped her head. Her hair swung forward and shielded her face as she mumbled a few words. Something caught in Ivy's chest, and she leaned closer.

"I'm sorry, Grace," she said gently. "I can't hear you."

Ivy reared back as Grace's head came up, big eyes blazing with resentment...and hope.

"I *said*, could you teach me how to ride a horse?"

Ivy took a moment to consider. "I could," she said, drawing out the words, "but we'd have to get your father's permission first."

Disappointment shadowed the little girl's face. "I wanted it to be a surprise. For Christmas," she added, and it was all Ivy could do not to smile. She had to give the kid credit for knowing how to lay it on thick.

If only Ivy didn't have to play the bad guy.

She moved to the sink, poured a glass of water and offered it to Grace. When the girl shook her head, Ivy chugged it. She set the glass back down and released a breath.

"That sounds like a nice gift," she said. "But I don't think your dad would appreciate our keeping something like that a secret."

Grace scowled and opened her mouth, and Ivy's phone rang. She practically launched herself at her purse.

"Excuse me, Grace." She grabbed her phone and headed for her office. When she reached the kitchen doorway, she spun around and waved at the fridge with her free hand. "You know you can help yourself, right?"

Five minutes later, Ivy was tracking Seth like a bird dog tracked quail. Not the most flattering comparison, but...whatever. The man had some nerve. He'd been helping out on the farm all week, and it hadn't taken long for Ivy and Dell to trust him with daily decisions like which of the Jersey girls needed special attention, how much hay and feed to order or whether the temperature on the holding tank for the milk needed adjusting.

This time he'd gone too far.

She found him in the tack room, cleaning one of the saddles. She'd thank him for it later, when she wasn't so mad. "Seth Walker. Who the hell do you think you are?"

7

IVY FUMED AS SHE waited for Seth's response. He'd been pushing the sponge in small circles, working the soap into the leather. Now his hand stilled, and he raised an eyebrow.

"Who do I think I am? You do realize you just said my name, right? So even if I don't know who I am, you clearly do."

"Oh, shut up, Walker." She waggled her cell phone. "I just got a call from Mrs. Quesenberry, one of the teachers at Thistle Hill Elementary. Imagine my surprise when she begged me to reconsider giving her kindergartners a tour. Thing is, I don't remember considering it the first time."

Seth rinsed the sponge in a nearby bucket and went back to scrubbing. "You can hardly keep up as it is." He dropped the sponge, picked up a wet rag and wiped the soap off the leather. "That's why I'm here, isn't it? To make your life easier?"

"Making decisions like that doesn't make my life easier."

"Ivy." He snapped up a clean rag and dried his hands. "She had a whole list of demands. I'm not going to apologize for caring enough about you to stop someone from taking advantage."

Her chest constricted, making it difficult to breathe. "If you cared about me, you wouldn't stop me from doing one of the few things I truly enjoy."

His gaze narrowed. Without warning he reached out and stroked a finger down her cheek. "How long have you been unhappy?" he asked quietly.

It shocked Ivy, discovering that not only did she have the strength to resist leaning into his touch, she had the strength to back away. "I'm not unhappy—I'm tired. Just...don't make any more decisions without consulting me, please."

"So when we talked about being partners after you lost two-thirds of your staff, you were just saying what you thought I wanted to hear?"

She jabbed a finger at him. "*I* never said partners. *You* said partners. Anyway, consulting is what partners are supposed to do."

"Partners are also supposed to trust each other."

She crossed her arms with such force they banged painfully against her ribs. "Well, I guess that leaves us out on both counts, then, doesn't it?" Which was a ridiculous thing to say, since she did trust him and they both knew it.

From behind them came the grating sound of a very deliberate throat-clearing. "Sorry to interrupt." They swung toward the doorway, where Dell stood fidgeting with the zipper on his jacket. "I'm getting ready to head out. The doc's on his way to take a look at Cabana Boy." He scratched his jaw. "Just thought you might want to know he'll be around, case one of you ends up drawing blood."

*   *   *

SETH HAD NO IDEA how Ivy did it. Eight o'clock on a Friday evening, and if he hadn't had two kids to feed and hustle in and out of the shower, he'd have been in bed an hour ago. After reading two chapters of the latest Molly Moon to Travis and singing "You Are My Sunshine" — twice — with Grace, he'd finally gotten them settled into bed. Then Travis had started singing the spaghetti song — make that pas-ghetti song — and Grace had joined in and they'd sung it twice, Grace in her bed, Travis in his and Seth standing in the hallway between them.

That was what he got for fixing spaghetti for dinner. He hadn't managed meatballs, though. He'd barely had the energy to brown the hamburger, let alone shape it into balls.

He grabbed a beer out of the fridge, threw himself on the couch and stabbed at the remote. This was his weekend to keep the kids, and as much as he looked forward to hanging with them, tonight he wished he'd just returned from dropping them off with their mother and had an entire weekend of riding the bed to look forward to.

Of course, *bed* and *riding* made him think of an entirely different activity he wouldn't mind indulging in all weekend. It had been too damned long. But Ivy was too stubborn to try things his way, and from the day he met her, he hadn't been able to picture any other face on his pillow.

He took a swig of beer and channel surfed until he found a black-and-white detective movie. He tossed the remote aside and settled in to watch, feeling pathetic for wishing he had someone special to kick back with. He'd had it for a while with Deb, until she was always in class and he was always on the job, and eventually they'd realized they each preferred doing their own thing.

He couldn't help thinking things would be different with Ivy. His wife had been sweet, but that sweetness had coated a self-centeredness that hadn't been a problem until the kids came along. Ivy was kind, but she wasn't sweet. Though he wouldn't mind taking a bite, just to make sure.

Considering the scolding she'd given him earlier, she probably wouldn't be up for that. She was right to be mad. He had been presumptuous. It rubbed him raw, though, to see the shadows under her eyes and the weary tilt to her shoulders.

Maybe a repeat of his apology was in order.

After another sip of beer and a jaw-cracking yawn, he put his sock feet up on the coffee table, wedged himself into a corner of the couch and squinted at the TV. Thought about what he'd say to Ivy in the morning while the television screen faded to gray.

"Daddy!"

Seth lurched up and off the couch, struggling to register where he was and what had wrenched him awake. He stood for an instant, swaying, and finally recognized that the hissing sound he was hearing was his jostled beer foaming up and out of the bottle. With a muttered curse, he set the bottle on the coffee table and hurried into Grace's room.

"Daddy!" she cried, the tears thick in her voice.

In the dim light provided by the circus-horse night-light they'd bought to replace the missing ballerina, he maneuvered around the piles he'd asked her to pick up a week ago and scooted into bed beside her. "I'm here, G, I'm here." He gathered her close and smoothed his hand up and down her back. She turned into him, her skinny arms wrapping around his neck as she sobbed.

After a long while she quieted, while he fought his own urge to weep. He had to make this better. First thing Monday morning, he'd arrange an appointment with her pediatrician. There had to be something someone could do for her. The poor kid needed her sleep.

"Want to tell me about your dream?" he asked softly. He was surprised she hadn't woken her brother, as well.

She shook her head. She pulled her arms from around his neck and wiped her face on his shirt. "Daddy?"

"Yes, G?"

"How can I make Miss Ivy like me?"

He winced. No sense in asking *why* she thought Ivy didn't like her. "Is it important that she like you?"

"I like being at the farm. Even though we have to do our homework."

"Do you like Miss Ivy?"

She shrugged.

He rested his cheek on her head and breathed in the smell of strawberry shampoo. "Maybe she senses you're cautious around her, and that's making her cautious around you." Though he was pretty sure it was the other way around.

"You mean if I'm friendly, she will be, too?"

"I think it would help."

She yawned and shifted on his lap. "What's it like to ride a horse?"

"I'll answer this question, and then it's time for you to go back to sleep. Deal?" She nodded, and he kissed her on the head. "You sit pretty high up off the ground, and you put your feet in the stirrups to help you sit straight. You use the reins to tell the horse which way to turn, and depending on how fast the horse is moving, it can be a smooth ride or a choppy one."

"Were you scared the first time you rode one?"

"Petrified. But I was maybe half your age, and the horse refused to stand still."

"What was his name?"

Seth smiled, recognizing a delay tactic when he heard one. "That was a long time ago, G. I don't remember."

"If I had a horse, I'd name him Rainbow."

"That's a pretty name."

"And it could work for a boy or a girl."

"Mmm-hmm."

"Daddy?"

"One last question, G, and that's it."

"What does Cabana Boy mean?"

Shit. He'd seen that one coming for days. "Uh, a cabana boy is kind of like a waiter, except on a beach."

"Like when we went to the peninsula?"

"The beach along Lake Erie is not the kind of beach I mean. I mean more like a beach in the Caribbean."

"Has Ivy been to the Caribbean?"

Seth had no trouble picturing Ivy lounging beneath a striped umbrella on some exotic beach, with a whole squadron of cabana boys at her feet. No way in hell would he visualize what she was — or was not — wearing, though, unless he wanted to guarantee himself another sleepless night.

Gently, he shifted Grace onto her bed and tucked her into her Barbie sheets. "I don't know where Ivy's been," he whispered, "but I do know where she is right now. In bed asleep, like you should be. Good night, G."

"Good night, Daddy."

*   *   *

MARCUS EYED PARVATI AS he finished scraping the griddle. The server had been flushed and preoccupied their entire shift, fumbling change at the cash register, dropping silverware and aiming glance after glance at the clock over the sink. Still, she refused to allow anyone to cover for her, which complicated things since Rachel had gone home sick. For some reason, Cal had agreed not to call anyone else in.

As they got closer to quitting time, Parvati got increasingly nervous. Even her tight curls seemed to quiver. He considered asking if she had a hot date — old Mr. Katz had tried more than once to bust a rusty move on her. But Marcus suspected Parvati's anxiety had nothing to do with romance.

All he wanted was the night to be over. Not that *he* had a hot date to look forward to. Liz still wasn't talking to him after that night at Audrey's. She didn't get why he wanted distance. If she ever did, she'd be sure to call him what he was.

A coward.

He reached for the grill brick that would scrape away every remnant of cooked food while Parvati finished washing dishes. Out front, the register buzzed its catchy end-of-day song as Cal closed out. A ripping sound, then Cal strode into the kitchen with the printout curled around his right hand and the day's stack of orders in his left. He shut himself in his office.

Marcus finished cleaning the griddle and turned to see Parvati trailing after Cal, her stride hesitant and heavy. *Shit.* He should do something. He should stop her. He should beat her to Cal's office.

Instead he watched her rap lightly on the door and open it without waiting for a response. She slumped down into the chair facing Cal's desk, not bothering to shut the door.

"I did it," she said, and Marcus closed his eyes. "I took the money."

Silence. Then a light *thwap*, as if Cal had dropped a pen onto his desk.

"Why?" he asked gently.

"You know how it is. Things are tight. I'm getting old. I don't make the tips I used to. Muscle rub isn't cheap, you know."

Marcus met Parvati's gaze. She gave her chin a little thrust in his direction, as if to say, *I got this,* leaned sideways and pushed at the door. Guilt surged. Marcus stared at the inches-wide opening to the office, then snatched the broom off the rack. He swept the broom across the floor, each stroke a whispered scolding.

Should have. *Should* have. *Should* have.

"You could have come to me." Cal's deep voice was muffled. "If you needed help, why didn't you ask?"

"I should have. I know that now. I'm sorry."

"I have to say, Parvati, I've never been more disappointed in you than I am at this moment."

Stifled sobs. Marcus flinched. His hands strangled the broom handle.

"What are we going to do about this?" Cal's tone suggested he was thinking out loud.

"I don't... I'm not... Excuse me, please." A clattering sound that must have been Parvati shoving up and out of her chair. Cal's door swung open and Parvati shuffled out, her head bent, the back of her hand pressed to her nose. Marcus swallowed.

Cal would fire her. How would she manage?

But Marcus already knew. She wouldn't. Even while pulling a paycheck, she'd been driven to steal.

While he...he couldn't be luckier. He had the entire second floor of a house to himself and a break on his rent every time he cooked for his landlady, who liked her steak rare and her vegetables in someone else's kitchen. He could survive just by eating all the greens she rejected.

He was young, and he wasn't afraid to work. At anything. He'd have a hell of a better chance finding a job than Parvati would.

Except for the whole ex-con thing.

He glanced around the kitchen and winced. He didn't *want* another job. And what about Liz? Sure as hell he'd never have a chance with her if he ended up out on his ass.

Don't you remember, dipshit? You ruined that sweet deal.

He exhaled. The thing with Liz was his fault. This wasn't. Parvati shouldn't have stolen from Cal.

Except...he didn't really believe she had.

The toilet flushed in the bathroom and flushed again, but the sound wasn't loud enough to mask Parvati's weeping. Shame soured his stomach.

He flung the broom into the corner and strode into the office. "Parvati's not the thief," he said. "I am."

Cal looked up from his laptop. Face grim, he nodded. "I wondered when you'd confess."

The shame morphed into frustration. Marcus knew his past would continue to fuck things up for him, but he hadn't expected Cal to give it a hand. "You did?"

Stiffly, Cal got to his feet. "Get Parvati in here."

Marcus had swept the entire floor and filled the mop bucket with soap and water before Parvati emerged from the bathroom, eyes rimmed with red. He followed her back to the office, where Cal leaned against the front edge of his desk, arms and ankles crossed. Flour was streaked across one shoulder of his black polo shirt, and a small puddle of batter had hardened on his collar. His office smelled like cinnamon, as it usually did.

Was this Marcus's last chance to notice?

Cal shook his head at them. "You're good people. Both of you. But a lie's a lie, and you should have more respect for yourselves."

Every muscle in Marcus's body went limp while Parvati looked from Cal to Marcus and back again, confusion plastered across her face.

Cal gestured at Marcus. "He confessed."

She sucked in a breath, then turned and gave Marcus a surprisingly strong smack.

"I know how you feel," Cal said drily.

"Ouch." Marcus clapped a hand to his arm.

"Neither one of you is stealing from me. I know that much." Cal ran both palms over his bristly hair. "So why tell me you did?"

Marcus rubbed his biceps. "Ladies first."

"Don't blame Parvati, Calvin, dear."

They all swung toward the doorway, where Marcus's landlady hovered, her lined face a study of maternal patience. She was a colorful sight in her knee-length purple sweater and puke-green purse. Every time Marcus caught a glimpse of that bag, he had the urge to whip up some guacamole.

"This was my idea," Audrey said. Her tone was contrite, but there was no missing the gleam of pride in her eyes.

Scowling, Cal pushed away from his desk. "I thought I locked the door."

"Not the back one, you didn't. The raccoons are in the Dumpster again, by the way." She started rummaging in her purse, pulling out handfuls of beef jerky sticks and summer sausages. "Do you have a tissue, dear? Parvati's leaking again."

Cal plucked a tissue from the box on his desk and thrust it at his server. "I could have fired you, you know. Don't you care that you'd be leaving this job with everyone thinking you're a thief?"

Parvati dabbed at her eyes with her left hand and fingered her yellow, star-shaped earring with her right. "It seemed a good idea when Audrey explained it to me."

Cal shook his head at Audrey. "You bullied her."

"Maybe a little."

He shifted his glower to Marcus. "What's your excuse?"

Marcus shrugged. "Hard to imagine Cal's Diner without Parvati."

Cal opened his mouth, closed it, and grabbed the back of his neck. He paced back and forth in front of his desk. "I don't like being lied to, and I don't like having my time wasted. You're each taking a week, and I don't mean with pay."

Marcus had never seen Cal so riled. Apparently, Parvati hadn't, either. The moment Cal herded them out of his office and slammed the door, Parvati scurried home. Audrey sighed heavily and wandered over to Marcus's freshly oiled grill.

"Don't suppose I could get a hamburger?"

"Sure." Marcus rolled the mop bucket into position. "Just not tonight."

She tried out a whimper. Ignoring her, Marcus dipped the mop into the water and lowered it into the wringer. "How'd you happen to come by tonight?"

"Parvati told me about Cal's meeting." She scampered out of the way as he slapped the wet mop onto the tiled floor. "She also told me about Sheriff Tate's visit. She was worried you'd end up taking the blame."

"So you asked her to take it instead."

"She was happy to do it."

"Yeah? After you promised her what?"

"The upstairs apartment."

He stilled. "The one I'm living in?"

"You won't be living in it for long, dear. I'm surprised you haven't already moved in with your squeeze."

His *squeeze*? "You know as well as I do that Liz and I broke up. If Parvati's moving in, I need to find somewhere else to live."

Please don't let that be the case. Where would he go? The motel wasn't an option anymore. Not that Joe had ever believed Marcus was the one who'd burned it down—it was his own girlfriend Joe had accused of *that*—but since Sleep at Joe's had officially opened for business, there were no pity rooms to spare.

Maybe Cal would let him bunk in the office.

"Move out? You'll do no such thing." Audrey patted his cheek with a meaty hand and he let himself relax. "Parvati likes the idea of having a man around the house. And that *is* a king-size bed you have all to yourself up there."

Marcus tried not to grimace. So much for relaxing. He didn't want to share a bed with his own grandma, let alone someone else's. Not that he even knew his own grandma.

Audrey patted his cheek again, this time more forcefully. One day she'd shove his jaw out of joint. "You know I'm joking, don't you, dear?"

"Yes, ma'am."

"Though if you're interested in sharing your bed with an older woman, you can't do any better than me."

Marcus chuckled weakly, ducked his head and busied himself mopping. If it wouldn't undo a righteous deed he'd practically had to cut his heart out to make happen, he'd have considered groveling to Liz so she'd let him move in with her.

Maybe he should talk to Noble. See if he could hang with him at his place. So what if the big man wouldn't lay off Marcus about getting his GED and ate gallons of chili despite his stomach issues? Marcus could deal.

Marcus and Audrey both jumped when Cal yanked open his office door, a pen in one hand and a bottle of aspirin in the other. He scowled at Marcus. "Next week I'll cover your shift myself." He jabbed the pen at Audrey. "You get to cover Parvati's."

He disappeared again. Marcus and Audrey stared at each other, and Marcus shook his head at the delight spreading across the old lady's face. At least someone was pleased with how things had gone down.

On the plus side, his landlady couldn't be holding canasta parties if she was here waiting tables.

He rinsed the mop, emptied the bucket and turned, about to ask Audrey if she needed a ride home. The words stuck in his throat when he saw she'd tied on the black apron Parvati had left behind and was pantomiming taking a customer's order. She even scooted out of reach and shook a finger when the imaginary diner pinched her. Marcus shook his head, jammed the mop into the bucket and wheeled it into the closet. Things were definitely getting weird in Tweedy land.

*   *   *

IVY SHIVERED IN THE early-morning cold, her breath fogging the air as she worked the Bobcat. She was tipping the last ingredient of the cows' feed into the Dumpster-sized TMR, or total mix ration auger mixer, when Seth appeared in the glow of the barn's floodlights. She jumped when she saw him.

"We need to talk," he said, loud enough to be heard over the grinding rumble of the mixer and the chug of the Bobcat's engine.

Ivy didn't care for the angle of his jaw. When she didn't immediately respond, he strode around to the front of the mixer and hit the kill switch. The unit trembled to a stop. He came back around again and waited for her to power off the Bobcat.

When she had, silence settled over them, made spooky by the thick dark that pressed in from behind the floodlights. It didn't take long for the cows to start lowing, their deep-pitched complaints echoing around them. The girls wanted their breakfast.

"We need to talk," Seth repeated firmly. "About Grace."

Crap. Grace must have told him she'd asked about riding lessons. Was he angry because Ivy hadn't mentioned his daughter's request, or because she hadn't turned the little girl down flat? Guilt niggled. She never had finished that conversation with Grace.

She slid to the ground, releasing the breath she'd been holding when her legs actually supported her weight. "One of these days when you stride up to me all sweaty and determined, the verb you'll be using won't be *talk*."

He stared, making her thankful for the shadows that hid her flush.

"It's a defense mechanism," he said slowly. "You don't like where a conversation's going, you bring sex into it and suddenly no one remembers what they were saying."

"Having sex is a better distraction than talking about it." She crossed her arms, the thickness of her plaid jacket unfortunately making the gesture appear more awkward than offhand. Meanwhile, his comment had her vacillating between pride and annoyance. "Good morning, by the way."

"Good morning. You and Grace. I want to know what the deal is."

"Why?" She licked her lips. "What did she tell you?"

"She wanted to know how to get you to like her."

Her arms fell stick straight. "She what?"

"Ivy. I want to know why you can hardly stand to be around my daughter."

The back of her throat pulled tight. "That's an exaggeration."

"I don't think it is."

Ivy thought of the phone call she'd been so happy to receive while she and Grace had been talking in the kitchen. She cringed. "She can tell?"

"That fence post over there can tell."

"Seth." A moment ago, she'd been headed for the mug of coffee resting on said fence post. Now the sharp roasted scent turned her stomach. "I'm sorry. I wouldn't hurt her for the world."

"I know." He rubbed both hands over his face, then moved his palms up to adjust his knit cap. "I don't think she's so much hurt as confused. She's used to women wanting to dress her up and do her hair and stuff." When Ivy started to speak, he held up a hand. "I don't want you to pretend something you don't feel, but I would like to know why you don't want to be around her."

"You think I'm taking my frustrations out on her."

"You're deflecting again. I want to know what's going on between you and my daughter."

"You sound like a father vetting a potential suitor."

"You sound like a woman desperate to change the subject."

Ivy looked down and toyed with her gloves, pulling them even tighter over her fingers. If she didn't explain, he'd forever consider her a ridiculous bully, holding something nebulous against his daughter just because she could. If she did explain, there was a slim possibility he could understand her hesitation around Grace, but there was an even greater possibility that he would consider her flighty and irresponsible. Cruel, even.

She lifted her head and saw his gaze locked on her hands. She was still fiddling with her gloves. Sucking in air that was so cold it seared her throat, she shoved her hands behind her back.

"My behavior doesn't have anything to do with Grace. I apologize if I made either of you feel uncomfortable. I'll..." She faltered.

"You'll what? Be more careful? Pretend? Suddenly get over whatever's bothering you? Your reasons have plenty to do with Grace. With me, too. I know you're unhappy, Ivy. Tell me why. Maybe I can help."

"It's personal."

"You've been trying to get us into bed for months." He spoke through clenched teeth. "That's not personal?"

"It doesn't have to be, no."

"Stupid question," he muttered. "Okay, how about this?" Before she could step out of reach, he snagged her left hand and pressed it between his. "Will you please tell me what's bothering you?"

"If I do, you'll look at me differently."

His lips quirked. "I have to say, it's nice that you care." When she didn't respond, he huffed out a breath and paced away. After a few moments of staring into nothingness, he returned, boots crunching over the frost-tipped ground. "I'm not trying to guilt you into telling me what's weighing on you, but I wish you would."

"You have to promise—" She swallowed the huskiness out of her voice. "You have to promise not to think I'm trying to play on your sympathy."

He cocked his head and gave her a nod.

The trembling in Ivy's belly quickened. She forced her legs to carry her to the fence, where she retrieved her mug. She poured the coffee out onto the ground, then looked over her shoulder at Seth.

"Can we do this inside? I could use something hot to drink."

Not coffee, though. Ivy had a strong feeling that even one sip would liberate the banana she'd eaten on her way out of the house that morning. Instead, once they'd entered the kitchen, she set a clean mug of water in the microwave to heat for tea and offered what was left in the coffeepot to Seth.

With a polite murmur, he accepted the steaming mug she handed him, his eyes never leaving her face.

"Why don't you sit?" he suggested quietly. "I'll bring your tea."

She accepted gratefully. She collapsed into a chair at the table, watching as he unwrapped a tea bag and placed it in her cup when the microwave beeped.

His boots thumped across the floor as he carried both mugs to the table. She wrapped her hands around hers and breathed in the gingery scent with relief.

Seth glanced out the window. Slowly, the predawn blackness was giving way to purples and grays. "Should I check in with Dell?" he asked.

She shook her head. "He can spare us for a few minutes. One of the perks of being the boss. Besides, I got an early start this morning."

"You get an early start every morning." He sipped his coffee and closed his eyes in brief appreciation. "When was the last time you slept in?"

She blew on her tea and considered. "Uh...1989?"

He set down his coffee. "Talk to me, Ivy."

The surface of her tea rippled. Her fingers were shaking. She clasped her hands in her lap and drew in a breath. "I know what you're thinking. You're expecting me to say I was abused. Or maybe you suspect I can't have children or that I have no interest in raising someone else's child. None of those is true."

She tipped her head and pulled in a quick contemplative breath. "Have you ever made a decision you believed with all your heart was right, or made yourself believe was right, because you needed to so badly? And that belief, along with the relentless insistence of everyone around you that there was no other option, helped you get through the day? Then came the time to act on that decision you'd made, and you did that thing you'd been so sure for so long was right. Only, with the very next breath you took, you knew you couldn't have been more wrong?"

Her fingers started to go numb. Because she was gripping them too tightly, or because they were cold? She dragged her hands back up to the table and wrapped them around her mug again. Then Seth's fingers were there, too, prying her hands free, enfolding them in his.

"Ivy. Hey. We've all made bad decisions."

"This isn't about a bad decision. This is about cowardice." She raised her head. "I had a baby and I gave her away. I gave away my baby girl."

8

A S MUCH AS IVY longed to, she didn't hide from Seth's gaze. He didn't hide from hers, either. She stared into his chocolate eyes and saw shock, yes, but also warmth and encouragement. Pity, too, but not so much she couldn't handle it.

She let out a long sigh and sat back. "I was eighteen. Preparing to start a four-year scholarship to college when I learned I was pregnant. The father was an ex-boyfriend who wanted nothing to do with the baby after I told him. My parents convinced me that I was too young to be a mother and that it would be in the baby's best interests to place her with a loving family desperate for a child. They didn't have to work that hard to coax me toward that decision. At the time, I couldn't imagine the horror of being tied to a baby when I wasn't done being a teenager. But the day my daughter was born..."

She was already battling tears when Seth untangled his fingers from hers. No way she could blame him for needing distance. He stood, but instead of moving away, he moved closer. A shimmering gratitude eased the ache behind her breastbone as he crouched at her side. He applied a gentle pressure to her legs, coaxing her to shift sideways in the chair so she'd be facing him.

He rested his hands on her knees. "Tell me about the day your daughter was born," he said gruffly.

He'd removed his knit cap when they'd entered the house, and his hair remained mussed. His palms on her knees provided a connection she sorely needed, but it wasn't enough. Then again, as much as she yearned to slide her fingers through his hair, the gesture would assume an intimacy that didn't exist. That couldn't exist.

She tucked her hands into the pockets of the jacket she still wore.

"She was born in the morning." Ivy raised her head and craned her neck to look out the kitchen window into the orange-hued dawn. "An October morning, like this one." Envisioning her daughter's tiny round wrinkled face made Ivy's mouth wobble. "I almost changed my mind," she whispered.

"But you didn't."

She jerked her head left, then right. "I went through with it. I said goodbye and let her go. I've regretted it ever since."

"I'm sorry." He stood, and lifted his coffee cup. He stared into it a moment and put it back down without drinking. "Grace reminds you of what you gave up," he said.

"Not gave up, like a bad habit. Gave *away*."

He rubbed the back of his neck, the rasp of denim as he lifted his arm loud in the cozy space. "You don't think you deserve another child."

"I wasn't very responsible with the first one. Anyway, it's more than that. To bring another child into my life..." She shook her head. "It wouldn't be fair, would it? Not to her. Not to the baby I gave away."

"Shit."

She choked out a laugh. "That's exactly how I've always felt about it."

He squatted again at her feet. "I'm not expressing disappointment—I'm judging your comment. It's bullshit. When are you going to stop punishing yourself? You made the best decision you could at the time. I get that you regret it, and I'm sorry you're still hurting. But, Ivy, we all have regrets."

"Condescending, much?"

"Deflective, much?"

Ivy sighed. "If you're trying to undo twelve years of conditioning, your technique needs a little work."

"Twelve? Is that how old your daughter is?"

"Eleven," she croaked. Despite her best efforts, her throat closed and her face crumpled.

Seth rose again, this time lifting her with him. He held her loosely until she settled in, forehead to his shoulder. Slowly, he skimmed his

145

palms up and down her back.

"Do you know where your daughter is?"

Ivy shook her head.

"Do you want to?"

She shuddered. "Could we...not do this? Or better yet, how about you take a turn at confession?"

His hands stilled. Then he pressed his lips to her forehead. "How about I fix you more tea?"

Reluctantly, she pushed away from his warmth, resisting the urge to press her palm against the spot where he'd kissed her. "How about you tell me why you and your wife got a divorce?"

His arms dropped to his sides. "I didn't realize sharing your secret came with a price tag."

"I didn't realize you'd consider this one-sided conversation sharing."

He let loose a frustrated growl. "Is this about what's fair or what you regret saying?"

"Maybe both," she whispered. "And maybe it's about wanting to know you better." When he tucked his hands into his armpits and looked at the floor, she nudged his boot with hers.

He lifted his chin and snagged her gaze. "We started wanting different things," he said. His chest rose and fell with a bottomless breath. The intensity in his eyes and the strain on his face made something squeeze deep in her chest, but since his body language said, *Hands off*, she resisted the urge to touch him.

"I'm a homebody," he continued, "and Deb wanted to get out more. She also wanted to switch careers, and I gave her a hard time about the hit our budget would take. The kids kept us together way past our expiration date. Still, I can't help wondering if I tried hard enough."

"Why doesn't she have custody?"

"Grace wasn't kidding when she said her mom likes school. Deb collects degrees and doesn't have time for much of anything else. In the end, we agreed the kids would have more stability with me."

He said it matter-of-factly, but Ivy could hear the undertones of disillusionment. She toyed with the zipper on her jacket. "She visits, though, right?"

"She lives near State College. Every other Friday we meet in Youngstown. She keeps the kids until I drive down again on Sunday."

"I've always understood why you're not into casual relationships," she said. "I don't like it, but I get it. Your kids come first. You should be proud of that."

His hands found his hips, and his fingers dug into denim. "They've been through enough upheaval. Grace is still having nightmares. I'll be talking with her pediatrician later today. Things keep disappearing around the house, and at first I thought the kids were playing some game. Now I'm wondering if one of them has developed sticky fingers. This morning I couldn't find the toothpaste, of all things."

"Sure that wasn't intentional?"

"Well, if it was, they know better now. Amazing what you can do with a little baking soda."

"Good to know." When an extended silence settled over the kitchen, broken only by Ivy's zipper as she jerked it up and down, she let her hands fall to her sides and gave an awkward shrug. "We should get back to work."

"We should," Seth agreed, his tone neutral.

"I'll adjust my attitude as far as Grace is concerned."

He leaned to the side and picked up his coffee, staring down at what had to be the now tepid liquid within. "A little awareness will go a long way." He drank several swallows and carried his mug to the sink.

Ivy considered. "And maybe look for an opportunity for some one-on-one time? With Grace, I mean?"

He took his time rinsing his cup. When he turned to face her, he had both eyebrows raised. "Immersion therapy?" he asked drily.

"Maybe. And maybe something a little less selfish, too."

"Take it easy with that. The more she likes you, the more she'll want to spend time with you."

"You want me to be friendly yet distant." She twisted her cup in slow circles on the tabletop. "That's what I've been going for."

"Try to remember she's a kid, not a business associate."

Ivy lifted her head. "You want me to treat her like a kid. Just not like your kid."

"We both know it's better that way."

Better, yes, and also seriously sad, that after everything she'd just told him, and after all these years of nurturing her disappointment in herself so she wouldn't be tempted by an opportunity to let another child down, she wished she could have a do-over with his daughter.

*   *   *

THE REST OF THE day passed in a blur for Ivy. She vacillated between feeling unburdened and embarrassed. Seth made no indication that she'd confided in him her deepest regret or that he'd been repulsed by it. He simply nodded whenever they saw each other and went about his business. That business didn't keep him long at the farm, since it was Saturday. After helping with the feeding and milking, Seth left to open his store. He came back late in the afternoon for the second round of milking, then left again. She'd told him not to come back until Monday. For once he hadn't argued, and she couldn't help a sense of abandonment.

Ridiculous, of course, but these days she found herself struggling to remember why she'd ever considered it paramount that she cope with everything on her own. Surely if her parents were around they wouldn't be able to deny she took the best care of the farm she possibly could, and she'd already vowed not to risk letting another Evan into her life. Plus, she felt guilty as hell for not being able to follow Seth to his store so she could give *him* a hand for once.

By the time Monday afternoon rolled around, Ivy had worked herself into a nervous panic over how to approach the situation with Grace. Interactions with Seth were friendly but wooden, and every time they spoke, she mourned the loss of their rapport. Maybe if she struck just the right note with Grace, Seth might unbend a little.

Besides, even if thinking Ivy didn't like her wasn't bothering Grace, it bothered Ivy. The shame of it had haunted her all weekend.

Late in the afternoon, Ivy finished feeding the calves and decided to do some work in her office. Dell was delivering more sand to the barn for the cows' bedding and Seth was on his way to start the second milking.

Inside the mudroom, she worked her feet out of her boots and headed for the kitchen. Grace and Travis were hunched over the dining room table, each with a pencil in one hand and a half-eaten pretzel stick in the other. The kids had asked for cookies and Hazel had said she was all for it as long as they did the baking.

Hence the pretzels.

Meanwhile, Hazel was standing in front of the open dishwasher, frowning at the dirty dishes in the sink, as if willing them to load themselves.

Ivy greeted them all brightly. Still, Hazel must have recognized the trepidation on her face, or — more likely — she was eager for a reason to end her standoff with the dishwasher, because she turned toward the dining room and clapped her hands.

"Okay, you two. Miss Ivy has some work to do, so let's give her a little peace and quiet. How about we walk down to the creek? See who's first to get their feet wet?"

Ivy chewed on the inside of her cheek. She should protest. She should offer to play a quick game or ask about their day at school, something, anything to avoid bolstering Grace's belief that Ivy didn't like her. If Grace believed it, her brother probably wouldn't be far behind.

And chances were, if they went down to the creek with Hazel, they'd end up with pneumonia.

But Travis was already shoving his arms into his jacket. "Can I have a jar? I might catch a frog."

Hazel cocked her head. "It's a little late in the year for that, honey." She frowned at Ivy. "What do frogs do during the cold season? Do they hibernate?"

"I think so. Underwater."

"Cool," Travis said. "Then I'll need a bucket, too. Or maybe a colander so I can scoop 'em out of the water."

Ivy put her hands on her hips. "You know what a colander is?"

"Yeah. We eat a lot of spaghetti." He pronounced it *pas-ghetti*.

Ivy laughed. "I'm afraid you're not doing any frog hunting today, kid. No going in the water at all. It's too cold."

Travis scowled.

"We'll think of something else to do," Hazel promised. "Ever played blindman's bluff?"

Ivy waved a frantic hand. "Not a good idea. Even if they don't fall in the water, they'll be sure to mess up their shoes."

"Cow pies. Right." Hazel pursed her scarlet lips, and gave Ivy a wink. "It's a lot less complicated when you play it in a bedroom." She shrugged. "I do have some calls to make, so maybe we can play graveyard instead."

Ivy didn't hold much hope that Hazel was kidding. Meanwhile, Grace stood motionless by her chair and refused to accept her jacket when Hazel held it out. "Can I stay here?" she asked.

Hazel shook her head and opened her mouth to reinforce that with a no.

Ivy sucked in a breath. This was her chance.

"Sure, you can stay," she said. "We can hang out until your dad gets here." She sent Hazel a *Wish me luck* glance and almost winced when the return look was about as encouraging as an air-raid siren. Hazel tossed Grace's jacket on the couch and hustled Travis out the door.

As soon as the door shut behind them, Ivy's cell phone rang. *Seth.* "It's your dad," she said to Grace. She snatched up the phone, giving herself a mental pinch for the breathlessness in her voice.

"Something came up and I'm running late," he said, the way a husband might say to a wife.

Stop that.

"Everything okay?" Ivy asked, the way a wife might say back to her husband.

I'm warning you, Millbrook.

"Two words. Mr. Katz."

Facing away from Grace, Ivy rested a hip against the counter. "Looking for more free samples for Mona?"

"His horse, this time."

"And I'm sure you sent him packing."

"Thanks," he said drily. "Between you and Bradley, I've officially reached my sarcasm quota for the day. Now I can move on to irony."

"You're a good man, Seth Walker."

After a few beats of silence, he said, "I called because I didn't want you to think I was sulking."

"You're not the type."

"I'm a man. I'm the type."

She hunched a shoulder, suddenly aware of Grace behind her. "But we reached an agreement."

"A cease-fire, you mean." In the background, a door slammed and an engine started up. Seth's pickup, Ivy assumed. "I'll be there in a few," he said.

Ending the call, Ivy turned back to Grace, who stood on the other side of the island, scowling, fingers pressed into the granite as if she were straining to ram the whole unit right at Ivy.

Hoo, boy. Ivy's smile went stiff. She'd have to chew over that conversation with Seth later.

"Sorry about that," she said.

Grace continued to stare.

Ivy folded her arms across her chest, then instantly unfolded them again. What she might find comforting, Grace would probably find unfriendly.

Now what?

You invited the kid to stay, Millbrook. Find something to do with her.

She spun toward the fridge and yanked the door wide. "Can I get you something to drink? Or something to snack on?"

"No, thank you."

When Ivy turned back around, Grace was eyeing her phone, as if considering flattening that instead of Ivy.

Crap. This was about Seth. Grace had sensed something from Ivy's side of the conversation. Something that obviously didn't sit well with the nine-year-old.

Time for a distraction.

"What would you like to do?" Ivy asked. "We could take some apples out to the horses or visit the calves or stay inside and play cards."

Or pin the tail on the dairy farmer. Ivy didn't say the last out loud, because the expression on Grace's face made it clear that would be the one to get her vote.

Grace pushed away from the counter. "I want to learn how to make ginger cookies."

The words hit Ivy like a fifty-pound sack of flour. Baking was what she'd always imagined doing with her own daughter. The whammy turned into a double when Grace continued, "That way I can make them for Daddy and he won't have to bother you. 'Cause you're always busy and stuff."

Message received, loud and clear. Now Ivy *really* didn't know what to do, because her weekend soul-searching had led her to decide she'd grant Grace's request for horseback riding lessons after all. Seth hadn't said no when she'd mentioned one-on-one time with his daughter, and as far as being in danger of bonding with Grace? She regarded the heart-shaped, mutinous face of Seth's older child.

That ship had sailed, baby.

Ivy leaned forward and braced her elbows on the island. "You know this is only temporary, right? Your dad helping me out? As soon as I find someone to manage the farm for me, I won't need your daddy's help anymore and things will go back to the way they were."

"That could take a long time."

"You're right. It could. But your dad doesn't have to stay."

Grace's thin body relaxed. "Does he know that?"

"He does." Ivy pushed upright. "But just to make sure, I'll tell him again."

"When he gets here?"

"The moment he gets here." Though Grace knew her father well enough to realize he would never leave if Ivy still needed his help. She probably hoped he'd take the words to heart if they came from Ivy.

Good luck with that, kid.

"Now about those cookies." Ivy moved to the sink and washed and dried her hands. "I'm happy to show you how to make them." She hid a smile when Grace eagerly stepped up and washed her hands, too. "But there's something I want to talk about first. What would you say if I told you I changed my mind about teaching you to ride?"

Grace turned and stared up at Ivy, eyes narrowed, hands dripping water onto the floor. "Why?" she asked.

Ivy hated that suspicion had overpowered Grace's longing. She hated even more that she'd likely only confuse the kid if she tried to fix it. Or worse, make Grace think Ivy was offering her a bribe.

Then again, wasn't that exactly what she was doing?

She bit the inside of her cheek and passed Grace a hand towel. "For one thing," she said, "I'm sorry if I gave you the impression I don't like you. I'm not good with kids."

"You give tours all the time. And you get along great with Travis."

"You got me there. Okay, here's the truth." Part of it, anyway. "If I had a daughter, I'd want her to be just like you. And sometimes being around you makes me sad that I don't have a daughter." Ivy's smile wobbled. "It's not your fault, and it's silly of me to act that way. So I'll stop. The other reason I changed my mind is that there's nothing I like better than teaching someone to ride."

Grace cocked her head and remained silent, the towel hanging unused at her side. This kid was a hard sell.

Ivy held up both hands in a *Trust me* gesture. "You don't have to like me. You do, however, need to like horses."

The front door opened and closed. Grace dropped the towel, wiped her hands on her corduroys and hurried out to the living room. Ivy followed more slowly.

Seth had brought in with him the fresh, earthy scent of a brisk autumn day. His thick brown hair was wind-rumpled, his handsome face ruddy with cold. Ivy had to wage a serious battle against the urge to walk up, unsnap his battered denim jacket and cuddle in close.

She didn't have the right. Even if she did, no way she'd do that to Grace.

Seth looked from his daughter to Ivy and back again, his expression a big fat question mark.

"Daddy!" Grace hugged his waist, then grabbed his hand and turned to press back against him, a challenge in her big brown eyes as she faced Ivy. "Ivy wants to tell you something."

Grace had dropped the *Miss*. Ivy really had ticked her off. She locked gazes with Seth, the shadows in his an echo of his daughter's suspicion.

"That's right," Ivy said lightly. "I'd like to make sure you understand you can cancel our arrangement at any time. If it takes too much longer to hire a manager, I'll work something else out. Please don't feel you have to stay."

Seth's smile faded. Grace had twisted around to peer up at him, but he didn't look away from Ivy. He nodded once, gravely. "I understand. Thank you for telling me."

Grace tugged on his hand. "So can we go now?"

Seth crouched in front of his daughter. "G. Listen to me. I'm helping out Miss Ivy because she's my friend. If you're trying to make her feel guilty for needing my help, that's not very nice. It's not fair, either, to Miss Ivy or to me. This is temporary, and I didn't volunteer you or your brother for anything other than staying here at the farm until I'm done with my work. If you're unhappy with the arrangement, I'm the one you should talk to. Understand?"

If Grace bent her head any farther, she'd be able to touch her nose to her knees. Finally, she gave a small reluctant nod, and Seth rose. "Where's Travis?"

"Out by the creek with Miss Hazel."

He spotted Grace's coat on the back of the couch and handed it to her. "Why don't you run outside and find them? I need a minute with Miss Ivy before I get started on the milking."

Ivy's stomach tilted, and she buried her hands in her pockets before she could start biting on her fingernails.

"I'm going to learn to ride a horse." Grace pointed at Ivy. "She said I could."

Hell. Ivy smiled weakly at Seth. But his unhappy expression was directed at Grace.

"You know better than to tattle," he said quietly. "You think there's something I need to know, you talk to me like a big girl. You don't throw it out there just to get someone else in trouble. Go on, now. We'll talk about this later."

"Yes, sir," she mumbled. She dashed to the door and wrenched it open. When she turned to shut it, her face was scrunched up tighter than a spitball. Ivy tensed, waiting for the slam. But the door closed gently.

Seth hitched a shoulder. "The rule in our house is, slam a door and spend fifteen minutes apologizing to it. The last thing Grace wants is to have a conversation with the inside of your front door, especially with you watching."

Ivy sighed. Tired of her impersonation of a statue, she walked over to the seating area, where she perched on the arm of the love seat that sat catty-corner to the sofa Seth stood behind. He turned as she moved, tracking her with his body.

"How are you?" he asked.

"What?"

"It's a simple question."

Ivy frowned. "You're not going to lecture me?"

"In a minute." He leaned over the back of the couch, palms spread wide on the nubby, dark sage upholstery. "Right now I want to know if you're okay."

"Because you suspect Grace may have duct-taped me to a kitchen chair and threatened me with a pastry cutter if I didn't agree to teach her to ride?"

His lips didn't even twitch. "Because telling me about your daughter this morning couldn't have been easy."

9

O KAY, THEN. IVY DUG her fingertips into the fabric on either side of her thighs. "If I say that on the inside I'm a weeping, wailing mess, does that mean you won't yell?"

"Ivy."

"I'm fine, Seth. Thank you for asking."

"You're welcome." His brows gathered, and he pushed upright. "Now, what the hell were you thinking, offering to put my kid on a horse without checking with me?"

"I thought you trusted me with your children."

"Oh, no." Seth gave his head a sideways shake as he rounded the end of the couch. "You don't get to make me the bad guy here. Yesterday you reamed me out for making a decision without consulting you, a decision that didn't involve pitting a hundred pounds of kid against a thousand pounds of horse." He paused. "Or is that what this is about?"

"Wow," Ivy said flatly. "Not only do you think I'm capable of holding a grudge, you think I'd use your kids to get payback." She pressed a hand to her chest. "It warms my heart that you know me so well."

He flushed. "I guess you do get to make me the bad guy." He sank down onto the arm of the sofa and braced his hands on his knees. "I'm sorry."

"You should be." Their knees brushed, and she resisted the urge to scuttle backward to the opposite end of the love seat. "Grace would never be in any danger, Seth. I'm a certified riding instructor, and you know very well that with the occasional exception of Cabana Boy, my horses are all gentle and well behaved. Besides. She said she wanted to surprise you for Christmas."

"She tried that last April, when I found her hiding a kitten in her room." He rubbed his chin with his thumb and forefinger, as if tracing the line of a beard. "Were you trying to get her to like you?"

"Ironic, isn't it?"

He grunted. "I did say this morning that irony was next on my list."

"I thought that granting her request might help make up for the way I've treated her. The guilt got to me, I guess."

"Which guilt are we talking here? Grace guilt or daughter guilt?"

Ivy jerked to her feet. "Low blow, Walker."

He stood, as well, and watched her steadily. "You asked about therapy for Grace once. Did you ever think about joining a support group yourself?"

"It's not something I can see myself doing."

"Because you know they'll tell you it's way past time to move on."

She wrapped her arms around her waist, her urge to cuddle replaced with the urge to pummel. "You don't understand. I know I made the right decision. The fact that I could give my baby away? That *that's* the kind of person I am? It tells me that wherever she is, she deserves to be there."

"Yet you were willing to piss me off so a little girl wouldn't feel unloved."

"Maybe I've learned something over the years."

"My point exactly."

"You need to butt out," she seethed.

"And you need to kick your own ass."

"Excuse me?"

His brows gathered. "Look. I know you've been hurt. Your parents hurt you, giving up your daughter hurt you, and that asshole ex of yours, Ethan—"

"Evan."

"Whatever. He hurt you. But you're using your daughter as an excuse. You're not so much worried about letting a child down as you are about getting your heart broken again."

Ivy jolted away from him. She turned and stalked toward her

office, swinging back to face him when she'd reached the doorway. "I confided in you this morning to explain my difficulties with Grace, not to open myself up to misguided speculation."

"I'm just trying to help, Ivy."

"Stop trying to save me from myself. I need your help out there." She pointed toward the porch. "Not in here."

"Understood." Slowly, he backed away, tipped the hat he wasn't wearing, and let himself out.

When he shut the front door, he did it ever so gently.

* * *

SETH DROPPED INTO THE booth and grimaced across the table at Gil.

"Whose idea was it to go trail riding today, anyway?" He clasped his hands together and blew on them, then tucked them under his armpits. "You couldn't have picked a warmer day? Like, say, in July? And who's covering for you at the hardware store? I want a name. I'll make damned sure they don't do it again."

"Don't be such a baby," his poker buddy said placidly. Gil picked up his menu, knocking over the pepper shaker and sending the napkin holder into a clattering wobble.

With a shake of his head, Seth shifted all of the condiments to his side of the table and glanced around for Parvati or Rachel, who usually pulled the Sunday shift at Cal's Diner. He seriously needed a cup of coffee. Hell, at this point he'd settle for a cup of hot water.

No one stood behind the marbled gray Formica countertop, probably because only two of the stools were occupied. Every booth besides the one Seth and Gil sat in remained empty, but three of the half dozen aluminum-rimmed square tables had been pushed together to accommodate what looked like a family out for an early dinner.

Three kids giggled while an older lady who could be their grandmother cleaned her glasses with pursed lips, and the couple Seth assumed to be the kids' parents shared a resigned yet contented look.

Seth yanked his gaze away. He missed his kids. It happened every time. The weekend he had them, he'd wish for peace and quiet. The weekend they were with Deb, he couldn't get them back fast enough.

He leaned toward Gil, muscles tensed as he fought the urge to shiver. "We break out our bikes again anytime soon and I don't care how dorky I look, I'm wearing my tights under my cargos. It got frickin' cold out there." Along with his shorts, he wore a long-sleeved wool jersey under a lightweight fleece pullover. Any other day he'd peel off the fleece, but after biking in the sun-starved woods in forty-degree weather, he wasn't ready to part with it yet.

He might never part with it again.

Meanwhile, his biking buddy sat there shudder-free, looking as if flying down the side of a mountain when the windchill factor was thirty-three was something he wouldn't mind doing again.

Seth scowled. "Aren't you cold?"

Gil shook his head without looking up from his menu. "I'm a man's man."

"Bullshit. You're wearing battery-heated boxers, aren't you?"

A black-aproned server appeared beside their table, coffeepot in hand. "Sounds like you boys need some coffee."

Oh, yeah. Seth jerked his right hand free of his left pit and fumbled the white ceramic cup into the fill-'er-up position. It wasn't until the steamy roasted goodness sloshed over the brim and onto the saucer that it registered — the server's voice hadn't belonged to either Parvati or Rachel. Seth wrapped both hands around the cup, took a gratified sip and sat back.

He blinked. "Audrey Tweedy."

That brought Gil's head up. Together they stared at the seventy-something retired high school history teacher, who was shifting from one neon purple sneaker to the other as she hovered beside their table. Usually she kept her gray hair out of her eyes by using a clip on one side — kind of like the psychotic nurse Kathy Bates had played in *Misery*.

No need for that clip anymore. She'd cut her hair. Now it was short and wild, and they could see her earrings. Silver chickens. No, wait — that was a chicken in one ear and a pig in the other.

Gil kicked him under the table and Seth got a load of Audrey's glower. He'd been staring too long.

"You look great," he blurted.

She flushed. "Thank you, dear."

Seth put his cup back on the table and his hands back in his pits. "What are you doing here?"

"Bringing you back from the brink of hypothermia, seems like." She motioned with the coffeepot and he nodded. "Where've you two been? Siberia?"

"He's the one who's cold." With a smirk aimed at Seth, Gil shrugged out of his jacket. He jarred his coffee cup in the process and it tumbled off the table.

Audrey caught it before it hit the floor. "Your lips are just as blue," she said placidly.

"A trick of the light." But Gil laid his jacket across his lap and held out his hands for his coffee. The moment she filled the mug and handed it over, he let it clatter back onto the saucer, snatched up a napkin and sneezed.

"Bless you," Audrey said.

"Man's man, my ass," Seth muttered.

"You boys know what you want?" Audrey had set down the coffeepot, and now held her pen and pad at the ready.

Gil glared at Seth and ordered a chef's salad and a milkshake. Seth chuckled and asked for vegetable soup. Tongue between her teeth, Audrey noted their choices on her order pad, then retrieved the coffeepot and strode away.

Seth leaned forward again. "What, no side of ice?"

Gil flipped him off, hesitated, then hunched over his coffee and wrapped both hands around his cup. He ignored Seth's snicker. "She never did say why she was working here."

Seth sobered. "This economy sucks. Maybe she needs the money."

"I figure that's why she took me on as a tenant." Marcus perched on the bench beside Seth and pushed until Seth made room. "Mind if I sit?"

"You already are, asshole." Seth gave him a fist bump. "What's up?"

Gil echoed the gesture, then cocked his head. "You look like hell."

"Yeah, well." Marcus shrugged. "I feel like it."

Seth exchanged glances with Gil.

"You on a lunch break?" Seth nodded at Gil. "He's buying."

"Sweet." But Marcus's grin wasn't all there. "You guys been out on your bikes?"

"Hubbard Ridge." Gil sat back and rested an arm along the top of the padded seat. "Once we hit the trail, Muscles here rode like he had two flat tires."

"Yeah, well, excuse me for needing a little extra time, but I've been riding the range. I haven't been this sore since Travis was teething and I spent three nights in a row sleeping on the swing on our front porch."

"'Riding the range'?" Marcus raised an eyebrow.

"I'm helping out at Millbrook Dairy Farm until Ivy can find a new manager," Seth explained. "I've been riding fence with the one farmhand she has left, checking to see if any repairs need to be made, making sure there aren't any hazards when her cows go out to pasture, that kind of thing. I had no idea how much acreage she had. That place is huge."

Gil straightened out of his slouch. "I read something online a few months back about a rancher who uses a remote-controlled quadcopter to keep an eye on his cattle."

Seth smelled steak frying and his belly grumbled. Maybe he should have ordered something a little more substantial than soup. "What the hell's a quadcopter?"

"A helicopter with four rotors. Since it carries a camera, the rancher can use it for long-distance surveillance."

Marcus scratched his jaw. "Is it a live feed? Though I guess it doesn't matter if it's real time or recorded—either way, someone's gotta watch a screen."

Seth jabbed a thumb at Marcus. "He has a point. You might as well be out in the field, ready to handle a problem when you come across it."

"Whatever, man." Gil shrugged. "Just trying to provide options."

"Provide them to Ivy. She's still pissed at me."

"What for?" Gil spread his hands, sending coffee sloshing onto his saucer. "You're doing her one hell of a solid, spending so much time away from your store and feeling up cows and such."

"Here's your tea, Marcus." Ice cubes rattled as a slender hand thunked a glass down on the table in front of Marcus. Seth looked up to see Rachel's big brown teenage eyes laser-sighted on *him*. She smiled widely, showing off a front tooth that bore a smudge of the bright pink lipstick she'd obviously just applied.

Oh, shit. Once upon a time, it was Joe she'd been crushing on. Now it looked like Seth's turn.

"Hi, Seth." She didn't even glance at Gil. "I just wanted to let you know your food will be right out."

Seth flashed a smile. "Thank you, Rachel."

As Rachel walked back to the kitchen, Gil reached across the table and poked Seth. "What'd you do to piss off Ivy?"

"I didn't do anything."

Gil smirked. "Maybe that's why she's pissed."

"Cute."

Rachel struggled up with a tray and started unloading plates. "Audrey's busy with her other table, so I thought I'd deliver your food. Let's see — we have two double cheeseburgers, two rib-eyes, two dozen butterfly shrimp and a double order of fries."

Marcus snagged a shrimp. "Way to keep Cal hopping, guys."

Seth and Gil stared at the plates spread across the table. With a shrug, Gil held his palms over his steak, taking advantage of the steam.

Seth scratched his head. "This isn't what we ordered."

"Oh. Right. I know. You don't have your drinks yet. I need to make Gil's milkshake. Can I make one for you, too, Seth?"

He shook his head, the thought of following a rib-eye with a shake doing dastardly things to his stomach. "Water, please?"

"My pleasure." Rachel smiled widely. Her teeth were pristine, so someone must have told her about the lipstick. She hugged the tray to her chest and made a little humming sound.

Audrey surged up to the table and set a third double cheeseburger in front of Marcus. "Eat up, boys."

Rachel scowled when Audrey nudged her aside.

Seth sat back and crossed his arms. "What happened to my vegetable soup?"

Gil didn't say a word about his chef's salad. He was too busy cramming fries down his throat.

Audrey wagged a finger. "You boys worked your bodies hard today."

"Hard," agreed Rachel, gaze glued to Seth's arms.

"You need protein to build your muscles back up."

"Muscles," breathed Rachel.

Audrey tapped Marcus on the shoulder. "You, too. Don't think I didn't notice you left the house without eating anything." She turned and strode toward the kitchen, turned back and snagged Rachel's wrist. Rachel stumbled backward, still beaming as Audrey tugged her behind the counter.

Seth glared at his tablemates. "Don't. Say. A word."

"Hey, I got my own girl troubles." Gil jabbed his fork into a bite of steak.

"Like what?" Marcus set down his own fork.

"Like I thought I was damned close to ending my dry spell, until she started coming up with conditions."

"What kind of conditions?"

Gil reddened. "The kind that involve a Caribbean cruise."

"Harsh." Marcus sat back.

"Yeah, apparently, big-ass boats really get her in the mood."

Seth squirted a puddle of ketchup on his plate. "So your dry spell continues. What are you working on, ten years, now?"

Gil tossed a fry across the table. "Fuck you, man."

"Only if you take me to Jamaica."

Not that Seth had much room to talk. The only action he'd seen in well over a year was the kiss he'd shared with Ivy. Remembering her sweet flavor and the teasing heat of her in his arms had him shifting in his seat.

"What about you?" Gil asked Marcus pointedly. "The reason you look like hell have something to do with a woman?"

Marcus curved over his plate, as if shielding it from an overeager busboy. "That's part of it," he said. He didn't offer anything more.

KATHY ALTMAN

Audrey brought their drinks over. "Rachel's in the bathroom fixing her makeup. If you planned on ordering dessert and eating it in peace, you might want to get it to go."

All three guys groaned. Dessert was not an option. Hell, Seth still had three quarters of a burger to plow through.

He was trying not to dwell on what Travis and G were doing at that moment when the bell over the diner door jingled and a tall man came in, glanced around and strode up to the counter.

"Let me out, will you, Marcus?" Marcus stood, and Seth slid out of the booth. Up at the counter, he clapped one hand on the customer's back and held out the other. "Wade."

Startled, Wade jerked toward him. "Seth." His cheeks took on some color as he shook Seth's outstretched hand.

"How are you, man? I didn't expect to see you in town still."

Wade pulled a twenty from his wallet and handed it to Rachel, who grabbed a to-go bag from the pass-through and set it on the counter. "Getting everything settled before we left turned out to be more complicated than we expected."

"You been by the farm at all?"

"I doubt Ivy wants to see me. Not after I left her high and dry." He accepted his change. "You know if she's hired anyone?"

"Not a manager, no. I've been helping out some. Did you know Gary left after you did?"

Wade winced. "No. Damn."

"You should come by. I'm sure she'd like to see you before you leave."

"Maybe I will." Under his mustache, Wade's lips twitched a sorry excuse for a smile. "I have to get back to the wife. Good seeing you, Seth." He scurried out of the diner faster than Seth's kids scurried to the door when the pizza delivery guy rang the bell.

Seth returned to the booth, where Gil was watching Wade through the window. "What was that about?"

"Guilt." Seth slid in beside Marcus, no longer interested in his lunch. "That was Wade, the man who used to manage Ivy's farm."

Gil slurped his shake. "I thought he moved out West."

"So did I." Seth shrugged. So did Ivy.

*   *   *

"I CAN'T TELL YOU how good it is to see you." Ivy lowered herself into the rattan chair set at an angle to the one Allison occupied. "The last couple of weeks have been..." She made a face.

"A bitch?"

"Yep." Ivy grinned and bobbed her head. "Pretty much."

They sat in the sunroom, where Ivy had bypassed the usual yellows and greens and decorated in soft blues instead. At three in the afternoon, the space remained toasty from the sun and offered a calming view of still-green fields that seemed to roll into infinity. Trees vibrant with changing leaves and velvety brown slow-moving Jersey cows dotted the vista. Soon the girls would make their way to the barn, anticipating the relief a milking would give them and the dinner they'd enjoy afterward.

"How are you feeling?" Ivy asked.

"So far, so good." Allison wriggled around on the cushions until she found a comfortable position. "I'm hoping I'll get to skip the whole throwing-up thing. Otherwise I guess I'll just be doing my part to break in our new bathroom." Her shoulders bounced. "At least the floors are heated."

Ivy laughed as she watched her bestie fidget. "What kind of vitamins are you on, anyway? You're antsier than Travis when he knows Hazel will be bringing over Baby Blue."

Allison bit her lip, then thrust out her left hand. "So, this happened."

"Oh, my God," Ivy squealed. She jumped up and grabbed Allison's hand, squeezing it as she admired the oval diamond on her friend's finger. She gathered her into a hug. "Congratulations! I can't believe I didn't even notice. *When* did this happen?" She sat down again, eyes locked on Allison's glowing face.

"Night before last. I've been walking around in a daze since then." Her expression turned earnest. "I hope you understand, Ivy. Yesterday I just wanted to keep it to myself."

"Of course. Oh, Allison, I'm so excited for you."

"I knew you would be. You're the first person I've told." Her grin turned sheepish. "You're not the first person to know, though. A couple from Texas checked out of the motel this morning and the wife admired my ring. I have to admit it was surreal, getting congratulated."

"And that's by someone you don't even know." She patted Allison's hand and sat back. "So tell me all about it. Does Joe give good proposal?'

Allison giggled. "Joe gives *very* good proposal." A moment later, she sobered. "I do have to admit, I'm not looking forward to telling Eugenia."

Ivy winced. Eugenia Blue was the owner of Thistle Hill's sole dress shop and was also the on-again, off-again girlfriend of grumpy, gum-chewing Harris Briggs, who helped run Parker's greenhouses. Things had taken a seriously romantic turn between Harris and Eugenia after Harris had experienced a health scare earlier in the year, but when Eugenia proposed marriage, Harris had turned her down.

Eugenia wasn't talking, but whenever Ivy went into her store, the other woman's sadness was almost palpable.

Allison frowned down at her ring, twisting it slowly. "I wish I knew what happened there."

"She's supposed to host the next Dollars and Divas meeting. Maybe we could talk to her about it then." After a few moments of pensive silence, Ivy pitched forward in her chair. "Okay, enough sad. Back to happy. Your most excellent news calls for a celebratory drink. I'll be right back."

When Ivy returned carrying two glasses of chocolate milk, Allison laughed and clapped her hands. After they clinked glasses, Allison sat back with a satisfied sigh. "Now. Your turn. Tell me about you and Seth."

Ivy gazed in the direction of her front porch. "Was it only four months ago I asked about you and Joe while we sat out on the steps?"

"You wanted to know if we'd really spent the night in my car."

"I didn't blame you for refusing to stay in the motel after you found Mitzi coiled up in the wall."

Allison shuddered. "Luckily, the rest of the renovations involved no such discoveries." She gazed down into her glass. "I have to say, as independent as I like to think I am, it's been nice having someone look after me. I mean, Joe supports me, but sometimes he also just...takes over. Usually when I need it most."

"That doesn't annoy you?"

"There are times. But mostly it makes me feel special."

Ivy set aside her glass and propped her elbow on her knee and her chin in her hand. "That would scare the hell out of me."

"Feeling special? Or being looked after?"

"Being looked after and enjoying it. Aren't you afraid you'll lose yourself?"

"Losing myself in Joe happens to be quite nice, thank you very much. But I know what you mean." Allison's features softened. "Joe and I are a team. We make sure we each get the time to ourselves that we need. The team works better that way." She patted her stomach. "Though that private time's about to go out the window."

"I admire the faith you have in each other, but I'm not sure I could offer someone that kind of trust."

"C'mon, Ivy. We both know you already have. And don't think I didn't notice the way you changed the subject when Seth's name came up."

Ivy jumped to her feet and wandered to the window. She gazed through the glass at the dimming sky, a sudden sadness leaching the heat from the air around her.

"What you said, about having someone to look after you?" She turned back to Allison and made a frustrated gesture. "That's Seth. He's not just helping me with the farm. He worries about how much sleep I'm getting and whether I'm eating enough. Sure, that sounds sweet, but at the same time he's making decisions he has no right to make. The man has a hero complex. How do I know it's not just instinct that makes him do what he does? How do I know he cares about *me* and not just about solving my problems?"

"Ask him."

"You make it sound easy."

"Don't dismiss me, Ivy," Allison said gently. "I was in a similar situation, and not that long ago." She rubbed her belly. "This happened so quickly. Neither of us was prepared for it and as excited as we were, we were also scared out of our minds. We *are* scared out of our minds. When Joe asked me to marry him, I couldn't help wondering—would he ever have gotten around to it if I hadn't become pregnant? He loves me—I know he does—but I couldn't get the question out of my mind. So I asked him."

Ivy moved back to her chair and perched on the edge. "What did he say?"

"He said, 'I take it this means you didn't say yes because of the baby.'" Allison offered Ivy a watery smile. "He'd been feeling as insecure as I was. In that moment, Ivy, my love for him—" She swallowed thickly and finished the thought in a whisper. "It bubbled up inside of me, so thick and intense and...and *right*. After that, we talked for hours. About all we'd been through and when we knew we'd fallen in love with each other and what it is about each other that keeps us in love and working to stay in love..." She wiped her eyes and chuckled. "It was sweet and cathartic and intimate, and afterward we knew exactly where we stood with each other."

"Intimate and cathartic? I'm guessing talking wasn't all you did."

"You'd be right, but that's not the point. Talk to Seth."

Ivy slumped back in her chair. Her braid made for an uncomfortable lump between her shoulder blades, but she was too lazy to tug it free. "We do talk. We are honest with each other. When we get around to it, anyway."

"Good. That means you trust him."

"But this is Seth. His rescue instinct isn't going to let him say anything but what he thinks I want to hear. Or what he thinks I need to hear."

"You trust him for a reason. Let him live up to that."

"What if he thinks that means I'm ready for a commitment, when I'm not?"

Allison produced an annoying kind of smile, something both smug and delighted, and toasted Ivy with the last of her milk. "I have a feeling the real question should be, what if you think that means you're not ready for a commitment, when you are?"

* * *

MARCUS LET HIMSELF IN the front door, and when he dropped his keys on the hardwood floor, he grumbled a swear word. The last thing he wanted to do was wake up Audrey. She'd been working hard all week, and even though today should have been Parvati's first day off suspension, she'd come down with the flu, so Audrey had covered for her again.

Cal should have been more grateful, instead of scolding her for doing her damnedest to talk her customers out of meatless choices. Never in the history of the diner had they sold so many rib-eyes. Still, at the end of the shift, Audrey had turned in her apron and walked out of the kitchen with a scowl on her face, and Marcus didn't think it was because she'd miss washing dried egg off plates or fishing her tips out of drinking glasses.

He hesitated after starting up the stairs to his room. He'd left the diner not long after Audrey but had driven around for a while, thinking about Liz. Only now did he realize how hungry he was. He hadn't managed much of that burger Audrey had ordered for him, and he'd been too busy grilling steaks to grab anything else before closing.

He backtracked and headed through the darkened living room for the kitchen. When he heard what sounded like a whimper, he froze.

What the hell? Was Audrey babysitting Hazel and June's schnauzer again?

The dim light in the hall didn't cast enough of a glow for him to see all the way into the room. He flicked on the light switch and blinked. Audrey sat slumped in the middle of the overstuffed couch, her head almost touching her knees. She'd taken off one purple sneaker and had shrugged out of one arm of her thick sweater. She held the material against her face, and he realized that what he'd thought was whimpering was actually muffled sobs.

His throat went all scratchy on him.

"Audrey." He dropped to his knees in front of her. Her shoulders were shaking so hard the entire sofa vibrated. He placed a tentative hand on her knee. "What is it? Are you all right? Should I call 911?" Dammit, no one should eat as much red meat as this woman put away. Not to mention the nitrates. She popped Vienna sausages like some of her peeps popped pills. He should have tried harder to make her eat her vegetables.

"Is it your heart?" he asked.

She started to choke. *Oh, shit.* Marcus watched helplessly as she leaned farther forward, pressing her head between her knees. If he hadn't been so worried, he'd have been impressed. She continued to gasp, and the thick, soggy, grinding sounds coming from her throat as she struggled to inhale and exhale had Marcus whipping out his phone with one hand and thumping her back with the other. Maybe she had something lodged in her mouth.

She sat up, batting at his hand, and slapped her knee. When the next exhale sounded more like a cackle than a struggle for breath, Marcus fell back onto his haunches.

No fucking way. The old girl was *laughing*.

"M-my heart," she wheezed. "That's a good one." She scrubbed the sleeve of her sweater over her face and plucked at her hair, which stood straight up. She whimpered again, and there was no mistaking the next batch of sounds ripping out of her throat. Desperately Marcus looked around for a box of tissues. When he spotted one, he lunged for it and pushed it into her hands.

She took a few minutes to get herself together. After she finished mopping up her tears, she offered a wry smile. "Sorry about that."

He lifted out of his crouch and settled beside her on the sofa. "Want to tell me what's wrong?"

"I charge you too much rent to expect you to listen to my troubles."

"I don't pay enough rent to get out of listening to your troubles." When she didn't respond, he gave her an awkward pat on the shoulder. "You're not sick, are you?"

She snorted. "Why does everyone assume a little melancholy means I'm dying?"

"Because you're —" she lowered her eyebrows and he licked his lips " —uh, mature."

"You mean old. And no, I'm not sick."

"When's the last time you saw a doctor?"

"Don't worry about me, dear. I believe in preventative maintenance. Why, just last week I went to the peeker."

"Who's the—?" *Oh.* He winced. "Never mind."

"Still want to know why I was upset? Might help get rid of that image of me in my altogether, flat on my back with my feet in the stirrups. They didn't use to put covers on those, you know. It was quite a shock to the system, having to subject your feet to that cold metal."

If he hadn't had an image in his head before, he did then. Frantically, he glanced around, finally tipped his head back and stared at the light fixture until his eyes watered and he saw nothing but spots.

"You remind me of him," she murmured. "Not your looks, but your manner. Even the way you move." She glanced over, tut-tutted and handed him a tissue. "I'm talking about Calvin."

"Calvin Ames? What did he do to you?"

"Nowhere near enough."

"You're saying...you and he..." God only knew how he managed not to blurt out, *But you're so much older than he is.* Audrey offered a knowing smile.

"I am a lot older, yes. But it wasn't so obvious twenty years ago."

"Is today an anniversary or something?"

She shook her head and traced the zigzag pattern on the tissue box. "Working with him brought it all back. He wanted to marry me. I was embarrassed about the age difference, so I put him off. By the time I made up my mind to accept him, he didn't want me anymore."

"Is that why he's been so hard on you? Because you turned him down?"

"No, dear. He's been hard on me because I'm a pain in the ass."

Marcus chuckled. An instant later, he could almost hear the snick as one thought hooked up with another and a realization was born. "Is that why you approached me about renting the second floor? So you could keep tabs on Cal?"

Audrey nodded, fresh tears dripping down her cheeks. "My bad," she sniffed.

Hearing that expression from someone with gray hair and perfect posture made him chuckle. "Doesn't matter why you decided to rent to me. You're the best landlord I've ever had."

"I'm guessing I'm the only one you ever had."

"Yeah." Wasn't as if they could count Uncle Sam.

"Let this be a lesson to you," she said softly. "You have a chance to be with the person you love, you should take it, no matter the circumstances."

"What if one of you's married? What if you're *both* married? Or one of you's a serial killer?" *What if one of you's just not good enough for the other?*

She slapped his knee. "Behave. You know exactly what I mean. If you're too stupid to take my advice, you're too stupid to be happy. And you're not stupid — you're just controlling."

"I'm what?"

"You need to be in control."

Head reeling, he rubbed his knee where she'd smacked him. "That would make for a nice change, especially when it came to sex."

"I would have thought that being with someone you love would make for a nice change when it came to sex."

"I thought…didn't I hear…I mean, what about Snoozy?"

"What about him?"

"You're not dating?"

"Each other? Hardly. Like most clueless men, he prefers younger women. Anyway, he'll never forgive me for what I said about Mitzi." She looked pensive for a moment, then sighed and pushed herself up off the sofa. "I could use a hamburger. No," she corrected herself, and put a hand on his forearm as he got to his feet beside her. "Make that an omelet. It's been decades since a man made me an omelet."

"What are my chances of talking you into a salad?"

"Piss-poor."

"How about I throw some mushrooms and broccoli in with the ham and cheese?"

"Fine. But could you substitute sausage for the broccoli?"

"How about I double the broccoli and mushrooms and substitute flax seed for the ham and cheese?"

"Is it too late to get that burger?"

He didn't even try to hide his grin. "Turkey or black bean?"

*   *   *

SETH IDLED HIS PICKUP at the end of Ivy's driveway and stared hard. Yeah, it was only three in the morning, but he was pretty sure he wasn't dreaming. Ivy's sign had undergone another transformation. It now read Millbrook Fairy Farm, with the word *Fairy* in bright green letters to match the Disney-esque outfit on a decent rendition of Tinker Bell, who hovered with her wand over a small herd of Jerseys. For some reason, Tink had turned the bottles of milk purple.

He shook his head. Someone had talent and way too much time on their hands. A vandalism charge, too, if they ever got caught.

Ivy wouldn't be pleased, but G would. She loved purple and still kept a Tinker Bell costume in her closet from trick-or-treating when she was three or four.

Seth lifted his foot off the brake and drove the rest of the way to the house. It had been nearly two weeks since Ivy had confided in him. They'd found a workable rhythm and the farm was operating smoothly, but things between them couldn't have been pricklier. She made sure he knew she was working her ass off trying to find a replacement for Wade. She'd increased the salary she was offering and advertised the position as far as Meadville and Jamestown. No bites yet. Her latest idea was to connect with other dairy farms and see if they had any suggestions.

He got out of his truck in time to hear a banging echo from the rear of the house. She was probably on her way to feed the chickens. He adjusted the fold of his knit cap over his ears and headed for the back yard.

Floodlights lit the way to the coop. He shuddered, missing the warmth of his bed but grateful for the cold that stripped him of any lingering drowsiness.

Ivy emerged from the coop with an empty bucket of feed and gave a yelp when she saw him. She pressed a hand to her heart. "Good morning. You're early."

"Not early enough to catch the sign guy."

Her expression turned annoyed as she locked the henhouse gate. "Again? What'd he do this time?"

He told her.

With a snort, she headed for the house. "Grace will love it, anyway."

"I had the same thought."

She hesitated at the door to the back porch and peered up at him, her eyes lustrous in the faint yellow glow of the overhead light.

"Is everything okay?"

"Yeah." He resisted the urge to touch a fingertip to the skin beneath her right eye, now empty of bruises. He indicated it with a nod instead. "Still hurt?"

She shook her head, a wary confusion seeping into her gaze.

"I hoped we could talk," he said. "Before Dell arrived."

She chewed briefly on her lower lip. "I was about to get a head start on breakfast. Want to come in and help? We can talk while we work."

Inside, they shed their jackets and hats and took turns washing up. Ivy pulled eggs, milk and butter out of the fridge and passed them to Seth, who set them on the table. Next she handed him two bowls and asked him to separate three eggs.

"What's on the menu?" he asked.

"Belgian waffles. The batter needs to rise for an hour or so."

He moaned his approval. "It's going to be hard as hell to go back to protein shakes every morning."

"What do the kids eat?"

"Egg sandwiches or granola. Shakes or trail mix when we're in a hurry. I try to limit the carbs in the morning."

She raised an eyebrow as she pulled a tub of flour out of the cupboard. "If only they could see you now."

"You aren't going to tattle on me, are you?"

Her response was a cagey smile. She heated milk in the microwave and gently stirred a packet of yeast into it, sneaking glances at him all the while as he studied the recipe card she'd left on the counter.

He put the card down and leaned back against the fridge. "I want to run something by you."

10

SETH HELD HIS BREATH and forced himself to remain silent. Timing was everything. Pushing Ivy would only make her push back.

She set the yeast aside and arranged a stick and a half of butter in another bowl and placed it in the microwave for melting. After shooting him a look, she picked up a bright red hand towel. "Why do I get the feeling I'm not going to want to hear what you're about to say?"

"Because you're naturally suspicious."

The caution came back into her expression, though she lightened it with a wry smile. "Another tour you want me to cancel?"

He shook his head. She was right. She wouldn't want to hear what he had to say. His words would make her defensive. Angry, even. But he cared too much to keep quiet on this.

When the microwave dinged, he pushed away from the fridge, retrieved the melted butter and drew in a breath. "Have you ever thought about farming more of your land? Growing your own feed so you don't have to buy it from someone else?"

With a scowl, she set the towel aside and took the butter from him, then whisked it together with the egg yolks and milk. "You've been talking to Dell."

"A bit. It is the business I'm in, Ivy. Also, Erie has a number of microbreweries. You could check and see what they're doing with their spent grain, which still has lots of useful protein and fiber. You could probably get a deal."

Ivy handed him the yeast mixture and pointed at the bowl. While he mixed it in, she added sugar, salt and vanilla. "Thanks for the suggestion."

"Thanks, but no thanks, is that it?"

Without a word, Ivy produced a hand mixer and clicked the beaters into place. Despite his frustration, he remained silent as he watched her beat the egg whites, loving the intent look on her face and the elegant curve of her back as she bent over the bowl. They mixed the remaining milk and flour into the batter, then folded in the egg whites. Ivy covered the bowl with plastic wrap and gave it a pat.

"When you taste the results you'll see it's worth the trouble."

No way he could let that go. "Exactly the point I'm trying to make. After the initial outlay, growing your own feed will be well worth the trouble."

The measuring cups, spoons and beaters clattered into the sink. "Raising crops isn't as easy as you make it sound," Ivy said crisply.

"Nothing worthwhile ever is."

She shoved away from the sink and headed for the jacket she'd hooked on the back of a chair. "When you're done spouting clichés, come on out to the barn. I'm going to get a head start."

He caught up to her at the front door, and braced a palm against it to keep it closed. She jerked on the handle a few times, then gave up and turned to face him.

"Remember those waffles you were looking forward to?"

"Remember when I said your face lights up whenever you talk about your horse?"

Her scowl cleared. "I believe the word you used was *radiant*."

"Radiant. Right." He lowered his arm and rested his shoulder against the door instead. Enjoyed the fact that she didn't back away. "You don't look like that when you're talking about the farm."

"What do you mean?"

"It's obvious you love your animals, but can you see yourself running this farm ten years from now?"

"Of course."

"Twenty? Thirty? When you do see yourself, are you happy?"

Now she did back away, jamming her arms into the sleeves of the jacket she hadn't taken the time to put on earlier. "Where is this coming from?"

"Humor me, all right?"

She grunted an exhale. "Yes, I see myself as happy. It's hard work, but it's satisfying."

"Dell says you've never seriously considered any of his ideas for expansion."

Resentment sparked in her eyes. "You know as well as I do that I can barely manage what I have."

"I know you're driving yourself too hard. I want to make sure it's for the right reasons."

"My livelihood and the reasons I chose it are none of your business."

"But you didn't, did you? Choose it?"

"So that bit about growing crops was just to see if my heart really is in dairy farming? What's wrong with you?"

"Was it your father who considered horse shows a waste of time?"

She went still. "How did you know?"

"Joe said something about you wanting to open a riding stable."

"I've thought about it. The farm keeps me too busy to seriously consider it."

"So give something up."

"You mean like feeding the cows? They wouldn't like that very much." She shrugged one shoulder. "Though I wouldn't mind giving up poop duty."

He pushed away from the door. "I mean like giving up the cows altogether." Her shocked expression made him relent. "Some of them, anyway. One-third. One-half. Whatever it takes to make that riding school happen."

She barked out a laugh. "You are crazy if you think I'm giving up my legacy."

"That's the point. That's why you're sticking it out. For your parents."

"And why not? They gave me everything."

He moved to the couch and leaned against it. "I'm sure they were very nice people. They did a damned fine job with you. Mostly."

"Mostly?"

"They saddled you with enough guilt to fill Lake Erie. They didn't respect you or your opinions. They made you believe they knew better when they didn't."

"Oh." She strode to the door and yanked it open. "But you. You do know better."

"I know *you* better."

"Because we kissed once?"

Seth exhaled. Ivy released a high-pitched, frustrated sound and marched out onto the porch.

Moments later, she marched back. "If you push me into something, how is that me following my dream?"

Seth levered away from the couch, resisting the urge to press a fist to the ache in his chest. Defensiveness? Check. Anger? Check. What he hadn't expected to see? Hurt.

"I just want you to consider the possibilities," he said quietly.

She nodded once. "Okay, then."

Seth followed her back out into the cold. Maybe he should have just kept his damned mouth shut.

* * *

MARCUS SAT WITH BOTH hands gripping the steering wheel, as if braced for impact, and for good reason. Reality was about to hit hard if Liz told him to go fuck himself.

It was no less than he deserved. It shouldn't have taken a lonely old lady crying on a couch to get him to see there was nothing heroic about pushing Liz away. That was taking the easy way out. Making her a part of his life, opening himself up to her, loving her, being there for her — that would take balls.

Still, he'd needed a few days to work up the courage to see her. He'd planned to wait for her outside Snoozy's and talk to her after she'd finished her shift, but did he really want to have his ass handed to him in public? He'd parked instead on the street outside her house. His pulse jumped higher the closer it got to ten, when her shift ended.

Twice he'd had to stumble his way through the dark to find a tree and take a leak.

At ten fifteen she pulled into her driveway. She got out of her car, tugged the clip from her hair and rubbed the back of her head. Marcus slid from his pickup and dragged deeply at the cool, pine-scented air. Liz didn't even notice the clunk his truck door made as it closed. He caught up to her as she mounted the cement steps of her porch.

"Liz."

She gasped and spun around, her purse swinging wildly, both hands pressed to her chest. When she saw him, her entire body sagged. "Marcus. What are you trying to do, give me a heart attack?"

"Sorry about that." He shoved his hands into the pockets of his jacket. "Can we talk?"

"I don't think so." She turned away, jogged up the remaining steps and jammed her key in the door. Harsh, but not unfair.

"Please." He paused on the bottom step. "I've missed you."

"Could have fooled me. I haven't seen you in a week." She opened the door and glanced over her shoulder. The glow of the porch light painted her ebony hair amber. "Besides, last I heard, we were over."

"You're not the kind of girl a guy gets over."

That brought her back to face him. She didn't say anything, though, as she paused in the doorway. Her lips remained thin.

"I owe you an apology," he said.

She marched back out to the edge of the porch and glared down at him. "No, you don't. You don't have to apologize for not wanting to have sex, and you don't have to apologize for not loving me. Stop. Apologizing."

They stared at each other. Her words echoed in the quiet dark around them. A dog barked, three sharp yaps, and Liz drew in a shuddering breath.

"There's no need to drag this out," she said softly. "I'm a big girl. I can take care of myself." She backed toward the door.

Marcus moved up another step. "I lied."

"About what?"

"I lied when I said you deserved someone better than me."

She spread her arms wide. One hand fumbled for the doorknob and the other braced against the jamb. "Is that supposed to be a compliment?"

"I mean that's not why I called it quits. I have this thing. About

179

control."

Her eyes went wide. "You mean like...BDSM?"

"BD what?"

"You know." She dipped her head and lowered her voice. "Domination and stuff. During sex."

His head went back. "You mean handcuffs and shit?"

He'd said it too loudly. The dog barked again and Marcus cringed. Meanwhile, the blood had seeped from Liz's face, and her mouth had gone slack.

She didn't know much of what he'd gone through as a kid, but she knew enough to know that restraints had played a cruel part.

"I did it again," she muttered. "God, Marcus, I'm so sorry."

"Now you're the one who needs to stop apologizing."

"Why are you here?" Her gaze was still stricken with remorse, but her body had stiffened. He hadn't expected easy, and he certainly didn't deserve it.

"Audrey helped me see it. For years I didn't have control over anything. Nothing important, anyway. Who cares if you get to pick out your clothes in the morning when in the afternoon your stepfather's picking up some pervert for you to—" He scrubbed his fist over his mouth. "Point is, once I ditched the son of a bitch, I figured I'd be calling my own shots. Except I landed in prison, where it's one goddamned rule after another. After I got out, I swore I'd never let anyone else control my time, my decisions or my emotions."

Liz pushed the door open behind her, turned and stumbled inside. She didn't shut the door, letting Marcus decide whether to follow or not.

Of course he followed.

She dumped her purse on the coffee table and rounded on him. "I've never heard you talk so much and I still don't know what you're saying."

"I'm saying I'm a goddamned coward. Because what I feel for you is out of control and it scares the hell out of me."

"Out of control...in a good way?"

"Yeah. And when I forget to be nervous about it—" he lifted his shoulders in an awkward shrug " —I kind of like it."

She crossed her arms. "Good for you."

"I'm really fucking this up, aren't I?" He walked right up to her then and gripped her shoulders. "I know I said you could do better. Thing is, I am good enough for you, but only when I'm with you. Being with you makes me the kind of man who deserves you."

A dawning glee lit up her face, like a flame touched to a rum-soaked bananas Foster. With a hiccupy sort of laugh, she jumped onto her toes and wreathed her arms around his neck.

"You're sweet," she said, and plastered her mouth to his.

Her kiss savaged him. Want pulsed in his veins and roused his paralyzed heart. He clamped his hands on either side of her face and tried to give as good as he was getting.

Her lips were warm and full and softer than silk. She gave him her tongue, and heat licked along every muscle. Discovery ached and hope stung.

The heady press of her body disappeared. Before he could protest it returned, minus the woolen bulk of her coat. His hands wandered her slim back and strong shoulders. Her moans drove him, encouraged him, and he slid his palms forward along her ribs and up to her breasts. He shuddered, and she moaned into his mouth.

All this time, he could have been touching her. Letting her touch him. Letting her *heal* him.

She yanked her hands from around his neck, shoved his jacket off his shoulders and scrabbled for the hem of his shirt. When her cool, clever hands touched his skin, he drove his fingers into her springy hair and eased her mouth away, panting against her cheek. She nipped at the underside of his jaw.

"You're so beautiful," he murmured. He buried his nose in her hair. "And you smell like tomato sauce."

"Yeah?" Liz licked his throat and inhaled. "You smell like pancakes." Her hands wandered up and down his naked back. "Remember when I said I recognized you?" Her voice was soft, softer even than the skin he'd touched at her waist.

He managed a nod.

"I know what you need," she whispered. "Because I need it, too. Affection. Closeness. Warmth." Beneath his shirt her palms trailed

181

downward.

He grabbed her wrists. She angled forward and rested her forehead against his heart. Her velvety, zig-zaggy curls brushed his chin.

"I know you want me," she said. "What's holding you back?"

"Liz."

"Tell me."

Where he found the brass to put it into words, God only knew. "I've...never been with a woman before."

Silence. His face caught fire.

She wrapped her arms around his waist and hugged him tight. "I find that incredibly—"

"Pathetic?"

"Hot."

Relief, warm and heady, flooded his chest. "I find *you* incredibly hot."

"So what are you going to do about it?"

He backed her up against the wall and raised her hands over her head. His muscles shook as he kissed his way from her temple down to her chin. "I'm going to find my way around this amazing body of yours." And hope like hell he could satisfy her.

"You're in luck," she said. "I'm an excellent guide." Her mouth sought his and he teased her, lifting his head away, pressing his lower body to hers as he trailed his lips along her jaw. When she began to writhe and her elbows thumped against the wall, he realized he was still holding her wrists. He yanked his hands away and stumbled back.

"Shit," he choked. *Again with the control.* "I'm sorry. Did I hurt you?"

"Of course not," she said. She fisted her hands in his shirt and tugged him close again. "I liked it. I'll tell you if I don't. So far the only thing I don't like is that your hands are empty."

Squeezing his eyes shut, he kept his arms rigid at his sides. "I'm going to fuck this up. I'm going to do something weird, or wrong, and you're going to realize this is a mistake. What I've done before—"

"Hey," she whispered. "We'll figure this out together. Your past is part of you, but good or bad, we don't have to let it hold you back. Do you want this, Marcus?"

"More than I've ever wanted anything," he said raggedly.

She went quiet. He'd surprised her. Surprised himself, too, with his admission that she meant more to him than the need for revenge that had driven him for so long.

Past tense.

She swallowed, and pressed a tender kiss to his throat. Groped for his hands and placed them on her hips. "Then do whatever feels good. There's no right or wrong way. There's only loving each other."

He made a sound, deep in his throat, that caused her lips to vibrate against his skin. His fingers slid around to her ass and tightened, and she moaned. This time when she lifted her face to his, he kissed her hungrily, urgently, his mouth all about demand. The passion she roused in him — it terrified him. She felt the strength of it, too, because when she broke away her expression was as shaken as his breathing. But her eyes gleamed as she took his hand and led him into her bedroom.

* * *

IVY WAS HALFWAY UP a ladder in the tack room, finishing up an inventory of the contents in the upper cupboards, when she heard a child's scream. Shock zinged through her. She half jumped, half fell to the floor and staggered upright. Where had it come from? She bolted from the barn, straining to hear over the thunderous drumming of her heart.

She hesitated between outbuildings, arms and legs loose with fear. A terrified shout from inside the house sent her hurtling toward the front porch. *Grace.* What could be wrong? *Oh, God, oh, God, oh, God.* Visions of Hazel gasping with a heart attack or Travis sprawled at the bottom of the stairs sent bile spiraling up toward her throat.

She took the steps two at a time and shoved through the front door. It bounced on its hinges with a splintering groan. Her blood bellowed in her ears as she paused on the hardwood.

Where were they?

Sounds of a struggle in her office. Hazel was scolding, Travis was crying and Grace was whimpering. *What the hell?*

"I said shut *up*," growled a deep male voice, and Ivy froze.

Gary.

Wild, outraged heat flashed through her body and launched her forward. As she charged through the living room, she snatched up the fireplace poker with her left hand and with her right snatched her phone from her pocket and dialed 911. It took her three tries, but her shaking fingers finally managed it. She lingered outside the office long enough to whisper to the dispatcher. Then she lurched into the doorway.

Gary stood behind her desk, his back to the window. One hand gripped a wad of cash, the other, Grace's hair.

Her insides iced over.

"Let her go!" she demanded.

Gary's eyes were desperate, and his shaved head gleamed with sweat, but pity was not one of the emotions that sliced at Ivy's heart. He stiffened when he spotted the phone in her hand and swore. Grace whimpered again.

Ivy brandished both the phone and the poker. "The police are on their way," she choked out. "Let. Her. Go."

This was her fault. All her fault.

"I'm the one calling the shots now." Gary pulled Grace closer. "Want the kid to get hurt? Keep bossing me around."

He didn't appear to have a weapon. *Thank God.*

Ivy glared. She prayed the sheriff would hurry and prayed even harder that Seth would come crashing through the window and take this asshole *down*. But he wouldn't be coming, because he couldn't have heard any of this. He was in the milking shed, running the skid loader.

Of all the days for her to send Dell on a supply run.

Her gaze dropped to Grace. Tears ran down the little girl's face. Ivy's hands shook as she gave Seth's daughter what she hoped was a reassuring wink. She glanced across the room at Hazel, who had lowered herself into a sort of warrior stance with a floor lamp balanced in her hands. The shade was gone, the bulb in shards, the jagged remainder pointed at Gary. Her silvery lipstick was smeared across her cheek and Travis had both arms wrapped around her waist, face tucked into the small of her back.

"Get your shotgun, Ivy." Hazel jabbed the lamp. "I'll hold him off."

Gary's eyes went wide and he raised the hand holding the cash. He'd found Ivy's lockbox. "I'm not looking to get shot here," he said. "I just want what's mine. You owe me."

It was all Ivy could do to contain an outraged scream, but losing her cool — what little of it she had — wouldn't achieve anything except upset Gary further.

"This isn't the way to collect a debt," she told him, as calmly as she could. "Terrorizing children and old women? What the hell is wrong with you?"

"Who's old?" Hazel demanded.

Ivy swallowed. What if he decided to *leave* with Grace? She couldn't let that happen. That would *not* happen.

She shifted her grip on the poker. She couldn't risk rushing him. Not with Grace in the way. For the same reason, brandishing her shotgun was not an option. "I'll write you another check, but you need to let Grace go."

Gary's thin face was redder than a summer tomato. He nudged Grace to her right, out from behind the desk. "Soon as I get to my truck, I'll let her go."

Oh, hell, no.

"Travis." The urgency in Ivy's voice brought the boy's head up. His chin trembled and Ivy's heart started to hurt. She turned her back and moved sideways into the room, far enough to block Gary from Travis's view. "Run and get your father," she said quietly. "He's in the milking shed." She held the poker out to her side, both in warning to Gary, and to help Travis believe the asshole couldn't get past her.

Travis was wagging his head. "He said he'd hurt Grace if I moved an inch."

"I meant it, too," Gary said. "You let that kid out of here and his sister's going to get knocked around."

Ivy bit her lip until she tasted blood, and fought to keep the panic from her face as she smiled down at Seth's son.

"It's okay, Travis. You can stay here with us."

The boy nodded and kept his grip on Hazel.

Behind the desk, Gary was breathing heavily. She needed Seth in here *now*.

His phone. He kept it on vibrate.

Ivy handed her phone to Hazel, who scowled, reluctant to set down the lamp. Ivy mouthed, *Text Seth*, then turned back to face Gary.

"Seth is on his way," she said. "He's going to hurt you. He's going to hurt you even worse if you're still holding onto Grace when he gets here."

The red in Gary's cheeks gave way to a sickly gray. He hesitated, casting frantic glances around the room. When footsteps pounded across the porch he burst into motion, shoving Grace aside as he lunged from behind the desk and toward the door. Ivy hustled out of his way at the same time Seth charged into the house, face thunderous, eyes wild. When Gary spotted him, he spun back toward the office. Meanwhile, Ivy rushed at Grace and gathered the crying girl in her arms. She shuffled her toward Hazel and away from Gary, who was scrabbling at the window latch.

"You son of a bitch," Seth shouted. "I'll kill you!" He rushed at Gary, who'd started snatching items off Ivy's desk and hurling them Seth's way. A stapler, a tape dispenser, a ceramic mug with two inches of tea inside. Liquid splashed across the carpet as the mug bounced off Seth's chest and thumped to the floor. Ivy winced, but none of it fazed Seth. He backed Gary into the corner and drove his fist into his jaw. The bald man's head snapped back against the wall. Plaster dusted the floor as he crumpled.

Seth stood over him, legs spread, fists tight, chest heaving. Veins bulged in his arms and neck. Ivy had a feeling he wouldn't have minded pounding on Gary some more, but the man was out cold.

Travis wrenched away from Hazel. "Daddy!"

Seth shuddered and pulled a hand down his face. He staggered back a step, turned and went down on one knee. Travis hurtled toward him. Seth squeezed his son against his chest and pressed a kiss to the boy's white-blond head.

"You okay, Tiger?"

Travis mumbled something and wriggled in tighter. Seth swallowed hard and looked over his son's head at Ivy. The torment in his eyes pulled a sob from her throat. He held out an arm. Ivy leaned down and rubbed Grace's back, whispering that her daddy needed to see she was okay. She gently guided her toward Seth, who crushed her close.

"You all right, G?" he murmured into her ear.

She nodded and started to cry again. Seth closed his eyes and gently rocked, whispering to his kids that it was all over, that everything would be fine, that they were brave and special and safe.

Ivy swallowed and turned to Hazel, who'd plopped down into an upholstered chair. The old lady's hand shook as she finger-combed her hair and wiped at the splotch of tears darkening the front of her pale blue blouse.

"How are you, Hazel? Can I get you a glass of water?"

"Water, hell. I need something with sass. Get the kids some, too."

Sirens whined in the distance. Ivy checked the corner. Gary hadn't stirred.

As quickly as she could, Ivy fetched a small glass of wine and watched Hazel swig it, then asked her to keep the kids occupied in the kitchen — and made it clear they weren't allowed anything stronger than juice. Seth managed to loosen the kids' hold on him and quietly asked them to go with Miss Hazel.

They both wanted to cling. Ivy couldn't blame them — she'd have liked nothing better than for Seth to fold her into his arms and never let go. But it was safer to keep the kids out of the way until Gary was en route to jail.

The sirens got louder as what sounded like a pair of patrol cars barreled up the driveway. Hazel herded the children into the kitchen and Seth moved back to stand over Gary. While car doors slammed outside, he shoved both hands through his hair.

"Why the hell didn't you come get me?" he demanded.

"It happened so fast." She couldn't help the defensive note that crept into her voice. "I was in the tack room when I heard Grace scream, and I ran toward the sound. You were on the skid loader. It would have taken too long to get your attention."

He swiveled, took hold of her arm and tugged. As he pressed his lips to her forehead, she wrapped her arms around his waist for a sideways hug.

"I'm sorry," he said gruffly.

"Police!" A female voice barked the word from the front of the house. "We're coming in."

* * *

SEVERAL TENSE AND TEARFUL minutes later, Ivy and Hazel stood back as Lily helped Gary fold his lanky frame into the back of her squad car. When Hazel pulled out her phone and took a photo, Ivy couldn't help a snort of laughter, but muffled it as quickly as she could. Seth watched grimly from the front steps, with Grace and Travis tucked on either side of him. Ivy figured Seth needed the distance to help him resist the temptation to land another punch.

She wouldn't have minded taking a turn herself.

Once her passenger was settled, the sheriff turned to Ivy. "I'll need you and Seth to provide statements." She glanced at the porch. "I'll send someone to Seth's house."

"I need to finish the chores first, but I can come in after that. An hour okay?"

Lily nodded and unhooked her keys from her belt.

Hazel squeezed Ivy's arm and beamed at the sheriff. "Do you need me to come in, too?"

Lily's impassive gaze locked on Hazel's fingernails, which were painted a surprisingly tame shade of baby blue. But putting the tame to shame was the decal on each nail—a pink baby bottle, in celebration of Allison's pregnancy. Ivy had a feeling Hazel knew damned well those baby bottles looked like penises.

"Wouldn't hurt," Lily finally said, in a voice that clearly indicated it probably would.

"Sheriff Tate." Seth and the kids joined them. "We want to thank you again."

She jerked a thumb over her shoulder, at the backseat of her squad car. "He's the one who should be thanking me. I'm pretty sure I saved him a butt-kicking by showing up when I did."

Seth shook Lily's hand and Travis did as well, eyes wide as he scanned her equipment belt. The sheriff hesitated, color leaching from skin already lighter than ivory. After a moment, she thrust her hand at Grace. Grace echoed Lily's hesitation, then squeezed her fingers once and scooted closer to her father.

Ivy winced. She didn't think Seth had noticed, but Grace certainly had. Ivy understood where poor Lily was coming from — Grace looked a lot like the daughter she'd lost.

A shaming heat rippled through Ivy. She dipped her head and brushed imaginary dirt from the legs of her jeans. Did she stare at Grace like that? Make her shrink like that? No wonder the kid thought Ivy didn't like her.

As soon as the sheriff left, Seth walked Grace and Travis over to his pickup and settled them in the extended cab's backseat. He shut the door and stared over the truck's bed toward the lake. Even from this distance, she could see his jaw working. He turned his head and snagged her gaze, and her heart trembled at the intensity in his face.

He opened the door again, leaned in and said something to the kids. After tugging off his hat and tossing it onto his seat, he shut the door and strode back to Ivy.

She waited, her heart thumping faster and faster. She knew what he wanted to say, and she didn't want to hear it. She'd tried to tell him. Now he was going to take them away, just when she'd resigned herself to caring about them. To caring about *him*.

He stopped in front of her, his gaze dropping to the arms she'd threaded across her stomach. "I'm sorry to leave you in the lurch like this," he said.

"Don't apologize. Of course you don't want your kids here anymore. I tried to tell you it could be dangerous." Her voice broke. "Though I never thought they'd be at risk *inside* the house."

"Ivy." He closed his fingers around her wrist, and a flash flood of heat rippled under her skin. He tugged twice, gently, as if to refocus her attention, but since the day she'd met him, no one had ever distracted her like him.

"Thank you," he said. The grit in his voice shredded her heart. "Thank you for keeping my kids safe."

"But I didn't." It hurt to breathe. "They were here because of me. He threatened them *because of me*. God, Seth, they're going to have *nightmares*—"

"Stop it." He cupped her shoulders and gave her a shake. "Just stop it. They'll be fine. Because of you, they'll be fine." His fingers dug in. "I want to hold you. I want to hold you so badly I can hardly stand it." He glanced back at his truck, squeezed her shoulders once and let go. "The kids have enough to deal with at the moment. I have to get them home. But you and I need to talk. Soon. I'll call you later." When she didn't respond, he stroked a finger along her jaw. "Ivy?"

"Take care of them," she said, and took a step back. "I'll be fine. I am fine." She choked out a laugh. "I guess it's time to get those security cameras."

He nodded once and cupped her chin. "I'll call you." No warning but a flexing of his fingers before his mouth covered hers in a quick, hard kiss. "It'll be okay," he said, and then he was gone.

* * *

IVY AWOKE WITH HER bladder in crisis mode. She yearned to stay in bed. Her muscles were lax and happy beneath her satin-trimmed comforter, her toes were toasty, and she hadn't yet finished with a dream involving sandy beaches and the mostly male cast of a Broadway play.

But the need to pee trumped all.

Somehow she made it to the bathroom, even with her eyelids doing their impression of a faulty garage door. She didn't dare look in the mirror as she washed up. She stumbled back to bed, opened one eye to check the clock and sagged with relief when she saw it was only nine. She hadn't been asleep for more than an hour.

Going to bed at eight was something she hadn't done since she was a kid. But after the day she'd had, she'd been looking forward to hitting the sheets the moment Seth and the kids left. By the time she'd finished taking care of the Jersey girls and running into town to let

Lily take her statement, it had been going on seven. Ivy had heated up a can of chicken noodle soup, taken a shower and crawled into bed.

Instead of sleeping, she should have been stepping up her search for a manager. She had to get Seth back to his life, back to his family, for everyone's sake.

But hallelujah, it felt good to crawl back into bed.

The moment she found the perfect position, her cell rang. She rolled over, snagged her phone off the nightstand and took the call under the covers.

Seth spoke before she could say hello. "It wasn't your fault," he said.

"It feels like my fault." She shifted her head on the pillow. "How are they?"

"Tired. Confused. I can't leave them."

"I wouldn't ask you to. Dell got back shortly after you left and helped me finish up. Not that it matters. Your kids need you."

"I can't come over there."

She frowned. "I know. I just said —"

"But you can come over here."

She threw the covers off, finding it suddenly hard to breathe. "Seth —"

"I want to hold you. I want to thank you properly."

"You're offering me gratitude sex?"

"Trust me, the gratitude won't be one-sided."

She sat up and scrubbed a hand over her face. "You're kidding, right? Do you honestly think I'd be good with this? Finally sleeping together after all this time, only because you feel obligated?"

"It's not obligation. It's need. I need you."

Ivy dropped her head to her knees while everything inside her shifted and tumbled. "You know that's not a good idea," she managed. "And not just because your kids might wake up and see me."

"You could wear a disguise."

"What, like a French maid's uniform?"

"Jesus, do you have one?"

She rolled her eyes. "No. I don't."

"I see." He sighed heavily. "I suppose you could come over anyway."

She got to her feet and started to pace, struggling to tamp down the excitement shimmering through her. "Remember what you said right before you left? The kids have enough to deal with."

He swore. "You're supposed to be trying to talk me into this, not the other way around."

At her bedroom window she closed her eyes and rested her forehead on the glass, not trusting herself to speak.

He exhaled. "I guess I want you here so I'll know you're all right."

"And if I'm not?"

"I'd do my damnedest to make it better."

"And how would you do that?"

"Superhero bandages and chocolate milk with a bendy straw."

She laughed.

"Hey, it works with my kids."

Her feet were getting cold, and in more ways than one, it seemed. She dropped onto her bed and shoved her feet under the covers. "Get some sleep, cowboy. This day has been rough on you, too."

"All right. But I know what this is."

"This is me needing my beauty sleep."

"No. You're starting to like them."

Her mouth went dry.

"You starting to like me, too?"

"I was," she said.

He chuckled, and wished her a gruff good-night.

She scooted down and settled on her back, her comforter tucked under her chin, her phone pressed to her chest.

*   *   *

TWO DAYS LATER, SETH was amazed by how quickly his kids had bounced back from their ordeal. He'd thought seriously about keeping them home from school, at least on Thursday, then decided they could use the distraction. He'd talked to their teachers about it, and they'd agreed. The school counselor offered to keep an eye on Grace, and her doctor had reminded him that kids processed things on their own timelines. As long as he made himself available to Travis and Grace and reminded them as often as possible that they were loved, they'd be fine.

Himself, he wasn't so sure about. The rage continued to simmer. Rage and guilt and naked-ass fear. He'd have gotten good and drunk Wednesday night if he hadn't had to be there for his kids. Especially after Ivy had turned him down. She'd been right to do it, for more reasons than one. Didn't mean he wasn't still thinking about it.

The sex part, not the drunk part.

Okay, maybe both.

That wasn't what had brought him to the farm tonight. The moment Deb had driven away with the kids for the weekend, Seth had attempted to get in touch with Ivy. He'd tried both her cell and her landline. No answer on either. There was a phone in the tack room, but Seth didn't know the number.

Yeah, it was Friday night, and Dell would have left earlier than usual. But what about Ivy? She'd never leave the place unattended.

Sheriff Tate had Gary in custody. Knowing that didn't keep panic from jolting through him.

"Ivy?" He walked the length of the bedding barn, cringing at the desperate edge to his voice. If she heard it, she'd be pissed, but he couldn't help it. Both her vehicles were here. Unless someone had picked her up, she should be here, too. He hesitated on the path to the horse barn.

Maybe someone *had* picked her up. Maybe Gary's stunt had shaken her more than she'd let on. Maybe she'd arranged for Dell to take care of the animals in the morning so she could stay the night at a friend's house.

An equal mix of relief and disappointment tugged at his shoulders. The damp, cool dusk that settled around him suddenly seemed more lonely than peaceful, the sharp scent of wood smoke from a neighbor's chimney more mocking than inviting.

He scrubbed a hand over his face. If he kept this up, he'd be standing under her bedroom window with a boom box on his shoulder. Earning extra points for pathetic because she wasn't even *there*.

He started moving again, gravel giving way to grass beneath his boots. He'd checked the house, the milking shed and the bedding barn. He'd give the horse barn a gander, then call Allison Kincaid, see if she knew where Ivy could be.

He grabbed the rightmost handle of the double sliding doors and pulled. *Dammit.* She wasn't in here, either. The lights were off, the emergency lights giving the interior a bluish hue. When a horse nickered a hopeful greeting from one of the rear stalls, Seth stepped inside. Might as well take a look.

Silver Dollar, the palomino Dell usually rode, pressed his muzzle through the grid that created the top half of his stall door. Seth chuckled and stroked his fingers along the velvety length of the gelding's nose. Silver Dollar blew a rebuke when he realized Seth had come empty-handed. And apparently would leave empty-handed, too—Seth saw no sign of Ivy. He pulled his cell from his pocket.

A muffled whimper, off to his left. His head came up and he went rigid, every muscle on alert. When he heard the noise again, he jammed his phone back into his pocket and strode farther along the row of stalls, slowing to peer inside each one. Three stalls down, he found her.

11

IVY STOOD WITH HER back to the stall door, arms wrapped around her stallion's neck, face buried in his chocolate-brown coat. Her slim shoulders shook. Her stifled sobs tore into Seth's heart.

"Ivy."

She gave no sign that she heard him. Cabana Boy swung his head toward Seth and stomped one foot, one clueless guy begging another to have his back.

"Thanks, buddy," Seth whispered. "I got it from here."

He moved in close and ran a palm down the length of her braid. The softness made him swallow. She stiffened and pushed tighter into her horse. Cabana Boy snorted, and Seth came up against Ivy's back. He slid his hands along her arms until his fingers tangled with hers. The choking sounds she was making reverberated against his chest.

"Ivy." He spoke quietly, his lips against her temple. "There's a real chance of getting stepped on here, and you're wearing slippers." He'd call her on that later. "C'mon, baby. Come with me."

Gently, he tugged her away from the stallion. Straw rustled beneath their feet as he backed her out of the stall. He kept her tucked against his side as he latched the door, then wrapped both arms around her, drawing her up against his heart. She'd kept her head bowed the entire time, but he could see her face was red and slick with tears. Cheek to his chest, hands grabbing at his shirt, she continued to cry. Her heavy tears soaked through cotton to skin in no time.

The strength of her anguish staggered him. He'd rarely seen her less than calm, cool and collected. She seemed...broken.

Jesus. Was she still feeling guilty about what Gary had done?

He slipped a hand beneath her braid and stroked her back. Up, down. Up, down. "Talk to me," he urged.

She jerked her head back and forth, pulled her hands free, and pressed her sleeves to her face. She shuddered as she struggled to collect herself. The tears kept coming.

"You're killing me, Ivy. Please. Tell me what's wrong. This isn't about Gary, is it? Because that's over. It's done. Travis and Grace are fine."

She clutched at his forearm. "I-it's her birthday," she sobbed. "Today's my daughter's birthday."

Aw, hell. His own eyes started to burn, and a stinging sadness crept into his throat. He rested his cheek on her head and held her even tighter.

He wished there were something he could say to make it better.

He concentrated instead on letting her feel his heat. His solidity. Letting her know she wasn't alone.

Gradually, her body relaxed, and her sobs mellowed to sniffles. Darkness pressed against the row of casement windows marching high across the opposite wall. How long had she been in here grieving? She must be exhausted.

He shifted his weight. "Let's go inside," he murmured. She wore a pair of thermal pajamas that were no match for the chilly night outside the barn doors. And she needed aspirin. With all that crying, she was bound to develop one hell of a headache.

She levered herself away and swiped her palms across her face. "Oh, God, I'm sorry," she said thickly.

"Don't." He framed her face with his hands and coaxed her chin up. The blue-tinged shadows weren't deep enough to hide her red nose, her swollen eyes, the tears that spiked her eyelashes.

She looked miserable.

She looked gorgeous.

He was an asshole for noticing.

He cleared his throat. "Anything that needs to be done before I take you inside?"

Her pupils expanded as she stared up into his eyes. Her head twitched a no. "Everyone's been fed and tucked in."

"Let's go up to the house, then, and get a drink. We can talk."

She tugged his hands away from her face. "Thank you," she said haltingly, "but I'll be fine. I know you need to get home." She glanced up at the windows, and her eyes widened. "Why are you here so late? Where are the kids?"

"With their mom."

"But—"

"They'll be okay. They're looking forward to a trip to the wildlife park."

"They're okay?"

"Okay enough to guilt their mother into taking them to the wildlife park. And a movie, I believe, on top of that."

"You're not worried?"

"Always. But she drove all the way here to see them, and they begged me to let them go home with her. They know I'm only a phone call away." He reached around and grasped her braid, pulled it forward, and let the satiny rope of hair slide slowly free. He stared at the tip as it settled in the center of her left breast. "Right now I'm more worried about you."

"You shouldn't be." She managed a thready laugh. "I deal with this every year. It's a kind of tradition. I'll be fine."

"You keep saying that. I'm not leaving till I know for sure."

* * *

SETH'S WORDS MADE IVY feel both cosseted and uncomfortable. "I can take care of myself," she said.

"I know you can. But everyone deserves a break, even from themselves."

She stared up at him. His brown eyes were soft with concern, but there was no mistaking the flush beneath his tanned skin and the uneven rise and fall of his chest.

He was turned on. A small forward motion confirmed it.

That wasn't a currycomb poking into her hip.

Confusion warred with wonder. He wanted her. Despite the sob-fest and the stuffy nose and the slime on her face, he wanted her.

If it hadn't been for the sobering burn in her eyes, she'd have done something about that, because her own libido was sitting up and taking notice. But it seemed ridiculously fickle, to be wailing one moment and seducing the next.

Although if Seth didn't mind, why should she?

And judging from the prod of his erection, Seth didn't mind at all.

She raised the hem of her pajama top and dried her face, then lifted her hands to his chest and stared at her fingers as they spread over his shirt. His heartbeat pulsed against her skin and she pressed harder, as if to prevent it from escaping. "This is going to sound incredibly selfish, but..." she tipped her head back "...I really hope your kids don't call and ask you to come get them."

His muscles bunched. "Does that mean you've changed your mind?"

"Depends. Did you come here hoping to change it?"

"Yes," he answered, and the gruff need in his voice had her brain sputtering like an engine low on fuel.

When she couldn't manage to do anything more than stare at him, he exhaled, and one side of his mouth tilted. "Since when are you out of moves?"

"Since I'm suddenly terrified I won't be able to live up to my own hype."

His hoot of laughter sounded strained. "I don't think you need to worry about that." He clasped her hands and trapped them against his chest, swung her around, and backed her up against Cabana Boy's stall. He dipped his head and let his mouth hover a quarter inch above hers. "But there's only one way to know for sure."

She sucked in a breath, which was just as well, since she didn't get to breathe for the next...God knew how long. Seth's lips covered hers and her state of mind careened from a self-conscious yearning to a hot, wet, brazen want and a jolting need so fierce she found herself climbing him like a tree.

He groaned. His mouth continued to plunder hers as his hands stroked down to her ass and lifted. He thrust forward, creating an exquisite trap between his lower body and the wall.

Ivy moaned and thrust back. When he captured her tongue with his and started to suck, she convulsed and heard a hollow thunk she didn't realize at first was the back of her head connecting with the wall. Dear God, if just the *promise* of sex nearly drove her to orgasm, how would she handle the act itself?

A nervous excitement coiled in her chest, the pressure building in her lungs as Seth's lips and teeth and tongue stole her breath, again and again. His kisses were relentless, as if he were afraid that if he let her come up for air, she'd ask him to stop.

That was *so* not going to happen.

This was exactly what she needed, in so many ways.

His chest heaved as he broke away and rested his forehead against hers. "Is this a mistake?" he asked. "Am I taking advantage because you're looking for a distraction?"

She winced at the words that so clearly echoed her thoughts.

"I am grateful for your timing," she murmured. "But you know that has nothing to do with wanting you."

"Good. 'Cause it'd be hard as hell to walk away."

She swayed forward and bit his chin. He'd shaved. The courtesy of the gesture, and the hope it implied, sent her belly into a slow, swooning roll.

"Please tell me," she whispered, "that we'll be doing more than kissing tonight."

His flush deepened. He cupped her jaw and ran a thumb over her lips. "We have all night," he said huskily. "Which is a good thing, since I intend to discover every inch of you, and not just with my mouth."

She whimpered.

The skin at the corners of his eyes crinkled as he smiled. "You're the boss. You give the orders, so yeah, I'm prepared to go beyond kissing." He leaned down and nuzzled her ear. "But I plan to give an order or two of my own."

He took her mouth again.

Sparkles of anticipation burst to life in her chest and shot outward, scattering heat all the way to her fingers and toes. She clamped her hands on his head and hung on for dear life as his tongue stroked hers. He squeezed her ass and slid his hands slowly up to her waist. There his fingers dipped under her pajama top and caressed her skin in a slow upward trail to her breasts. When he scraped the sides of his thumbs across her nipples, she gasped. The throbbing pressure in her core spiked and she brought her legs up and linked her ankles against his lower back. Her hips started a slow piston, moving faster and faster as he teased her breasts.

"Easy," he gritted, and lowered his hands to her thighs.

"No," she cried. "Don't stop."

Gently but firmly, he tugged her legs loose from his waist. "We're not doing this out here."

"We're not?" She could barely get the words out, she was panting so hard.

"No. Number one, it's our first time. We'll be taking this slow."

She licked her lips. "And number two?"

"If I take you here, I'll be thinking about it every time I step inside this barn. I'll never get any work done. Trust me, I can't afford to get into any more trouble with the boss."

She slumped against the stall, gladness making her light-headed. "You're coming back?"

He frowned. "You haven't hired any help, have you?"

"No."

"Then I'm coming back. I thought you understood that. I just needed time with my kids."

"Thank you, Seth." She cupped his face and gave him a fervent kiss, then took his hand. "Let's do this thing."

His deep, husky chuckle hummed along her skin, raising goose bumps. She led him to the barn door, a giddy impatience quickening her stride. He shoved the door open and Ivy dashed out into the — rain? She was drenched instantly, the icy, relentless downpour sucking the air from her lungs and freezing her in place.

When had it started to *rain*?

Seth appeared beside her, equally soaked, hair flattened to his skull. Rivulets that flashed silver in the moonlight dripped from his nose and chin. He grabbed her hand. "Come on!"

They sprinted to the house, slipping and sliding on the grass. The row of tall, spindly pines to their left swayed and writhed in the wind, the cows' uneasy lowing a distant, eerie soundtrack. Ivy kept up with

Seth as best she could, but somewhere along the way, she stumbled and lost a slipper. Cold seared the sole of her foot, but she almost fell down laughing.

They made it to the porch and turned, gasping, to watch the storm. Thunder rolled and grumbled. Blades of rain thumped at the roof and walloped the mulch in the flower beds. Ivy breathed in quick, rasping shudders, and Seth swore. He grabbed her hand again, pulled her in and shut the door against the fury outside. "We need to get you out of those clothes."

"Isn't that the whole idea?"

He gave her a look, dropped to the floor and fumbled with the laces on his boots. He stared at her mud-splattered foot.

"You lost a slipper."

"I'll find it tomorrow."

He stood and moved to her side, his socks making squelching sounds on the hardwood. "You'll get sick."

She waggled her eyebrows, grabbed his soaking-wet sleeve and led him toward the stairs. "So come warm me up."

"You know what you need?"

"As a matter of fact, I do. If *you* don't, I'll be happy to show you."

*   *   *

SETH LET IVY LEAD him to her bedroom on the second floor. When she turned at the foot of the bed and offered him a come-hither smile, he smiled back, bent at the knees and scooped her off the floor.

She gasped out a laugh, her arms automatically winding around his neck. "Don't you dare throw me on the bed. I'll get the sheets wet."

He didn't answer, just carried her into the bathroom. He set her down, shoved back the shower curtain — the rows of bright pink ruffles shocked him, as he'd never have taken her for a girlie girl — and turned on the water.

"Strip," he said.

She hesitated, then reached for her braid. Slowly, her fingers unraveled her pale blond hair. "You first," she countered, all seductive and throaty, and his body tightened painfully. Hell, he

201

couldn't have gotten any harder even if she'd been on her knees and wrapping her lips around him—

His thighs went rigid and he groaned. All right, so he *could* get harder.

Her mouth curved as she watched him, her cheeks losing their fever stain of insecurity. Her gaze dropped to his groin, and she licked her lips.

Jesus.

But he couldn't move, didn't dare take his eyes off her. How many times had he fantasized about seeing her hair free of its braid? He told her as much and her lips curved into a startled smile.

Seth stood, transfixed by the slow rise of her arms as her hands climbed their way up her braid. Her breasts pushed forward, the rigid nipples poking at her pajama top. His palms itched to cup their fun-sized warmth. Despite the wet chill of his clothes, he started to sweat, and it had nothing to do with the steam rapidly filling the white-tiled room.

He took a step forward and she froze. He was about to choke out a question about second thoughts when her eyes went wide and she shoved her face into the crook of her elbow. A pair of sneezes jolted her and echoed around the bathroom. She lowered her arm and with a blissful sigh slumped back against the counter. The soap dish rattled out of her way.

"I'm not certain I need you after that," she said, her voice languid. The feral gleam in her eyes put the lie to her words.

"Oh, you need me." He leaned back and without looking turned the water off, then moved in on Ivy, gripping her hips and pushing in between her thighs. Her harsh inhale as he flexed against her went straight to his head, the sound more potent than a double shot of—

The thought imploded when she flung her legs around him. The heavy tension in his groin tipped him toward madness when she nestled him against her red-hot center. She was rubbing up against him again, even before wrapping her arms around his neck. She closed her teeth on his chin.

He moaned, and his vision grayed. Or was that the damned steam?

Skin. He needed skin. And mouth. And tongue.

He reared back and winced at the scrape of teeth as she released his chin. He imagined that same sensation on his torso as she worked her way down his body and his pulse went damned near through the roof. He fumbled for the hem of her shirt and shoved his hands beneath the sodden material. Her skin was chilled and so smooth. He rubbed his palms over her back, lowered his head and helped himself to a mouthful of neck.

Damn, she tasted sweet.

So strong and yet so delicate.

She shuddered. He rubbed harder, warming her, tormenting himself. She continued to writhe against his hard-on, pulling his breath out of his lungs in harsh, heaving gasps. Much more of that, and he was going to blow.

"We need to get into that shower," he mumbled. He nipped the underside of her jaw and forced himself to step back. She tensed her legs, trapping him, and trailed her fingers down his chest to his abs.

"You're shaking, too," she said.

"Not from the cold." One upward tug, and her top was off. *Oh, yeah.* He stared at her perfect breasts, with pink nipples jutting in sweet invitation, and licked lips gone suddenly dry. *Beautiful,* he tried to say, but what came out of his throat wasn't even a word.

Shit, had that been a whimper?

"*Seth,*" she choked out, and grabbed for him. Her top landed on the floor with a wet slap as their bodies collided. She stretched upward, mouth seeking, hands shoving at his shirt. Her hips returned to shimmy mode as she urged his arms over his head. With a muffled sound of protest, she broke their frantic kiss so he could peel off his waterlogged tee. She leaned forward to help, and her nipples grazed his chest. He jerked, swore, and fought to free himself. Ivy giggled.

Finally, he tossed aside his tee and reached for her. She leaned away, eyes round, breasts trembling.

"My God, you're ripped," she breathed.

She touched him almost reverently, half moaning, half humming as she smoothed her palms over his pecs and across his stomach. Then she yanked him close again, her knees high and tight against his lower back. She tugged his head down for another frantic kiss.

"Easy," he begged against her mouth.

"Walker," she panted.

"Millbrook," he groaned.

"This obsession with the shower. You planning to do me in there?"

"I was hoping you were planning to do *me*."

"Can we get on with it, then," she huffed, "because I really do need to—"

She went rigid. Her head dropped back and her body followed. He caught her before she smacked into the mirror, reveling in the keening sound she made and the convulsive movement of her sweat-slick throat as she climaxed. Her hips jerked against his, over and over, and it was all he could do not to follow suit.

Finally, she went limp. Hand cradling her head, he kissed her lightly, then pulled free and pushed upright.

He ran a shaking hand through his hair. He'd never witnessed anything sexier.

"I need to see that again," he said.

She laughed weakly. "I wouldn't mind a repeat myself."

He took advantage of her relaxed state, pulling off her pajama bottoms and the satiny bit of material he was in too much of a hurry to admire. He dropped the clothes on the floor and stared at her legs and her hips and the glory in between.

His erection swelled further and he hissed in a breath. His junk felt as if it were trapped in a condom five sizes too small. Ivy rose up onto her elbows, caught him staring and flushed. She reached for him.

He pulled her to her feet. "Not on the counter."

"First you say no to the barn, and now to the bathroom... Choosy, are we?"

"I said no to the bathroom counter." He stood back and, with extreme caution, unzipped his fly. Since everything was soaked, it took more effort than he'd expected to peel off his jeans and boxers. By the time he had them down to his ankles, he'd bitten out every cuss word in the book and was breathing as though he and Ivy had already gone two rounds.

A snort had him glancing up as he tugged his feet free. She had her arms crossed under her breasts, smirking as she watched him struggle. Then he straightened, and the amusement on her face shifted to greed. He let her give him the once-over, the hot wonder in her expression damned gratifying.

"Just to make it clear," he said, "this isn't gratitude sex. It's not comfort sex, either."

"Then what is it?"

"Desperate sex. As in, I've been desperate to get your clothes off for a year now."

"They're off. Now what are you going to do?"

He looked at the pile, then back at her. "Hide them."

* * *

IVY BACKED UNDER THE spray of water and moaned. The delicious warmth pelting her skin was bliss compared to the chilly rain outside, but that wasn't why she'd let loose a sensual hum. Seth stalked her, his face taut with erotic intensity, his jutting erection as impressive as the rest of him.

Hoo, boy.

He pressed against her, and finally, *finally*, she was free to take what she'd been craving for months.

"Hello," she rasped. She raised a hand and stroked her thumb over his lips. She lowered her other hand and gripped him.

He jerked, and his eyelids fluttered. "Hell-*o*."

Slowly she stroked him, her fist caught between their bodies, her mouth lifted and open, desperate for his kiss. He braced his palms on the shower wall behind her and lowered his head. With his lips, tongue and teeth, he seduced her mouth, while she worked his shaft with one hand and tangled the other in his sopping hair. The steam rose around them, cocooning them in an intimate mist.

"Ivy," he groaned. He lowered a hand to her breast and began to play. She twitched and squirmed and finally released his rigid length. Pried his left hand off the wall and clamped it to her other breast.

"Fair is fair," she panted.

She felt his chuckle deep in her belly. He cupped and plucked and caressed until she could barely stand upright. Then his hands swooped down to her ass and he lifted her up and lip-locked a breast. She gasped, sucking in water along with air. She started to cough.

He pressed her into the corner, guiding her legs around his hips. "You okay?"

She palmed his shoulders and nodded, staring down into his half-lidded eyes with their X-rated gleam and spiky lashes. Dear God, the man was sexy. His cock blazed against her core and she couldn't keep her hips from starting up a gentle bounce. Her entire body throbbed and tingled.

She leaned down and caught his ear between her teeth. "I can't believe you're in my shower," she whispered, and hugged him tight. "Of all the fantasies I've indulged in since we met, the shower is one place I never pictured us having sex."

"I'd like to hear about those fantasies." He gripped her hips and backed away. Jaw rigid, mouth tight, he slowly coaxed her legs to the floor. "But this one we'll have to indulge another time."

It was all she could do not to wail. *"Why?"*

"I forgot the condoms in the truck."

Ivy blinked. "I have some. Somewhere. Hazel gave them to me." She laughed at his expression and shook her head. "Don't ask. We don't need them, anyway. I'm protected." She tipped her head. "Plus I owe you one." With a cheeky smile, she slid her hands down his chest to his waist and sank to her knees.

*   *   *

IN THE DIM GLOW cast by the floor lamp on the far side of the room, Seth stared down at Ivy, wondering how the hell he'd held out against this for so long. He knew *why*, and his reasons still existed, but they were damned difficult to bring to mind when he had this gorgeous, giving woman sprawled beneath him, her pale skin luminous against dark purple sheets, her hips pressing up against his in breathtaking demand.

Her damp wavy hair lay spread across her pillow, her face flushed, her lips pink and swollen. The thought of what those lips had done for him just a short while ago sent him surging against her. She caught

206

her breath and wrapped her legs around him, offering herself up to him, begging for him. When he hesitated, she dug her fingers into his scalp, reared up and nipped his lower lip.

"It's not nice to tease," she growled against his mouth.

"You should know something," he said. "This is going to be embarrassingly brief."

"Don't worry, I'll let you make it up to me."

"That's big of you."

She dropped back onto the pillows and grinned up at him. "Fishing for compliments?"

"Would it hurt so much to point and gasp?"

That earned a full-fledged laugh. "Trust me, I did. At least in my head." She sobered and pressed her hand to his heart. "I can't believe you're in my bed."

Beneath her touch, his chest blazed. "I can do better than that," he said huskily, and pushed forward.

Her eyes widened and she arched off the bed. "Seth," she gasped.

He eased out and pushed again, filling her this time, gritting his teeth when she squeezed him so tightly he feared "brief" might be an overstatement.

She stiffened and drew in a ragged breath. Her hands clenched his biceps. "Wait," she murmured.

He froze. "Did I hurt you?" He started to pull out, stopped when she pressed her hips tighter to his. His arms shook as he fought the urge to move.

"No, it's just..." She quivered. Her eyes went soft as she stroked her hands down his back. She gripped his ass and tugged and squirmed even closer when he groaned. "I can't believe you're in my—"

He shut her up by taking her mouth, then thrust his hips and took her breath.

* * *

IVY LAY STRETCHED AGAINST Seth's right side, her leg across his thighs, her palm pressed to his left pec. Her skin was so sensitized that whenever she shifted position, the rough brush of his leg hair against her inner thigh had her vibrating. Or maybe that was still the aftershock from two of the most intense orgasms she'd ever had.

And those were on top of the one she'd thrashed her way through on the bathroom counter.

Wind pressed the dark against the windows, and the panes gave a muffled rattle. Her room was dark, as well — Seth had turned off the light when he'd gotten up to fetch them water. They both needed sleep, since three in the morning insisted on arriving daily at a ridiculous hour.

She was too stirred up to sleep.

Seth, in her bed... She could hardly believe it. The sex had been fantastic. The cozy intimacy afterward? Better still. The drugging combination of the consideration he'd shown her and the demands he'd made?

Scary as hell. She'd never enjoyed a man more.

He lifted his arm and bent it behind his head, and the flex of muscle made her mouth go dry. She shifted against him. His fingers stopped their lazy travels up and down her arm.

"Cold?"

She shook her head. She wasn't sure she'd ever be cold again.

"You're quiet," he said. When she didn't respond, he scooted down and turned on his side so they lay face-to-face. He rested his head on his bent arm and smoothed her hair behind her ear. "You okay?"

"I'm trying to decide whether or not I'm speaking to you."

"You just did."

She pushed at his shoulder, found she couldn't let go and caressed his skin down to his elbow. Damn, the man had muscles. "From now on, I mean."

"Because..."

"You've been holding out on me. All this time, we could have been doing *that*."

He grinned. "You liked that, huh?"

"I did. I liked it a lot."

"You know what I like?"

She tensed, and he took his time finishing the thought. Finally, he gripped her thigh and rolled over onto his back, bringing her with him. She sprawled on top of him, amazed when she felt him stirring against her stomach. He didn't make any moves, though. Instead he spread his arms and legs and moved them up and down, as if he were making snow angels.

"I like these sheets," he said.

She let her hair drape over his chest as she bent her head and licked a nipple. "You have good taste. Also, you're weird."

"They're too smooth, though. They could use a few wrinkles." He flipped her over again and bounced a few times.

Ivy squealed and threw her arms over her head. "Wrinkle away."

* * *

WHEN IVY AWOKE, HER back was pressed against Seth's front, her head beneath his chin. He traced lazy circles on her hip under the covers he'd pulled up and tucked around her. She huffed a contented sigh, shoving away the knowledge that morning was coming at them faster than the Jersey girls after spotting her with a bucket of feed.

Slowly, she registered that Seth had stiffened behind her. Every part of him, not just the star of last night's show.

"Do you have to go?" she whispered.

"Not unless you want me to."

"No." She turned her head and stared through the darkness at the ceiling. "What's bothering you?"

Sheets rustled as his legs moved restlessly. "Can I ask you a question?"

She nodded and held her breath.

"I was thinking about your daughter."

Ivy swallowed, the sound a loud gurgle in the quiet of her bedroom. It took a few tries to squeeze words out of a throat gone narrow. "I think of her as Hannah."

"Hannah," he repeated. "That's beautiful. The other day, you said she was eleven. Since yesterday was her birthday, she's twelve now?"

"Yes." She rolled over onto her back. Seth scooted aside to give her room, his hand remaining warm on her stomach. It was easier to talk about her in the obscurity of night, prodded by friendly curiosity rather than judgment.

What a sweet relief, actually, that someone else knew the story.

"I think about it a lot," she murmured. "What it might be like to meet her. To spend time with her."

"Is that why you give tours for the kids? Because you're looking for her?"

Ivy gasped, feeling as though someone had stuffed her lungs with dryer lint. "Maybe. I'd...never thought of it that way." It was amazing how insightful Seth could be. Amazing and terrifying. "Anyway, I keep coming back to — why would she want anything to do with the woman who gave her away? I've seen enough Lifetime movies to know it rarely works out the way you want it to."

"How do you want it to work out?"

She rolled again, pushing Seth onto his back. She slid on top of him, stacked her palms on his chest and propped her chin on her hands. He sat up enough to jam a folded pillow under his head, then lay back down, one hand between the pillow and his head, the other toying with her hair. She hummed in appreciation at the up-close-and-personal view of his bulging biceps.

"Ivy?"

She sighed and met his gaze in the scant light, courtesy of the moon. His brown eyes were sleepy and warm with caring.

"You look at me like that," she muttered, "and it's all I can do not to..."

The hand in her hair stilled. "Yeah?"

He hardened beneath her and she gave a slight snort. "Even the suggestion of a suggestion perks you up."

"Hey. We have a lot of catching up to do." When she licked her lips and started to wriggle downward, he tightened his hand in her hair to stop her. "Ivy," he groaned. "I can't believe I'm asking this, but could you hold that thought? I'd like to hear what you have to say about Hannah."

"You're relentless."

"You're not answering my question."

She sighed and rested her cheek on her hands.

He pressed his lips to the top of her head. "Tell me."

"I...hope she's growing up knowing she was adopted." She swallowed a surge of tears. "I hope they told her she's extra special because they chose her. I dream it's no big deal to her, being adopted, because she knows she couldn't be loved more. Because —" she was barely choking out the words now " — maybe then she won't hate me so much."

"Ivy." He banded his arms across her back and squeezed tight. "Shh. She doesn't hate you, baby."

"I would. I would hate me."

He shook her lightly. "Stop beating yourself up for making the best decision you could at the time."

"I should have kept her. I was her *mother*. I should never have let her go."

"But you did. Because you were eighteen, and because you loved her."

Ivy breathed in the salty, musky scent of warm, well-worked male, lifted her head and kissed his hard chest. She didn't know about all that, but she loved that he was trying to make her feel better.

Seth to the rescue. Frowning, she nudged the thought aside.

"Thank you," she said.

"You're welcome."

"Speaking of kids." She lifted her head again and gave a contented sigh when his fingers tunneled through her hair. "That's a big deal, isn't it, that you let them leave with your ex?"

"I wouldn't have if I thought they needed me."

"Often I wonder if you need them more."

His hand stilled. "You're saying I should let them be more independent."

"A little."

"So today was a good start." He lifted up and squinted at the clock on the nightstand. "*Yesterday* was a good start."

"A very good start."

"For you, too." He slid his hands along the sides of her chest and pulled, his erection paying more and more attention as she slid up his body. "For such an independent woman, you seemed awfully needy a little while ago."

Despite his teasing tone, panic flickered. She willed it away.

"Still am," she said. Leaning in for a hot, heady kiss, she worked her pelvis. "Now about that thought you asked me to hold."

*　*　*

THE RAIN WOKE HER. It had started up again with a vengeance, slapping against the windows and tapping steadily on the roof. Damn. Slogging around from building to building to get the animals fed promised to be an unholy mess. No doubt the cows were already gathered in the bedding barn, eager to fill their bellies.

Her own belly muttered at her. She'd been too upset to eat last night, and a sudden spurt of nausea had her tossing back the covers and feeling for her slippers.

Oh. Right. Her slippers had been ruined. She'd have to get a new pair.

She shifted around gently and stared down at Seth. He lay on his stomach, both hands tucked under his pillow, the covers gathered at his hips. His back rose and fell with steady breaths, and even in the dim light, she could see the start of a beard shadowing his jaw.

Her hands tingled with the need to stroke his skin and her chest ached. She'd wondered what it would be like to work at his side, day after day. Now she couldn't help wondering what it would be like to spend her nights with him, too. To laugh and cuddle and talk and explore and make love.

To not be alone.

She surged to her feet and grabbed her robe. *Make love.* Not a good idea to think of it like that. Better to call it...affectionate sex.

Quietly, she made her way downstairs, not bothering to turn on the lights. In the kitchen, she snagged a banana from the bowl on the island and wandered into the sunroom as she chewed.

She stared through the glass into the darkness beyond, watching the night weep, despairing because she'd just spent the most fulfilling, challenging night ever in a man's arms, yet felt like weeping herself.

He'd heard her secrets. He wanted her anyway. The freedom was intoxicating, the burden crippling. She didn't want to hurt him.

Now there was no way to avoid it.

A light flicked on in the kitchen, and Seth's bare-chested reflection appeared behind hers in the glass. She was relieved to see he'd found his boxers and pulled them on. He wrapped his arms around her and grunted when he felt her shudder. "Come back to bed. I'll see what I can do to get you warm again."

"Seth," she said, squeezing her eyes closed, hating that she was about to turn this into yet another cliché. "We need to talk."

12

SLOWLY, SETH LOOSENED HIS hold and backed away. "That doesn't sound good."

"It's not bad." She set her half-eaten banana aside and tried a smile. "Remember when Grace asked me to remind you you're free to walk away from this, at any time?"

"You know I wouldn't do that. Not when you need help."

"I do know that. I'm not talking about the farm."

He lowered himself into one of the rattan chairs, and settled an ankle on the opposite knee. "What you're trying to tell me," he drawled, "is that whatever this is between us, you want to keep it casual."

"What's between us *is* casual. It always has been. You're the commitment guy, and I'm the good-time girl. Nothing has changed. Maybe I'm not so scared of your kids anymore. Maybe we've proved what we already suspected—that we can rock a bed. I still value my independence."

He leaned back in the chair, hands linked behind his head. Ivy looked away from the lure of his abs.

"I find it hard to believe that someone with the label 'good-time girl' would give a man an entire year to make up his mind about having sex with her."

"I've been busy, and..." Ivy dipped her head and concentrated on retying the belt on her robe "...you were worth the wait."

"Good to know," he said softly. He stood. "You're wrong. Plenty has changed. You're learning to trust. Me, my kids, yourself, too. You know what that means, don't you? You will forgive yourself."

"You think just because you know my biggest regret, you know me, but you don't. You don't know me."

"You won't let me." He reached out and trailed his fingers along the silk arm of her robe. "I couldn't be sorrier about your daughter. But you're kidding yourself if you think you'll ever be fully independent. For twelve years, you've been letting that decision dictate your relationships. Your career, too. You can't tell me there's no connection between your dedication to this farm and your regret over your daughter. Doesn't sound free to me."

"You're making my argument for me. I don't feel free to commit to anyone. I admit I care about your kids, which is why we need to leave them out of this."

"Let me get this straight." He pulled his hand back and crossed his arms. "You and I can hang out as long as the kids aren't around?"

"If you want to, or you might want the weekend to yourself. That wouldn't hurt my feelings." Her mouth tasted sour as she spoke.

His jaw flexed. "You're using her. You're using your daughter as an excuse. You don't believe you have what it takes to be in a committed relationship, and who could blame you, considering what your parents put you through? Not to mention Ethan."

"Evan."

His face changed. He stalked out into the living room, swore under his breath and stalked back, his bare feet making slapping sounds over the hardwood. "Tell me you don't think I'm after this place."

She shoved her hands deep into the pockets of her robe so he wouldn't see her fingers shake. "You tried to talk me into selling, just like he did."

His head went back and his nostrils flared. Moments passed as they stared each other down.

"Besides the fact that downsizing isn't the same as selling, I'm going to let that go because you're scared," Seth finally said. "You're afraid I'll figure out what's behind your need for independence. Yes, you gave up Hannah for adoption, but you didn't deny her a family. She has one, and you have one, too, waiting for you. You may not think you deserve us, but we deserve you."

"Wait." Ivy rubbed her forehead as an unpleasant tingling started up in her belly. "What?"

He moved close again, pulled her hand from her head and pressed it to his chest. "I love you. I've loved you for a long time. Seeing your smile, hearing your laugh, watching you with your animals —" he gave a strained chuckle " —watching you with *my* animals... It's what keeps me going. Last night was mind-blowing. But I don't want to be in your bed, and I don't want you in my bed. I want the two of us in *our* bed."

Ivy was shaking her head as she backed away, but he wouldn't let go of her hand. "Seth—" she choked.

"Ivy Millbrook, will you marry me?"

Oh, God, oh, God, oh, God. When she had nowhere to go because she'd backed all the way up against the window, she closed her eyes, blocking out the earnest hope in his expression. *Coward,* her mind whispered, and she opened her eyes again. A small part of her rejoiced in his words, while the rest of her mourned the loss of their friendship.

"No, Seth," she whispered. "I can't marry you."

His fingers tightened around hers. "Why not?"

Tears scalded the backs of her eyes. "You know why not. You've always known. I'm happy with my life the way it is."

"We both know that's not true. But nothing I say will make a difference because you're hell-bent on punishing yourself." He lifted her hand to his mouth and kissed her fingers. She almost protested when he let go. He pressed his thumb and forefinger into his eyes and shuffled back a few steps. His chest lifted and fell. When he met her gaze again, his expression telegraphed a wrenching distance.

"You matter to me, Ivy," he said, his voice a painful rasp. "I love you, and I want you in my life." He swallowed, and one half of his mouth twitched upward. "This discussion isn't over. We were honest with each other, once upon a time. Maybe you can try to remember how that used to be."

He left the room. Ivy turned back toward the wall of glass. She heard his bare feet going up the steps, and a short while later, he came back down, his boots a steady thud. Regret pushed on her shoulders. She'd meant to put his clothes in the dryer.

But maybe she'd known all along he'd need to make a quick

getaway.

He didn't head straight for the front door. She stared at his reflection in the glass and he stared back, his posture stiff, his face brooding. Her gaze shifted back to her own mirror image, and she swallowed a manic giggle. With her loose hair and oversize robe, the two of them looked like the cover of a 1960s gothic novel.

"You should get some sleep," he said finally. "I'll be back in a few hours to help with the chores."

The drum of rain got louder as he opened the door. She smiled wryly. Just as well she hadn't bothered to dry his clothes, after all.

She sank to the floor and dropped her head to her knees.

* * *

"MARCUS!"

Marcus jolted out of a vivid, sweaty daydream and blinked at Rachel. She stood beside the grill, frowning, hands braced on scrawny hips.

"You're burning my steak sub," she complained.

Shit. The smell of over-caramelized onions finally registered and Marcus jerked the spatula, scraping the ruined beef off the heat, all the while careful not to turn away from the stove. Rachel did *not* need to see the inconvenient side effect of his thoughts of Liz and how they'd been spending their time together. Cal would fire his ass quicker than Noble Johnson could polish off a T-bone.

Though if Marcus kept burning orders, he'd end up fired anyway.

"Give me a minute and I'll cook another one," he said.

Rachel rolled her eyes and went back out front.

Slurping at a diet soda, Parvati tossed her gardening magazine aside, wandered over to Marcus and patted him on the back. "You might want to get your mind back on the business at hand," she said. "At the very least, step away from the stove before you end up roasting your weenie and serving it up on a bun."

Marcus jerked backward and looked down. His apron lay perfectly flat. He turned to scowl at Parvati and spotted Cal standing outside his door, arms crossed.

"Come see me as soon as you finish up that order." Cal shot an indecipherable look at Parvati, turned and disappeared back inside his office.

"That's a pretty shade of pink," Parvati said, head tilted as she studied his face. She winked, picked up her magazine and sat back down. Soda slurped.

Five minutes later, Marcus knocked on Cal's door. Cal swung it open and led Marcus out to the counter. The diner was busy for a Thursday night, but Cal didn't look happy. He peered around, as if to make sure the servers were occupied in the dining room, and gestured for Marcus to step closer.

"I went back through my records and found something interesting," Cal said. "Most of the money goes missing on this shift, as you already suspected. The week you and Parvati were gone, we ran pretty much on target. We both know neither of you is guilty." He sighed and rubbed a palm over his bristly hair. "I'm thinking about that camera idea, though I hate the thought of spying on my employees. You know I consider you family."

"Someone in your family is stealing from you."

Cal gestured and Marcus stopped talking. They moved out of the way as Rachel came up to the register to ring up an order, at the same time asking Parvati to get her a to-go container. Parvati had to ask the teen to repeat herself, and it gratified Marcus to hear Rachel patiently grant the older woman's request. The cash register drawer dinged open, Rachel leaned to the side to grab a bag, and when Parvati turned back around with the container, she caught the edge of the drawer she didn't realize was open.

"Ouch," she muttered, and rubbed her side.

Marcus went still. He glanced around the dining room, touched Cal on the arm and returned to the kitchen.

Frowning, Cal followed him. "What is it?"

"Two hours till closing." Marcus took off his apron and held it out. "You're going to have to man the grill tonight. I have an idea."

* * *

FOR THE NEXT NINETY minutes, Marcus sat wedged in a corner in the rear portion of the dining room, out of sight of the diner's front door. Cal had asked Parvati and Rachel to act as if he weren't even there. He said he'd given Marcus some paperwork to do that required total concentration. The servers had been bewildered but obedient. They hadn't so much as looked Marcus's way.

When Cal sent Rachel home early, Parvati hadn't complained. She was grateful for the extra tip money, though there weren't many more customers to wait on that evening.

Twenty minutes before they were scheduled to close, one of Cal's regulars, Jasper Cole, came in and shuffled up to the counter. He owned a landscaping business and in the winter months did a brisk trade selling firewood. Since he was wearing faded overalls, a padded plaid jacket and work boots, Marcus figured he must be coming off a long day.

Jasper greeted Parvati, then started to cough. He held up a finger and coughed a good long while, Parvati making sympathetic noises the whole time. Finally, he turned back to the counter, ran a hand through his thick gray hair and ordered half a dozen cinnamon rolls. Parvati told him she'd have to check in the back. As soon as she disappeared into the kitchen, Jasper began hacking again. He kept it up as he leaned across the counter, hit a button on the register and started plucking bills out of the open drawer.

Marcus sighed, pushed to his feet and strolled up to the counter. "That's a nasty cough you got there, Mr. Cole."

Jasper jerked away from the register. His elbow caught the plastic charity jar and it hit the floor with a hollow, jingling rattle, then rolled across the linoleum. Red faced and wheezing, Jasper watched the jar until it came to a rest beneath the gumball machine. His gaze lifted to Marcus. He swallowed.

"I, uh..." His jaw twitched toward the counter behind him. "I was looking for some cough syrup."

"In the cash register?"

Jasper went still, then pressed a hand to his chest and burst into a coughing fit. He struggled to suck in air, and his face turned tomato red. *Oh, shit.* Marcus lunged forward, digging for his phone so he could call 911. Jasper opened one eye and closed it just as quickly.

Marcus jolted to a stop. "Cut the act, Mr. Cole, or when the EMTs get here I'll tell them you need your stomach pumped."

Jasper let out one last choking gasp. When Marcus stood unmoved, the landscaper straightened and heaved a gusty sigh.

"EMTs?" Cal stood behind the counter, a stack of receipts in his hand. His gaze landed on the open cash drawer. "Jasper? Want to tell me what's going on?"

Jasper tossed the bills on the counter. "Guess you can figure it out."

For a long moment, Cal stared down at the money. "Want to tell me why?"

"Does it matter?" Jasper asked sourly.

"Marcus, call the sheriff."

Marcus nodded. *Fucking A.*

"Wait. *Wait.*" Jasper lifted shaking hands. His jaw bobbed, but words didn't emerge.

The door to the walk-in fridge closed with a metallic clunk and Parvati appeared, a bakery box in her hands. Sensing tension, she stopped short.

"What's going on?" Her voice wavered.

Cal leaned on the counter, his expression grave. "That's what I'm trying to find out. I thought business was good, Jasper. The weather's changing, so plenty of folks will need firewood. Your customers not paying their bills?"

Jasper was shaking his head. "Business is fine, and I already got more orders for wood than I can handle." He scrubbed his fingers across his scalp, hard enough to draw blood. "It's my wife."

Marcus shifted his feet as sympathy stirred. "She's sick?"

"She's a bitch."

Cal pushed upright and slapped the countertop. "This is about being able to pay for a *divorce*?"

"Hell, no. Just because she's a bitch doesn't mean I don't love her. Nah, this is about being able to pay for cigarettes."

Marcus eyed Jasper doubtfully. "Your wife doesn't know you smoke?"

"How is that possible?" Cal asked.

Jasper shrugged. "Separate bedrooms." He glanced at each of them, then slumped down onto the nearest stool. "Thing is, I get an allowance, and it doesn't cover the cost of my smokes."

Cal rubbed a hand over his face. "Sorry I asked."

Jasper swiveled around to face him. "I know it was wrong. But it was so easy." His expression turned crafty. "Too easy. You might even say I did you a favor. Parvati here needs to—"

"Do not go there."

Marcus blinked. Never before had he heard that spike of danger in Cal's voice.

"Fine," Jasper said hastily.

"Go ahead and start closing up," Cal said to Parvati, then gave Marcus a nod. "You can call the sheriff now."

After Sheriff Tate had hauled Jasper Cole away, the landscaper begging the whole time for another chance, and an indignant but relieved Parvati had headed home, Cal walked Marcus to his pickup and thanked him for cracking the case.

"How'd you figure it out?"

"When Parvati backed into the cash drawer because she didn't hear it open, I realized that if someone were to make a lot of noise at the counter, we'd never know what they were up to. All they had to do was get rid of Parvati for a few minutes."

"Hence Jasper's addiction to my cinnamon rolls."

Marcus nodded. "He'd figured out we keep the leftovers in the walk-in."

When they reached Marcus's truck, Cal offered his hand. "I can't thank you enough. The peace of mind you've given me tonight... I'm damned grateful."

Marcus flushed. "You're welcome."

"There'll be a bonus in your next paycheck." Cal raised an eyebrow. "Assuming you can stop wasting food while daydreaming about your girlfriend."

Marcus should have been embarrassed, but he couldn't stop a wide-ass grin from spreading across his face. "I'll see what I can do."

*   *   *

AN ENTIRE WEEK HAD passed since Seth had proposed. On the farm, they managed as they had before, working together efficiently, if not harmoniously. Off the farm — there was no such thing. No phone calls, no late-night visits. She and Seth never did have that talk he'd threatened, which relieved Ivy. Things were complicated enough.

Besides, he was right. There was a time when she'd prided herself on the honesty they'd shared. Then it got to be too damned difficult to tell the truth, even to herself.

No wonder she was finding it harder than ever to get to sleep. Seth had spent a matter of hours in her bed and she missed him as though it had been months. His warmth, his solidness, his scent — she wanted it all back. But having it meant questioning her entire way of life, and opening herself up to hurts she'd spent years burying. She couldn't bring herself to do either.

The fact that he'd asked her to marry him... She still couldn't wrap her mind around that. How could he possibly know, after one night together, that he wanted to spend the rest of his life with her? Still, she couldn't help replaying his proposal over and over in her brain. His expression, his grip on her hands, his words... *You matter to me.*

Choked her up, every time.

He mattered to her, too, and she didn't know if she'd ever have the guts to tell him.

She knocked off work early that Friday afternoon. She had cheesecake orders to fill over the weekend, so she let Seth and Dell finish up the milking while she got down to business in the kitchen, grateful she wouldn't have to see the grim beauty of Seth's face every time she looked up.

The house was relatively quiet. Since the kids had finished their homework, Hazel and Travis were playing a surprisingly pedestrian card game at the dining room table, while Grace watched an animated mystery series on TV. Why did the characters always have such high-pitched, know-it-all voices?

Still, Ivy welcomed the normalcy of it. She and Seth had both been concerned that after what had happened with Gary, the kids wouldn't want to return to the farm. He'd offered them an alternative, having them stay with their neighbor Mrs. Yackley, but once Travis and Grace had been assured that Gary wouldn't ever be coming back and had in fact been transferred to the city jail miles and miles away, they'd settled in again, more easily than anyone could have imagined.

Ivy was cracking eggs when Grace screamed. The sound ripped through her and she flung two halves of a shell up in the air before grabbing a dish towel and dashing out to the living room. She found Grace shaking in Hazel's arms, muttering about a snake. Travis was turning in eager circles, and Hazel was shooting Ivy a *What the hell?* look.

"I saw a snake!" Grace cried.

Ivy blinked. It was too cold for snakes. Wasn't it too cold for snakes?

Had the damned thing been living in her house?

She suppressed a shudder, tried not to think of Snoozy's python and curved her lips in what she hoped was a calming smile.

"Where did it go, sweetie?" she asked Grace.

Grace pointed behind the TV.

"Cool," Travis crowed, and rushed in that direction. Ivy headed him off at the pass and told him to sit on the couch. Grumbling, he complied. When he suddenly went quiet, Ivy glanced over her shoulder. His gaze was swinging from his sister's face to the TV and back again, a scowl scrunching his nose. He'd realized how upset Grace was at the prospect of a creepy-crawly in the house.

Ivy wasn't thrilled about it, either.

She moved between Grace and the television, promising herself that if something *was* back there, it wouldn't attack her from behind. This time the shudder got the best of her.

She drew in a breath. "What color was it?"

"B-black."

Good. That was good. Black was much better than brown.

"I'm going to get a flashlight and take a look," Ivy said. "No one move, okay? I'll be right back."

When she came back toting a broom, as well, Hazel snorted.

Ivy shrugged. "No shame in being prepared."

The television sat in a bulky cabinet pushed against the far left corner of the living room. Ivy had always meant to find a better place for it, but since she rarely watched TV downstairs, she'd never made it a priority. The TV was old, the cabinet older, but at least the thing had rollers. She gripped the flashlight in one hand and the broom in the other, gave momentary thought to summoning Dell or Seth, then settled her weight against the cabinet. Slowly, it rolled to the left, giving her just enough space to peer behind it.

Please, God, don't let there be anything moving back there.

She leaned around the cabinet cautiously and played the flashlight all around the cramped space. Nothing but dust. She exhaled.

"Is he back there?" Travis asked. The quiet concern in his voice just about melted Ivy's heart.

"All clear," she said, and straightened. Too late, she realized the thing could have crawled *underneath* the cabinet and at that very moment might be slithering across her feet. She did a little backward dance, not blaming Hazel a bit when the old woman snorted again. Just to be sure, Ivy lowered herself to her knees and took a cautious look.

She caught the squeal before it left her throat. She fished the cord free, got to her feet and beckoned to Grace. Her heart squeezed when she saw that somehow Grace had gotten hold of her lavender cashmere scarf. The little girl had draped it around her neck and was petting it.

"Mystery solved," Ivy said lightly, and brandished the coaxial cable. "You're absolutely right — it does look like a snake. It must have been loose and just happened to fall while you were watching."

Grace bit her lip and nodded, while Travis chewed a thumbnail.

Ivy turned away. She'd have to make sure Seth knew what had happened. Regret pinched as she attacked the dust in the corner with the broom, then pushed the cabinet back into place. She'd worry about the cord later.

Meanwhile, Hazel clapped her hands. "Okay, Travis. Shall we get back to our card game, and let Miss Ivy get back to her baking? You, too, Grace. Leave the scarf, hon. Come help your brother trounce me at Uno. Winner gets to give Baby Blue a bath the next time I bring him over."

As Ivy turned the corner into the kitchen, she heard Travis mutter something about forgetting his cards. At the same time she realized she'd left the dish towel by the television. When she took a step into the living room, she noticed Travis standing by the sofa, craning his neck toward the dining room, as if making sure he couldn't be seen. He rolled something up and tucked it into the sleeve of his jacket. Then he scooped up his cards and hurried back to the table.

Ivy backed into the kitchen slowly. Travis had taken her scarf. To get back at her for some reason? To tease Grace by hiding it from her? He must have realized how much it comforted her.

She let her head drop back against the wall. Should she say anything? Or should she tell Seth and let him handle it?

Why don't you grow a pair, Millbrook, and take care of it yourself?

Seth had already mentioned Travis's sticky fingers. She wouldn't be doing anyone any favors by letting this slide.

Besides. The kid had nabbed her favorite scarf.

She walked back through the kitchen into the dining room, where Grace was giggling into her fist as Hazel drew card after card from the stack on the table—and not for the first time, considering the number of cards she already held.

"Would you mind if I borrow Travis?" Ivy asked lightly. "I could use some help checking on something outside."

"You couldn't have come for him a few minutes sooner?" grumbled Hazel. She shifted her cards to her other hand and shook her fingers.

"Miss Hazel's losing." Grace smirked, and Ivy blinked. G hadn't frowned at her once today. Because she knew their time at the farm was about to come to an end?

Her shoulders curved inward. She concentrated on hanging on to her smile and turned to Travis. Wariness had dimmed the blue of his eyes.

"What do you say?" Ivy was already wondering what on earth had made her think she could handle a situation like this. "Want to take a quick walk with me?"

He squirmed in his chair. "Can Grace come?"

"Your sister's going to help me organize my hand," Hazel said, with a sly wink at Ivy. "You go on ahead, hon. We promise not to look at your cards while you're gone."

Ivy pulled her plaid jacket from the closet and shrugged it on. Behind her, Travis was struggling with his own jacket. She gave him a few moments, then turned just as he was tugging the tail end of her scarf free of his sleeve.

"Thank you, Travis," she said cheerfully. She took the scarf from him and wrapped it around her neck. "All set?"

Glumly, he followed her to the door and down the porch steps. The late afternoon sun gilded her driveway, her outbuildings, her fences and her fields with a glow that after a hard day's work she normally would have regarded with satisfaction. But today it just reminded her of the passing of time.

Her chest began to ache with a fierceness that yanked the breath right out of her. Suddenly, she found herself blinking back tears at the prospect of never again taking a walk with the boy at her side, who smelled like magic markers and had a smile sweeter than apple juice.

"Where are we going?" he mumbled. "Are we checking on Priscilla Mae?"

Ivy shook her head. "See that tree over there?" With her left hand, she pointed at a crimson maple on the far side of the milk shed. "That's where we're going."

Scattered leaves crackled and crunched as he trotted to catch up, eyes glued to her right hand. "What are those for?" He'd spotted the binoculars she'd grabbed from the closet shelf.

"Follow me and I'll show you."

Five minutes later, a wide grin split his face as he angled the binoculars upward and spotted the tree dweller Ivy had nicknamed Chubs. Chubs was a plump ball of white and gray fur, with beady black eyes and long pink toes curled tightly around the branches he was perched on while he stared down at Travis as intently as the little boy stared up at him.

"Cool," Travis said reverently, leaning so far back Ivy expected him to fall on his butt.

"He likes horse feed," she said. "And chicken feed and cat food and pretty much anything he can scavenge. But he likes horse feed best. One evening after I shooed him away from the barn, it was still light, and I followed him here."

Travis stumbled two steps closer to the tree, binoculars still pressed against his face. "He's not scared," he said breathlessly.

"I guess he knows we won't hurt him."

Finally, Travis lowered the binoculars and frowned up at Ivy. "I thought possums only came out after dark."

Ivy chuckled. "I think Chubs likes to get a head start on dinner."

They watched the possum watching them for a few more minutes. Then Travis reluctantly surrendered the field glasses.

"Thank you for showing him to me," Travis said.

"You're welcome."

He stared at the binoculars in her hands and bit his lip. "You know what I did, don't you?" He stole a glance upward and spotted her nod. His shoulders collapsed, while the toe of his sneaker explored an exposed root. "It's easier when everyone's in bed," he said.

"That makes sense." Ivy couldn't help a smile. "Kind of like possums. It's harder to spot them in the dark."

Travis swallowed. "You going to tell my dad?"

The vulnerability in his expression reminded her of Seth, when he'd asked her to marry him. Ivy's heart tumbled. She lowered herself to her knees and squeezed the boy's shoulder.

"Travis. You should never take something that belongs to someone else. Not without permission. You know that, right?"

His shoulder lifted. Part shrug, part objection to her touch. She pulled her hand away and he plastered his chin to his chest. "But if I asked, you'd want to know why."

"I think I already know why."

His head came up. "You do?"

"You want Grace to have it."

He nodded, his eyes wide.

"Is it her birthday?"

Disappointment clouded his face and he shook his head.

"Is it because it made her feel good?"

Another nod. The wariness had returned to his face.

Now what? She had a strong feeling she should have left the parenting to Seth.

She shifted, her knees already stiffening from their exposure to the cold ground. "So, these things you've been...collecting. They're for Grace?"

"She has nightmares." Nylon rustled as he pushed his hands into his jacket pockets. His chin came forward, as though he expected Ivy to make fun.

She folded her arms, hugging the binoculars to her chest. "I'm sorry to hear that. But...have you actually given her any of the things you've taken?"

"I'm saving them."

"For what?"

"For when a snake comes out of the wall."

And just like that, it all made sense. Her throat throbbed with a hot, thick swell of compassion. *Oh, Travis.*

She forced herself to swallow. "Like at Joe's motel."

Travis nodded energetically. "If a snake comes out of the wall, we have to run. We won't have time to get our stuff. But I have everything Grace needs in my pillowcase, so I can just grab that, and wherever we end up, she won't have nightmares, 'cause I'll have all her favorite things with me."

"That's good thinking," Ivy managed. She dropped back on her heels and took a moment to blink the searing damp from her eyes. "But, sweetie, I promise you, there isn't a python living in your walls."

He couldn't have looked more doubtful if she'd told him Priscilla Mae was an international assassin in disguise. "How do you know that?"

"Because the python Joe found was a pet that accidentally got loose. She was looking for a warm place to live and came across the motel. It was old and run-down and had a lot of holes and openings, so it was easy for her to get in. Your house isn't like that. Besides, I don't know anyone else in Thistle Hill who owns a python. Do you?"

Travis rubbed his chin with his thumb and forefinger, as if testing for a beard. "Could be a copperhead."

"Could be. Except copperheads would rather live in the woods than in the walls, with a bunch of dust and insulation. You wouldn't want to live in the walls, would you?" When he shook his head, she pushed to her feet. "Have you heard any noises that would make you think there's something in your walls?"

The front door opened and Grace came out onto the porch. She wrapped an arm around a column and looked around and, when she spotted them, waved them in. "Are you done yet?" she yelled.

"We'll be right in," Ivy called back. Grace hesitated, then went back inside. Ivy leaned down and tugged lightly on the zipper of Travis's jacket.

"You need to talk to your dad about this. Maybe all three of you could have a family meeting and figure this out together."

He stuck out his bottom lip. "Think Dad'll be mad at me?"

"I think he'll wish you'd talked to him sooner. I also think he'll be proud of you for doing such a good job looking out for your sister. In fact..." she tugged the scarf free of her neck and held it out "...you're absolutely right. Grace needs this more than I do."

Travis beamed up at her, the delight on his face rivaling the gleam of the sun on his hair. "Thank you, Miss Ivy." He tucked it under his arm and tipped his head back, angling for another glimpse of the possum. "Can we come back and check on Chubs again?"

"Whenever you want."

"Cool." He spun away and broke for the house, legs churning so fast they were practically a blur. One end of the cashmere scarf trailed behind him. He stopped suddenly, kicked at something on the ground, then started running again. Twenty steps later, Ivy spotted what had captured his attention.

The slipper she'd lost in the rain. She picked it up with two fingers and carried it to the trash bins behind the house.

*   *   *

AN HOUR LATER, WHEN Seth came in to pick up the kids, Ivy asked Hazel to stay a few extra minutes and invited Seth into her office.

He shut the door behind him, his eyes as guarded as his son's had been when she'd invited Travis for a walk. She rushed to explain.

"I know why things are disappearing at your house." She told him about the incident with the "snake" and what Travis had confessed. "He's been making a go-bag in case someday you find a snake behind one of your walls."

"Jesus." Seth clasped his hands on top of his head.

Ivy leaned back on the edge of her desk. "Grace seems to have recovered from her scare. Hazel distracted her by challenging her to a let's-see-who-can-hold-their-breath-the-longest contest. Travis agreed to talk to you about this tonight, but I thought I'd give you a heads-up in case he forgets."

"Or chickens out," Seth said wryly. He dragged a hand down his face. "Thanks for paying attention in the first place. I'll get your scarf back to you as soon as I can."

Ivy stiffened. "Do you realize how condescending that sounds? As if I wouldn't notice Travis acting oddly?"

"You're being awfully defensive about something you don't want in your life."

Ivy gritted her teeth so hard her jaw ached. She pushed to her feet and walked stiffly to the door. "I already told Travis he can keep the scarf," she said. "Please don't take it away from him."

She stalked out of her office and back to the kitchen to finish her baking.

* * *

MARCUS TRUDGED UP THE stairs to his room, looking forward to a shower after manning the grill during what had to have been his busiest shift since he'd started working at the diner. Fridays had always been the most hectic night of the week, but he'd never seen the place like tonight.

Neither Cal nor Marcus had said a word, but someone had spread the news about Jasper Cole. Noah, Marcus figured. Customers crowded the counter, demanding details, speculating about jail sentences, hungry to know if the rumors about gunplay were true.

Damn, people were gullible.

Cal hated the attention, but Marcus was glad, for his boss's sake.

Maybe he'd recoup some of what he'd lost. Though the nasty comments about Jasper Cole almost made Marcus feel sorry for the man.

Almost.

He opened his bedroom door and blinked, surprised to find the light on. An instant later, he registered Liz on his bed, and his chest swelled with pleasure. She lay asleep on top of the covers, in jeans and a purple sweater, curled toward the wall. He smiled at her pink socks, shook off his jacket and sat on the bed behind her.

"Hey, sleepyhead." He stroked her hair.

She moaned, stretched and rolled over. When her face brushed his knee, her eyes opened. She blinked a moment, then smiled up at him. "You're back." An instant later, she lost her smile. She sat up and combed her fingers through her hair.

Marcus leaned in and kissed her. Her lips trembled against his.

"What's wrong?" he asked.

She shook her head. "You smell like pepperoni," she said, but he hadn't missed the quaver in her voice.

"You wouldn't believe the number of pizzas we sold tonight. I was about to take a shower." He picked up her hand. "First I want to know what's bothering you. Are you feeling all right?"

She choked out a laugh and nodded. But tears swam in her sweet dark eyes, and panic started thumping in Marcus's chest. He stood, pulled her to her feet and hugged her close.

"You're scaring me," he said into her hair. "Please tell me what's going on."

She leaned away and, with her head bent, ran a finger under each eye. Her pink lips were parted, to help her breathe. Finally, she looked up and gulped.

"Marcus?"

"Yeah?" He braced himself.

"I'm pregnant."

*   *   *

SATURDAY AFTERNOON, IVY WAS fastening the latch on the pen

after feeding the calves when a deep male voice spoke behind her.

"Hello, Ivy."

She whirled, a grin stretching across her face. Already her cheeks ached, as if her facial muscles had gone stiff from disuse.

"Wade!" She stopped short of hugging him when he dropped his gaze and shifted his feet. She offered him her hand instead. "I heard you were still in town. Shame on you for not coming to see us sooner."

Beneath his mustache, his mouth drooped. She hid her dismay. He looked older and thinner.

"I should have stopped by," he said gruffly, "but I was feeling awful for leaving the way I did."

"Don't feel bad. We've been making it work." She gestured toward the house. "Want to come in for a drink?"

He shook his head. "I heard about Gary and what he did. I never would have guessed he'd have resorted to something like that. Then again, lately people have been surprising the hell out of me."

Ivy picked up the handle of the wagon she used to transport the calves' bottles and headed in the direction of the milking shed. Wade walked beside her.

"We were lucky no one got hurt," she said. "*He* was lucky no one got hurt. Seth was ready to tear him limb from limb."

"That's a good man you got there."

"Seth and I are not..." She flushed. "We're good friends, but that's all."

Wade nodded and glanced around. "Place looks good. You all seem to have it well in hand."

"Oh, good God, no. Far from well in hand. But we are managing. It's not the same without you, though." She paused outside the barn. "When do you think you'll head out to Montana?"

Under his beat-up sheepskin jacket, he shrugged. "Matter of fact, I've been having second thoughts about that."

"About the dude ranch, or about Montana in general?"

"About Becky."

"Oh, Wade. I'm so sorry." She dropped the wagon handle and squeezed his arm. "Is there anything I can do?"

He shook his head and kicked at a small pile of sand on the

ground.

Ivy bit her lip. "I don't know what your plans are, but you know you're always welcome —"

He held up a hand. "Stop right there." After sending a sheepish glance her way, he apologized. "What I mean is, you don't know the whole story. You need to hear me out before you start extending any invitations."

"What's this about, Wade?"

"Cabana Boy doing all right?"

Ivy nodded and leaned a shoulder against the exterior wall of the barn. "I guess you heard he got out. He's fine now. Gary swore to the sheriff he didn't do it, but he's the only one who makes sense."

"Gary didn't do it."

"How do you know that?"

"'Cause Becky did."

Ivy gasped and jerked upright. "Your wife let my horse out of the barn? *Why?*"

He turned his head and spit. "She was mad at me for having second thoughts about the dude ranch and mad at you for making this such a fine place to work that I didn't want to leave. Like I told you the day I quit, we were supposed to head out to Montana straightaway, but I kept finding reasons to linger." He spit again. "Seems I married me a spiteful woman."

"When did you find out?"

"Couple days ago." He saw Ivy's face and held up a hand. "I've been keeping an eye on her since."

Thank God she hadn't come back to do more damage. Ivy wrapped her arms around her waist. "I don't understand how she could do something like that."

"Me, neither." Wade cleared his throat. "I thought we were partners. I thought she had my back. That kind of betrayal... I don't know if I can get over something like that." He sniffled, pulled a hankie from his back pocket and blew his nose. "Damned allergies," he muttered.

"I'm sorry, Wade."

"Me, too. I called Sheriff Tate. She might be contacting you for a statement."

He tipped his hat and walked away.

* * *

ALL SATURDAY EVENING AND long into the night, Ivy considered Wade's words. *I thought we were partners. I thought she had my back.*

Despite what she'd insisted, she and Seth *were* partners. He'd had her back.

Had she ever had his?

The question kept her from sleeping. After several restless hours in bed, she rolled to her feet, exchanged her pajamas for a pair of jeans and a sweatshirt, and headed downstairs. If she wasn't going to sleep, she might as well get a jump on her chores. She could use the time to figure out what she'd say to her lawyer on Monday. After starting a pot of coffee, she pushed her feet into a pair of boots, clomped down the porch steps and headed toward the barn. Nothing like a good mucking to help put things into perspective.

Halfway to the barn, she hesitated. She'd heard something from the direction of the road. A thump. On her property or beyond? She heard it again.

Definitely within the borders of the farm.

Her heart shuddered in her chest. It couldn't be Gary. Becky, then? Back to stir up more trouble, despite Wade's promise to keep an eye on her?

A growl ripped from Ivy's throat as indignation shot through her veins. *Oh, hell, no.*

She dashed back inside, grabbed her phone and pulled her shotgun from the safe — not that she had any intention of using it, but there was no reason not to be prepared — and walked quietly along the edge of the driveway, toward the road and the sound she'd heard. She was almost at the final curve in the drive before she realized she wasn't seeing the usual glow from the floodlights positioned on either side of the Millbrook Dairy Farm — well, *Fairy* Farm — sign.

Then she heard a different sound. Wait. Was that...? Was someone...*humming*?

She pushed herself forward again, creeping around the bend until she had a clear view of the bottom of her driveway.

He'd parked his rusted orange pickup, engine still idling, in front of the sign. He'd covered both floodlights with what looked like bath towels and stood on the lowered tailgate of his truck, a cardboard box top serving as a tray for several open containers of paint balanced in his left hand as he leaned into the sign and worked a brush with his right.

If she hadn't recognized him by his truck, she'd have recognized his wordless rendition of the theme from *Spider-Man*, which happened to be Travis's favorite cartoon.

"Okay, then," she said loudly, and couldn't help a chuckle when his entire body convulsed and he nearly lost his balance. As he turned and stared, she strolled around to the back of the truck and peered up at him. "Now I know who my vandal is. And here I thought you were always nervous around me because you liked me."

His lips split into a grin, albeit a shaky one. "Awk-ward," he sing-songed. Carefully, he bent down and set his "tray" on the tailgate, then straightened and ran a not-quite-steady hand through his hair. "I do like you. You don't paint over my work. I appreciate that." He nodded at the sign. "What do you think?"

He was adding a second fairy, one wearing a deep purple tulle skirt and ballet slippers. She stood on tiptoe, her hands curving toward each other as her arms stretched gracefully above her head.

Ivy sighed. "A sugarplum fairy, I presume?"

"Yeah." He sounded distracted. When she turned her head and found him staring at the shotgun propped against her leg, he shook himself and offered up a weak smile. "You're not planning to use that, are you?"

"Of course not." She motioned with her chin at the sign. "You're only half-done."

He gave a strangled chuckle.

Her gaze lingered on his work. "You really are talented. Why aren't you in art school?"

"I've been thinking about it." He looked from her to his painting and back again. "You really think I'm that good?"

"Good enough that I can't bring myself to shoot you."

"Good to know." As he scratched his jaw, his boot nudged at the tray of paints resting on the tailgate. "So what are you going to do?"

She yawned widely and thought about it. Not for long, though — the cold had made short work of her sweatshirt and she was starting to fantasize about flannel nightgowns. "I'm going to go back to bed," she told him. She cradled her shotgun and turned toward the house. "And let sugarplum fairies dance in my head. Good night, Bradley."

"Good night, Ivy," he croaked.

She'd taken maybe half a dozen steps when the humming kicked in again.

*   *   *

AS SOON AS HER lawyer's office opened Monday morning, Ivy called to make an appointment. She spent the rest of Monday and all of Tuesday and Wednesday fidgeting. Wednesday evening she received the call letting her know her paperwork was ready.

When Seth and Dell came in for breakfast Thursday morning, Ivy told Seth she had something she wanted to talk about with him after the meal.

She could hardly eat and paid little attention to the conversation, which Dell had steered to the dehorning debate. Some animal-welfare activists considered the process of removing or stopping the growth of horns to be cruel, but anyone in the livestock business knew that horns posed a real danger, not only to humans but to other animals. The subject was relevant, and usually Ivy enjoyed a heated debate as much as anyone, but today she just wanted Dell gone.

Finally, he did go, and Ivy was alone with Seth for the first time in days. He helped her clear the table, then leaned back against the counter, arms clamped across his chest.

"What's this about?" he asked quietly.

"Sit down," she said. "I'll be right back."

She fetched the paperwork from her office and returned to the kitchen. Seth had straddled the chair at the head of the table. He watched her impassively as she settled at his elbow and slid the envelope across the table.

"Open it." She held her breath.

One eyebrow raised, he kept his gaze locked on hers as he ripped the envelope open and withdrew a sheaf of papers. He unfolded the stack and looked down.

Ivy eventually had to take a breath, and she struggled to do it as silently as possible. She didn't want to miss the moment Seth registered what she'd done. Couldn't wait to see the pleasure spread over his face as he realized —

His hands thumped back down to the table. The papers shuddered in his grip. He didn't raise his head.

"What is this, Ivy?"

She frowned. Wasn't it obvious?

Her left leg started to bounce.

13

PARTNERSHIP PAPERS," IVY SAID. She cleared the gritty uncertainty from her throat. "Because we're partners. I wanted to make it legal so you'd know I'm committed. You already do close to half the work around here, so it's only fair you should be part owner. I'm not expecting you to give up the feed store, of course, and I just found out Wade's not leaving town after all. If I can convince him to come back, you can stop working these crazy hours. Anyway, I owe you. You helped save my farm. You could even" — she swallowed noisily — "move in, if you wanted to."

By the time she was done speaking, her voice was little more than a whisper. Seth's shoulders had grown more and more rigid, while his hold on the papers had gradually loosened, until finally the sheaf landed on the table with an ominous rustle.

"You say you're committed," he said, almost idly.

Yes, she had to mouth, because her voice had deserted her. His head came up then. Emotion blazed in his eyes and she gasped.

"Wait a minute. You're *angry*?"

He jerked to his feet, the scrape of his chair the opening salvo to what she instinctively knew would be their ugliest disagreement yet.

"Yeah, I'm angry. Angry, confused and so damned disappointed..." He crossed his arms over his chest, tucking his fingers into his armpits.

She rose to her feet, as well, confused by the distance that had sprouted between them. "I thought you'd be happy."

"I thought you'd know better."

"What did I do wrong?" she whispered. "I only wanted to share."

He aimed a frustrated glance at the papers her lawyer had drawn up. "What's wrong is that you think this represents a commitment. But it's nothing more than an excuse to avoid getting married. I *proposed* to you, Ivy. I didn't ask for a business arrangement." He picked up the chair and spun it so it faced in the right direction, then banged it back down again. "I have children. Two impressionable kids I have to set a good example for. Shacking up with you won't set a good example. They deserve a mother, not a roommate."

"So I can't be a mother to them without my name on a marriage certificate?"

"You can't be a wife to me."

Ivy felt behind her for the island and sagged back against it. "I thought I'd found the perfect compromise."

"We both deserve better than a compromise."

"You're just saying that to get your way."

"Ivy." He shook his head. "I don't want half of your farm. I want all of you."

She gripped the island behind her, fingers curling around the edges of the countertop at her hips. "All or nothing?"

"Those are my terms. I made that clear from the start."

"I put my all into that contract." She tried for a shrug, but her shoulders did little more than twitch. "I'm sorry that isn't enough for you."

He walked toward her slowly, as if he thought any sudden motion would scare her off. He stood two feet away, the rapid rise and fall of his chest belying the calm in his expression. "I'm not like him," he said. "The asshole. Ethan. Evan. Whoever. Still, you can't bring yourself to trust me."

"Don't take it personally. I don't trust myself, either."

"Jesus. We're trying to settle our future and you're cracking jokes?"

"You don't get it, do you? This *is* me trusting you. This whole partnership thing? I almost hyperventilated on the way to the lawyer's office. And while I was in there. And after I left. And five minutes ago, when I handed you those pages. But I reminded myself, over and over again, that you're different. That you're in it for the long haul. I'm realizing that's only true if everyone else plays by your rules.

That doesn't sound like a partnership to me."

"Ivy—"

"I think our future is settled, Seth. Yours will involve a nurturing wife and stay-at-home mother and mine will involve someone who can respect my warped view of the world."

"I can respect your worldview without agreeing to it."

"But you can't live with it." She offered a strangled laugh. "Literally." She crossed her arms and tucked her shaking hands out of sight. "Someday I'll tell you how much I appreciate what you've done for me and the farm. Right now I need you to leave."

"We can work this out."

"I think you know that's not true."

He laughed abruptly, the sound harsh and lonely. "This is exactly what I was fighting to avoid. Falling in love with a woman—letting my *kids* fall in love with a woman—only to have it all turn to shit."

She couldn't keep her voice from shaking. "Your kids are in love with the farm. They'll be okay."

When he reached the kitchen doorway, he turned back. "What will you do?"

"Put your last check in tomorrow's mail."

He flinched, and gave her a final nod. "Goodbye, Ivy."

"Goodbye, Seth."

* * *

SETH HAD NEVER BEEN so grateful for his kids as he was that weekend. They kept him too busy to mope, and with their presence in the house, he wasn't free to spend all night driving by Ivy's farm and thinking up new reasons to convince her to marry him.

The bottom line was, she didn't want a husband. Probably just as well, too, because she'd never told him she loved him.

Sorrow sliced into his chest and he kicked at the bag of horse feed he'd just loaded in the back of his box truck. The bag split and feed spilled out onto the floor.

"Fucking perfect," Seth muttered, and kicked it again for good measure.

"Everything okay in there?"

Get it together, Walker. Seth ran a palm down his face and walked to the back of the truck. Marcus stood at the bottom of the ramp, squinting in the late-afternoon sunshine.

"Marcus." Seth loped down the ramp and offered up a knuckle bump. "What's up?"

"Allison said I might find Joe here. He around?"

"He was here. He stopped in to say hello before he and Gil left to hit the bike trails. You just missed him." He lifted his ball cap and resettled it on his head. Panic shadowed Marcus's face. "Something I can help you with?"

Marcus shook his head. "S'okay. I just needed to check with him on something. Thanks." He swung toward his pickup. "I'll see you later."

"If you have a minute," Seth called after him, "I could use some help."

Slowly, Marcus turned back around.

Seth gestured at the stack of bags waiting to be loaded. "Bradley's busy keeping an eye on the kids. I sure would appreciate it if you could give me a hand."

Ten minutes later, they had half the bags loaded. Seth gave a mental shrug. Looked as though Marcus wasn't going to open up to him after all. But when he turned from stacking his latest load, he found Marcus staring down at a bag of puppy chow.

"Joe's pretty freaked out about the whole baby thing," he said.

"Everyone is, the first time." Seth grabbed two bottles of water from the cooler inside the bay door and tossed one to Marcus. "The second time? Not much easier."

Pensively, Marcus unscrewed the bottle cap. "Ever have any regrets?"

"About my marriage, yeah. About my kids? Never."

Marcus drank deeply, replaced the cap and stared off toward the highway. "Liz is pregnant."

And there it was. *Shit.* Seth propped one boot on a stack of feed. Somehow congratulations didn't seem to be in order.

"What are you going to do?" he asked quietly.

"I have to do the right thing. I have to marry her."

"Marcus. As noble as that is —"

Marcus swung back to face him. "There's nothing noble about getting a woman pregnant, then walking away."

Seth pushed upright. "I wasn't going to suggest you walk away."

Marcus held up a palm in silent apology. "I've been thinking about this all weekend. I don't know much about healthy relationships, but I do know that if you love someone and you want them in your life, you have to make adjustments. Sometimes it's your own expectations that need adjusting."

Seth chuckled. "Shit, Marcus. You know more than I do, and I was married almost eight years."

"I love her," Marcus said simply.

"And she loves you?"

"She hasn't said it yet, but...yeah."

Seth tossed his empty bottle back in the cooler. "You're young."

"Only in years."

"Sounds like you've made up your mind."

Marcus blinked, then grinned. "I guess I have."

Seth offered his hand. "Then let me be the first to offer my congratulations."

* * *

OH, NO. OH, NO, no, no, no, *no*.

"No," Ivy groaned out loud. Fate couldn't be that unkind. Could it? She contemplated the clean white ceramic as she hovered over the toilet. They did say bad things came in threes. First Allison, then Liz, now... *No*. Allison was thrilled about her pregnancy, and according to Liz, she was, too.

Ivy, not so much.

Though it would certainly explain the headaches and fatigue she'd chalked up to missing Seth.

Why hadn't she let him run out to his truck to get those damned condoms? *Why* hadn't she taken the time to find the roll Hazel had given her? *Why* hadn't she reminded herself that the 99 percent effectiveness of oral contraceptives meant that 1 percent of women ended up sobbing into maternity bras?

After ten minutes of puking up mostly nothing, she crawled into the shower and stayed there much longer than she should have. Luckily, Wade had been back as her manager all week, and by the time she made it downstairs, he and Dell had finished the morning chores and were scrambling eggs for breakfast.

Ivy thanked them both, then lied and said she'd already eaten.

"I'll be away from the farm for an hour or so at lunch," she told them. No way would she risk buying a pregnancy test in downtown Thistle Hill. After pretending not to see the perplexed side eye Wade and Dell exchanged, she hurried outside to escape the smell of fresh-brewed coffee.

And the absence of Seth.

*   *   *

SETH SAT IN THE bench swing on Ivy's front porch, feet braced to keep the damned thing from swinging. It wouldn't take much to push his stomach from grumpy to pissed and the last thing he needed was for Ivy to drive up while he was spewing into her bushes.

Shivering in the hoodie he should have exchanged for his heavy denim jacket, he stared across Ivy's farm at the lake beyond. He didn't know how to fix this. He wasn't certain he could, and that one sad, miserable detail had turned his world gray like no rainstorm could.

He missed her like crazy.

Sometimes it's your own expectations that need adjusting.

Marcus's words continued to scold Seth.

He exhaled, and rubbed his palms over the worn denim at his knees. Maybe this was a bad idea. Maybe he should have given Ivy a heads-up. Bradley had been fine with staying at the store — in fact, the kid had been all kinds of helpful lately, as Grace and Travis tended to be after they'd done something sure to give him heartburn — but Seth could brood at his own place just as easily as he could at Ivy's.

The rumble of an engine neared. Seth pulled off his ball cap as Ivy parked her dark green Volvo. She strode toward the house, head down, muttering to herself. She had her purse clutched in one hand and a small white drugstore bag in the other.

Her long legs made short work of the steps and his body tightened, his brain teasing the rest of him with erotic flashes of those legs wrapped around his waist.

He didn't dare stand.

He did manage to find his voice as she opened the screen door. "Ivy."

She jerked, shock stamped across her pretty, pale face. Paper rattled as the hand clenching the bag flew to her chest. "Seth. I didn't see you there."

He tipped his head toward the driveway. "Didn't see my truck out there, either." When she continued to stare, he pushed to his feet and swallowed hard against a rise of bile. The swing bumped the backs of his knees. "Can we talk?"

"Now is not a good time." She rubbed her throat and registered that she still had the bag in her hand. She dropped it to her side and lifted her chin.

Seth tapped his hat against his thigh. "With the way I acted the other night, I pretty much guaranteed no time would be a good time. I know you're busy. But I have some things I need to say."

"I'm not kidding, Seth." She aimed a longing glance at the front door. "Your timing sucks. We can talk later."

"Bullshit. You think I don't know a brush-off when I hear one? Last week you offered me half your world and I blew you off. Forgive me if I refuse to let you return the favor."

"Okay, then." She stuffed the bag into her purse and crossed her arms. "Say what you came to say."

He filled his lungs, hoping like hell the air would calm the nausea roiling in his gut. "Thing is, I'm an asshole. I tell you that I love you, that I want to make a life with you, then I turn around and sulk when you get on board but not on my terms." He swallowed. "I need to let you know that I'm honored to be invited into your life."

She didn't appear moved. "What brought this on?"

"A conversation with Marcus. He helped me see that being hell-bent on changing someone else's expectations probably means we're too blockheaded to see that we need to change our own."

"Did he really say *blockheaded*?"

"More like *head up my ass*."

She stifled a smile. "Whether that's true or not, no one changes their belief system that quickly."

"No," he said slowly, "but accepting that not everything has to be black or white is a solid first step."

"Seth," she whispered. "I don't want you to change for me."

"Because you love me the way I am?"

She dipped her head. Her chest rose and fell with an inhale, and she adjusted her purse, tucking it closer to her body.

"You were right," she said, and raised her gaze to his. "From the very beginning. We see things differently, important things, and it was wrong of me to push us into something we already knew wouldn't work. I'm sorry, too."

Alarm iced his insides and he pushed himself closer. "You love me, Ivy. Those partnership papers you had drawn up — that was you doing your best to make me happy. You were willing to sacrifice some of that self-reliance you treasure to give me what I wanted, because you love me. Let me sacrifice my stubborn vision of the perfect family so we can be together. I love you. I waited a long time for you to love me back and I know you do. We make a good team. We can figure this out."

She was shaking her head and backing away, pushing the front door open behind her. "I'm not what you need, Seth. Any of you."

"I might be an asshole, but I'm not stupid." His hand clamped around the edge of the screen door. "I'm not giving up that easily."

"You should, Seth. Travis and Grace deserve better."

The door closed gently in his face.

* * *

IVY SHUT THE DOOR and leaned back against it, her heart pounding so hard it sounded like someone knocking behind her with a closed fist.

It wouldn't be Seth. Not after she'd so casually dismissed his apology.

Tears threatened and she pressed the heels of her hands against the burn, grunting when her movements swung her heavy purse against her hip.

We make a good team. We can figure this out.

They might have more to figure out than he could ever begin to guess.

Oh, God, what was she going to *do*?

She pushed away from the door and scrabbled for the small white bag in her purse. Pee before panic, *that* was what she was going to do.

On her way to the stairs, she dropped her purse on the sofa, tucked one corner of the bag in her mouth and shrugged out of her coat. She was halfway up the steps when her phone rang.

"Crap," she muttered. But she couldn't ignore it. Not when it could be farm business.

She hurried back down the stairs, half expecting her cooked-noodle knees to give out on her. Shoving her bangs out of her eyes, she plucked the phone from her purse and peered at the screen.

Liz. Ivy answered, calling herself all kinds of coward for jumping at the chance to delay the whole peeing-on-a-stick shtick.

"Hey, Liz. What's up?" She slumped down onto the arm of the sofa.

"Oh, Ivy."

Ivy bounced right back up onto her feet. "What's the matter?"

"Nothing. Everything. Marcus proposed. He *proposed* to me."

Ivy closed her eyes. The burn was back. Liz sounded as excited as Ivy should have been when Seth popped the question. Was this a sign that she'd made the right choice, or one more example of just how screwed up she was?

"Ivy?"

Stop being a selfish you-know-what, Millbrook.

She leaned her butt against the wall and bent to take off her high-heeled boots, one at a time. "I want to say congratulations, but it doesn't sound like that's what you want to hear."

"I'm twenty-four, Ivy, and Marcus is barely legal. I mean, he acts like he's thirty, but...twenty-*one*. This is a huge step. Two huge steps.

246

Marriage and baby, boom, boom, like a one-two punch. What should I do? I don't know what to do."

Ivy winced as her friend's voice started to rise. "Did you talk about it with him at all? Or did you run for the door the moment he said the *m* word?"

Ivy padded into the kitchen in her sock feet while Liz made a choking sound that was probably supposed to be a laugh.

"We talked about it," Liz said. "And it all made sense at the time."

"Because you love each other." Ivy hiked her shoulder to trap the phone against her ear. She snagged a wineglass from the cupboard and the half-empty bottle of pinot noir she'd shoved to the back of the counter. She set both on the island and worked the cork free of the bottle. "But you're home now, and you're having second thoughts?"

"Actually, I'm in his bathroom."

Ivy stilled. "Wait, you mean he *just* asked you? Just now?"

A clanking sound, as if Liz had put down the toilet seat to give herself a place to sit. "A little while ago. He had to go downstairs and help Audrey with something, but he'll be back soon. With plates and forks because he made a cake. A cake, Ivy. Coconut, with Please Marry Me piped on top."

"Oh, how sweet. Chocolate icing?"

"Dude." Liz's voice dripped with *duh*.

"Marcus knows you well." Ivy shifted her phone to her other ear and poured herself half a glass of wine. "Okay. Here's what you need to do."

"What?" Liz asked eagerly.

"Save me a piece of that cake."

Liz laughed. "Consider it done."

"And as for the other? You already know what you want to do. I can hear it in your voice. Even if I didn't, I'd tell you what I once heard Parker tell Joe. Follow your heart."

"That's what I want to do," Liz said softly. "We're in love. We love each other. I can't imagine being happy with anyone else. But I can't help wondering — did he ask me to be his wife because he's ready to get married, or because I'm having his baby?"

Ivy's glass was halfway to her lips when the word *baby* registered.

She froze and, with a rueful glance at her own belly, set the wine aside. Her fingers tightened on the glass, then released.

"Can I ask you something, Liz?"

"Sure."

"Did you ever consider...giving your baby up?"

"No." The answer came swift and sure. She gave a hiccupy sort of sigh. "I probably would have if I were younger. You know. A teenager. It would be tough if Marcus didn't want to be a part of this. I thought about that before I told him, what I'd do if he cut me loose. How I'd make it as a single mother. But the thing was, deep down, I knew he wouldn't walk away. What I didn't expect was that he'd want to marry me."

Ivy pushed away from the island, moved to the sink and poured herself a glass of water. "Did you ask him about that? About whether he proposed because of the baby?"

"He said he was going to ask me anyway. But what else could he say?"

"You know who you need to talk to about this."

"Oh." The word was one long, drawn-out sigh. "Allison. You're right."

"I know."

Liz laughed again, and the sound was so full of joy that Ivy couldn't help her own giggle, even as she leaned over the sink to avoid crumpling to the floor.

"Thank you, Ivy." A rustling on the other end of the phone. Ivy pictured Liz getting to her feet and checking her face in the bathroom mirror. "I have to go now, before Marcus thinks I'm in here getting sick. He might not let me have any cake."

"I think Marcus is likely to let you have whatever you want."

"Maybe." No mistaking that she was delighted by the prospect.

"Liz?"

"Yes?"

"I'm so happy for you." Ivy hoped the truth of that came through in her voice. "Congratulations, to you both."

Liz thanked her warmly, then hung up so she could go get engaged.

Ivy stood at the sink, staring through the window at the greens, golds and oranges of the legacy her parents had left her. A legacy of hard, honest work. A legacy of blue skies and fresh air and a product she could be proud of.

A legacy of loneliness.

She gulped her water before heading upstairs with her drugstore purchase.

Time to find out just how drastically her life was about to change.

* * *

THAT NIGHT, AFTER WADE and Dell had left and Ivy had heated and then rejected a bowl of soup for dinner, she sat in her kitchen. She stared through the glass at the brick patio, at the tall blob-like trees beyond, at the nearest length of pasture fence, weathered boards glimmering under the fading moon. She'd left the kitchen light off because otherwise she'd be staring at the reflection of the most pathetic woman she knew.

Follow your heart, she'd told Liz.

What a hypocrite, that she couldn't even take her own advice.

A buzzing sound, at her elbow. She picked up her phone and found a text from Liz, the only message a happy face and a photo of Liz's left hand. Encircling her ring finger was a silver band adorned with a bright blue sapphire.

Ivy choked out an approving laugh. Marcus had chosen wisely. She texted back her admiration and best wishes and added a string of exclamation points. She set her phone down and slowly pushed away from the table. She was barely out of the kitchen before her uncertain amble toward the stairs had turned into a run.

An hour later, she stood outside Seth's door, her hair loose and her lips red. She'd wriggled into her plum-colored sweater dress and finished off her outfit with a pair of black high-heeled boots.

When Seth opened the door, his eyes went wide and his gaze went south. "Ivy."

He was dressed casually, in jeans and a faded sweatshirt, and she suddenly felt like a monumental idiot. At least if he kicked her out, she could pretend she was on her way to somewhere fabulous.

Or maybe she could just be honest.

"I'm sorry to bother you at home," she said.

"No bother. Come in."

She moved into the living room, spied the cards and chips on the dining room table and winced. "Poker night?"

He nodded. "Deb has the kids for the weekend. The guys'll be here in a few." He rubbed the back of his neck and gave her outfit another once-over. "You look great. Going somewhere?"

The tightness in his voice both cheered and shamed her. She shrugged and managed a smile. "Actually, I dressed up for you."

"For me?"

"In case you weren't in the mood to talk, I figured I could vamp my way in."

"Vamp?" His lips twitched. "Is that even a word anymore?"

She sighed. "You know what? You're expecting company. I'll come back later."

"Will you still be wearing that?"

She tried to laugh, but she didn't do a very good job of it. He followed her to the door and reached around her to hold it shut.

"Why are you here, Ivy?"

"I wanted to tell you something."

His body went rigid behind her. She knew because the muscles stood out in his forearm.

"What did you want to tell me?" he asked gruffly.

She turned and leaned back against the door. "I thought I was pregnant."

He shot upright. "You *what*?"

"I know, right? I'm not, though. False alarm. A stomach bug, maybe, or... I don't know." She licked her lips.

He exhaled, picked up her hand and led her to the sofa. He snatched up a book, a pillow and a stack of folded boys' underwear and tossed them on a nearby chair, then sat her down. He pressed her hands between his and held tight.

"Are you all right?"

She nodded, fighting tears because he was always so good to her and she didn't deserve it.

Stop it. If she started thinking like that, she'd never get through this.

"Can I get you something?" Seth was looking at her strangely. "Water? Something stronger?"

"Water would be great." She didn't think she could stand it if he kept holding her hands. Not if he didn't want to hear what she had to say. Though they had a phrase for that.

"Poetic justice," she murmured.

"I'm sorry?" He handed her a glass of water. Instead of sitting beside her, he sat facing her, on the coffee table. His knees settled outside of hers.

She took a sip and met his gaze. "Allison was right. It does make you feel special to have someone look out for you."

He started to say something, then exhaled. "What did you mean when you said 'poetic justice'?"

"That's what it would be if you'd rather not hear what I came to say."

"There's more?" He scratched his jaw. "You thought you were pregnant with triplets?"

"It scared the hell out of me."

"I'm sure it did."

"But at the same time I felt...peace."

Hope flashed across his face. She felt the echo of it in her heart.

"In what way?" he asked softly.

"I was overwhelmed and facing a host of options all over again. When I was a teenager making this decision with my parents, I felt so alone. I knew I wouldn't be this time. What you've been saying all along finally sank in. The choice I made when I was eighteen was right for Hannah, even if it wasn't right for me. Things are different now, and I'd have made a different choice." She swallowed. "I finally found acceptance."

He rested his hands on her knees and squeezed. "I'm happy for you, Ivy."

"I knew you would be."

Someone thumped on the door and hollered about a six-pack

getting warm.

Ivy jumped and held out her water. "I should go."

"Stay put." Seth stood and strode to the door. He opened it a crack. "Plans have changed," he said. "Give Noble a call—see if you can hang out there." He shut the door on a barrage of protests and walked back to the sofa, but didn't sit.

Ivy blinked up at him. "You didn't have to do that."

"Gil will get over it. Joe always wins anyway, which means I just saved myself some dough." He perched on the sofa's arm. "When did all this happen? The pregnancy scare, I mean."

"I suspected earlier today, when you came to see me." Ruefully, she toasted him with the glass. "I know I'm giving you one more reason to resent me."

"Jesus, Ivy. I don't resent you. You were hurting and overwhelmed and I was probably the last person you wanted to share anything with at the time." He frowned. "Are you sure you're all right?"

"No." She shoved to her feet, sloshing water as she moved. She rounded the far end of the couch, then shook her head when she realized she'd put the piece of furniture between them. Did she really believe it would shield her from the pain of his rejection? She set the water down on an end table, tried to find something to do with her arms and ended up folding them under her breasts.

Seth watched her carefully. "What's going on, Ivy?"

"I *couldn't* tell you. I couldn't let that pull us back together. Then when I found out it was a false alarm, that I wasn't pregnant after all, I was crushed." When he jerked toward her, she held up a hand to ward him off. "Not because I suddenly found this deep desire to have a child, but because it would have made it so easy to get back together with you." She gasped a laugh. "And now I have to try it the hard way."

"Ivy."

"No. Let me say it. You expressed your feelings and I never returned the favor. Yes, I'm screwed up, and you know I'm screwed up, but that's no excuse. Seth, I'm so sorry. I'm sorry I didn't listen to you when you tried to give us another chance."

"You don't have to apologize." He approached her cautiously, as if expecting her to take off again. But she couldn't have moved if her life depended on it. Not when he was looking at her with all that naked relief on his face.

"You took a huge step," he continued, "and instead of appreciating that you were ready to trust a man again, I threw it back in your face."

When he stood in front of her, pupils dilated, pulse twitching at his throat, she found it easy to say. "I love you, Seth."

He blew out a breath, clamped his hands around her face and kissed her, hard. "I never thought you'd be able to admit it."

She slid her arms around his neck. "I love you, and I love your kids. I love your stupid truck and your sense of honor and your brilliant ideas and your arms. I really love your arms."

His expression turned pained. "You called my truck stupid."

"But your ideas brilliant."

He kissed her again and pulled her tight against him. "I have an idea right now."

Yeah, and it was a big one. She shuddered, leaned back and touched a finger to his lips. "Can you hold that thought? Because I have to say, being a mom scares the hell out of me."

"Grace and Travis already love you. Just keep doing what you're doing." He hesitated. "When you say 'being a mom...'"

"I know. We have to talk about that."

He nodded, moved his hands up her back and started combing his fingers through her hair. "I love you."

"Why?"

He flashed a dimple. "Why?"

"Yes, why? Marcus told Liz that she makes him the kind of man who deserves her. I want to be the kind of woman who deserves you."

"Ivy, if I ever made you feel like you're not good enough..."

She shook her head. "I've done that enough for both of us."

His fingers slowed as he considered. "I love you because you're smart and sexy and the hardest worker I've ever known. You're tough but vulnerable and honest when you're not trying to pay some imagined penance. You have a huge heart and a fun sense of humor, and I don't even have to be around you to feel better about the world. I just have to think of you, and the sun comes out." He peered down at her. "Will that do?"

"Oh, yes," she breathed. "That will do nicely."

He dipped his head and she lifted her mouth. Her eyes fluttered closed as she breathed him in, inhaling sweat and musk and desire. She trembled and passed her tongue over her lips. His fingers tightened in her hair, his breath whispered over her mouth, and for long moments she knew nothing but pure bliss.

When they came up for air, Ivy sighed and tucked her forehead against his throat. "If I'm rushing you, please tell me, but I was thinking we could combine households."

"Yes."

"Yes?"

"We'll move in with you. You're right. It makes sense. The kids love the farm, your place is bigger, and you know what? A marriage license doesn't guarantee a loving, stable home. That's what my kids need to see, and the way you and I feel about each other" — his arms tightened around her — "that's exactly what they're going to get. I'm sorry I couldn't get that through my thick skull sooner."

She tipped her head back. "It means a lot to hear you say that."

His smile faded. "I hear a *but* coming on. Didn't you just say something about combining households?"

"Yes, but I wasn't going to ask you to move in with me."

Frowning, he looked around. "You want to live here?"

"Still not quite what I had in mind." She reached for his hands and interlaced her fingers with his. Their joined hands dangled between them. "During this past year, I've been both the happiest and the most miserable I've ever been in my life. Having you as a friend and a lover, and almost losing you as both—" Her voice wavered and she coughed. "You and your children helped me work through a terrible regret that has haunted me for what feels like forever. I love you so much. I don't just want you in my life. I want you to *be* my life. You and G and Travis. So, Seth Walker." She strengthened her grip on his hands and dipped her left knee until it touched the carpet. Swallowed against a frigid rise of panic. "Will you marry me?"

His fingers spasmed around hers as he stared down at her. "That wasn't what I expected to hear," he said finally, his voice cracking.

Tiny trembles racked her shoulders, despite the stunned pleasure in his eyes. She waited for him to tug her upward. Instead he sank to his knees, as if his legs would no longer support him. He searched her gaze. "Ivy." He disentangled his right hand and gently smoothed her hair back from her face, then cupped her cheek. His thumb traced back and forth over her cheekbone. She could hear the thump of his heart. Or was that hers?

He canted his head. "Are you sure?"

"It's not a choice anymore, Seth. Not for me. It's all I want." She couldn't help chuckling at the disbelief on his face. "Are you okay?"

"I've never been on the receiving end of a marriage proposal." He swiped a hand over his face, then laughed. "Did you get me a ring?"

She scowled. "What's so funny?"

"Back when Joe was thinking about proposing to Allison, he told the guys he was considering getting a ring. Noble asked whether it was for his nose or his 'love muscle.'"

Ivy grinned. "I can just picture Allison leading Joe everywhere by his nose."

"We were thinking it was the 'love muscle' part that was funny."

"If that's what you want, I could get you one as a wedding present," she said helpfully.

"Cute, but I'll pass." He cocked an eyebrow. "Mind if we take this discussion into the bedroom? I can show you what I'd rather have."

She threw her arms around him before he could get to his feet. "Thank you for not giving up on me," she whispered into his neck.

"Hey." He tugged her arms free. "We're here because we didn't give up on each other." He kissed her nose. "We're not giving up on that riding-school idea, either. I'm not ready to let the feed store go, but if I can find a partner half as amazing as you are, I can help with the farm while you're handling the stable."

A breathless heat radiated through her chest. God, she loved this man. She stroked her palms down the thin gray fleece of his sweatshirt. "Seth?"

"Yeah?"

"My knees are starting to hurt."

"Mine, too." He stood, pulling her up with him. "Come with me," he said. "You can tell me how much you love me while I kiss your knees and make them better."

* * *

Thank you for making THE LONG GAME a part of your library! I hope you enjoyed reading Ivy's and Seth's story as much as I enjoyed crafting it. :-)

Have a sweet tooth? Subscribe to my mailing list and get instant access to an exclusive collection of recipes for the sweet treats featured in the Thistle Hill series. Cupcakes, muffins, cookies and more — inside THE SWEET STUFF you'll find a baker's dozen of recipes and story snippets guaranteed to whet your [romantic] appetite. :-)

You can subscribe on my website (www.kathyaltman.com) for access to the download (ebook only), or scan this handy dandy QR code:

Interested in helping other readers find this book while earning my endless gratitude? Please consider leaving a review. I would love it so much if you did. Thank you!

To find out about upcoming releases, including the next book in the Thistle Hill series, check out my website at www.kathyaltman.com.

ABOUT THE AUTHOR

Author, wife, cat mom, hardcore chocolate chip cookie fan, Kathy Altman prefers her chocolate with nuts, her Friday afternoons with wine and her love stories with happy ever afters. Her contemporary romance and romantic suspense books are an award-winning, feel-good blend of the heartfelt, the humorous, and the seriously sexy.

www.ingramcontent.com/pod-product-compliance
Lightning Source LLC
Chambersburg PA
CBHW020313200626
46814CB00006BA/2223